VEILED

-- Book 1--

CYANA GAFFNEY

Dream Always!!

Copyright © 2016 Cyana Gaffney

Published by Blue Sky Publishing

All rights reserved.

ISBN-13:978-1540496089
ISBN-10: 1540496082

(2nd edition)

TO HE WHO IS THE CREATOR OF DREAMS
&
TO MY BIG TREE

CHAPTER 1

The small, metal coils of the cot pressed into her side through the thin, stained mattress. Her ribcage was throbbing. He may well have broken a couple of ribs, and she feared there would be some pain if she tried to move. It was, for this reason, she remained still; discomfort was better than pain. The chill in the room had already reached down deep into her bones, so she didn't bother to rearrange the ragged blanket that lay across her torso.

What good would it do? She thought to herself.

Footsteps.

Her mind screamed at her to turn towards the door and see who might be approaching, but the humiliation coated her body like a straitjacket, pinning her in place. The hope she had felt only hours earlier had completely vanished, leaving her not only fearful but more terrified than she ever thought possible. She squeezed her eyes shut, hoping that whoever it was would keep moving.

The footsteps faded down the hall without even a slight pause.

Her body relaxed a bit. Silent tears ran down her face as she thought about the unlikelihood that she would ever escape these

1

confines.

She was glad she wasn't alone. But with the uncertainty that the other woman, who lay just a few feet away, wouldn't be taken as well, made that fact of little comfort. The screams from the day before still haunted her as she wondered who would be next.

How silly she felt when she considered how broken up she had been over Jeremy. It all seemed so pointless now. All these events that had led her to this point seemed so ridiculous. The regret and foolishness that she felt nearly smothered her; if only she could go back and make different choices.

=======

Pushing through the glass doors of his office, the smell from a hot dog vendor's cart encircled him and caused his stomach to groan. Ryan had been stuck in meetings all day, and at the time it had seemed like a good idea to press on and work through lunch, something he was now regretting. As he stepped out into the sun, Ryan's attention drifted to thoughts of her.

He had tried to give her some space, but it was so hard to wait for her to contact him. Ryan worried that Hailey had been pushed too far this time and he was concerned she wouldn't return to them and that she might sever ties with everyone who had a connection to Jeremy.

He could only imagine how betrayed she felt that none of them warned her. He should never have listened to Sheila.

With each phone call, only Hailey's voice mail would talk to him. Even when he stopped by her dorm, either there was no answer, or she would just talk to him through a small crack in the door and inform him that she wasn't up for a visit.

Ryan was constantly tormented with trying to decipher when it was appropriate to push and when to just back off. It was a dilemma that was driving him mad. He so wanted to be close to her and reassure her that she wasn't alone. Yet neither he nor his brother Thomas, had any luck getting past her defenses to get through to her.

He stepped down off the sidewalk with one foot and raised his arm to hail a cab. Seeing how his office was on the edge of the financial district, he never had a problem getting a ride within minutes of exiting the building. After giving his destination to the driver and leaning back against the seat, Ryan resorted back to his thoughts. Then it hit him.

No way... it couldn't be. Have I actually been thinking about Hailey constantly over these last few weeks?

Ryan tried to convince himself that it wasn't the case. He had been playing Thomas's party repeatedly in his mind and also what happened after she...

Wait! That evening.

The memories of holding Hailey in his arms while she cried in the street, picking her up and having her nuzzle herself protectively against his chest with her arms around his neck, and bringing her home, tucking her safely in bed. It was those thoughts that had been the actual source of his distraction at work, and they had consumed him. He was, of course, concerned about what his friend was going through, but it went beyond that, way beyond that.

I've been such an idiot.

A small smile appeared on his lips.

CHAPTER 2

Ryan was nervous, and it caused him to laugh at himself. He hadn't felt like this since his high school crush. All throughout his senior year Ryan had tried to avoid that girl so he wouldn't make a fool of himself. Although the difference here was he wasn't avoiding Hailey; she was avoiding him.

Ever since Thomas's party, Hailey had been very erratic. Then when Ryan heard about Hailey's run in with Sheila after the party, he had tried to give Hailey some space. But usually they wouldn't go so long without seeing each other, and it was driving him nuts.

When they talked on the phone, she seemed so distracted. It was as though she was limiting her words in hopes of not prolonging the conversation any longer than politeness would demand of her. But Ryan wasn't offended. He understood, and it made it easier for him not to push, but he was about to explode from lack of contact. It had now been a week from the time when he realized how he truly felt about her.

However, this space away from her this past week was probably a good thing. Ryan needed that time to think and plan what he would do with these feelings. But even after having time to sort through them, he wasn't quite ready to call her up and have "The Talk." Ryan decided he needed someone else's input and his little brother, Thomas, would be the perfect guinea pig.

Closing his front door, Ryan zipped up his jacket, shoved his hands in his pockets, and jogged down the five steps leading to the sidewalk below. The air held a bit of a chill, but Ryan decided to walk the hour to his brother's place. He needed the fresh air to clear his head and replay one more time what he would say. Thomas was a pretty supportive guy, but Ryan did worry a bit about whether Thomas would try to deter him. Ultimately, it would be great if he only showed support.

It seemed mere seconds since he left his place, but here he was standing outside the door knocking. Ryan took a deep breath as the door opened.

"Hey, buddy. What are you doing here? Didn't you have to work late tonight?" Thomas questioned.

Ryan shrugged. "Not as late as I thought. Actually... I really need to talk to you. Do you have a sec?"

"Sure," Thomas said as he led the way into the living room and took a seat along the far wall. "So, what's up? Is everything OK?"

"Yeah... um... it's great." Ryan leaned against the back of the couch and ran his hand down his thighs. "Actually... really great. I got some good news last week, and I wanted to run it by you and ask for your advice."

Over the next ten minutes, Ryan unfolded everything that had happened over the last month: his feelings, the few times Hailey and he spent together, everything. When he finished, he looked at his brother. His face was stunned.

"So... what do you think? Am I crazy? Do you think I should go tell her now or wait till she recovers a bit more?"

"Um, well." Thomas's tone seemed like he was trying to stall. *Oh no, maybe this was stupid.*

It was obvious Thomas didn't know what to say so Ryan gave him a few moments to collect himself. It seemed a little awkward, but Ryan tried not to break the silence and provoke an answer even though it was killing him that Thomas wasn't saying anything else.

Thomas finally spoke. "Oh man, this is big. How long do you think you've felt this way? And how come you didn't tell me sooner?" His words were calm but a little hurt.

"No, it's not like that. I honestly just realized it myself. But it's true. I'm… crazy about her. Although with everything that has happened over this last while, I don't know how she would take it." Ryan paused. "Look at you. You're barely involved, and you're having trouble recovering from the shock." Ryan shrugged. "I really do need to know what you're thinking bud."

"Yeah, of course." Thomas shook his head and leaned forward, placing his elbows on his knees. "Sorry, this is just so… so huge. But apart from the shock, honestly it's great." Thomas chuckled. "So, what are you going to do about it? Are you going to tell her?"

"Well yeah, I want to. I want to run over there right now and tell her, but I'm scared I'll freak her out. Although, the real problem is that I don't know how to be around her and not tell her. It's like it's oozing out of me and I know she will be able to tell something's up." Ryan let out a frustrated sigh.

"Well, at least you have almost a month till you have to see her." He gave a playful punch to Ryan's shoulder. "Come on, let's grab some coffee."

Thomas rose and headed into the kitchen. "That should give you lots of time to settle yourself so you can keep your cool until you know how she's doing," he said over his shoulder as Ryan followed him.

"Wait, what do you mean I have a month before I see her?" Ryan questioned him as he perched himself on a kitchen stool.

"On your trip to Saudi. Aren't you planning on seeing her and Anna when you're there?"

"Yeah, but I can't avoid her until she leaves. That's over three weeks away."

Thomas grabbed two cups from the cupboard. "Ryan, stop messing around. When I was dropping Hailey off last week, she said she was looking forward to your visit. So you can see her when you go." Thomas had an amused tone to his voice, and it was starting to bug Ryan.

"What are you talking about? Dropped her off where?" Ryan asked, trying to keep the frustration from his voice.

"Uh... Tuesday, last week. I drove her to the airport to go visit Anna." Upon seeing Ryan's face, Thomas continued. "You really didn't know? After she had called me for a ride on Monday, she was going to call you and tell you about it."

"No..." Ryan got off the stool and leaned against the counter. He ran his fingers through his hair. "I was in a meeting all Monday, and it went really late. I must have missed her call. My stupid voicemail was full." Ryan paced across the kitchen and banged his fists on the kitchen table. "I can't believe this. She's already gone?"

"Yeah, sorry buddy. I thought you knew." He paused. "It's strange she didn't mention anything to me about not getting a hold of you. But hey, look at it this way, with her being in Saudi she will have a chance to cool down. Then, by the time you see her, she'll be in a much better headspace to hear you out when you tell her about how you feel. If you think about it, this

7

actually could be the best-case scenario." Thomas shrugged and turned back to the coffee.

"I guess. I just wish I had a chance to say goodbye. I miss her. It's been killing me to keep my distance this long, and now I have to wait another three weeks?" Ryan groaned and walked back to the counter and leaned on it in a huff.

How am I going make it until the end of the month when this past week has been near impossible?

God control my heart, please.

As calm eased its way throughout his nerves, he turned to Thomas. "So you think it's a good idea? Me and Hailey I mean?"

"Are you kidding, I think it's great. Just don't get ahead of yourself." Thomas handed him a steaming mug. "Pray about it lots and wait on His timing and you'll be fine."

"Right! Thanks."

"Oh, and I wouldn't bother asking Jeremy about it. After what they pulled at the party, I don't think he gets a say anymore." Thomas took a sip of his coffee. "So much for him being our wise, older brother."

"Seriously hey?" Ryan said, with a disgusted chuckle.

After leaving Thomas's, Ryan headed back to his place. On the walk, he thought about how thankful he was for the faith his parents taught him and his brothers. It was during times like this that he needed guidance and was glad he had God to give it to him. Ryan just wished Hailey still felt that way.

They had had several talks about faith and beliefs, but after the last conversation, Hailey had ended it by saying "I just don't believe anymore and there isn't any way to change that. Please, if you really are my friend, you will need to learn to respect that."

It went without saying that Ryan would. He stopped

confronting her outwardly about it, but inwardly he refused to stop praying for her. He knew if she had any hope to cut the chain of guilt that was strangling her, she would need God to do it.

The next morning came after a very restless sleep. It was Thursday, Ryan's day to go to work a bit late. He tried unconvincingly to go about his Thursday routine as normal, but in all honesty, he was just trying to keep busy.

He made a pot of coffee, poured himself a cup, and sat at the kitchen table to read the paper. His eyes kept reading, but his mind wasn't processing it. After reading halfway through an article and still not having a clue what it was about, his eyes rose over the top edge of the paper and glanced at the counter where the phone was sitting.

NO! You are reading this, now pay attention. Ryan chided himself.

After reading the next sentence of the article five times, his eyes wandered to the phone again. It was late afternoon in Saudi Arabia, and the girls might be home. He could just call and say hi.

And say what, you dork? 'Hi, just wondering how things are going?' First, you'd sound like an idiot and second, it's not like you can tell her over the phone that you are madly in love with her. Snap out of it and read the paper! Maybe another cup of coffee would help.

After downing half the cup, he looked into the cup while he leaned on the edge of the sink.

Yeah stupid, that will make you more relaxed: more caffeine.

Ryan dumped the rest down the drain and set the cup down. Bracing himself with one hand on each side of the sink, he craned his neck to look over at the phone again. It had been two weeks since he talked to her and he desperately wanted to see how she was doing.

This is ridiculous. Just call her.

He crossed the kitchen and picked up the phone and dialed, trying to keep his hands from shaking.

God, keep me focused and steady my heart till the right time.

The phone rang and rang then Anna's dad's voice came on the phone saying, "You have reached the Harington's. We're sorry we missed your call. Please leave a message, and we will call you right back."

After the beeps had sounded, Ryan left a message. "Anna, it's Ryan. I hope you girls are having a great time. When you get in, can one of you give me a call? Thanks… bye."

Ryan hung up the phone and returned to the table. When the clock finally rang 10:00 a.m. he couldn't wait for their call any longer, he needed to get to the office. So with a shrug, he grabbed his suit jacket and headed out the door.

- - - - - - -

Thursday couldn't have passed by any slower. Even with a short day and Ryan trying his best not to watch the clock, it dragged on. The weekend came and went with no phone call from Hailey or Anna.

When Monday came and went with no response, Ryan tried Thomas and even Hailey's aunt to see if either of them had heard anything but still no luck. It was now Tuesday, two weeks after Hailey had left and he was starting to worry that she was intentionally not calling.

Ryan wondered if the feelings Hailey was currently experiencing brought up vivid reminders of her family. Of course, she never forgot or needed reminding. No one could ever forget something like that. Ryan didn't know much about Hailey's family life before the accident. She did talk about them a little, and they had seemed close and happy.

Hailey had been born in the US, but when her father accepted a job transfer, they all packed up and moved to London. Hailey was only three at the time. She lived there until she was seventeen. But after the accident, Hailey moved back to New York to live with her aunt for a year while she finished high school. She then moved out on her own as soon as she had returned from her post-grad trip to Europe and had been independent ever since.

Ryan always wished Hailey would talk more about her past because, in his understanding, it seemed that she was still running from it. Maybe she thought that if she never acknowledged it, then it didn't really happen? But maybe it was for some other irrational reason. Nevertheless, he tried to respect her boundaries and remind himself that, unless he walked in Hailey's shoes, he had no basis for judgment.

When he had last talked to her about Saudi, Hailey had said she was really looking forward to getting away, really away. Did that mean away from everything, even him?

I hope not; he thought as he pulled back the shower curtain and stepped into the bathtub.

The hot water poured over his shoulders and gave him a bit of relief from the very stressful and busy day at the office. There had been what seemed like an endless schedule of boring meetings, most of which could have been done via email. But the worst part came just before leaving the office. He was almost to the elevator when his boss handed him the budget analysis report. It was now sitting on the coffee table.

Ryan sighed and realized how sore and tired he was. But

unfortunately, with that dreadful report to read tonight, he knew he couldn't possibly stay under the water as long as he would have liked.

Turning off the taps, the sound of the water ceased, and that's when he heard it.

The phone! It was ringing.

Scrambling over the edge of the bathtub to make it before it stopped ringing proved to be anything but graceful. Ryan's right foot landed clear on the floor, but his left caught the edge of the bathtub. He instinctively reached out and grabbed the closest thing to slow his fall. Unfortunately, it was the shower curtain. Along with each pop, pop, pop as the curtain ripped off of each loop, the closer he got to the floor. He landed with a hard thud.

Hearing the answering machine pick up and Anna's voice, he threw the now completely free shower curtain into the bathtub and rolled to his stomach. Doing a quick push-up, he was on his feet, racing to the living room.

Ryan grabbed the phone. "Hello? Hello? Anna?"

Silence. The answering machine then beeped, and the light started to flash.

"Dang!"

Ryan, seeing that the living room curtains were open, threw the phone onto the couch, ducked and rushed back to the bathroom. After he had wrapped a towel around his waist, he snatched the hand towel off the rack. Returning to the living room, he mopped up the little water puddle he had left and then backtracked to the bathroom catching all the wet footprints. After throwing the hand towel into the laundry basket, he left the bathroom to grab his cell.

It wasn't on the front entry table, nor on the kitchen island.

ARGH!!

After frantically searching around the house for it, Ryan finally located it behind the couch. It must have fallen off the back when he came in and collapsed on it. As the frustration from tearing the house apart started to ease, he reprimanded himself again for not implementing his New Year's Resolution to be tidier.

Sitting down on the ottoman, he located Anna's number in his contacts list, grabbed the house phone, and dialed her number.

She quickly answered. "Hello?"

"Hey, Anna, it's me. Is everything alright?" Ryan tried to keep a calm, light tone to his voice, but his worry poked through.

"Yeah, of course, we're great. We just got back from a surprise trip to Europe my dad took us on. What's up?"

"Oh, nothing much. I was just worried when you didn't call back. But hey, are you gals having fun? How was Europe?"

"Um, yeah us... girls are fine. My mom says hi by the way."

"Oh yeah? Say hi back for me." Ryan rose to pace the room.

"I will," said Anna. "Yeah, Europe was great. We saw so much. It was a nice break. Are we still on for the end of the month?"

"Yup, you bet. Hey, I was wondering... are you girls OK with me crashing your girl party early? I would love to come out sooner and see you guys and hang out a bit." He sighed. "I could use a bit of a vacation."

"Um... Ryan? Is everything alright? You can't miss my mom that much." Anna chuckled yet sounded a bit confused.

"No, no... I mean... yeah, I miss her, but I want to hang out with you and Hailey. Can I talk to her?"

"My mom?"

"No, Hailey. Can you give her the phone?" He sat back down to steady his nerves.

"Uh, Ryan what are you talking about? Hailey's not here."

Ryan sat back down. He would have accused her of joking, but the tentativeness in her voice had no hint of sarcasm, and it caused his heart to sink.

"What do you mean she's not there?"

"She isn't coming until sometime after the sixteenth when finals are over. You know that. What's going on?" Her worry coated each word.

The color drained from Ryan's face. Despite feeling a little light headed, he rose off the ottoman, walked over to the window, and looked down to the dark street below. Resting his head against the glass, he closed his eyes and sighed.

"Anna, Thomas drove Hailey to the airport a couple of weeks ago. She left early to surprise you guys. She has to be there."

"Ryan, she isn't here." The dread in Anna's voice poured through the phone line.

If Hailey wasn't with Anna, then where was she?

CHAPTER 3

– Six weeks earlier –

"Hailey, are we keeping you from something?"

"What?"

Hailey jolted out of her daydream and realized the whole class was staring at her. She felt the color flood her face like a can of crimson paint being poured over her head. Embarrassed, she sat up straight and returned her attention to the front.

Professor Gladstone was glaring at her, licking his lips and impatiently tapping his fingers on the podium. From the angry heave of his chest, she could almost smell the staleness of his breath.

He always wore the same dull, gray suit, ebony-rimmed glasses, which were too big for his face, and a scraggly beard that usually had some crumbs in it from his lunch. He was a brilliant man, no question. But Hailey wondered why he had to be so ruthless about pointing out, what he perceived to be, other people's lack of intelligence. It was that arrogance that felt like the sound of fingernails on a chalkboard to Hailey.

After her grades had started falling, he seemed to single her out at every chance that presented itself. Lately, this happened at least once every class, and it made Hailey feel incredibly small.

Why can't I concentrate?

She already knew the answer to that, and it drove her crazy.

Why can't I just let it go and move on?

She hated the fact that it was so cliché. Hailey tried to pride herself on being a strong, independent woman, one who didn't need a man to be whole or give her the ability to define herself. But here she was, a total mess.

"Shake it off Hailey," she whispered quietly to herself.

"Excuse me? Miss Pearson, if you actually have an answer then you must speak up," the professor hissed as he moved his glasses even further down his nose.

"Oh, um... nothing, sir. I didn't... ah... hear what you asked. Could you please repeat the question?" She wished her voice hadn't come out sounding so timid.

"Are you trying to make a mockery of this institution?" he said with a sneer. "Miss Pearson, we are not a class of one here. If you came to this fine establishment to learn and not just to take up space, then pay attention or I will give you an F for this class, regardless of the quality of your past assignments."

Hailey apologized and slumped down in her seat, wishing she could become invisible at will.

The rest of the forty minutes of philosophy class ticked by painstakingly slow. Learning nothing, Hailey eased out of her seat, grabbed her things, and quickly left the classroom as soon as it ended. She headed down the hall, out the main entrance of the philosophy building, and into the sun.

I so wish I could graduate without that stupid class. I'd drop it in a second.

Hailey couldn't believe that even though she was already more than halfway through her fourth year attending Columbia, she was still confused about what she wanted to do with her life.

To date, she had changed what she wanted to major in three times. This meant Hailey wouldn't be graduating at the end of this semester with the rest of her friends. Although that wasn't the worst part, it was that she still wasn't satisfied or confident in the direction her life was going even in this major. More and more often these days she felt as if she was on a rollercoaster set on cruise control, but Hailey couldn't remember why she had gotten on in the first place.

"Hey, Hail, wait up!"

Hailey craned her head over her shoulder to see Sheila rushing towards her, arms full of books. Sheila was the only one that called her Hail, and she loved the nickname, regardless of the harsh weather reference. She was a great friend, although if Hailey was honest, she was also a bit of a rival. Sheila was an ideal student, and it caused Hailey to be a bit jealous.

"Sweetie, where have you been?" Sheila paused to catch her breath. "It's been a week, and you haven't called me back, how was your time off?" Her voice was cheerful, but at that moment, it grated on Hailey's nerves.

"Ah… spring break wasn't that great. Mostly uneventful." Hailey kicked a rock with her shoe, trying to hide her frustration. It didn't work.

"What's wrong?" concern drenched Sheila's tone.

Hailey huffed. "I just came from philosophy with Mr. 'I'm mightier than thou,' and I'm kind of freaking out. He nailed me again."

"Well, were you paying attention?"

Why did she have to do that? Hailey thought to herself. *It's not my fault I can't concentrate. It's Jeremy's.*

Hailey hated him even more because of it.

"Well… no, not really," Hailey admitted. "And yup… he saw

me. Why can't Gladstone just ignore me and get on with his class? I swear that man has the radar of a bat. If anyone in his class even remotely thinks about something other than what he is discussing at that exact moment in time, an alarm goes off in that huge brain of his and he nails them." Hailey, exasperated, threw her hands in the air. "It's not fair being expected to even be in the same room with that sort of ability. It's impossible. He's impossible. The whole class is impossible. I hate this." Hailey groaned and looked at Sheila with sad eyes.

"Yup, I'm so glad I'm done that class. Hang in there. You will get through it," Sheila said with annoying optimism. "Only six more weeks and classes will be done. They will fly by. You'll see. Then summer will be here, and you will be free for a whole three and a half glorious months." Sheila's tone made it all sound so easy.

"Is that all?" Hailey groaned. "I don't even know if I want to come back. Really, what am I even doing here?"

"Hail, listen to me. You are a passionate woman and with that comes some confusion. You don't get one without the other. But don't give up, you're so close. Just a couple more semesters to catch up. I'm certain you'll find your way. You just have to hang in there."

Sheila reached out and squeezed both her shoulders and playfully shook her until a small smile broke through Hailey's defeat. Hailey felt a bit of guilt for being so annoyed with her.

"Well, I'll try, but I'm not promising anything." Hailey flashed Sheila a quirky smirk. "Anyways, how are you?"

"Great actually! It was nice to get away for a bit and clear my head."

"It's good to have you back. Campus was lonely without you."

Hailey was about to end the conversation, say goodbye and head for her dorm, when Sheila stopped her.

"You know, you should really think about coming to Thomas' party, especially because you won't let us throw you one for your birthday." Her voice held a begging quality. "I think it will do you good to have some fun. It should be pretty small, just a handful of people and we will just be hanging out, nothing crazy.

"Oh... I don't know," Hailey stalled. "With the track meet this weekend and trying to survive another birthday... honestly, I'm not sure if I'm up for it. Besides isn't Jer going to be there?"

Sheila sighed. "Ah... yeah! But Ryan and I will be there too. You can't avoid Jer forever. Please come." Sheila pleaded.

Hailey hated that she still had such a fear of running into Jeremy. The pain was still so fresh, and the confusion over why it happened was still in abundance. She didn't understand it, and she didn't want to explore the reasons as to why he didn't want her.

Hailey thought for a moment. *If I did go, what would I say? I... could just ignore him and pretend he wasn't there. But really, how ridiculous is that? This isn't high school, stupid. It would be so much easier not to see him at all. Then that way I can just ignore it and try to forget about the whole mess.*

"I'm sorry. I'm just not ready."

"You'll be missed."

After convincing Sheila to give Thomas her apologies and saying goodbye, she headed off to her dorm room.

Sheila was great, no question. They had hit it off from the moment they bumped into each other on orientation day, over three years ago. They were both on the track team and loved the theater. They had gotten even closer this year, especially after

Anna had left to go back home.

To Hailey, it seemed that Sheila was someone who had it all together. She had a kind spirit, a brilliant mind, and a goal orientated personality that tenaciously went after anything she set her heart on. Then there was her beauty. Sheila's dark, raven hair fell in soft waves over her shoulders, which highlighted her ivory, blemish-free skin. Her blue eyes were gentle and welcoming. Her smile and goofy expressions showed off perfect white teeth. As a whole, Sheila looked more like a painting than something resulting from a mix of genes.

In a way, Hailey envied her, and she wished she could summon up even an ounce of Sheila's focus. Sheila had such a positive outlook on life, which probably helped her to focus.

After the accident when she was a teenager, Hailey had lost all the authentic optimism she had. She had faked it for years now and convincingly so. She fooled everyone. Yet despite her constant attention to her façade, as time went on, it was getting thinner and thinner.

As soon as Hailey got in the door of her room and dropped her book bag, she collapsed on the bed. Thinking of running into Jeremy brought up all the emotion to the surface again. The tears stung her eyes and soaked her pillow. It wasn't one of those movie cries, where a few tears peacefully roll down each cheek. It was a cry that came out from the depths of her soul, from a broken heart and shattered expectations.

She felt so alone and now lying on her bed, weeping away, she found herself missing Anna so intensely that it genuinely, physically hurt.

This would all be so much easier if she were here. Hailey continued to sob as she reminisced about their first meeting.

- - - - - - -

After saying goodbye to her aunt outside, Hailey had just settled into her dorm room at Columbia when the door to her room flew open. In came a bubbly and spunky girl, overloaded with suitcases and bags. Both the girl's hands were full of belongings. Bags also hung around her neck and from both shoulders. She was even kicking a small box.

The girl had an exotic beauty. Her dark hair was a messy mass that was held up by a strip of earth-colored cloth on the top of her head. Her clothes had a cool, thrift store, hippy vibe.

The girl waddled over to the other bed and collapsed. She didn't take the bags off her hands or let go of the suitcases, she just went over to the bed and fell face down and let out a small groan.

"Um, hi?" Hailey said tentatively.

"Oh, ah..."

The girl struggled to get upright again but became tangled in her bags. The more she tried to sit up, the more tangled she got. She looked like a fish flopping on the deck of a boat. As the bags were still tying up her hands, it made it impossible for her to get them under herself and push off the bed.

Hailey stifled a laugh.

"Sorry, I didn't know anyone was in here yet. Just a second. Be with you shortly." The girl finally broke free by half sliding, half rolling off her bed. She stood up and frantically pushed her hair out of her face, adjusted her shirt and smoothed out her pants.

Hailey kept silent as she watched the comical scene play out in front of her.

"Hello," the girl said, extending her hand as she took a step towards Hailey.

But before she could finish the movement, her toe caught on the top of her largest suitcase. The girl went sprawling forward, and when she came to a stop, she was in Hailey's arms.

"I'm Anna, it's very nice to meet you," the girl said casually.

Both girls burst out laughing and fell to the floor in a big mess of limbs.

- - - - - - -

Hailey thought it was the perfect start. From that moment on, there was no pretense or info required to see if their personalities or interests matched up. They were friends as soon as they hit the floor that day. And they weren't the kind of friends that just hung out to be a safety net for each other so they wouldn't appear or feel alone at such a big university. They were the kind that told each other everything, every gory detail of who they were, what they thought and experienced.

I miss her so much, Hailey thought to herself as she grabbed more tissues from her nightstand.

With Anna, there was no competition or judgment. They accepted each other for who they were and who they weren't. And if Hailey was honest, Anna was the closest thing she had to a family.

Hailey, of course, loved her aunt. But seeing how Aunt Norah looked so much like her mother, it hurt too much to be around her for long or to open up to her.

Anna had decided to take classes throughout the summer last year to get through her fine arts degree faster. When she finished her final exams mid-December, she headed back to Saudi Arabia where her parents were stationed. It was only a few days after Jeremy had broken things off with Hailey.

"You can call me anytime, whenever you need someone to talk. Day or night, OK?"

At the time, Anna's words were comforting, but calling Anna now and disrupting her life yet again, seemed selfish.

Hailey still had Sheila, but it wasn't the same. Not to be misread, Hailey loved being friends with her. It was just that there was that touch of competition and reserve with Sheila. They were close, but Sheila just wasn't Anna.

The sobs continued to assault Hailey's body, causing it to shake violently. She was scared, alone, and questioning everything. She didn't even hear that soft voice calling to her. After about an hour of tears, fatigue finally took over, and she fell into a restless sleep.

=======

Sheila banged on the door.

Where is that girl?

The track meet was this weekend in Richmond, and their coach made it very clear that they needed every second of practice until then. Sheila had already waited for her in the courtyard for ten minutes, and they were now running late.

Hadn't Hailey said she would meet me and walk over to practice together? Where is she?

Annoyed, Sheila banged on Hailey's door again.

With the exception of a few people coming and going from their dorm rooms, the hallway was mostly empty. The smell of fresh laundry mixed with macaroni and cheese filled the air. After a few moments of standing in the hallway, shifting her weight from one foot to the other and getting more and more impatient, Hailey finally opened the door.

23

Right away Sheila could see something was wrong. Hailey's face was puffy and blotchy, her eyes swollen, and in the distance, the whole bed was littered with crumpled tissues.

"Sweetie, hey what's wrong?" Sheila, her frustration forgotten, went to her with arms open.

Accepting Sheila's support, Hailey leaned into her. Her chest heaved again.

"It's so... stupid, it's been... over for two months and..." Her words became incoherent, her sobs masking the end of her sentence.

Sheila didn't need the rest, she knew. Hailey was heartbroken. Her friend was hurting, and here she was with Hailey in her arms, sobbing away. And where a friend should be feeling empathy, compassion, and concern, Sheila only felt guilt.

CHAPTER 4

The track meet was a great distraction even though it didn't have the outcome she had hoped for. Coming in fourth in most of her events frustrated Hailey, yet she made sure to keep up a smiling face until she was off the bus.

After a quick goodbye to the other girls, she grabbed her bag and headed for her dorm. She was desperately hoping to place so that the accomplishment might help cover up the lack of control she felt. With every step, her frustration grew.

What's wrong with you?

The question just kept repeating itself over and over, forcing her anger level to rise with each repetition. When she reached her room, she unlocked the door and slammed it behind her, rattling some of the framed photos hanging on the wall.

Hailey stormed around the room, pacing like a caged lion. Throwing her gym bag across the room, it landed with a huge thud as it hit the leg of the desk. Surprisingly the act liberated a small portion of the anger and frustration that was almost entirely consuming her core. But the walls still felt like they were closing in on her and it made it feel like the air was being sucked from the room. She could hardly breathe. Hailey's lungs felt like they were on fire and the room started to spin.

She hated herself getting so emotional, and she tried to will herself to calm down. She hurled herself on her bed. But before the tears of frustration had a chance to be released, she felt something jab into her side. Rising off the bedspread, she looked down to find a small rose-colored envelope with her name inscribed on the front.

Hailey's fingers made quick work of the sealed flap and pulled out the card from inside. A smirk quickly took over her face, washing away her frustration. She gazed at the card. She didn't even need to look inside to know who it was from.

The bright colors splashed across the front of the card were common on all child birthday cards. It had originally been a card for a two-year-old, but in the classic style of the giver, there was a five drawn with a purple marker to the right of the sparkly number two.

In all the years Hailey had known Ryan Foster she had never received a card that was originally designated for the occasion for which they were celebrating. Ryan was normally quiet and carried himself with a shy confidence. Although in contrast, somewhere in his personality, there was a dry wit that loved adding "special touches" to the cards he gave out.

Whether it was crossing out words and inputting his own or just adding numbers, it seemed impossible for Ryan to buy a card, sign his name and leave it at that. However, Hailey didn't mind. In fact, she liked Ryan's cards more than any of the others she received, no matter the occasion.

Even on the anniversary of her family's death, Ryan sent her a congratulations card, originally meant for a graduation. She was so confused until she read the inside. The original context had been 'Congratulations on your achievement.' However, Ryan had added a few dots and then added "of making it through another year without your family. I admire your strength."

If it had not been for the fact that she had been dating his older brother at the time, she might have taken offense. But in the light of now knowing more about Ryan, his heart, and his goofiness, she was glad she gave him the benefit of the doubt rather than jumping to the judgment that it was a little "off taste."

Her birthday was tomorrow, a fact she had been trying to run away from for weeks now. Hailey didn't feel old enough to be already halfway through her twenties, and she didn't feel like she had much to celebrate this year or the next. The past year was bleak, and the next didn't look any better. On the other hand, seeing Ryan's card and having it cause her to smile, she was reminded of something.

Yeah, things suck, but I do have some really great friends.

Her mind played over memories of the incredible support that those friends had shown her over these last few months and her mind drifted back to Anna.

If Anna were sitting beside her right now, she would offer her a shoulder to cry on. Anna wouldn't assault her ears with advice or judgment. She would just hold her and repeat 'Oh honey, I'm so sorry. I promise it will get better'. Hailey's soul ached to hear those words now, and with the realization that the room was filled with a deafening, empty silence, fresh tears welled up in her eyes.

As they brimmed over and rolled down her cheeks, she looked over at the phone, and before she could even second guess herself, she reached out for it.

Hailey curled up. With her knees to her chest and her back pressing into the corner of the wall at the head of her bed, she cradled the phone in both hands. She leaned back across her bed, opened the small drawer of her nightstand and withdrew Anna's number, then leaned back against the wall.

She knew Anna would love a call from her, but seeing how they had just talked last week, Hailey didn't have anything new to tell her. Minus sharing the disappointment that was the track meet, there wasn't much to say except to reiterate all the things Anna had heard a million times. If only they could see each other and have some fun like they used to. Hailey desperately missed seeing her every day.

Anna was an amazing artist, and she loved to peruse the many art galleries in New York. And although Hailey's artistic ability was pretty much non-existent, she loved to join Anna and see things through her eyes. Anna relaxed by being in nature and found a way of transporting herself away from this concrete jungle whenever she was looking at art. Whenever Hailey joined her, Anna could transport her as well, and she missed that.

Oh, how Hailey wished she could be transported now. She wanted to be anywhere but here, surrounded by all the pain of not being able to move on with her life and not knowing where to move onto, even if she could. As soon as the thought of being somewhere else graced Hailey's mind, a plan started to form.

Why shouldn't I?

To leave and go somewhere to clear her head sounded wonderful. Anyone could easily see she wasn't accomplishing anything by staying at Columbia. Hailey was pretty much just going through the motions of a routine she didn't even understand anymore.

She lifted the phone off her knees and made quick work of Anna's long phone number. The connection was horrible at first, but after the assistance of an operator, the sounds of ringing filled Hailey's ears.

Anna had been living back in Saudi Arabia with her parents for three months now. Her parents, Chuck and Linda, had lived in Saudi ever since Anna was a little girl. Her Dad was an executive at Entrata, a booming oil company.

As Hailey listed to the ringing, she wondered how Anna liked being back there.

- - - - - - -

"The situation in Saudi is a touchy balance for westerners." Anna had told her soon after they had met. "Inside the compounds, life is a Polaroid replica of western resort-living. We have our own grocery stores, beauty shops, gyms, pools, and other recreation centers and amenities. My family and the other residents, who are mostly from places in Europe, rarely even need to leave the compound. Apart from work and venturing out to some restaurants and malls, which are located close to the compounds, we pretty much stay within the walls."

"I would have never guessed that."

"It's true. On the other hand, when someone does go out of the compounds, life for us foreign women is... anything but effortless. Once outside the walls, women are required to wear the traditional dress that is mandatory for the Saudi woman. It's called an abaya. It's a long dress like garment with long sleeves that ensures complete coverage of any skin, apart from hands and feet. Saudi women are also required to wear a scarf to cover their head and hair. Some locals are even required to wear a veil that barely leaves a shadow of their eyes visible."

"Oh yeah, I saw a woman dressed like that the other day."

"Fortunately, the religious police aren't allowed to enter the compound to harass the residents; which is a good thing. That kind of dress code only pertains to the gates and beyond. Inside the compound, we're free to choose to wear whatever we want, including bathing suits, tank tops, and shorts. This is something that would most likely get us imprisoned or thrown out of the country if such freedoms were taken on the streets outside."

- - - - - - -

As Anna relayed such stories to Hailey, she always tried to stress that, regardless of the hassle of living in a different culture, it was good to learn from and be respectful of another society. Hailey admired Anna for that outlook.

Hailey had done a bit of traveling, but she now wondered how she would fare in such a place which was so drastically different from what she was used to. Nevertheless, she felt she needed to move ahead with her plan.

"Hello?" a woman's voice answered.

"Hi, I was wondering if I might speak with Anna please."

After a few moments, Anna's voice came on the line.

"Hey, Anna, it's Hailey. Sorry to call you again, but I have something to run by you."

After being jokingly chastised by Anna on how it was never a bother, Hailey divulged her plan.

=======

Even though he loved parties, the one he was throwing next weekend had Thomas a little nervous. He didn't blame his brother. It had been three months, but knowing that she would be at the party with him and that Hailey would be there too, made it a potential for a volcanic situation.

What if they didn't play it cool?

Questions like that had been occupying his thoughts for the past week.

Thomas cared for Hailey as though she were his little sister. He had felt that way soon after meeting her when Jeremy introduced them. Hailey was sweet and sincere, and Thomas was sure she would soon become his sister-in-law, everyone did. Everyone, even Hailey, he had assumed, was expecting to see a ring on her finger come Christmas.

Even though the three brothers were inseparable, not even Thomas or Ryan saw Jeremy's change of heart coming. It came as a shock when Jeremy called him a few days before Christmas late one night to tell him it was over.

Why did Jeremy have to break up with her in the first place, and just before Christmas? Sure, he said he just knew she wasn't the one. But seriously, they had been together for three years and if she wasn't the one I don't know how anyone else could be; they seemed perfect for each other. I guess You must just have different plans.

It hit Thomas hard as he listened while Jeremy explained his decision, but his thoughts soon drifted to how Hailey must have been feeling at that moment. And over the last three months, he had a front-row seat to experience just how hard she took it. Those three months would go down as the most awkward and painful in the group's history. This was the exact reason why he was now dreading the party.

Oh Lord, help it work out. She has to find out sooner or later.

And with that, Thomas tried to let it go and wait to see what transpired at the party.

=======

"Hailey, you know we would love to have you and I miss you so much. But are you sure you want to come to Saudi? If you need to get away after finals, I could always meet you in Europe or even somewhere closer to you."

"Thanks, but I think I really need to get away, really away. I mean everything that is familiar to me is eating away at my will to keep going. I know I sound like a heartbroken idiot, but I can't fool myself anymore." Hailey had to sneak a quick breath to keep the tears at bay. "I really can't keep going like this, and I think a trip to somewhere so different from what I'm used to might be just the thing to snap me out of this self-pitying ditch I'm trapped in. Does any of that make sense?"

"Hey, it totally does, and it is no wonder you are feeling the way you are." Anna chuckled. "And you are not an idiot; you're a woman who had her heart broken. You're responding in a completely normal way. So don't worry about that, there is absolutely no judgment from me."

Those few words from Anna hit their mark, and Hailey's nerves settled a bit. Anna had this amazing way of reminding Hailey to feel what she was feeling and to accept it as being OK. Up until then, Hailey had tried to ignore her feelings, and it wasn't working; they were growing and taking over.

Hailey instantly knew she had made the right choice to go visit Anna. It was the perfect change she needed, the perfect plan to start over. Of course, there were numerous details they needed to figure out, and for the next hour, that's just what they did.

"Well, first things first. You will need to get an entrance visa, which my dad will have to sign. He will act as your sponsor while you're here. This usually takes quite a while, but my dad has a contact that can probably get it for you in about four or five weeks. The entrance visa my dad will get you, is good for a year so you can stay as long as you like. But keep in mind that you will also need an exit visa, or you won't be able to leave the country. So if you are thinking of only coming for a few weeks, then my dad can apply for that at the same time."

"Oh, well if you and your parents don't mind," Hailey interjected, "I would love to stay for a bit longer than a couple of weeks. I haven't planned things out in detail yet as far as a time frame goes. All I know is that I desperately need to get away. Is that OK?"

"Yeah definitely. Just keep that in mind and give us a two-week heads up when you are ready to head home. My dad will take care of getting it all organized. And don't worry about my parents. They have a hotel-like attitude when it comes to my friends. You are more than welcome to stay as long as you like. We would all love to have you, even in your 'woe is me' phase." Anna chuckled again. "We can help you get up the other side."

Hailey could almost hear Anna smiling.

"Well, what about one of those abaya things all the women have to wear? Do you know where I could even get one of those? I guess I will have to wear one when we go out and about, right?"

"Don't worry about a thing. I can take care of all of that. Just look for a package in a little more than a month and inside will be everything you will need: a visa, clothes, directions and your plane ticket. It will be all set, and all you'll have to do is catch the plane, make your transfers, and give me a big hug at the airport when you see me."

"Wait a second. There is no way I can let you cover the ticket. Just tell me how much it is, and I can forward you the money," Hailey protested.

"Not a chance. You've had enough hard knocks this last year, and the last thing you need to do is try and plan a trip to somewhere you've never been. You might as well get used to a little TLC because that's all you'll get when you're here." Anna's empathy felt refreshing, and Hailey was so grateful for the offer.

After another half hour of reminiscing and making a few rough plans, Hailey leaned over and laid her phone back on her night stand. Peace and excitement flooded her soul, and a small amount of relief took up residence in her heart. She knew the next month and a half would go by painfully slow, but she was thankful that at least she would have finals to distract her; studying would take up most of her time.

CHAPTER 5

The next week was very uneventful. Apart from taking a few calls from Ryan urging her to get out of her dorm, Hailey went to her classes and studied. She didn't go out for coffee with the girls on Tuesday morning, a tradition Hailey took part in ever since she started at Columbia. She didn't grab lunch with Sheila, Thomas, and Ryan, which she would normally do at least a couple of times a week when Ryan could pull himself away from the office. Hailey was just too focused on the trip, and apart from prepping for her exams, everything else just seemed futile.

Hailey didn't feel like she was any fun to be around and so she saw no point in subjecting her friends to the pathetic existence she was leading. Hailey secluded herself and implored Ryan to make excuses for her. It worked up until Friday night when Ryan finally refused.

"No Hailey, I'm not doing it anymore. If you don't come, you can call Thomas and tell him yourself that you aren't coming to your party." The frustration in Ryan's voice grew as he spoke.

"Wait, what? My party? What are you talking about?"

"That's right, your party." Ryan let out an exasperated breath. "You've been moping around for months, which we all completely understand. But seeing how you are so overwhelmed and wouldn't let anyone throw you a party for your birthday, Thomas thought he would anyway and just not tell you. I wasn't supposed to say anything. But honestly, what you're doing is not healthy, and we are all really worried about you. You need to get out of the house." He took a deep breath and signed. "And yes, before you ask, Jeremy will be there. But either you go and learn how to be in the same room with him, or you separate yourself from the rest of us. I totally disagree with what he did to you, but I'm not going to exclude my brother from everything. We are a group package, and we don't leave anyone behind." Ryan's voice softened a bit. "Please come, Hailey. You'll see that it will start to get better. The key is, you have to keep moving for that to happen."

Following a few more convincing points from Ryan, Hailey gave in.

"Great, now go get dressed. I will be there to pick you up in half an hour. The party already started a... little over an hour ago, and people probably have given up on the idea that you will be coming. But it will be great; we can surprise them. How does that sound?"

If Hailey was honest with herself, it did sound like fun.

"OK, sounds good. I will see you soon."

Hailey clicked the phone off and threw it on the bed as she hurled herself towards the bathroom, leaving a trail of clothes behind her.

- - - - - - -

"Wow, you look beautiful." Ryan's eyes danced as they fell on Hailey as she opened the door.

"Thanks, do you think it's too dressy?"

"Nah, you look great."

Seeing Ryan's response to her new dress boosted her confidence that this night just might not be the end of the world.

So what if Jeremy was there. Ryan was right. I need to learn to be Jeremy's friend again... OK, maybe that's a stretch. I'm not willing to lose any friends because of him, so I can at least learn to tolerate his presence.

There was also her small, dark wishful desire to make Jeremy eat his heart out. Considering Ryan's response to the dress, that just might be accomplished tonight.

"Thanks for kicking me in the butt. I think I needed this."

Hailey locked her dorm room and headed to Ryan's car. Once inside, Ryan turned on some music and headed for Thomas's place. Hailey was grateful that Ryan seemed content just listen to the music and leave her with her thoughts. She needed some time to pump herself up so she could remain in a positive frame of mind and not ruin the evening for the others.

Hailey appreciated Ryan's authenticity and that their friendship remained intact when Jeremy ended things. He was shy, but what he lacked in outward confidence, he made up for in sincerity. Ryan was one of those guys who would be on your 'first to call' list if you were in trouble or just needed someone. He had a way of giving you his attention without causing you to doubt his intentions, as well as, a sensitivity that didn't give question to his manliness. Ryan was a true friend in every way.

Hailey had first met Ryan through Jeremy. Although in such a small world, the Foster brothers also had a connection with her through her best friend. Ryan, Thomas, and Jeremy had met Anna when they were little. Both their fathers worked together at Entrata. Tim, the boys' dad, was stationed in New York while Anna's dad, Chuck, remained stationed overseas in Saudi.

On Tim's business trips, their fathers would hang out and play golf together. During Christmas holidays, when Anna and her parents made it to the states, the Fosters and the Haringtons would spend it together.

Now that Ryan had followed in his father's footsteps and worked for Entrata, he now stayed with Anna and her parents. Entrata always expensed a room at a ritzy hotel or a rented apartment in the compound for him, but Ryan never stayed at either. He had sort of adopted Anna's parents as his second family.

- - - - - - -

As Hailey thought about them hanging out as kids, it helped to reroute Hailey's train of thought away from Jeremy.

"Oh hey, I talked with Anna last week."

Ryan glanced at her. "Yeah? How is she?"

"Great, she misses everyone. I'm actually off to see her at the end of finals."

"Really?" he said hesitantly, concern clouded his face.

"Yeah... why not? I mean I'm not doing anything for the summer and I really, really need to get away." Hailey got excited again just thinking about it.

"Well actually," he paused, "I think it is a great idea. And... it turns out I'm scheduled to go there for a business trip at the end of May. We'll be able to hang out." Ryan smiled. "I mean if you're OK with that."

"Yeah, that sounds great."

Ryan spent the rest of the drive telling her about some great places to eat and others to avoid. Ten minutes later, they pulled up to Thomas's. Ryan turned off the car and turned to Hailey.

"You ready for this?" He winked at her and smiled.

With a deep breath, Hailey replied, "You bet, let's go."

And with that, they exited the car and headed to the door. With one quick knock, Ryan opened the door and ushered Hailey in with a supportive arm, for which she was grateful.

"Hailey! Happy birthday," the crowd in the living room chimed out in unison.

Warmth filled her heart, and she grinned at the realization that she had been overreacting and foolish for even thinking of not coming. These people loved and accepted her. Even though Jeremy didn't want to be with her, these friends would help her pick up the pieces and move on.

There were a lot of faces she recognized and a few she didn't. This didn't surprise her. Even though Thomas threw the party for her, he always had the mentality of "the more, the merrier" and tonight was no exception. It seemed the house was full.

So much for a small gathering Sheila! But in all honesty, Hailey didn't mind.

She did a quick sweep of the room. Jeremy was nowhere to be seen. So far so good. Hailey needed a moment to settle herself. Ryan took her coat and disappeared down the hall. Hailey waved to the crowd and excused herself to the kitchen, where she heard Thomas yelling at the coffee machine.

"You know you can always buy another one; she will forgive you."

Thomas glanced over his shoulder. "Are you kidding? This is the best coffee machine; you know that. It makes the best cup, and I'm horrified you would suggest getting rid of her when I know she still has so much more to give."

Hailey leaned against the doorjamb and crossed her arms as she raised her eyebrows at him.

"I think she'll understand," Hailey teased him.

Thomas placed his hand on either side of the machine as if covering its invisible ears. "How dare you suggest such a thing." His voice oozed sarcasm. He couldn't keep up the ruse for long, and a smile broke out.

Hailey loved hanging out at the house, especially with Thomas. He always made her laugh and was a master at making people feel at ease, a friend to everyone he met. He crossed the room, picked her up and twirled her around in a huge hug.

"Hey, baby girl, how are you? We were pretty sure you weren't going to make it. I'm so glad you did."

"Hmm, me too. Thanks for not listening to me. I love the party. I've been a sour puss for far too long."

"Yeah, I know. It's been a total bummer. You're lucky we stuck around." Thomas joked, trying to push her buttons. He put her back down but kept her close.

"Oh shush," she said accompanied with a playful slap to his arm. "You know you love me and you couldn't get by without me."

"Well, you got me there." Thomas held her in his arms and grinned at her. "You know we love you right and that we're here for you?"

"I know."

"Well then, don't push us away. Come on now, how would you survive without me? Now that really would be impossible." Thomas was certainly a charmer.

"Oh, I don't know." Hailey moved back and dramatically placed the back of her wrist against her forehead. "I'm sure I would manage somehow."

"Oh no, you wouldn't. But don't worry I'm not going anywhere kiddo." Turning his attention back to the counter he said, "Give me a hand with the food will ya?"

Hailey grabbed a platter of cheese and crackers from Thomas and headed into the living room. He followed, carrying a large spinach bowl.

Thomas had a perfect place for parties. The living room was large with couches lining three of the dark brown walls. He had installed hardwood floors and put a DJ platform in one corner. Even though the Foster brothers weren't into drinking at their parties, there was a small bar against the opposite corner that had soda on tap and other non-alcoholic drinks. Sporadically placed in front of the couches were little, round coffee tables and square ottomans, which were used as extra seating. The lights were low and created a jazz bar-type setting that was warm and soothing, making it easy to relax and converse with friends.

The house also held a fantastic game room with high tables and bar stools, a bookcase filled with card and board games, a pool table, and a foosball table. To top it off, it had an old-fashioned jukebox.

Thomas had built stairs next to the entrance of the game room, which led up to a small door. It opened onto the roof so you could get fresh air yet still be close to the party.

The roof was one of Hailey's favorite places in the city. Thomas had set up two poles parallel to the roof's peak, then strung strands of white, Christmas twinkle lights on the rooftop above the door to each of the poles to create a square. The strands continued down the length of each pole. There were two patio furniture sets and a porch swing for seating. He even installed a couple outside heaters to ward off the chill, which was welcomed this time of year. But it was the view that gave the spot a real romantic getaway feeling.

Thomas's house was perfectly placed along his street, so you got a clear view of the Chrysler Building: Hailey's favorite in all of New York. She loved sitting up there. Seeing the lights and hearing the busyness of the city invigorated her. It didn't matter if she was alone or if it was in the midst of a party and the place was packed; it was peaceful and breathtaking.

After a few more trips to the kitchen to help with the food, Hailey plopped down in the corner of one of the couches and grabbed a handful of taco chips from one of the little tables. She curled her feet under herself and struck up a conversation with a girl from her English-lit class. After a few minutes, it struck Hailey that she hadn't seen Sheila yet.

"Hey, have you seen Sheila? Did she make it?" Hailey questioned the girl.

"Oh yeah, she's been here a while now. I last saw her heading up to the roof."

Hailey excused herself and headed over to Ryan. "Hey, Ryan, can I borrow your sweater, please? I just want to head up to the roof."

Ryan slipped off his sweater and handed it to her. "Do you want some company?"

"Nah, Sheila's up there, so I'll be OK."

Donning Ryan's sweater, she headed towards the back of the house and up the steps. Grabbing the door handle, she pushed it open. The sight before her did take her breath away. Although it wasn't the view of the city she saw, it wasn't the lights, and it wasn't the sounds that assaulted her senses. It was a manifestation of her worst unknown fear. Something that could only be born in a bad dream and not a conscious understanding of a fear she had or thought was even possible.

Panic took over her body, and before she could even process what was happening, her feet went into autopilot, knowing all on their own that they had to get her out of there.

Hailey turned back towards the stairs and slammed the door behind her. Her foot hit the first step, but it caught on her dress, and before she had a chance to grab the railing, gravity took over and pulled her forward.

Down she went.

The stairs were so steep that she completely missed the next five stairs, only to land hard on the last few steps with her left shin and elbow. Her head cracked onto the floor at the bottom of the stairs. Pain seared through her body. With the amount of adrenalin flowing through her, she was able to struggle to her feet and start running towards the hallway before the door opened above her.

Tears ran down her face and even with her best efforts to contain the sobs until she reached the safety of seclusion, they came anyway. She tore through the living room, reached the door and hurled herself outside. The cold air stung the wetness of her cheeks as she bolted down the street towards the subway. As these horrible emotions coursed through her body, she only had one thought, one goal: home.

=======

Ryan had been sitting on the couches in a deep conversation with a few of his buddies when he saw Hailey appear from the hall. Panic filled her face, and she was crying. He instantly jumped up off the couch and started to push by the mob of dancers. But before he was able to break free from the crowd, Hailey had reached the door and was gone. Once past the edge of the living room, he glanced down the hallway to see Jeremy and Sheila running hand in hand towards him.

Ryan's eyes narrowed and burned with anger as Jeremy's eyes met his. In that one expression, Ryan said everything he was thinking.

How could you? You both knew she might have come tonight. You idiots!

By the look on their faces, they received the message loud and clear. They stopped in their tracks. Ryan didn't have time to yell at them. He had to reach Hailey. He turned back towards the door and stormed out of the house.

As soon as he reached the street Ryan looked left, nothing, and then right. There she was. Her distant figure was drawing farther, and farther away and he knew he would never catch her on foot. Even if he were the one with the head start, she would most likely outrun him. He headed to his car.

As he pulled up behind her, he saw that her body was still racking itself with sobs. Ryan's heart filled with empathy. Her dress was ripped, and she was carrying her heels in her hand. She must have taken them off to flee the house faster, causing her nylons to be ruined from the rough concrete.

He slowed the car so not to startle her and rolled down the window.

"Hailey!"

There was no response. She just kept staring ahead and continued to run.

"Hailey, please stop!" He tried to keep his voice soft yet firm.

She stopped and fell to the ground in a ball of sorrow. Ryan stopped the car, jumped out and ran over to her. Scooping her up in his arms, he sat there in the middle of the road with her, holding her as she continued to cry.

"How… could they… Sheila… and Jeremy? How long… have…. they been…" she couldn't finish, but Ryan knew what she was asking.

"I think it's been… about a month now. I'm so sorry Hailey, I know they didn't want you to find out this way. None of us did. We pushed them to tell you sooner, but Sheila thought you were still too upset to handle it. I am so sorry they did this. They shouldn't have been so careless."

"She… she was sitting… on his lap… he had his hands around her. They were… kissing. How could he… how could… she?" Between her sobs, Hailey barely managed to force out her sentence.

Ryan just sat there and let her vent and process all the emotions from witnessing such an event must have brought up for her. She swung from anger to confusion to understanding and back again. Hailey needed this, and he wasn't going to squelch her with his advice or even comforting words, so he remained silent. He just listened and held her.

After a while, she started to shiver, and she was more whimpering now then sobbing. Ryan picked her up, carried her to the car and placed her gently inside. As he drove her home, Hailey just leaned against the window and stared silently at the blur of all they passed. Within minutes she fell asleep.

When they reached her dorm, Ryan carried her inside. Fortunately, she had given him a key for emergencies. He used it as he assumed her purse was still at Thomas's. Unlocking the door, he flicked on the light with his shoulder, went over to her bed and softly laid her down. Ryan then went over to the closet, removed a blanket, covered her up, and then stepped over towards the desk. Upon leaving a brief note to call him as soon as she was awake with an offer of breakfast, he turned off the light and left.

God, heal her heart and protect her from their stupidity.

CHAPTER 6

Time lost its meaning and monotony reigned. Hailey kept going to class and studying but with no productivity to speak of. Her face only inhabited a blank stare and an occasional tear. No sobs, no smiles, nothing that expressed an emotion other than shock.

One might think this girl was overreacting, a girl who didn't know what real pain or heartache was – just a love-sick kid. So what if a man dumped her? Couldn't she use a little growing up? But the truth is, Hailey had endured extreme loss when she was a teenager. So when Jeremy broke her heart, it was more than she could just "get over."

Hailey still blamed herself for the accident. Of course, it was something she would never admit to anyone. She couldn't chance that they would talk her out of feeling responsible. It was her guilt and shame, and she wouldn't allow anyone to take that away. It was for this reason that Hailey hadn't let people get close to her since that day.

When she met Jeremy, it had been years since her loss, and he was the first person she opened up to. She couldn't help herself, she grabbed on to him with her whole being. It wasn't with a puppy dog type love. It was with a passion that would have lasted far beyond gray hair and walkers. But in the end, that passion didn't do her any good.

- - - - - - -

It had been a few days before Christmas and Hailey had been running around most of the day trying to find a few last-minute gifts.

She burst through the front door almost tripping completely on a scarf that found its way out of one of the many bags looped around her wrists. With her feet in a tangle and her hands holding too much to provide any type of support if she fell, Hailey quickly threw her weight and slammed hard into the wall of her aunt's mud room. She hoped to gain some type of friction so she wouldn't end up in a pile atop all her bags. With relief, it worked, and she leaned against the wall to catch her breath.

Once composed and with a less than elegant flick of her foot to slam the door closed, Hailey headed into the living room to unload her arms. No sooner had she dropped the last bag and thought of plopping herself on the couch, did the phone ring and grab her attention.

"Hey," she said with excitement after seeing his face light up her screen.

"Hey, how was your shopping?"

It was Jeremy and her heart, forgetting all the stress of the mall mayhem, soared with excitement. It was just a couple hours before he would pick her up for dinner. They were going to her favorite restaurant on the Upper East Side. She had been giggling with her girlfriends about the possibilities this night might hold, and she was antsy just thinking about it.

"It was great apart from the crowds and parking." She flung herself onto the couch. "I can't wait to see you. We're still on for seven, right?"

"Um, yeah." He paused, and Hailey could hear the tiredness in his voice. "I have to run now," he continued, "to get ready, but I will be there."

He must have had a busy day at work, and Hailey was now glad that she had chosen the black dress. It would certainly make him forget the worst of days at the office. There was the red dress that she had favored, but knowing Jeremy loved her in black, she went with her second favorite.

"Sounds good. I will be ready and waiting." Her grin was almost audible.

A couple hours later, she opened the door. Jeremy's response wasn't quite what she expected or hoped for, but she was glad she wore the dress she did.

The cab ride to the restaurant was taken up with her telling Jeremy all the events from her day. Hailey tried to keep the conversation going because she worried that if she paused, her mind would go places she was trying to keep from thinking about until the event happened.

Her friends had been teasing her all week that this was "the night." Hailey wasn't so sure. She was fairly certain Jeremy would wait till his whole family was together Christmas morning. She had told him a few weeks ago that she wanted an iPad for Christmas. However, she suspected she would see a small ring box in Jeremy's hand instead.

As the cab pulled up to the restaurant, Jeremy invited her to go inside and check her coat while he paid the cabbie. She accepted.

Hailey looked at the line that was formed to the right of the door. It was a place she would now be standing in if it weren't for Jeremy's client gifting him with his table for the night. The waiting list at Senses was over a three-month wait, and Hailey had actually been there only once, yet it was still her favorite.

Shortly after checking her coat, Jeremy appeared at her side, and they were soon seated. Their table was nestled into the back corner on the far end of the restaurant, away from the kitchen. Warm lighting encircled the velvet seats and dark mahogany tables. A piano, saxophone, and cello played softly in the background from a small raised stage a few meters away. It was an amazingly romantic setting.

Jeremy, ever the gentleman, pulled out her chair and then took his seat across from her. Hailey glanced at the candle, which resided in the middle of their table, and then looked at Jeremy. She smiled coyly at him. He smiled back and quickly looked away. It was then that Hailey saw it. He was nervous. Jeremy was actually nervous. It was an emotion she very rarely got to see on him. With all that made up Jeremy Foster, nerves just didn't seem to be among them. It was refreshing actually. Hailey kind of enjoyed seeing his discomfort.

But wait! Could these nerves mean that I was wrong? Could this be the day? Hailey couldn't think of another explanation.

She decided she would be kind to him. She politely excused herself and departed to the bathroom. She was barely able to contain her shriek of glee until she pushed through the lady's room door. Upon meeting her reflection in the mirror, she grabbed the edge of the counter and leaned forward. Hailey's face exploded with a smile that seemed like it would take up permanent residence on her face until she returned home after the honeymoon. She rinsed her hands and dabbed some cool water on her neck.

"Mrs. Hailey Foster," she whispered confidently to her reflection. It sounded beautiful. It was a name she would quickly get used to. Like most girls expecting a ring, she had practiced her new signature numerous times and had already settled on one she liked. Taking a deep breath and nodding to her reflection, she exited the bathroom and returned to the table.

=======

Jeremy watched her gracefully return to her seat. *She absolutely has no idea, does she?*

Jeremy would have loved to think this was the first time he realized this fact, but self-denial seemed to be his closest friend of late. Although being seated here now, confronted with the reality of what was happening, he wished he had just let the reservation go and picked a different location. This morning it had seemed like such a good idea to come. It would have taken him months to get a reservation so when Joel Snider gave him his table for the night, he felt pressure to not cancel.

Just breathe Jer, it will be alright. He had no option but to tell himself anything else.

The beginning of the evening passed with Hailey animatedly discussing this and that. She reminded Jeremy of a little hummingbird. She went from one subject to the other, her hands never settling and her endless facial expressions punctuated her sentences. It was an endearing trait that he enjoyed watching.

=======

They ordered their drinks and talked casually until the waiter came to take their order. Once he left, silence crept over the table. Looking out from under her brow, her chin resting playfully on her hand, and elbow on the table, she gave Jeremy a bashful smile. Hailey saw him take a deep breath and she held hers.

Could this be it? She had to scold herself to restrain from fidgeting from the adrenalin that surged through her.

"Hailey," he murmured.

This is it. I am about to be engaged. Hailey finally released a breath and relaxed.

"I don't think we should see each other anymore."

As soon as the words hit her ears, confusion set in. "Excuse me, what?" Hailey shook her head and looked at him.

She leaned closer to make sure she could hear him, but before Jeremy could answer, three waiters returned with their meal, stalling the conversation. Hailey stared at him, but he wouldn't meet her eyes.

Was he joking? He had to be, but then why isn't he looking at me? I must have misunderstood him.

As she waited until the waiters were out of earshot, her eyes darted about as they looked inside her mind for some sort of explanation.

"Jeremy, I know I miss some of your jokes, but this one isn't funny on any level. What are you doing?"

"I'm serious Hailey," he said with a hard swallow. "I have been trying to convince myself that you were the one, but I can't deny it any longer. We're not right for each other, and I don't want to waste your time, it's not fair to you."

Waste my time? Not fair to me? What is he talking about, this has to still be some kind of sick joke? Why is he doing this? Hailey's mind swarmed with questions, but she let him continue.

"I mean, don't get me wrong. I love you. And not to sound cliché... I'm just not in love with you." He paused and took a deep breath. "I think it would be wrong for us to continue when we aren't seriously heading towards something."

"Wait! Just stop!" She lowered her voice a little so as not to draw any attention. "Jeremy, you're serious?"

"Yeah, of course, I am." He sounded so matter of fact.

At that admission, the blood drained from Hailey's face and nausea strangled her core. Her breaths started coming in short bursts, causing the air not to fill her lungs. The room started tilting, and she was having difficulty fully making sense of the situation. Hailey wanted to jump across the table and slap him, anything to make him stop saying the things he was. But she was frozen, fear and embarrassment shackled her to her chair.

The rest of the night was only a blur of raw emotion. She couldn't remember the details, only that Jeremy kept going on and on explaining himself, something she was sure was more for his benefit than hers. Well that, and the memory of her raising her voice at some point stopping it.

She couldn't remember what he said to end the conversation or him even saying goodbye, just that he got up at one point and left the restaurant. It was that memory of him walking away she remembered vividly, every detail, every step.

As the space between them grew, the spaces between the fragments of her heart grew as well. Hailey sat motionless until he was out of sight, then slowly, she lowered her gaze and stared at her plate of untouched food. She let out a short huff. She found it sadly ironic that the coldness of a once fabulous meal now resembled the lifelessness of the last three years they had spent together.

Well, I guess that's that.

She didn't know how much time had passed. But when a waitress approached her and asked her with a compassion filled voice if they could call her a cab, Hailey realized they all must have been waiting for her for some time. She thanked her and accepted the offer.

After getting home, she went straight to her bed. Without removing her shoes or coat, she lay down and pulled a blanket over her entire body. It was the only protection she could find from a reality she didn't want to be in.

- - - - - - -

And that is exactly where she found herself now. When Hailey wasn't in class or at the library, she was here on her bed trying to feel protected from the outside world. The emotions in her heart mirrored those of the night when Jeremy broke her heart, and her dreams were ripped away.

She wasn't pathetic enough to think they would still have a chance to end up together. But seeing Jeremy with Sheila brought the small bit of progress she had made in separating herself from him, come to a crashing halt. Even though three weeks had passed since the encounter, Hailey was still not able to move past it.

BEEP, BEEP, BEEP.

Hailey was startled out of her thoughts by her alarm clock. Glad she remembered to set the alarm, she rolled off her bed and headed to her closet to get ready. Tonight was a lecture on women's rights around the world at the Deutsches Haus building. It was something Hailey was very interested in. She had signed up for it months ago, and she didn't want to chance missing it.

After quickly getting ready, Hailey went to the door and opened it.

A small scream escaped her lips. She was startled to see

someone standing on the other side. His hand was raised as to imply he was attempting to knock. In his other hand, he carried a package.

"Oh... um, sorry!" the scrawny, uniformed courier said, embarrassed. "I'm looking for Hailey Pearson. This package is for her."

"Oh, no my bad. Sorry. I'm Hailey," she said with a small, uncomfortable laugh.

After signing for the package, Hailey looked at the packing sticker. It was from Anna. Warmth flooded her heart. Even though she was excited to rip into it, Hailey restrained herself and went back inside and placed it on her desk. She would need to wait until after the lecture. She was already leaving later than she wanted to and Hailey didn't want to try to find a seat after it started.

CHAPTER 7

The lecture was fantastic. Hailey tried her hardest to concentrate and take in everything each speaker had to say, but she found it difficult not to allow her thoughts to drift to the package. It was a large, brown box with her name on it, sitting there with anticipation on her desk, just waiting to be opened. Hailey closed her eyes and shook her head, and upon opening them, she tried to muster a newly determined attentiveness.

The current speaker standing at the podium was a representative from a human rights group that had been founded at Columbia. She was a native of India and had been shunned by her whole family when she chose to change religions. Hailey was struck by her confidence and passion and soon found herself envious of this woman's faith and certainty.

Hailey's parents had also had faith like that, and it had made an impact on her when she was little. Hailey wasn't considering going back to her old beliefs, but it was the last time in her life when she was certain about anything.

Her mind drifted farther. *If only my mom were here to help direct me.*

"I'm glad you came."

Startled, Hailey jumped back into the present. Glancing up,

she saw Sheila scooting her way past some knees and settling herself into the empty chair next to hers.

"I don't want to talk to you. Please, just leave me alone." Hailey wouldn't even look at Sheila and continued to stare at the speaker. The betrayal was still so fresh, and she wasn't about to let Sheila explain away her offense.

"Hail, please. It's been so long. I miss talking to you, and you need to hear what happened and let me explain."

"No!" Hailey's voice came out louder than she intended, causing a few stares and shushes to come from those around them. Hailey lowered her voice and continued in a firm whisper, all the while glaring at Sheila. "No, I don't need to hear it. I don't want to hear it, and I don't care if you miss me. You are a vile friend. You and Jeremy have broken my heart all over again... and worse. If that's even possible." Hailey paused for a moment to regain her composure to ensure her voice stayed low. "How could you Sheila? No, forget it. I don't want to hear it. Our friendship is over. I can't even look at you."

With that, Hailey rose, grabbed her jacket and pushed past Sheila, leaving her sitting there with tears in her eyes.

Once out of the lecture hall doors, Hailey burst into a run. The coolness of the night stung the tears which were sliding down her cheeks. They weren't tears of hurt but of anger. Furious, hot anger rose deep within her and caused her to shake.

The nerve of Sheila to think that enough time had passed to believe it was alright to initiate a conversation with me. And, to top it off, choosing to come at me in the middle of this lecture. Sheila knew I had been looking forward to it. Did she want to ruin it on purpose?

"AHHH!" Hailey's frustration echoed through the campus.

Bursting through her dorm room door, Hailey dropped her jacket and kicked off her shoes. She grabbed Anna's package and walked over to her bed.

Setting the package on her bedspread, she tore the outer brown wrapping off of the box and threw it on the floor. She looked at the box. Anna must have used most of the roll of packing tape because the whole box was shimmering. Hailey would need scissors.

After rummaging around in the top drawer of her desk, she was able to locate a pair and return to her bed. Within minutes, after fighting with all the tape, Hailey had the box open. She took a deep breath to calm herself, then started going through its contents.

On top was an envelope with "OPEN FIRST" written on the front. A smile grabbed hold of Hailey's lips when she saw what was inside. It was a picture of Anna and her in Florida, sitting under a palm tree, both with huge smiles on their face. On the back of the picture was written:

> *"Remember the good times? For even though we have to go down some hard roads, there are more great times to be had around the next corner."*

Hailey's heart ached to remember that first trip they took together. She craved to be in Saudi so badly that it was physically frustrating to every inch of her skin. Hailey felt tired and deeply miserable. The only thing that seemed to be keeping her going was the idea of this trip.

Shaking her head, she told herself not to drown in all that was happening. She would be away from it soon enough. She continued on.

Next in the box was a canvas bag that contained a beautiful, black Abaya. The large piece of black fabric was plain apart from a thin, small, black, satin ribbon lining the neck and each cuff. Even though the Abaya wasn't going to be flattering, Hailey tried not to let her opinion of it darken the idea of the trip. She was totally willing to be respectful of other cultures and knew that one shouldn't travel if not prepared to do so. However, looking at the blackness and heaviness of the fabric, Hailey couldn't help but feel that the ribbon was merely art hanging on a prison wall. She shrugged off the feeling and chose to replace it with an appreciation for their modesty and left it at that.

At the bottom of the box was a large brown envelope that contained her entrance visa, sponsor papers, a plane ticket, and detailed instructions. She quickly read through the instructions. Anna had given her a step by step details to follow from when she stepped off the plane in Saudi's capital, Riyadh. There were also directions and tips on how to make her transfer, and then what to do once she reached Dammam, the city where Anna lived.

Hailey was grateful for such a friend. She then noticed there was a small yellow sticky note posted to the front page of her entry visa:

Hailey,

    As you can see from the date, this is good for a full year (until April 20th) - so feel free to stay as long as you like. We can't wait to see you.

                                    Chuck

Hailey's excitement burst into high gear as she realized the visa was good right now. She hated everything about being here, and there was no point in staying until finals were finished. She knew she would only fair so-so anyway. Because she didn't even really care if she had the credits or not, there really wasn't anything worth staying for.

She set the papers down and looked at the clock. It was almost 11:00 p.m. and that meant that it wasn't even 7:00 a.m. for Anna. Hailey was excited, but she would wait an hour before calling. She decided to take a bath and read a book to relax, so she wasn't just watching the clock.

Still dripping from the bathtub, she crossed the floor an hour later and started dialing Anna's number. There was no one home, and the disappointment showed on Hailey's face but only for a few minutes. A new plan began to form.

After thinking it through a bit, Hailey was glad Anna didn't answer; it would work out better this way. The fun of a surprise would be a good start to thank Anna and her parents.

Finding it almost impossible to sleep, Hailey awoke early the next morning and instantly started making the final preparations. The next flight she was able to book was on Tuesday, three days away. This would give her enough time to tie up some loose ends: she needed to pack up her room, put her things in storage, withdrawal from her classes, forward her mail to her aunt's, and say her goodbyes to her friends. Then finally, hope Thomas arrived in time to drive her to the airport before her plane took off. All her final preparations, except one, went smoothly.

When Hailey was making her calls on Monday night to say goodbye to her friends, she couldn't get a hold of Ryan. She tried numerous times, but it would just ring and ring, then a message would come on saying his voicemail was full. She hated to leave without saying goodbye to him, but he'd probably had it turned off for a late-night meeting. Hailey knew he wouldn't mind; he had Anna's number. He also had that business meeting in Saudi a month later, and they could hang out then. So, with that, she hung up and headed off to bed.

This was going to be just the kind of adventure she needed. As she watched the distancing of the ground as her plane took off, she was finally able to look at the future with anticipation and not boredom or dread.

CHAPTER 8

– Present Day –

Panic came in waves, rushing over his soul. They weren't the kind that rolled over your body then passed until another came in. They were waves that pulled you under and just as you thought you were coming to the end of one and were able to catch your breath, another would grab you and pull you down again.

Everything about that day seemed to be moving in slow motion, and even though it was ridiculous, Ryan was annoyed with everyone. He knew it was unfair, but he half expected them to understand what was truly happening in his life and stop everything that was normal to them so they could help.

Sleep eluded him all night, and he was exhausted. If it weren't for all the adrenalin, he would have collapsed long ago. He had spent the last number of hours calling everyone Hailey knew that he had a number for, in hopes that someone had heard from her. Apart from her aunt, it was foolish to think Hailey would have called someone other than Anna or him, but he was desperate.

After saying goodbye to yet another person who hadn't heard anything, Ryan finally decided it was time to call the airline. Thomas had passed on her flight details to him, and she had two

61

transfers before she landed in Dammam, where Anna originally was to meet her. One transfer was in Frankfurt, Germany and one in Riyadh, the capital of Saudi Arabia.

Ryan needed to talk with the airline authorities to see if she had made either of those transfers. He then needed to get on a plane as soon as possible and try to retrace Hailey's steps and see if he could find her.

After being transferred a few times, he finally reached the right department.

"Airport authority, this is Greg Bronson. How may I help you?" The voice was cheerful.

"Ah… yes. I desperately need some help." Ryan paused to steady his voice before continuing. "My name is Ryan Foster, and a friend of mine caught Lufthansa flight 405 on April 29th. I have just found out now that she never made it to her destination and no one has heard from her in the two weeks since she left." Ryan had to strain to keep his emotions out of the conversation. "I need to know what I can do to see if she made either of her connections. So… um… how do I do that?"

"Well, I'm sorry, but we aren't at liberty to give out that sort of information to you. You…"

"What am I supposed to do?" Ryan cut in. "Sit here and wait for her to never call?" Ryan tried to keep his tone level, but his irritation came through.

"No, sir. There are many things you can do. First, contact the police to file a missing person's report and then contact the American embassy in the destination country, as well as the embassies in both of the transfer countries. Provide as much personal information about your friend as you can, even down to blood type."

With that comment, nausea pummeled his stomach.

What if she's not OK?

"The police will then be in contact with us to get her flight information."

They talked for another twenty minutes, and Ryan received all the info he needed. Greg gave him phone numbers, websites, and names of organizations that he could contact for help.

"I'm sorry I can't be of more immediate help to you, but good luck."

Ryan thanked him and hung up.

He immediately dialed Norah, Hailey's aunt. She answered on the first ring.

"Ryan, have you heard anything?" her dread filled voice trickled tentatively over the line.

"I contacted the airport, but they can't help directly. Something about stupid privacy and security issues. However, they did give me some steps to what we could do next." Ryan reiterated all the information to her. "Norah, could you do all the paperwork stuff here? Seeing how you are a relative, you might have fewer issues, and I think I can get a flight out tonight."

"Yes, definitely. Just text me the information, and I'll get started right away."

"OK. Um... I guess I will call you once I get to Germany and you can hopefully know by then if Hailey made her connections. If she did, then I will continue onto Riyadh and then onto Dammam. But if she didn't make either of those transfers, then I can stay where we know she was last and work with the embassy to start looking for her. Does that sound OK with you?"

"Yes, that's a good plan. Ryan, we have to find her."

"We will. Hey... Norah?"

"Yeah?" Her words were choked with emotion.

"I don't know if you pray or not... but... could you? I will need a lot of help to do this."

"Honey, I don't very often, but I'll try. Be safe and call me as soon as you land."

Ryan hung up the phone and sat there. The emotion broke suddenly.

Where is she? Is she OK? Is she hurt or in trouble?

Ryan tried to push those types of thoughts from his mind and not to think the worst, but he loved her, and he couldn't help but be terrified of the possibilities. Saudi Arabia is a tricky place, and he feared what trouble she might have run into, that is if she even made it there. Then another thought stole his attention. He tried to block it out, but it took hold and wouldn't let go. It oozed into him and made him shiver.

What if she hadn't contact anyone by choice? What if she ran from all of us?

Honestly, he couldn't decide which possibility was worse. Hailey hurt and/or in trouble or her leaving them and never looking back. At least with the first option, he could find her and help. Ryan couldn't see how she would even think about the later, but with all the stress and pain she had been through this last while, maybe it was possible. However, neither explanation changed his course of action, so he called the airline, booked a flight, texted Norah, and then rose off the couch to go pack.

- - - - - - -

The airport was surprisingly busy for so late at night. The traffic mostly comprised of businessmen coming or going from trips and families getting a jump on the long weekend. Ryan had an unexpectedly long wait to go through security. Fortunately, he made sure to be at the airport long before he needed to be, so he still made it through with time to spare... actually, too much time to spare. He hadn't had anything else to do at home and saying he was a bit overzealous to get going was an understatement. He now had to wait in the lounge for more than two hours until his flight boarded.

As the coolness of the last sip of his drink slid down his throat, Ryan pushed the glass to the edge of the bar and rested his head in his hands. This was all supposed to go so differently.

Ryan had initially planned to meet Anna and Hailey in a few weeks. They would go sightseeing to show Hailey what their childhoods had been like when their families got together. But mostly, they would hang around the compound, laughing and having fun. He missed them both. His heart ached to hold Hailey. He hadn't seen Anna for so long, and he wished their reunion wasn't tainted with such dire circumstances.

How did this happen?

Anna was simply a wreck, blaming herself for everything, despite Ryan's reassurance. He had called her just before leaving for the airport to fill her in, and his heart broke as he had listened to her sobs.

"Ryan I... shouldn't have let her... come to Saudi. What was I thinking? I should have talked her into meeting me in Europe." She sniffed. "I'm so stupid to put her in a situation that is so different than what she is used to."

"We don't even know if she even made it to Saudi. This could have happened either way. It's not your fault." He tried to reassure her.

"We have to find her Ryan. I miss her and I won't be able to live with myself if we can't. Call me as soon as you know anything. I'll talk to my dad and see if there is anything he or his friends can do."

Ryan had ended the call with those promises, and now he was here, sitting alone. It was such a contrast to a week earlier when he was flying as high as a kite telling Thomas about his feelings for Hailey.

"Excuse me did you want another soda?" The bartender interrupted his thoughts.

Ryan lifted his head. "Oh, no thank you. Just the bill please."

After paying, Ryan wandered around the airport and went into the few stores that were still open until he heard the boarding call for his flight. He made his way over to his gate and boarded the plane. Ryan knew it was silly, but he felt closer to her already. At least now he was able to do something and not just sit at home waiting.

The seats on the plane were comfortable, but the smell was awful. The perfume from a woman a few rows over was making him queasy. He tried taking a few deep breaths to relax, but the scent was overwhelming, and he could only manage short quick breaths.

Why did older women do that? Was their sense of smell going in their older age that they didn't realize that there is such a thing as too much? Or maybe after using the same perfume for years, they had to add more and more each year as they were becoming immune to the smell.

He shook his head to clear the questions.

Glancing around, he caught sight of a few passengers walking by to find their seats. They were trying to hide it, but it was evident they were also struggling with the smell as it wafted in front of them. Ryan smiled to himself and took his seat. Hopefully, it would dissipate soon. As a precaution, he turned the fan above his head on full before he rested his head against the headrest.

OK God, there is only one way I'm going to make it through this flight. Please calm my soul. I trust You, and I know You are watching over her. Please work in me to let my heart know that truth as well. It's kind of freaking me out. In Your name…

Someone touched his arm, and he opened his eyes.

"Excuse me, sir. Are you Ryan Foster?"

The young flight attendant was hovering over him with a friendly yet concerned smile on her face. Ryan sat up abruptly.

"Yes, what is it?"

"Well…" She glanced down at a little piece of paper in her hand. "Norah just contacted airport security with instructions to get this message to you before we took off. She said that you don't need to remain in Germany because Hailey made her connection to Saudi Arabia." She lowered herself into the seat next to him and spoke softer. "However, when she was in Riyadh, she didn't make her flight to Dammam."

"Ok," Ryan said as he rubbed his chin.

"They aren't sure what happened after that. The only thing they do know is that she never claimed her luggage after it was taken off the plane and that she didn't come to the service counter when she was instructed to." She dropped her hands in her lap and looked at him. "You see once a passenger doesn't board a connecting flight, we are required by law to remove their luggage and page them." She looked once more at the paper and then returned her attention to Ryan.

"That's not the news I was hoping for, but thanks for letting me know," Ryan said with a sad smile.

"I am so sorry to hear about your friend. If there is anything you need or if there is anything I can do to make this flight more bearable, please let me know."

Ryan choked back the emotion that was rising from the knot

in his stomach. "Um... no." He glanced at her name tag. "Thanks, Sarah, but I'm all right."

"This may be little of consolation, but we do have a few...," she lowered her voice further, "vacancies in first class. You are more than welcome to one if you'd like." She raised her eyebrows and smiled.

"Yeah, that would be great." He could maybe get some proper rest, as well get some distance from the perfume drenched woman. "Thank you."

The flight was long and dull, but Ryan was glad for the extra room in first class. He was even able to get some desperately needed sleep. It was in short bursts, but it was by far more than he would have accomplished back in his original seat.

Sarah kept checking in on him. It was if he had his own private flight attendant. She was sweet, and her friendly, empathetic smile finally gave him the satisfaction that people did understand what was happening, something he sadly lacked earlier.

Ryan soon realized God was already providing because she was also on his flight from Germany to Saudi. Sarah had to go to Saudi to catch her next flight, a red-eye to China and she was able to bump him up to first class again. The continuity gave him a sense of comfort.

As the plane circled the city of Riyadh before landing, he looked out the window. It was huge. The city stretched over hundreds of square miles and being able to see the whole city at once was overwhelming.

How am I supposed to find her? How am I going to find just one person in a sea of more than seven million people?

Ryan realized it would take a miracle. He couldn't even think of where to start.

=======

She was just sick with worry. The fear that came from the news that Hailey was missing coated Anna's body like a dark cloak. Sleep, or even rest for that matter, seemed to run away from her and the cause of all of it was due to Anna blaming herself. Despite all the reassurance from her parents and Ryan, she couldn't shake the responsibility that hung around her shoulders.

How could I have been so irresponsible? I should have insisted that I would meet her in Europe and then we could have come here together. Why didn't she give me her flight details and tell me she was coming?

Anna's regrets made her stomach knot up as she wished Hailey hadn't been so impulsive.

The sound of her footsteps echoed down the hall as she ran towards her father's office. She had just gotten off the phone with Ryan, and she was thrilled he was coming. He was like a brother to her, and she desperately needed his support. Ever since they were little, he had been a rock for her, and with this horror smothering her, the distance between them couldn't shrink fast enough.

They had played together all throughout this house as kids. Endless hours of hide-and-seek used to fill these halls with laughter, but now they were filled with the thundering of her footsteps on the tiled floor. The sound caused her heart to beat even faster.

Bursting through the double doors, she fell in a heap into one of the armchairs facing her father's desk.

"Dad, it's confirmed. No one knows where she is. We have to do something, anything. We have to find her." Tears came rolling down her face. "What if she's hurt or in trouble." She smeared the tears across her cheeks with the back of her hand. "What have I done?" Anna mumbled the question to herself.

"Hey, slow down," her father instructed. "I will call the office and get in touch with George. He'll know what to do and who best to call. We will find her sweetie."

Before Chuck had even finished his sentence, he was reaching for his Rolodex. Flipping through the little white cards, he found the number and reached for the phone.

Anna loved how strong and calm her father was in stressful situations, the exact opposite of herself. She took after her mother in that regard, along with most of her other traits.

George was the liaison for Entrata employees when they were planning to transfer to Saudi. He knew all the policies, red tape, and procedures of the country and was a good friend of her father.

Entranced, Anna listened to their conversation.

"Hi George, it's Chuck." A pause. "Yeah everything is great with us, sorry I don't mean to be rude and cut you off, but we have an emergency. A friend of Anna's was on her way to visit us, and she's missing. We need some assistance on where to start." Another pause. "No, we don't know for sure yet. We know she made her flight leaving New York a couple of weeks ago." Pause. "April 29th. Then she had a transfer in Germany and then another in Riyadh. But we are still confirming if she even made either of those. But I want to assume she made it to Saudi and not lose any time." Chuck looked up at Anna and smiled.

Anna's heart leaped. *Maybe George could help.*

"Yes." The look on her father's face looked positive. "OK, thank you so much, George. I will wait for your call." Chuck hung up the phone and looked at Anna. "George is going to call around to his contacts with the police and in the government. He said that if she made it to Saudi, then there is a good chance his contacts will be able to help confirm it. Once we know that, they will know what the next steps are. We will find her." He leaned forward and rested his arms on the top of his desk.

Anna's tears broke the surface again causing her shoulders to shudder. Rising from his chair, Chuck rounded the desk and knelt in front of her. Pulling her into a hug, he stroked her hair to comfort her.

"What if… we can't Dad?" Anna whispered into his shoulder.

"We will. Shhh now. We will."

CHAPTER 9

The flight to Germany seemed longer than Hailey remembered, and her body was stiff and achy from sitting so long. It was definitely time to stretch her legs. Glancing up, she was relieved the seatbelt light was off.

Rising slowly, she excused herself past the woman who was seated beside her. It was a bit awkward due to all the extra fabric swarming around her legs, but soon Hailey reached the aisle and made her way to the bathroom.

She knew the abaya was necessary, but Hailey felt clumsy in it. It was foreign and confining. Initially, it seemed like a good idea to put it on during her layover in Germany. Although now feeling all hot and sticky, she realized she should have just waited until they were in the air and were getting close to Saudi.

With both hands on either side of the sink, she leaned in and looked in the mirror. Seeing the dark circles under her eyes, she exhaled forcefully and pulled back.

Yikes... I look even worse than I feel.

She reached into her purse and pulled out her makeup bag. After freshening up with a face wash, she reapplied her makeup and returned to her seat. She would thankfully be landing in Riyadh in an hour and would have a chance to grab something to eat before her connecting flight boarded. She was starving.

=======

Ryan had called from Germany before he boarded his flight to Riyadh, but Anna had nothing new to tell him. George was still tracking down some of his contacts. To Anna, it almost seemed like there was red tape in this country to go through to even have a phone call returned. Her patience was greatly being tested. But at least Ryan had a bit of information for her.

Hailey had made her connection to Saudi. This was bittersweet news. It was good that they at least knew people here in Saudi who could help them. They didn't know anyone in Germany with those types of contacts. The bad news was that it was in Saudi: a very culturally different country than Hailey was used to. Saudi was definitely going to be challenging to search.

Anna and Ryan decided that it would be best if he just continued right on to Dammam and that they would meet at the Airport and take it from there. It was better to work together on this, and hopefully, by then, her father would have heard something that could help them. They needed more information before making a game plan.

Hanging up the phone, Anna went to update her father. "His flight lands tomorrow at one o'clock. Have you heard from George yet?"

"No, not yet sweetheart. Nothing in the past ten minutes since the last time you asked. We will just have to wait and see."

Frustration coursed through Anna. She felt useless just waiting around while her friend could be in danger or worse. Shivers coursed through her body. Any one of the thousand thoughts that jumped into her mind were too much to even explore for more than a moment. She shook her head to try to dislodge them.

"Dad, how can we just sit here?"

"We have no choice."

Anna was frustrated by his short answer. "Do you think she could be...?" But Anna couldn't bring herself to finish.

=======

Ryan exited the plane. Bidding farewell and saying thanks to Sarah, he followed the crowd through the corridors. The smell of the airport was thickly spiced. He knew it was foolish: the probability that she was here was so low, but he still glanced down every hall and tried to scan each group, hoping to see her face.

The airport was beautiful. Tall columns stretched to the multi-level ceiling and cream, marble tiles covered the floor. The ceiling was spectacular. It was covered with triangular windows and triangular tiles that created a dynamic, geometric pattern. The center of the ceiling was the highest point, and it stepped down in lower and lower sections as your eye looked closer to the outer walls.

Ryan passed a beautiful fountain in the center of a large garden. The flowers which surrounded the fountain were vibrant and rested in cream angular planters. Even though the site was striking, he barely saw any of it. His eyes only noticed that the random faces he passed weren't Hailey's.

He found his connecting flight with ease, and within the hour he was in the air again. It was a short transfer window, and he was thankful he didn't miss the flight to Dammam. The plane was almost empty, and he was grateful that he didn't need to sit beside anyone. He didn't feel like talking.

As soon as he was settled and belted in, Ryan's mind started to wonder.

If Hailey made her connecting flight to Saudi, was it possible for her to have gotten lost at the Riyadh airport? Anna's directions were so simple and were better than what I would have given. If she did get lost and missed her flight, why hadn't she called? Surprises were great, but there was a limit, and she shouldn't have played around.

Would she have been so foolish as to have left the airport until the next flight? Had she run into trouble before she could make it back to the airport? Or if she did catch her flight, what could have happened in Dammam? It was an easy cab ride to the compound. How could she have gotten lost? Anna told her that there were plenty of taxis waiting outside every door of the airport. It would have been simple to make the trip.

To Ryan, it seemed so straightforward.

What in the world could have happened?

Ryan was glad it was a short flight to Dammam, but it was still frustrating to have to sit there with just his thoughts. The questions seemed to have no solution, they just kept rattling around and leading him back to the start, then around he'd go again.

Finally, the captain's voice broke his concentration, announcing their arrival. As soon as the plane had finished pulling up to the gate, he sprang from his seat, grabbed his bag and hurried down the aisle before the other passengers could block his way. Jogging up to the baggage claim, his eyes searched for Anna.

With no sight of her, he turned his attention to the bags. Ryan wished he could fast forward through this part, everything was moving so slowly. He looked briefly around at the others standing around him. People hugging and greeting their loved ones created an ache in his heart that seemed to radiate into each part of him. He felt so alone.

Where are you, Hailey? I need you to hold on, wherever you are. I'm going to find you. Just hold on.

"Ryan!" A woman called out from a few feet behind him. He turned to see Anna running towards him. "Ryan!"

"Anna!"

They both ran towards each other and embraced. Holding onto each other as though they didn't know what would happen if they'd let go, Ryan and Anna stood and sobbed into each other's shoulder. Ryan had felt so helpless, but having Anna in his arms gave him a surprising amount of strength and relief.

A large hand grasped his arm. Ryan pulled away to see Chuck standing there, empathy etched on his face.

"Ryan it's OK. We will find her."

After a handshake and a firm hug from Chuck, Ryan wiped the tears from his face with the back of his hand and took Anna's hand with the other. They all stood in silence while they waited for his bag.

Even though they had not heard back from George as of yet, Ryan didn't head straight for the exit after grabbing his bag but walked to the left. He wanted to see if the security personnel at this airport would help. It was a long shot, but there was no harm in at least trying.

There was a fairly long line at the desk, so Ryan took his place behind a small woman. She was dressed in a black abaya and wore a full face veil, leaving only a small slit that showed her eyes. She was almost the same height as Hailey.

The line moved up slowly, but with each movement, the woman glanced around nervously. Ryan followed her darting gaze, yet couldn't see anything that would be the cause for her perceived distress.

After a half hour had passed, the line had only moved up a few people. He now only had the woman and another man in front of him. Ryan was getting very impatient, and it was obvious that he wasn't the only one. He took a few deep breaths to try and stay calm.

"I'm just going to go call Linda to let her know you've arrived. I will wait for you two outside." Chuck excused himself and started towards the pay phones outside.

Ryan watched him go, but his attention was quickly averted. A man approached from behind and brushed past him, apparently upset. He drew near to the woman in front of Ryan and grabbed her arm. Pain flashed in her eyes.

Ryan's body tensed. Anna touched his elbow to signal it wasn't wise to interfere. Anna kept her head down and continued to look at the floor, and Ryan tried to do the same. The scene played out in his peripheral vision.

Continuing to hold onto the woman's arm, the man, speaking in Arabic, made his frustration very clear. He shoved the woman out of the line and took her place. The woman slunk off towards some waiting children standing against a nearby column.

Ryan shook his head and could have burned holes into the back of the man standing before him. There were many differences about this country that Ryan had become used to, but he would never get used to abusive behavior towards women. The country had come a long way compared to where it had started. However, Ryan worried that men like this one would forever stay adamant that women were mere possessions. Saudi would have a long, difficult road ahead of her to separate the bad from the good.

Ryan was all for modesty and protecting women, but thought that it can take an ugly turn when done as a means of dominating, showing power, or pride of ownership. He shivered as he thought of how many women in the country experienced that ugliness on a daily basis. Seeing the scene before him play out so openly in public, evaporated his naivety. He realized he had no clue or could even imagine what this woman had to endure behind closed doors.

After another twenty minutes, it was Ryan's turn. He politely asked if anyone spoke English. The officer behind the desk looked him up and down with a raised eyebrow, turned and walked away. Ryan looked at Anna with concern.

"Just wait. He'll be back," Anna reassured him.

He came back moments later and pointed to the end of the counter and told them to wait. Ryan was exhausted. He leaned against the hard counter where the officer had requested and turned his attention toward the rest of the airport. Anna joined him. He continued to look around.

"You too huh?" Anna asked.

"You mean looking for her? Yeah. I mean I know that she's not here, but I can't help trying to catch a look at everyone's face." He shrugged his shoulders. "Even though I know it's stupid, some part of me is holding out this bizarre hope that maybe I will look over… and she will be there, safe and sound, with a strange story to tell us of why we haven't heard from her in seventeen days." He paused. "Yikes, seventeen! I knew it has been that long, but saying it out loud is so overwhelming." He paused again. "I mean I know it won't happen, but I can't help it. I keep looking."

"No, it's not stupid. I'm doing the very same thing." She sighed.

Anna leaned her head on his shoulder, and he leaned over and kissed her forehead. Both their parents had hoped they'd end up together, but there never was any romantic feelings between the two. Early on, both had entertained the possibility, but they felt more like family than anything else, and so the possibility was dismissed before anything could ever come of it.

This was something that Ryan was glad for now in retrospect. It would be a little awkward to have Anna there if something had transpired between them and too lonely not to have her there. Ryan wondered when he should tell Anna about his feelings for Hailey, but that could wait. They had too much on their plates to deal with at the moment.

"Ahem," someone annoyingly cleared his throat behind them.

They both turned to see a very large, stern officer standing there with his hands on his hips.

"I speak English. What can I help you with?"

"Um... well, you see..." Ryan stumbled through the explanation.

"You said it was your friend that is missing? What about you, are you her family?" he said as he motioned towards Anna.

"Um... no." Anna shook her head. "She is a friend of mine as well."

"I'm sorry, only her... uh... close family can be given that information."

"What do you mean her close family?" Ryan interjected.

"I don't know the English word for it... but only her mother, father, or siblings can ask those things. I'm sorry, but you'll have to get them to come here. I can look into it for them... only them." The officer turned to leave.

"Wait! I can't do that. She doesn't have any close family."

Ryan barely succeeded in keeping his voice calm.

"Then, I'm sorry. I can't help you." He again turned to leave.

Ryan slammed his fist on the counter, causing everyone in the area to turn and look at him. There were a couple of police officers standing thirty feet away. They stopped their conversation and placed a hand on the assault rifles that were slung over each of their shoulders. Ryan was so focused on the officer across from him that he didn't notice.

"Wait! You can't just leave us like this. We need help."

Anna grabbed his arm. "Ryan, we have to go. Now! Calm down and turn away slowly."

Ryan looked at her, confused by her passivity. She nodded her head to look behind him. The police were now slowly moving towards them, obviously concerned now with the disruption that Ryan had caused.

When Ryan followed her gaze, he immediately backed down, apologized to the officer, and followed Anna away from the security desk. They moved into the crowd before the men could reach them. They didn't dare turn around to see if the officers were gaining on them.

Ryan and Anna progressed through the crowds towards the exit as quickly as they could, their hearts pounding. Once they were quite a distance away from the desk, Ryan stole a quick glance and breathed a sigh of relief, the officers had returned to their station by the far wall.

The heat hit Ryan like a bucket of hot water being poured over him as he exited the doors. Although the heat didn't drip off like water would, it hit him and then seemed to pass through him and then rested all around him. Sweat instantly started pouring down his forehead.

Chuck was sitting on a bench just outside the doors and

jumped up as soon as he saw them. "What happened, you guys look scared?" There was a tone of slight panic in his voice.

"We're OK Dad. Just some over-zealous officers is all. Did you get a hold of Mom and George?" Anna's eyes were full of hope.

"Here, come sit." Chuck gestured towards the bench. Once they were all seated, he continued, looking at Ryan. "Linda is so glad you're here. She's starting on supper and insists you come over right away. She wanted me to tell you that she misses you and that she's just sick with the news about Hailey."

Ryan smiled gratefully.

"As for George," Chuck looked at Anna with a reassuring grin, "he said he was able to get a meeting with the head of airport security of the Riyadh airport tomorrow, sometime late in the afternoon. It turns out that Hailey didn't make her connection to Dammam and so he thinks the Riyadh airport would be a good place to start." Chuck leaned over and wrapped his arm around Anna giving her a small, comforting squeeze.

Ryan didn't really know what he was feeling. Relief yes, as they finally had a starting point, but there was also fear. Hailey did catch the flight from Germany to Riyadh, which meant she had intended to go to Saudi to see Anna. She wasn't off gallivanting by herself somewhere, which was great, and she wasn't cutting them out of her life. But it also meant that something had happened to her in Riyadh that caused her to miss her flight to Dammam. Ryan's guess was that it wasn't by choice.

=======

The Riyadh airport was a busy place. It seemed like thousands were coming and going all around her. Even in the multitude of endless faces, Hailey felt singled out, as though all eyes were on her. She continued down the hall, ensuring to hold her head high. Hailey wanted to be respectful of different cultures, but she couldn't change who she was. She was proud to be a woman and an American.

Although now being in the midst of this ominous crowd, she regretted leaving the headscarf in her luggage. Her auburn hair, piercing green eyes and porcelain skin made her stand out even at home, but now with her only wearing the abaya, she felt silly.

So much for blending in. I feel ridiculous.

Hailey made her way through the crowd and over to the closest wall. She needed to look over Anna's directions again and preferred to not bring even more attention to herself by causing a traffic jam by stopping in the middle of the corridor.

After reading them all through, Hailey reentered the flow of the mob to follow each step.

1. *Depending on the flight, you could fly into any one of the gates. So once you get off the plane, turn left when you come through the gate and head to the end of the hall.*

Check

2. *Turn around and head back the other way. This could make you backtrack quite a bit, but at least I can give you exact directions from this point, regardless of which gate you come in.*

Check

3. *Once you turn around, continue until you*

have passed two foyers on your left.

Check

    4. *Take the third foyer, it has a hall that will lead you to the connecting domestic flights.*

Check

    5. *Once through that hall, there will be a huge flight board on the wall to your right. You can double check the gate that your flight is departing from. They sometimes change so be sure to look. If you can't figure out the gate number, just ask the attendant standing at the small stand. They always post someone there that speaks multiple languages, and they'll be able to help.*

    6. *Then once*

She looked up to make her way through the hall before reading on. As she looked to her right, a small feeling of fear tapped at her mind and made her shoulders slump. There was no flight board, there was no attendant, and there was no stand.

Oh no!!

Hailey spun in a few circles to look around.

Where did I go wrong? Was this even the hall? Did I miss a hall or forget to count one of the foyers?

She turned back around and retraced her steps through the hallway. Upon reaching the other side of the hall, nothing looked familiar. Most of her attention had been on the piece of paper gripped in her hand and on trying not to trip over her abaya or anyone else.

Frustrated, Hailey looked around again. She noticed a group

of businessmen standing beside a huge fountain, deep in conversation.

This is ridiculous. I could be here forever trying to figure this out.

Hailey was worried about missing her connecting flight to Dammam, so she made her way over to the men to ask for directions.

She was completely unaware that she was closely being watched.

CHAPTER 10

Being in a foreign country is a funny thing. It's hard to know all the ins and outs of a culture, and admittedly the social behaviors can be the trickiest of all. Being watched by the man across the room wasn't the only thing Hailey was unaware of. Had she known more about Saudi life, she wouldn't have been so naïve to even entertain the idea of approaching the group of men for directions.

Hailey had one hand firmly on the handle of her small carry-on suitcase and the other holding tightly to Anna's directions. As she waited for a stream of people to pass, she noticed that one of the men was standing a few feet from the others and had just finished a phone call. Hailey decided he'd be her best bet as he was speaking English during his call. As she came nearer to him, he looked up and returned his cell back into the pocket of his suit jacket.

The man's eyes were warm, and a smile graced his face in an unthreatening and welcoming way. Apart from the wrinkles around his eyes and mouth, it seemed like a corporate life had treated him very well. He was dressed in a tailored, black suit with a white dress shirt and a black tie. His head adorned a traditional Saudi red and white striped headdress with a black cord to hold it in place.

"Excuse me. I'm trying to find my connecting flight to Dammam. My friend told me where the flight boards were, but I can't find them. Could you, by any chance, point me in the right direction please?"

"Certainly. Just continue down that hall." He gestured with his hand to the hall she had just come from and continued to direct with his hands as he spoke. "You'll have to wait till it curves to the left, as all the flight boards for connecting flights are now located there. Once you get there, you can check your gate number. Then from there, the gates are in numerical order running down the far wall. You can't miss them."

He hesitated and waited till Hailey nodded her understanding.

"Where are you flying from?" he asked.

"I flew from Germany, but I'm from New York... in America."

"Ah yes. I've been there many times. Welcome to Saudi." He gave a slight bow of his head. "I don't mean to be rude, but you shouldn't be traveling alone. Do you have anyone meeting you?"

Smiling, Hailey started to explain. "I'm actually here to surprise..."

As Hailey was in the midst of relaying her story, a strong hand reached out from behind her and forcefully grabbed her elbow.

Yelping from part surprise and part shock from the pressure of the hand, Hailey turned to see that the man standing behind her wasn't intent on just getting her attention. It was clear he wanted to invoke a bit of pain as well. His face was not welcoming; it was a mass of anger. The stranger started yelling at her in Arabic. Hailey was terrified and looked at him confused. The man switched to English. It held a very thick accent, and she had to concentrate to understand what he was saying.

"You American whore! You think you can come into our country and entice our men. Allah will judge you greatly. You wear an abaya, yet you don't wear a niqab. Are you trying to play with men's minds?" He paused, disgust flashing in his eyes. "Answer me!"

For a moment, all Hailey could do was stare at the man and those who accompanied him.

There were four men in total. The one who still had her tightly by the arm had a long black beard and was dressed in a long white dress and the same traditional headdress as the man who gave her directions. The man to his left was dressed identically. The man to his right was dressed similar but had a long brown flowing robe over the white dress.

None of the other men spoke, but they were all glaring at her. However, it was the fourth man who triggered the most fear in her. He was a uniformed officer, and although he was standing slightly off to the side, appearing to just be observing, he maintained a strong grasp with both hands on a black assault rifle.

Hailey's pulse raced.

The officer's tan uniform was pristine, and he wore a black beret. The brass badge he wore depicted a wreath encircling a tree with crossed swords, and it rested beneath a crown. A few insignia were pinned to his uniform and likely stated his rank. Hailey had no clue what any of it meant.

"Speak woman or do you have no defense?" the bearded man shouted at her and clenched his hand tighter.

"I'm sorry," Hailey sputtered out. "I don't know what a niqāb is." Her mispronouncing of the word seemed to infuriate the man further. "I was just asking for directions," she said as she gestured behind her.

Hailey's eyes darted around trying to seek out a friendly face. She looked back to the man whom she'd been talking to but noticed that he had backed off and now was slowly making his way away from her and the other men. She turned her attention back.

"I'm sorry, I got turned around. I'm just trying to get back to…"

"Enough!" the bearded man cut her off. "It was very clear to all of us what you were doing. You must come with us immediately." He started to pull her towards him.

"No, wait!"

Hailey tried to shake free of his hand, but his grip just tightened and caused her to wince again. The man to his right came around to her left and took hold of her other arm.

Hailey panicked. "Stop! Please, this is just a misunderstanding. Just let me call my friend, and she can explain everything."

"Silence, this is not a joke. You should not even be here," he hissed as he gave another jerk to her arm to punctuate his point.

"I have all my visa and sponsor papers in my bag. Please wait a minute, and I can explain."

Unyielding, the man started to drag her away from where they had been standing. The officer circled behind them and grabbed the handle of her suitcase and began to wheel it off toward a door a few meters away.

"Wait! I need that!" Hailey shouted after him. "My passport is in there."

The officer kept on walking, not even bothering to look back.

He went to the door, entered a code on the small keypad, then disappeared through the door.

The man on her left jerked her in the opposite direction, towards where the bearded man was trying to pull her. The force caused Anna's directions to fly out of her hand. Hailey watched helplessly as they slowly floated to the floor. They were trampled by the man with the brown robe as he moved to follow her and the men who were now forcefully escorting her.

Hailey tried to pull back from the two men and make her way back to the paper resting on the floor, at which point they put their full weight into towing her along. She was no match.

"Please, I beg you," she looked over her shoulder with pleading eyes to the man in the brown robe, "I need that paper. It has my sponsor's phone number and address. Please... please go back and get it."

Rigid, the man just continued to follow with a blank expression on his face.

Hailey didn't know what else to do, and although it seemed foolish and useless, she couldn't control herself. "Help me! Someone, please help me," she screamed out to all the strangers around her, as she continued to struggle against her escorts.

No one came to her rescue. No one even looked at her apart from a few quick stolen glances. She might as well have been invisible.

Like a camera zooming out during a film scene to show how small and alone the actress is, Hailey felt like everything that she knew, everything and everyone she loved was being pulled away from her. What she was experiencing wasn't that different than falling down a dark hole. The farther she fell, the more the light seemed to be swallowed up by darkness and fear. Panic overcame every inch of her.

The men took her to a similar looking door to that of the officer who had taken her suitcase went through. It was a large, white, metal door with a silver handle. On the wall, a few inches above the door handle sat the same small keypad.

The two men stopped but kept a firm hold on her while the man in the brown robe punched in the code, opened the door, and stepped through. He held the door for the three of them to enter.

Beyond the door was a long hallway with random doors running the length of the hall. It reminded Hailey of a hospital or a mental ward you might see in the movies, the kind that caused you to feel uneasy because it was too dim and all a bit too clean.

They opened the third door on the right and shoved Hailey into a small, windowless room. The force of the push caused her top half to move faster than her feet could manage under all the fabric and she toppled to the floor. She only slightly missed hitting the metal table that sat in the center of the room. Hailey raised her hands, grabbed the edge of the table, and hoisted herself up. They closed the door behind her before she could even take one step.

As Hailey heard their footsteps fade further down the hall, she made her way over to the door. She knew it was futile, but she still tried the handle.

Locked.

She looked around the room. There were three wooden chairs with brass legs surrounding the table, a small clock on the wall, and nothing else. She took a seat on one of the chairs, leaned on the table and rested her head in the crook of her arm.

What the hell! What am I going to do?

Her sobs filled the tiny room. Even though she knew they were expected in such a situation, the force of the tears surprised her. They were in part from exhaustion, physical and emotional, but mostly they came because she had no clue as to what to do. She had no way to contact Anna, she didn't know where her passport or visa papers were, and she had apparently greatly offended these men in some way.

Hailey glanced at the clock. She didn't check the time when she was put in the room, but she guessed it had been closing in on twenty minutes. The sobs softened to quiet whimpers and mixed with her sniffles. They echoed in the room, which only magnified the fact that she was all alone.

Stomp! Stomp! Stomp!

The sound of heavy boots resonated in the hallway, drawing closer. Hailey reached up and dried her eyes and cheeks with the edge of her abaya and tried to compose herself. Resting her hands in her lap, she sat as straight as she could and stared at the wall on the other side of the table.

The door opened behind her, and two men entered. One was the bearded man who had yelled at her, causing Hailey's heart to sink. She was not fond of him. He terrified her. The other was an officer. Hailey was relieved that he only had a clipboard and not one of those intimidating assault rifles.

This was not the officer who had taken her carry-on but an older man with a few more insignia on his jacket. He was definitely someone higher up the chain of command.

This fact was bittersweet for Hailey. Sweet, since he might be able to help her sort out this whole mess; but also bitter, since she had to be so careful with her words to avoid inadvertently offending him. She instinctively knew she couldn't afford to make this man an enemy if there was going to be any chance of her getting out of there soon.

The men took a seat in the two empty chairs across from her.

"What's your name?" the officer asked.

"Hailey Pearson. Please, I didn't mean for any of this to happen and if you just tell me what…"

He put up his hand to silence her and wrote on the clipboard with the other.

"Where are you from?"

"New York City in the USA."

Hailey made sure not to talk more than what was asked of her. Her very core was terrified to anger this man. He wrote her answer down.

The bearded man was obviously still furious with her, and he made no effort to hide it. He sat with his arms crossed and glared at her from under the edge of his brow.

"Why were you traveling alone?" the officer continued.

"My friend's parents work at the Entrata Compound in Dammam." Her voice sounded so small. She cleared her throat and continued. "I was going there to surprise them."

The admission sounded so stupid to her now in hindsight.

So much for good ideas.

His voice wasn't angry but direct. "Sameen, here tells me you were flirting with a group of men. Can you please explain this?"

"I wasn't flirting." Hailey felt her defensiveness rise in her throat, so she paused to get her emotions in check. "I wasn't flirting," she repeated and managed to say it calmly and matter of fact. "I was lost, and I was just asking for directions. That's all."

"Liar!" Sameen stood and slammed his hands on the table, sending his chair crashing to the floor behind him.

Hailey jumped and almost shot out of her chair to get away, but she managed to remain in her seat.

"Sit down and control yourself Sameen or I will ask you to

leave the room."

Sameen snatched the chair from the floor and returned to the table.

"I will get to the truth," the officer reassured the bearded man and then turned back towards Hailey. "Please, tell me why you are not wearing a niqāb or at least a hijab?"

"Sir, I'm sorry I don't know what either of those are." She shrugged her shoulders.

Sameen hissed at her, "Well American, you should have done your research before coming into our country. You don't own the world, and you should know that you aren't welcome here with the attitude you have. You have to respect our customs and faith, and it is evident to me that you are one who does not."

"But I do want to show respect. That's why I'm wearing an abaya, and if you tell me what those are I can get one and..."

The officer cut her off. "A niqāb is a veil that women are required to wear at all times when in the presence of any man she is not related to. You should have one or at least have hijab, which is a scarf, to cover your head. In my opinion, a hijab is not ideal but to have neither... is an insult and a crime in my eyes." The officer lowered his gaze and started to write again.

Hailey's stomach sank, and she chided herself for not remembering about the scarf. How many stories had Anna told her about head coverings?

Stupid!!

Now thinking about it, she could have easily used the sash she had in her carry-on. She was going to wear it as a belt for her new capri pants at the compound. It probably would have been long enough to cover her face and neck. At the very least, it would have been better than nothing.

Hailey had been so excited to get off the plane and to see

Anna, that she hadn't even thought about it at the time. But that would have only solved one of the problems that faced her now. The other problem was certainly larger, and it was one she didn't know how to fix it.

"After hearing what you've told me and hearing Sameen's account of you talking to those men, I'm officially turning you over to the Mutawa to be processed for your crimes."

"Who are the Mutawa?" Hailey asked tentatively.

Sameen answered in a calm, prideful voice, "I'm a Mutawa, a member of Saudi Arabia's religious police."

Sameen reached his hand up to his chest and pointed to a small badge clipped to his robe and tapped it with his finger. Hailey hadn't focused on it before.

He continued. "We are the authority for the promotion of virtue and prevention of vice. Sharia law is a very traditional, pure form of Islam and I am devoted to upholding this with the Saudi people… as well as with you foreigners." He shot her a sneer. "Though some of my brothers don't agree with my methods." He looked at the officer. "Praise Allah, that you aren't one of them my brother."

The officer nodded his support to Sameen, and they both rose, leaving Hailey sitting speechless. The officer slowly slid his clipboard off the table, and the scratching sound made Hailey's skin crawl.

"I will have some officers come for you shortly, and you will be transferred to the Mutawa holding office until further action can be arranged."

"Wait, don't I get a phone call or something?" As soon as the question left her mouth, she realized how stupid it sounded, and she wished she could take it back.

Both men left the room laughing.

- - - - - - -

The next couple of hours passed by painfully slow. Hailey was thinking that being handed over to the religious police was probably going to make things worse for her. Nevertheless, she was starting to go crazy in the little room, and she hoped they would come for her soon.

The ticking clock, the overhead flickering fluorescent light, and the windowless walls were testing her limits. She resorted to pacing the room.

The room was small, so she started doing laps around the table, first one direction for a few laps and then switching. The ticking seemed to amplify with each pass and began to make her head pound.

"I'm Henry the Eighth I am, Henry the Eighth I am I am." She sang to try and drown out the sound of the clock. "I've been married to the girl next door. She's been married seven times before, and everyone's been a Henry, a….."

The door suddenly swung open, shutting Hailey's mouth.

Two officers entered. They both had the same insignia as the first officer who took her suitcase, probably denoting that they were guards or something similar. The taller one asked her to come with them. She complied.

As she approached the door, the smaller one spoke. "If you trouble, we handcuff you."

His English was quite broken, but Hailey understood the message loud and clear. She nodded her compliance. They handed her a scarf, and she quickly draped it over her head and loosely crossed it to cover her hair, cheeks, and neck as much as possible.

They moved out of the doorway allowing her to stand between them. The taller one lightly grasped her elbow. It was obvious he wanted to remind Hailey that she was still in serious trouble despite the absence of handcuffs. Not that she needed reminding.

They led her down to the end of the long hallway in the opposite direction of the door in which she'd initially come through. It felt like an Alice in Wonderland or a Matrix moment as the hall seemed to bow and get longer. Once at the end of it, they made a left and reached a set of double glass doors. They entered and passed through an office. There was a door to her left that led to the outside, which Hailey looked at longingly. A long counter sat to her right where a long line of people was waiting. Some of them were fanning themselves with papers and others just held papers motionless in their hands.

Everyone had their eyes on her.

Hailey tried to just stare at the floor as she wondered about the intent of the officers.

Do they have other ways to get to wherever they are taking me? Or do they want to make an example of me and this is the most public place to do that? Hailey questioned to herself.

To Hailey, it seemed as if they were silently announcing: "Yes, we are dealing with these outsiders harshly when they don't obey and we don't take their crimes lightly."

Parading her in front of the crowd of locals must not have been enough. When they were right in the middle of the room, the taller officer gave a forceful downward yank to her elbow forcing her to trip and stumble to one knee. The smaller one, as if on cue, came beside her and grabbed the other arm. Both yanked her to her feet and dragged her through the next set of metal doors.

Hailey felt her nose tingle, and her eyes start to water. She wished she could stop it, but the sobs came rolling up her throat. She tried to stifle them, but that just seemed to make them break forth with more force. Her body started shaking, and she could see that her escorts were growing more uncomfortable. They increased their speed, dragging her along.

After going through a few more doors, they rounded a corner and pushed her towards a small door. It was adorned with a few small Arabic characters. Hailey had no clue what they said.

"Go and get control of yourself and clean up. You have two minutes." The taller officer's English still held an accent, but it was easy to understand him, and if Hailey wasn't mistaken, his tone held a bit of empathy.

Ah, a bathroom. Hailey was grateful.

"Thank you," she said as she pushed the door open.

She headed straight to the mirror. Mascara was running down her face, and her eyes were red and puffy. She removed the scarf and looked at herself.

Oh, Hailey! Not your best day by far, huh?

She ran some water and filled her hands. Splashing it on her face, she washed the mascara rivers off her cheeks and combed her fingers through her hair, then replaced the scarf. After she had finished, she stood there, looking at her reflection. Seeing herself standing there in the all that fabric made her lip start to quiver. She felt so afraid.

No, Hailey, hold it together.

She looked up at the ceiling to stop the tears and took a deep breath.

"Time's up. Come out now!" An angry voice said, followed by a banging fist on the door.

Hailey exited the bathroom, thanked the officers again and

took her place between them. The three continued down the hall in silence. It was then that a different fear overtook her.

Being in the small room with the table, three chairs, and the little ticking clock, she had only wanted to get out of it, but now she yearned to go back. After the short break from the shock she was experiencing up until entering the bathroom, she now realized that what waited for her within the hands of the Mutawa was unimaginable.

The fear of the unknown crept all over her body like hundreds of tiny, poisonous spiders. She wanted so deeply to run and get away, but the knowledge that any sudden movement could possibly lead to her death kept her compliant.

Externally she remained silent, whereas on the inside she was screaming out in terror.

CHAPTER 11

Hailey might have found it all a bit comical how things transpired and got out of hand so quickly, but her intense anxiety kept all humor at bay. Thinking it was a good idea to leave without Anna knowing that she was coming, had to be the most foolish thing she had ever done.

After exiting the airport security wing, Hailey was loaded into the back seat of a black van. The smaller officer remained at the airport, but the taller officer got in the passenger side and now was staring straight ahead. Hailey tried to ask him about her luggage. When he didn't even acknowledge her, she chose to sit quietly and stare out the window.

She wasn't sure how long they'd been traveling. The intense heat made it seem like an hour, even though it was probably only fifteen, maybe twenty minutes. The driver was quiet the entire time and didn't even make eye contact with her in the rearview mirror.

Everything that passed by the window just blurred by, a smear of brown mixed with a few colors here and there. Nothing made an impact or stuck in Hailey's mind. Just as the officers were treating her, she, in turn, treated the rest of the world. The fear hadn't lessened, it just changed and made Hailey numb and defeated.

The van jerked and stopped briefly in front of a large building. It loomed above her, and her eyes scaled its entire height as she craned her neck further towards the window. It was made of light, red brick. Five windows were symmetrically placed every few feet on either side of the door, they continued on each level right up to the top floor, which loomed ten stories above her. Even though it was naive of her, Hailey was shocked at how industrial the building looked.

She had not seen many pictures of Saudi from outside the walls of Anna's compound. In all honesty, she had expected the country to be filled with light-brown clay, one or two story buildings, surrounded by small, dirt streets and beyond that... only desert. She had assumed there would most likely be tall steel buildings, like this one, in the downtown core of the big cities, but seeing it now seemed odd and out of place.

After the short pause, the van continued around the side of the building, down a small alley, and stopped in a small parking lot next to the building. The tall officer got out, said something to the driver in Arabic and closed his door. The driver remained seated with the engine running. The purpose of the trip was clearly to drop her and go.

The tall officer opened her door and was waiting for her to get out. She hesitated as her stomach lurched. Each transition, each change from one place to another seemed to bring a new wave of fear, and she was finding it difficult to push herself forward.

"Come with me. Now!" If there was any empathy in his voice before it was now gone.

Hailey quickly got out.

He kept one hand on her upper arm, guiding her towards the

building and one hand on the assault rifle slung over his shoulder. The tall officer pulled open the metal door after tapping the security panel with a key card.

Hailey turned and glanced toward the main street that they had come in on and, before disappearing into the building, she could have sworn she saw a palm tree and a coffee shop. A little, sad chuckle caught in her chest. It looked like Florida.

There were people everywhere. Most of the people were coming and going through the large, double glass doors at the front of the building. The majority of the men that passed had on the same badge as that wretched man from the airport. They were chattering to each other or yelling at others who did not have a badge. Hailey wondered what they might have done to end up here.

Is it even half as preposterous as my situation?

The officer moved her past them all and rounded a long, oval desk. The officer sitting behind the desk smirked at her as she went by. Upon reaching the far side of the desk, they came to some frosted double glass doors and continued through them. The wall of air-conditioning hit Hailey, and she shivered. The heat of the van had covered her body in sweat underneath the dark fabric, and she welcomed the chill.

They seemed to be in some sort of processing office, and shortly after entering the room, another officer holding a clipboard joined them. The two men talked for a few minutes, and then the tall officer took the clipboard from the other, signed a form, returned it, and turned towards her.

"Good luck."

That was it. The tall officer turned and left without another word.

As Hailey watched him return to the frosted doors, she again felt all familiarity being sucked away from her. It hadn't been much, but the tall officer had been the only ray of friendliness she had encountered since talking to the businessman at the airport. She didn't want him to leave.

A cold hand tightened around her arm.

Hailey had tried not to make eye contact with anyone in the building. She didn't want to have more accusations thrown at her, but she raised her eyes slowly to meet the eyes of her new escort. His smile caught her attention first. It was welcoming but the kind that made her skin crawl. Like a wolf welcoming a sheep into his den.

He was dressed in the same tan uniforms like the other officers, but the insignia on his shirt far outnumbered that of the tall officer and the officer who had interviewed her back at the airport. A white t-shirt peeked out of the v of the uniform but not enough to cover all of his salt and pepper chest hair.

He looked to be in his mid-forties. His black hair was slicked back and was showing some signs of receding. He wore his goatee short, with one or two day's growth filling in the rest of his beard. His dark eyes bore into her, and she tried not to imagine what he might be thinking.

"My name is Faisal bin Hakim Al Zahrani. I'm..." he searched for the words, then continued. "I'm not sure what the American equivalent would be, but let's just say that a lot of the officers here report to me. Waheed, the officer that interviewed you at the airport, called me and made me aware of your situation and that you'd be coming to me." He waited till a few people passed, then continued. "Let us go somewhere a bit more private, and I will explain what is going to happen. But before we do that, I must make one quick phone call beforehand. Please stay here, and I will come for you shortly."

"OK," Hailey mumbled quietly.

He led her a few feet over to the closest wall where five small wooden chairs sat, and she took a seat on the closest one. Hailey didn't watch him leave but kept her eyes fixed on the black and blue tiled floor. His footsteps faded away, and she dropped her elbows on her knees and let her head fall into her hands.

Her eyes started to water as the day replayed in her mind. Hailey had to bite her lip to keep the tears from coming. The ache and fear she felt in her heart were starting to take over, quicker than her resolve to stay strong. But then...

Footsteps.

They were drawing nearer. Hailey sat up but kept her eyes down. A swirl of black fabric to her left caught her eye, and she looked up to see a Saudi woman passing with quick little steps. It was as if she were gliding along the tile.

"Don't fight him and it will be quick." Her whisper was so quiet, Hailey barely heard her.

"Silence!" the officer who had her by the arm yelled, as he jerked the woman away from Hailey and kept her walking towards a hallway on the other side of the room.

Hailey's heart quickened. Her abaya felt like it was tightening around her throat, like two hands strangling her. Despite the air-conditioning, a bead of sweat started to trickle down her forehead.

A door opened, Hailey looked up to see Faisal exiting an office and start making his way towards her. She turned her head the opposite way towards the frosted doors and tried to calculate her chances if she made a run for them. Despite the fact that the cause of her fear was just a few yards away, the same fear also paralyzed her, keeping her on the chair like an invisible cage. She couldn't get herself to move.

Faisal approached.

"Come with me please," he said.

Hailey rose and allowed the cold hand to grip her arm once more.

=======

The drive was almost painful. As the distance between the airport and the car increased, Ryan felt like it was creating a bigger distance between Hailey and him. After a debate with Chuck, Ryan surrendered and agreed to come back to the compound for the night, but he now regretted conceding.

"You can come back first thing tomorrow and catch a flight back to Riyadh. You will be there in plenty of time for the meeting with George."

Replaying Chuck's words as they drove to the compound still didn't bring him any comfort. He knew that they needed to meet with George before they could start any productive action, but still, he wanted to start looking for her now. This lack of action was going to drive him mad.

It was nice to see Linda again, but as soon as dinner was finished, he retreated to his room. He couldn't handle any more small talk. Ryan called Norah to see if she had made any progress. She hadn't. She was still waiting for people to return her calls. He tried Thomas, but there was no answer. Ryan didn't even want to bother trying Jeremy. In his mind, Jeremy was responsible for Hailey taking off early, and he couldn't guarantee he could control his tongue if they spoke.

Hailey, where are you?

Ryan looked over at the phone where he placed it on the nightstand.

God, please... if she's able, get her to call.

Ryan repeated the prayer over and over until he fell asleep. Soon a dream flooded his mind...

> ... A thick, red blanket lay over Hailey. She was surrounded by light. A dark figure emerged out of the light and moved to her lay beside. The fear that cut into Hailey's face was heartbreaking to witness.
>
> Ryan screamed at her to run, but she lay there unmoving. Ryan tried to reach out to her, but he couldn't move his arms. The figure grasped her shoulder and pulled her towards himself.
>
> Ryan screamed at her to pull away, and Hailey looked at him with emotionless eyes.
>
> "I can't," she said.
>
> Hailey squeezed her eyes shut and turned her head away. Ryan tried to reach out to her again, but he was being sucked backward. Unable to stop his fall, the image of her and the figure was wrenched out of view.
>
> Then there was blackness...

His eyes flew open. Ryan was breathing heavily. The sheets were a sweaty, twisted mess at the bottom of the bed.

"Hailey!" Ryan whispered her name to the empty room.

He turned onto his back and ran his hands through his sweat soaked hair. Staring up at the ceiling, he felt God speak softly into his heart. Ryan poured out prayer after prayer for her until the sun rose.

=======

Faisal led her through a few small white doors into a room not much bigger than the room she'd first occupied at the airport. However, this room had a black one-way mirror spanning the far wall, and the table was tall and thin. It looked like a table her aunt had behind the couch back in the States. There were no chairs, only two small three-legged, metal stools.

"Please sit." Faisal motioned to the stool farthest from the mirror in the center of the room.

Hailey expected he didn't want to obstruct the view of whoever was in the other room watching. Faisal took the other stool and dragged it across the floor, making a horrible screeching noise as the metal scraped the black and blue tile. He moved it off to the side, took a seat, and leaned his back on the wall to the left of the mirror.

Hailey looked towards the mirror and only then noticed a small video camera sitting on a tripod in the corner of the room to the right of the mirror. She also noticed how Faisal made no intentions of turning on the video camera. Hailey shuddered.

"Have you ever heard my name before? Faisal?"

"No."

Hailey looked him in the eyes but kept her head tilted downwards as an attempt to not seem confrontational. She hoped to not offend or aggravate him in any way. Hailey was still trying not to let her mind go to the worst explanation when she replayed the woman's warning.

She could have meant the interview and nothing more, right?

"It means insightful arbitrator. Have you ever heard the name, Hakim? It was my father's name." He didn't wait for her answer. "His name means wise or insightful. I believe Allah, in all his wisdom, gave my father his name so he could give me mine. When I heard what you did, I thought it would be best for me to see you in person and discuss things with you. You may remove the scarf if you'd like. I know it is quite warm in these rooms."

Hailey had noticed there was no air conditioning in the room, undoubtedly an interrogation tactic. Her first instinct was to decline. However, when she glimpsed a small frown creeping across his lips as she hesitated, she changed her mind and took his offer.

As she placed the scarf into her lap, she felt the heaviness of his gaze upon her. She returned her eyes to his. His look made her swallow, and she now regretted her inability to try and run when she had the chance.

Faisal continued. "Please start by telling me how you saw the events of this morning unfold."

Hailey did just that. For the next half hour, she explained her reason for leaving America unannounced, her trip through Germany, and her arrival at the Riyadh airport. She told him of her trouble with Anna's directions and her innocent attempt to ask for assistance from the businessman and how Sameen and the other men had misinterpreted her actions and had approached her. She laid out the details of how her belongings were separated from her and how she had tried to explain that she meant no disrespect by not wearing a veil or scarf. She described the interview with the officer in the little room and her transfer. She made sure not to leave out a single detail.

"You see, I truly meant no harm, and I apologize for my foolishness." Hailey glanced down at her clasped hands before going on. "All I want is to reach my friend in Dammam. Is there any way for this mess to be straightened out so I can leave?"

"Hailey, you see Saudi is a very different country than your America. We place a high importance on respect and modesty, something many of my countrymen feel that the West has forgotten all about. So when they see a young, beautiful woman," his eyes made a trace of her whole body, "like yourself, not abiding by our laws, they feel like you are bringing the cancer of your country into ours. Sameen is one of those countrymen to whom I am referring and, unfortunately for you, he is highly respected among our police and those in our justice system. Once he has made an accusation, his word is usually taken as truth. I, on the other hand, understand how your intentions were misinterpreted and I am willing to help you." He allowed his eyes to run over her again. "Well... maybe we could help each other out."

Hailey swallowed hard.

There was a knock from the other side of the glass. Faisal stood abruptly and went over to the door. Beside the door, hung a small phone attached to the wall. Faisal picked up the receiver, listened for a moment, frowned, and hung up.

"I guess sadly our time is coming to an end... quicker than I would have hoped." His shoulders made a small, sad shrug.

Hailey's heart exhaled with relief.

"The officers at the airport sent over your possessions and your papers, including your sponsor's contact information and your passport. They are sitting on my desk as we speak. I'm sorry to say, however, that it appears you have made quite an impact on Sameen. He is on his way over here personally to try to sway our courts to administer the strictest punishment. It seems he'd like to make an example of you. Even though Sameen has a lot of friends," Faisal smirked and leaned towards her a bit, "I have more, and I will speak on your behalf.

"You will still have to be processed and placed in one of our holding cells until I can work this all out, but it shouldn't take too long. I'd like to process you myself and have you placed under my charge before Sameen can stack up other charges against you when he gets here. So how about we get started?" He gestured for her to get up.

Hailey cautiously stood as Faisal slowly made his way over to her. Every step sent alarms coursing through her core. Hailey looked pleadingly towards the unseen form on the other side of the mirror. Her eyes darted about the room, and her mind raced.

What did "process you myself" entail?

The woman's warning surged through her mind again. By the way Faisal was speaking, Hailey didn't have much doubt left as to what his intentions would have been before the knock on the glass came. She assumed his plans had been interrupted, but why was he looking at her that way again: like a sailor who had finally laid his eyes on a woman after being at sea for months.

Wasn't Sameen on his way?

Faisal kept approaching with a slow stride. He reached her and raised his hand, she flinched. He paused and looked into her eyes, then continued to move his hand to the side of her face. He grasped a few strands of her hair and pulled them away from her face.

"You see," his voice was barely above a whisper, "before we allow anyone into one of our holding cells we need to ensure they have nothing on them that they can use to hurt themselves or anyone else. Now I can help you undress, or you may do it yourself."

His hand went to her shoulder causing her to jump.

"No!" the word came out of her lips with more force than she intended.

"Now, now. Don't fight. I usually enjoy a little fight in a woman, but we don't have time for that or much of anything sadly. I promise I won't touch. If you choose to undress yourself, then all I will do is follow protocol." He chuckled. "I think a glimpse of you will be more than enough compensation for speaking on your behalf. Don't you?"

Hailey felt more trapped than she ever had before. Without saying it, it was obvious he was giving her an ultimatum. Either she undresses for him, and he would help her get out of trouble, or he would undress her himself.

"I… I…" Hailey's eyes searched the walls senselessly for help.

"I know this can be tough," Faisal cooed in her ear as he leaned into her.

He smelled of cigars, and it turned Hailey's stomach.

"How about we do this together?"

He reached one hand to the V of her abaya to undo the clasp hidden under the collar. Hailey closed her eyes and wished she could disappear at will. Hearing the little pop of the clasp, brought Hailey over the edge of what she could handle. She tried to stop herself, but her hand flew up.

Slap!!

It was if she was standing outside of her body watching herself make her second foolish mistake since entering this country. When her hand made contact with the side of Faisal's face, his whiskers and the force of the slap stung her hand. But the sting from the slap didn't compare to the look that now blazed in Faisal's eyes. Hailey shrunk underneath his stare and dropped her eyes to the floor.

"I told you we didn't have time for that," he bellowed and the words reverberated off the walls.

He lunged at her, grabbed either side of the abaya and ripped it open, exposing her. He stood back a bit and stared at her with his mouth open. He was breathing faster.

"Now that I've got it started, please finish." His voice held a calm, sinister tonality.

Hailey cringed.

She didn't know what to do so she just stared at him. He took two quick steps towards her. She hardly had time to react as his hand made contact with her left cheek and her lip, splitting it. She put her tongue on the cut and tasted the blood. It was bitter and made her stomach tilt. Her hand protectively covered her throbbing cheek.

He wasn't leaving her with much of a choice.

Do I even have a choice anymore?

Hailey had never been faced with such a situation, and her mind was racing to make sense of it. Faisal returned to his spot a few feet away and turned to watch, arms crossed. Hailey dropped her head in defeat, raised her hands to either side of the now torn abaya, and started to slide it over her shoulders.

A knock!!

Hailey let out her breath and relaxed a bit. As Faisal turned towards the door, she immediately pulled the top of the abaya back over her shoulders and around her body. Then she crossed her arms protectively in front of herself.

Faisal opened the door, and a short officer came up to his side. He had to raise himself on his toes to reach Faisal's ear. The short officer finished whispering something to Faisal in Arabic, handed him something, and retreated around the corner out of Hailey's view. Faisal closed the door and turned back to face her.

"Here put this on," Faisal said as he threw a piece of fabric at her.

Hailey unfolded the cloth to reveal that it was another abaya.

"You can leave the one you've torn on the table and take a seat back on the stool." From the tone of his voice, he was furious. Not the fury that caused his voice to rise to a scream, but the kind that caused him to become eerily calm. "You have wasted our remaining time together. Pity," he frowned a mock sadness, "you could have used my help." Faisal turned to leave.

"WAIT! Please! What do you mean?"

He didn't even pause, he just continued to the door.

"I'm sorry. Please. Wait!" Hailey let the new abaya fall to the floor as she took a step forward.

Faisal left and closed the door behind him, leaving Hailey standing there mouth agape.

The tears came in small rolls of whimpers. Hailey's hands rose up to her head. She ran her fingers through her hair but stopped halfway and pulled.

"Ahhhrrggg." It was a scream of anger and defeat. She closed her eyes tightly. *Did I just waste the last chance I had to get out of this mess?*

Hailey removed the torn garment as the whimpers trickled out of her and replaced it with the other. She made sure to keep her back towards the mirror in case there were any peeping eyes still lurking behind the glass. Her shaking hands made it difficult to do it as quickly as she would have liked, but soon she was covered again. The new abaya was black but was plain and made of a heavier, coarser, synthetic fabric than the one Anna had given her. Nevertheless, Hailey was happy to be covered again, a small comfort she warmly welcomed.

Once she had set the torn abaya on the table, she took a seat on the hard, metal stool again. Hailey placed the scarf back over her head and waited.

Feelings of utter hopelessness flew all around her.

CHAPTER 12

Another knock at the door. The door swung open and an officer, whom Hailey hadn't seen before, came in. Behind him was that awful man from the airport, Sameen. Seeing him drove Hailey's hopelessness to a new low. Faisal was nowhere in sight.

Hailey kept her attention from Sameen as a silent protest to his presence and rested it on the officer. His face was mostly covered with a curly, black beard. He was older than the high-ranking officer at the airport. He had a small, oval mouth and narrow, brown eyes. His left eye had a large scar above it. His stomach hung out over his belt, and he limped when he walked. He looked tired.

When Hailey's eyes did drift to Sameen, he looked the same way he did the last time she saw him. However, he did seem to be looking at her with even more disgust. Hailey didn't even think it was possible, but he somehow had managed to draw up more repulsion towards her. It caused her fear to rise so she looked away.

After both of the men had entered the room, Sameen leaned against the wall to the left of the door. The officer walked over, grabbed the other stool, and placed it a few feet away from her. He sat down with a thud and a sigh.

"I'm sorry to keep you waiting all this time. This must be frightening for you."

Hailey noticed he was holding a small brown file and watched silently as he leaned forward and placed it on the table.

"I was under the impression that Faisal, one of my officers, had been in here to search and process you."

Hailey kept silent to see how this would play out before admitting anything.

"You've met Sameen" he gestured towards the cruel, little man. "He is here to... assist me. My name is Ahmed bin Naif Al Harbi. I usually don't get involved with such cases as yours, but when Sameen contacted me, I choose to look into it personally. It seems you have crossed a line that he is unwilling to overlook." He opened the file and glanced down at the contents, read for a moment, then returned his eyes to hers. "Hailey Pearson, I'm here to inform you that you are formally charged with being alone with a male non-relative, intent for prostitution, and..."

"Now wait just a second. I never did that," Hailey interjected.

Ahmed held up his hand. "Please let me finish. You are formally charged with being alone with a male non-relative, intent for prostitution, and are also charged with not obeying hijab. You see Saudi is a very modest country and hijab is the practice of women covering themselves. This is something you should have been aware of before entering our country. When Sameen was witnessing these actions, he became outraged and is very intent on using you as an example. And, even though he and I have differing views when it comes to foreigners, I am supporting his claims, and I will be transferring you to one of our prisons until your trial." He tried to smile empathetically, but it fell flat. "Do you have any questions?"

Hailey didn't even bother to try and stop the sobs as they

violently rose in her throat. She was terrified. "Please… this can't be happening. I can't… go to prison for this. This is… all a big… misunderstanding. Please, please have mercy. I meant… no harm." Her words came out sporadically through her sobs.

How is this happening? How did everything get so twisted?

Her chest was so heavy that it was hard to breath and the fear that squeezed her was unbearable. Hailey looked at Ahmed with pleading eyes.

"I'm very sorry." His tone was softer but still direct. "Our country is different from yours. We don't tolerate your kind of behavior. Whether you meant any harm or not, you need to understand that you caused harm nonetheless."

Hailey hung her head in her hands and continued to cry. Ahmed stood and started towards the door. He stopped halfway and turned back to her. Hailey raised her eyes in hope. His eyes were kind, and he smiled compassionately.

"I assume you have a sponsor here?"

"Yes, of course!" A small bit of adrenalin seeped into her bloodstream.

"If they can be contacted and they agree to come get you, I will permit you to stay with them here in the city until your trial. You are not allowed to return to the compound with them nor are you authorized to try and leave the country. If you give that information to me and agree to those terms, I will put a hold on your transfer and try to contact them."

Before Hailey could answer, Sameen cut in and addressed Ahmed in Arabic. Hailey had no idea what he was saying, but it was clear he wasn't happy. Ahmed listened for a moment, then raised his hand and replied in a forceful tone. Whatever Ahmed said in return must have been a rebuke because Sameen immediately ceased his objection and stormed out of the room.

Ahmed turned back to Hailey with raised eyebrows, waiting for her response.

"Yes... yes, of course, I accept those terms. Thank you. Thank you so much."

He nodded his head.

"I don't have my sponsor's information with me, but Faisal does. He said they are on his desk."

"So you've spoken with Faisal?" Ahmed questioned.

"Yes, he was in here before, just like you thought. I didn't want to be rude and interrupt you. Please go ask him for them. He has my passport, my visa papers, and my sponsor's contact information, everything." Hailey beamed as she wiped the tears from her cheeks.

Ahmed turned for the door. "I will go discuss that with him and return shortly." He peered back over his shoulder. "Don't fret, I will try and settle this with as much ease for you as possible. But please know that I am unable to ignore your offenses. You will receive punishment for your crimes... however... as you did them unintentionally, I will try to aid you in any way I can." He smiled at her and left.

Hailey's fear subsided dramatically. At least she finally had some sympathy from someone in this place and not just from a low-level guard but from someone very important it seemed. A sigh blew through her lungs and passed over her lips. Suddenly aware that her legs were cramped, she rose from the stool and did a few circles around the small room.

Time seemed to be ticking by so slowly, and Hailey started to wonder where Ahmed had gone.

Maybe he had already called Anna's parents, and they were just arranging the details of my release.

A slight smile rose to her face.

Maybe they were packing up their things to come and get me right at this very moment. Maybe Chuck could clear everything up so that I wouldn't need to even have a stupid trial. Or, even if I did, maybe his lawyer could easily straighten it all out with the judge. Maybe this trip can return to normal and then just be something Anna would tease me about later.

Her growing excitement made it harder to stay in the small, muggy room. To distract herself, Hailey started thinking of what it would be like to see Anna again. She began to play the different scenarios out in her mind.

Each version of how the reunion might happen was sweet, and thinking of them lifted her spirits considerably. Even the scene where, right in front of all the officers, she broke down in tears in a bumbling mess while telling all the Haringtons about what had happened to her would be okay. She didn't care how it played out, Hailey just longed desperately for it to be over and to see her friend.

Soon thoughts of the compound came into mind, and she longed to be in the safety of its walls. It felt so close, and she felt more at ease with each thought of what awaited her. Familiarity was by far the thing she longed for most: Anna, her parents, her own clothes, but most of all: no guards with guns or perverted officers or religious police, and no stuffy little rooms with stupid clocks or one-way mirrors. With each realization of all that the compound represented to her, each of the steps she made around the room became a little lighter. It was even getting easier to breathe.

Hailey stopped walking and leaned against the far wall, opposite the one-way mirror.

Did they know? Did anyone even know that I had gotten in trouble?

Hailey doubted anyone did. It had been only a few days since she left New York and her flight wasn't due to land in Dammam until later that night. Anna was about to get one crazy phone call and would be completely shocked...

> "I'm sorry, but your friend has been arrested for prostitution and this and this. You must come immediately and bail her out of a Mutawa holding station. If you don't, she will be immediately transported to a prison to await trial. Blah, blah, blah."

Hailey laughed to herself and shook her head.

Poor Anna! Sorry girl.

Not even her friends back home would believe it. Thomas would just look at it as a crazy adventure minus the whole Faisal incident. He would, of course, give her a hug for that. And Ryan... Ryan, for some reason, all Hailey could imagine about his response, would be to just take her in his arms and hold her like he did after she had run out from the party. Hailey's heart started to ache, she missed Ryan. She now regretted her choice to keep her distance from him during that last month.

A month, had it really been almost a month since the party?

Hailey shook her head at her idiocy. What she had really needed during that time was a friend, and he was the best. She felt more alive when she was with him. He made her laugh and was always there for her. She wished so much that he was there with her right now and even though she would see Anna soon, she could sure use his strong shoulders to help her through this last bit.

Although... I'm not sure the officers would enjoy having him here.

Hailey chuckled and was just starting to imagine how those conversations might play out when another knock sounded at the door and interrupted her thoughts.

=======

Eighteen days. It had been eighteen days since Thomas had dropped Hailey off at the airport and the last time anyone had seen her. Ryan was still awake and had just finished calculating and recalculating the count of how long Hailey had been missing when the alarm clock went off. He felt sick to his stomach.

I shouldn't have given her so much space. Maybe if I would have pushed she would have talked to me sooner, and I would have known she had left. Heck, I would have been the one to drop her off or… gone with her, for that matter. Way to go Ryan!

Kicking off the covers, he took a brief shower, got dressed, and headed downstairs.

The smell of breakfast was amazing. Linda was an incredible cook, but Ryan would have to force himself to eat. His stomach was still uneasy from the nightmare. He trusted God had answered his prayers and protected her from whatever was happening to her, but he wasn't sure what God was going to do with all of this. He was still worried for Hailey, and he had trouble not letting doubt creep in.

What if that figure lying beside her, whoever it was, had hurt her? Stop it! It's in His hands.

He rounded the corner and came into the kitchen.

"Ryan!" Chuck said as he looked up from the newspaper in his hands. "George called just a moment ago and confirmed the meeting at the airport for late this afternoon, and you're all booked on a flight, which…" Chuck checked his watch, "leaves in three hours. More than enough time. Once we finish up breakfast and get all packed up, Linda will drive us to the airport."

"Actually, I wanted to talk to you about that." Ryan glanced from Chuck to Anna and back again. "I was thinking that... maybe... I could go alone, and you and Anna could stay here. I mean if Hailey calls or makes it here, then it would be good to have you guys here to help her out in whatever way she needs. George will be with me in Riyadh, so it doesn't make much sense to have us all in one place."

"You really want to do the 'don't keep all your eggs in one basket' thing now?" Anna asked sadly.

"I know you'd like to stay together... but... we know that Hailey didn't catch her connecting flight, but who knows, maybe she made a different flight or got to Dammam another way. You never know. I'd just feel better if there was one of us in either place she might be."

Chuck nodded his head. "Yes, I totally agree. Anna, I think it would be good for you to stay in case she does get here."

"I'll go call you a cab." Linda smiled and squeezed Ryan's arm as she rose from the table and made her way over to the counter where the phone was sitting.

"Ryan, are you sure you don't want me to come with you?" Anna's eyes were pleading.

"Yeah, I am. I mean I know Hailey has met your parents before, but if she makes it to the compound I think she is going to need a friend and if we both aren't here... I don't know... something tells me she will really need us."

Memories from his dream tried to come forward again, and he had to push them away.

For the next hour, they planned their strategy as best they could. Ryan would go meet George and contact them once they had more information from security. Anna would call the train station in Riyadh to see if she could speak to the ticket counters. Maybe someone remembered seeing an American girl fitting Hailey's description. It was a long shot but worth it. Chuck would head out to the Dammam train station with a photo and do the same. They went through all the scenarios they could think of and made contingency plans if any of them had any luck and found a lead.

"Be careful!" Anna said as she hugged Ryan when the cab pulled up. "Find her and don't take no for an answer from anyone... OK?"

"I will." And with that Ryan hopped in the back seat of the cab.

The cab smelled of coffee. The air conditioning must have been broken as the fabric of the seat was hot and hurt the back of Ryan's legs when he sat down. As the cab pulled away, he turned around and looked out the back window. Anna, Chuck, and Linda were still standing on the porch, arms around each other. When they saw him turn to look back at them, Chuck and Linda waved. A big smile accompanied his return wave. Ryan felt blessed to have them in his life.

If he had only known that this would be the last time he would ever see them.

CHAPTER 13

The door slowly opened. Hailey's heart sank as she saw who it was entering the room. It was Faisal. The moment his eyes met hers her skin started to shrivel. He wore a smirk of victory on his face like he had won something.

"Ahmed will be here in a moment, so I don't have long, but I wanted to inform you of something before he gets here. You see here at this particular holding station I am sort of like the prince, and Ahmed is like the king. When he is not here, I'm in charge. I also handle the transfers, and it is up to me if they go smoothly," he walked over to her, "or if they go... uncomfortably."

He reached down and grabbed her arm and twisted. Hailey winced but sat still.

"It's really the choice of whom I'm transferring."

Footsteps sounded outside the door, and he backed away from her. Hailey raised her hand to massage the throbbing in her arm that his grip had left behind. She looked towards the door. Ahmed stepped in, concern showing on his face.

"It seems we have a bit of a misunderstanding. Faisal never received any of your belongs from the airport. I made a call to the airport security, and they informed me that you didn't have anything with you when they approached you. Now this confuses and saddens me."

He took a few more steps into the room. Hailey held her breath.

"I told you I was willing to help you, but adding dishonesty to your list of offenses has changed my mind." He rubbed his temples with both index fingers and continued. "I was confused as to why you would lie to me, but Faisal said that you haven't stopped lying since you arrived. Without a sponsor or a way to confirm why you are in my country, there is no other choice but to transfer you to our prison. Goodbye." He turned his back to her.

Hailey leaped from the stool to interject. "No, he's lying. They're all lying. Wait! I wouldn't lie to you. Why would I lie about this?"

Hailey almost made it to the door, but Faisal's face came within inches of hers. He cut her off, and Ahmed disappeared around the corner.

"Funny thing," Faisal snickered as he walked over to closed the door, "it seems I was mistaken, I don't have your paperwork after all. It's also strange, but my friends at the airport sadly don't remember taking anything from you and giving it to me. Odd isn't it? Well, I guess it doesn't pay to anger me."

His head snapped around, and his eyes bore into her. Faisal slowly advanced towards her. He lifted his hands. It took everything in her, but Hailey forced herself not to move. His touch was light as he placed them on her shoulders, Hailey closed her eyes.

Then all of a sudden his touch changed drastically, he shoved her. He put so much force into it that Hailey went sprawling backward. Catching her heel on one of the legs of the other stool, she started to fall. Her arms got tangled in the abaya, and she was unable to use them to break her fall. Pain seared through her head as it smacked against the tiled floor.

Faisal loomed over her, smiling down at her like a Cheshire cat. Before Hailey could scurry away, his boot connected hard with the side of her ribcage. Hailey cried out and rolled into a protective ball. She waited for the next blow, but Faisal only circled her once and then left the room. His laughter carried down the hall and echoed in her ears.

=======

Faisal appreciated his brothers at the airport. They were always very gracious to call him when a female foreigner was being brought in. They knew how he enjoyed having a little fun with them before they were processed and then transferred to the prison. Usually, the women were from the Philippines or Africa: not his first choice but still very enjoyable. Once in awhile, he would get a call about an American, his favorite.

Americans were different. They knew the least about Saudi, which gave a sweet taste to their fear. Also, their women were accustomed to freedoms Saudi woman knew nothing of, nor should know. Some demanded rights that he found laughable, whereas others were so terrified with their surroundings that they were almost catatonic. He liked both responses but for different reasons.

With the first group, the fighters, he enjoyed the challenge of chipping away at their resolve bit by bit until they accepted their circumstances. With the latter, the mice, he found it similar to watching a beautiful, moving painting, silent but stunning. However, the girl he met today was different. She was a mix of the two, which was somewhat difficult to categorize. It was frustrating that he didn't have sufficient time with her to work it out.

When she was first brought in, she didn't fail to capture his attention. This American beauty almost made him blush when she caught him staring. He usually never tried to hide his lust, but he felt like a school child getting caught looking at his crush. He was initially excited to process her, but after her flip flop act between noncompliance and acceptance had taken up so much time, he thought he would have to write her off after being interrupted. But surprisingly, the events of the afternoon had played out quite nicely.

It was fun to play with her and watch her squirm. Not unlike a cat playing with a terrified mouse, Faisal took pleasure in catching her, batting her around a bit and then letting her go, only to squash her hopes of freedom by catching her again.

The power he felt flowing through him as he made his way down the hall was intoxicating, and he couldn't remember the last time he had had such a satisfying laugh.

Arriving at the end of the hallway, he pushed open the doors that led back to his office with one hand and wiped away the tears from his eyes with the other.

He reached his office and, after drawing the blinds, he took a seat and opened the locked file cabinet behind his desk. He withdrew the papers the officers at the airport had sent over. Faisal quickly glanced through them, thought for a moment, and returned them back to the cabinet. He originally had planned to destroy the girl's documents after receiving reassurance from his brothers that their story would match his. However, after enjoying his last moments with her, he thought he would save them. Who knows what occasion might arise later.

The woman would be staying at this Mutawa holding office,

his holding office, before she was transferred and if he was at all able to gain even a few moments with her, having some leverage might come in handy. Typically a prison transfer would take place the next day, but he would try and delay that a little longer. He had a large number of responsibilities, and they wouldn't be easy to get out of. The longer she would be able to remain here, the better. He'd have to make a call immediately to delay the paperwork.

After hanging up the phone, he leaned back in his chair. With Ahmed in the office this week, he would need to come up with some good excuses to see her. A large smile crept through his lips as his plan started to take form.

=======

Hailey was so confused about how quickly everything had changed. The hope she had felt when Ahmed had left after the first meeting tasted bitter in her mind now. She was shaking. However, her shaking was not from room temperature; the room was still muggy. It was from a deep fear and loneliness.

It had been a little while since Faisal had left the room, but she remained on the floor and was trying not to move. The pain that cut through her rib cage had dulled to a sharp throb, but she didn't want to attempt getting up for fear that it would return.

Two officers entered the room. They each took one arm and lifted her slowly to her feet. As the guards hoisted her up, the pain shot through her again, causing her knees to buckle. A small cry escaped her lips. The guards gripped her arms tighter and steadied her. They half escorted, half dragged her out of the room and down the hall to another room. One guard, the larger of the two, supported her weight as the other unlocked a metal door containing a small postcard size barred window.

The sound of the key in the door and it unlocking terrified Hailey.

"Please, please," she whispered, "can I speak to Ahmed again?"

She couldn't take in a full breath to speak any louder; her ribs wouldn't allow it. Regardless, it didn't matter, her question was only met with silence as the large, metal door was swung open and she was led into an even smaller room.

There were no windows, apart from the little one in the door, no double-sided mirror, no clocks, no chairs, and no table. A small, metal bed rested in the far corner with a thin, discolored mattress. It was void of any sheets or pillows.

In the opposite corner, at the far end of the room was a three-foot square tiled area. The tiles continued up the wall and reminded Hailey of a shower, although there were no glass doors or a curtain.

No, it probably isn't a shower.

In the center of the tiled area was, what looked like, a very shallow, square, plastic sink with a large hole in it – four times the size of the hole in a standard sink. The depth was only about half an inch. The top and bottom edge of the basin was the width of an average sink, but the sides of it were flat, roughly three inches wide, and were ribbed.

Leading out from the top of the basin was a thin, metal pipe that ran up the wall and disappeared about four feet up from the floor and into the wall. Next to the pipe, a white hose protruded out of the wall. It had a small nozzle at the end, which was resting on a hook on the wall. Upon seeing the hose, Hailey reconsidered, *maybe it is a shower.*

"What's that?" Hailey questioned.

"Where you relieve yourself," answered the smaller guard.

Hailey's face instantly scrunched in disgust. It looked like it hadn't been cleaned in some time.

That is going to be extremely difficult to use, especially wearing this. Hailey dreaded the thought as she pictured it.

The larger guard guided her to the bed and let go of her arm, she slumped down with a small yelp. Both guards left, locking the door behind them. Hailey whimpered as she gingerly raised her legs onto the bed.

She spent two days in the dark, little room. She didn't see a soul apart from the door opening once each day as a tray of food was shoved in. The lights were turned off and on by another, and so she slept and woke on their schedule. The ache in her side had diminished, and a dark bruise emerged as evidence of Faisal's attack. Hailey was thankful that nothing seemed broken and even more grateful that she hadn't seen Faisal again. However, she was surprised that he hadn't come back.

Voices.

Yesterday there were voices in the hall from a few men going from door to door. They weren't officers, but they seemed to be discussing something as they paused outside each door. Hailey guessed they were discussing each detainee. One of the men made notations in a book after each case was presented.

Hailey wanted to watch again, so she cautiously rose off the bed and made her way over to the door. She had to stand on her tippy toes to see out the little window.

There were four men today. The three from yesterday had returned. When her eyes met the face of the fourth, her fear and anger raged simultaneously. It was Faisal. None of the men paid any attention to her peering through the window, so she continued to watch. One man spoke, then the other. The third was about to write in the book, but Faisal grabbed his arm, keeping his pen off the page. Faisal seemed frustrated and spoke with a forced calm.

Hailey was dying to understand.

The other three men seemed forceful with their initial statements as each of them took another turn to speak. Faisal spoke again but was cut off by the third man with one loud word. Faisal pursed his lips, looked from one man to the next, let out a small sigh, and spoke one word. Then with a bow of his head, he turned and left. The third man finished making his notations while the first man spoke into a small, gray hand radio. A moment later an officer joined them.

The officer turned right for her door, and she was now standing face to face with him only inches apart, peering at each other through the window. He said something to her, and even though she didn't know what the Arabic word meant, she understood and moved away. The officer unlocked the door and entered the room with the three men in tow.

Hailey backed up towards her bed, arms protectively around her middle. The third man came around the officer. Hailey had no idea what was going on, but she was happy Faisal had left.

"You are being transferred to our prison today. This matter should have been completed yesterday. However, it seems like you have made a… an impact and delayed our protocol. I would apologize except it did allow you to remain in these nicer conditions for an extra day," the man said as he looked around the room. "So I would count yourself fortunate."

Nicer conditions? He's got to be joking.

Hailey shuddered as she wondered where she might be headed.

The man continued. "This officer will handcuff and escort

you outside. You will board a vehicle that will take you to the prison. You will remain there to await the court's verdict on your case. Do you have any questions?"

His dull tone aggravated Hailey. It was one that came from frequently reading detailed procedure. He wasn't even trying to hide the fact that he didn't care her life was falling apart and that each of his words caused a deep terror to pulse through her. He had uttered these sentences a thousand times, and as the question seemed only part of the routine, Hailey remained silent and only shook her head in response.

"Very well then. But if you resist or cause a scene... well, let's just say... I would advise against it. You will save yourself much trouble if you comply."

And with that, the three men left the room.

The sound of clanging handcuffs filled the room as the officer approached her.

- - - - - - -

The sun was blaring bright. It burned her eyes, and she had to shut them for a few moments until they adjusted. The difference between the dim, little room and the Arabian sun was vast. The officer hadn't guided her back through the offices, through the frosted doors, and out through the metal side door where the tall officer from the airport had initially taken her. That path would have helped to adjust her eyes: dim room, office fluorescents, and then the sun. Instead, the way they took went deeper into the back of the building and then exited out a door located in a back alley behind the building.

The smell of garbage was the second thing that hit her senses, and Hailey choked on the stench. The third attack on her senses was the heat. Sweat broke out over her whole body, and it trickled down her back. How the Saudi women manage to wear this outfit and others, which had even more coverage, day in and day out in such heat, Hailey would never understand. It had only been moments, and her skin was already crying out for shade and cold water. She missed the lighter fabric of Anna's abaya.

There was a vehicle sitting on the other side of the alley, and the guard started to lead her over to it. Halfway there, the door they had come through opened and another officer exited with a Saudi woman, also in handcuffs. Hailey's officer gave her a little push to keep her walking.

They all reached the large truck just as a third officer jumped out of the truck, unlocked a big padlock from the back doors. The vehicle reminded Hailey of a cross between a delivery truck and a large passenger van. The back was the size of a big delivery truck with double doors, secured by a large pin. The roof was curved like a van.

Once the doors were opened, Hailey saw that there was one other woman already in the truck. She was seated on one of the metal benches lining each side of the vehicle. As she was dressed in a full abaya, Hailey couldn't see many of her features – only her dark eyes. The woman shifted her weight as they approached.

Both Hailey and the other woman were pushed into the truck. The length of each of their abayas and the fact that their hands were handcuffed, made this act less than graceful. Once seated, the officers swung the doors closed, slid the pin in place, then replaced and locked the padlock. Hailey watched as their heads bobbed past the two small, barred windows set into each of the back doors.

Hailey wondered if the other women were as terrified as she was.

Do they at least know where we are headed? Had they been there before?

Hailey wanted desperately to talk to the women to find out their stories and to tell them hers, but there were listening ears too close. She couldn't see the front seat as there was a small partition separating the front and back, but she could clearly hear the driver and the other officers talking. So with that knowledge, Hailey didn't dare get herself into more trouble by attempting to speak. The other two seemed to have the same understanding, and after exchanging small empathized smiles, all three of them turned their eyes to the floor and rode out the trip in silence.

=======

Ehsan's day had not been going as he had hoped. He hated visiting the prison because he found it lowly and an insult to be requested to do so. However, if the king had matters that he wished for only Ehsan to deal with, then he would comply.

Ehsan stretched and rubbed the back of his neck. He rose from his chair and grabbed a glass of water from the small table near the office door. He desperately needed a break but instead returned to his seat. He wanted to tie up matters quickly and be on his way with his report before the mid-afternoon prayer time. Things had already taken much longer than expected and he loathed the fact that he was still there during the after-midday prayer.

He took a long sip of water and then wiped his hand across his mustache and down his beard to clear off the few drops the glass had left there. He glanced at the clock once more and turned back to the task at hand.

CHAPTER 14

The drive to the prison was long, and with each minute that passed, Hailey's body continued to protest. Her legs were cramped from trying to keep herself seated upright on the hard bench, her wrists were starting to chafe from the constant rubbing of the handcuffs, and the rest of her body felt stifled under the dark, thick material that lay over it.

The truck was stuffy, and Hailey was starting to feel a bit nauseous. The driver had only stopped once, during what Hailey guessed had been over an hour drive, to give them a quick drink of warm, stale water. When the liquid touched her lips, her body yearned for more despite the awful taste. After a few, small sips the officer drew it back and they continued on their way. Hailey soon wished she had refused the water. Before the drink, she didn't notice her thirst, but now her mouth was outrageously dry, and she felt faint.

The truck lurched back and forth as it made its way through the streets. Hailey and the other women bumped and jolted around like rag dolls with each turn, pot hole, and swerve. It caused Hailey's ribs to sharply object.

More time passed. Hailey had no idea how much. Then the truck slowed and came to a stop. Hailey raised her head to look out the back window. The windows were dirty, so she had to squint to see out. Between the bars and the muck, she saw only sand, gnarled trees and the road they were driving on snaking out behind them.

After a short pause, a loud creaking noise emanating from beyond the front of the truck. Once the sound dissipated and they drove a few more feet, it became visible that they had driven up to a guard shack and were now passing through a massive gate that bridged the two sides of a tall, thick stone wall.

Hailey saw a handful of armed guards standing on either side of the opening. There were also more guards within the walls. All of the guards were holding assault rifles.

Hailey's heart sank.

Soon the truck came to a quick stop, and all three women toppled over, Hailey fell hard on one elbow as she caught herself. The back doors were once again unlocked and opened, allowing the sun to flood in.

Hailey was escorted roughly off of the truck by one of the guards, who then turned his attention to the other women and pulled them off the truck one after the other. They were all shoved into an already formed, long line of women. The line was making its way into the eastern side of a large building.

Not all the women were proceeding voluntarily, but Hailey witnessed that a jab into a few of their ribs from the butt of a guard's gun silenced them and kept them walking. The act also proved to actively persuade the rest of the group to pick up the pace, and the line started to move more quickly. Hailey hurried and took her place in line behind the dark-eyed girl from the truck and kept her head down.

"Where are we?" Hailey whispered.

"The prison just outside Riyadh. Now please no more

words."

Hailey soon understood the need for quiet. The guard to her left and a few paces behind them started to pick up his pace and come closer. Hailey continued walking quietly, with her eyes to the ground, heart racing. The guard grunted and slowed. Hailey let out the breath she noticed she was holding.

Hailey guessed there were around fifteen women, or maybe twenty, as some were already inside. They were all being led into the building and down a few switchbacks of a zigzag ramp, similar to the wheelchair ramps in the States. The room seemed to have no lights, but after a few moments her eyes adjusted and Hailey took a look around.

At the bottom of the zigzag ramp, there was a deep-set room with about thirty shower heads poking out of the walls at three-foot intervals. The floor was made of a light concrete, with a handful of drains randomly peeking through. It looked like a locker room had been built at the bottom of an empty indoor swimming pool. The fluorescent lighting flickered and buzzed overhead. Along the wall on Hailey's right sat five squat toilets, similar to those that were in her room at the Mutawa holding office. Again they offered no privacy and Hailey shivered to think that she might have to get used to not having privacy again for some time.

Although all the women were strangers, Hailey, like them, felt they'd all be safer if they stuck closer together. They all huddled together in the center of the room. The woman standing next to Hailey was a tall, dark, African woman, probably in her late forties. She put a protective arm around Hailey. The act brought Hailey a small bit of comfort, and she leaned into the woman, accepting the maternal care.

One of the guards entered the door they had just filed

through, came over to the railing and looked down at them, twenty feet below. He spoke in Arabic, which of course Hailey didn't understand, but she did hear whimpers and gasps trickle through the crowd in response to his words. Hailey shuddered. He pointed to a large door behind her.

What is he saying?

The guard then switched to English.

"You must take clothes off, put them where your feet are, shower and line up at door," he said as he pointed again to the door behind her.

Hailey instantly shared the women's responses, her chin quivered, and she buried her head into the woman's shoulder. Hailey was thankful that she kept holding onto her.

Hailey looked at the door again then returned her attention to the other guards. There were six of them now. They were all walking down the switchbacks and then spaced themselves around the room. The guard who gave the directions was the only one that remained above.

All the women seemed to be doing the same thing, hesitating. Each of them waited, silently pleading the men to leave the room. After a few moments, it was obvious they would not be leaving them, but still not one of the women moved.

The guard above them yelled out a strong word in Arabic. The other guards took one military step toward them, stopped, swung their assault rifles off their shoulder, and clutched them with both hands in front of them.

Before Hailey realized what was happening, the African woman dropped her arm from around Hailey's shoulder, screamed a warlike cry and lunged at the guard standing directly in front of her. The crack, crack, crack of the gun resounded in echoes off the walls and stabbed Hailey's ears.

Hailey's hands went up to her ears, and she squeezed her eyes shut. The room instantly filled with women wailing and screaming, but Hailey refused to open her eyes.

"No... no... no," she whispered softly to herself. It was all Hailey could do.

Swoosh!

The sound of running water filled Hailey's ears, despite the attempt of her hand to shut out all sound. Something was trickling down her cheek. Hailey opened her eyes to see that the showers had been turned on and she raised her hand to her cheek to wipe off the spray of water. As she pulled her hand back, it was red. Hailey's red stained fingers became blurry as her gaze shifted past her hand. Nausea hit her stomach like a rush of wind hitting her face.

The woman who had been standing beside her, protecting her just moments ago, was now lying on the ground. Her head was turned unnaturally towards Hailey. Her veil had fallen away from her face but still hung around her head and neck. Her neck... the smooth dark brown skin on her face didn't continue down her neck. Instead, there was a bloody mess of skin and tissue. She had been shot.

The woman's eyes were vacant and unblinking. A trail of blood flowed away from the woman's body, Hailey's eyes followed it. As Hailey's eyes moved farther and farther away from the body as they followed the trail, she noticed that the blood was starting to mix with the running water from the showers.

Both water and blood swirled together and moved in unison down the dips in the floor. Hailey violently jumped backward as her eyes reached the end of the trail. The blood was swirling around her shoes. She had been standing over a drain.

A panicked whimper jumped out of Hailey's throat as she grabbed the bottom of her abaya and shakily wiped the blood splatter from her face.

Get it off, just get it off. Hailey's mind screamed at her.

The guard yelled the same word at them, causing Hailey to jump. All the women around her suddenly started removing all of their clothing. Some were in full abayas with a complete veil and head covering. Hailey focused on one woman. Her dark, thick hair fell over her shoulders and brushed the tears that were raining from her eyes. Others were dressed as Hailey was: an abaya with a headscarf.

Hailey's eyes met the face of one of the guards and his eyes narrowed. She then noticed that she had been frozen, unmoving in a sea of activity. Her inactivity was drawing a lot of attention to herself. Immediately she removed her headscarf and followed directions. Every movement seemed to be ripping her apart. Her hands kept moving, but her mind screamed out '*NO!*'.

After the flurry of fabric subsided and the showers had washed away all dignity, the women huddled by the large door. Soaking wet, they all tried desperately to regain some decency and hide their nakedness behind each other and with their arms and hands. However, after undressing and showering under the watchful eyes of the guards, it was a pointless attempt. They were all left humiliated, shivering, and scared.

Hailey felt numb and empty. Her bottom lip quivered and her eyes blurred with fresh tears as she watched two more guards jog down the switchbacks and remove the woman's dead body. They left a path of blood in their wake as they dragged her up the switchbacks.

With all the cries and moans of the hopeless women surrounding her, Hailey's resolve broke, and she joined them.

They became unified in their mourning and fear. Their cries rose up and filled the room with such sadness. It was excruciating, and Hailey felt as though she were splitting in two.

- - - - - - -

The prison cell was cold and exactly the way you'd imagine a prison cell to be. It was not one from a country club-type prison in the States but that of a harsh, foreign country you might see in a movie. It was a tiny room with three cots, which left little walking around the room. Two cots sat end to end along one wall, and the other sat across from them in front of the squat-toilet area. There was no tile around the toilet, just concrete. The floors, the walls, the ceiling – all concrete. A small sink rested on the wall in the back corner, opposite the toilet area.

Hailey was thankful to see a set of new clothes sitting at the foot of each of the beds, but the embarrassment she had gained as they paraded naked down the hallway, through the complex, and into a cell, remained as a dead lump in the center of her stomach.

After dressing in the new abaya, she took a seat on the floor and leaned against the wall farthest from the bars. Pressing the top of her thighs to her chest, she rested her forehead on top of her knees and wrapped her arms around her head. After a few moments, came a clang followed by another and another. All of the women were in their cells, and all the doors were now being shut.

Hailey didn't raise her head. She couldn't bring herself to catch the eye of another guard after being on display like that. Hailey shuddered and tried to shake the memory away from the front of her mind. The effort was futile.

There were two other women in the cell with her. Hailey assumed one of them didn't speak English and now sat beside the toilet area, staring at her open hands as she rocked back and forth. The other was very quiet. Aside from a quick hello to Hailey in English and something similar to the other in Arabic, she had immediately gone to one of the cots, dressed, laid down, and turned towards the wall.

Hailey didn't really feel like talking, but she was desperate to know what she should do or if there was even anything she could do. She got up and slowly made her way over to the cot, knelt down, and gently placed her hand on the woman's shoulder. The woman jumped and shrieked.

"I'm sorry, I'm so sorry." Hailey stumbled backward, startled. Her eyes started to fill with fresh tears as she fully realized her loneliness.

"No, no. I sorry. I have better days than this." The woman offered a small smile of condolence, which Hailey returned.

"I guess we all have," Hailey said as she watched the other woman who hadn't even looked up. She turned her attention back. "My name is Hailey, are you from Saudi?"

"Yes, yes. I born here in Riyadh. You from America?"

"Yes. I'm supposed to be here visiting a friend, but everything got so messed up, and now I have no idea what to do."

"There is only one thing." The woman sadly looked down at her folded hands. "Wait."

"Wait? For what?"

"Them to come." The woman looked towards the hallway, through the bars. "The guards will come, and you find out your... ah... I don't know word, but it is what they do in return for what you do."

"You mean punishment?"

"Yes, yes, punishment. Once you in here," she glanced around to each of the walls, "you can't do anything but wait... unless you have done what I have. I don't need to wait. I know what they do, just don't know when."

"What did you do?" Hailey's curiosity was captivated before she could bridle her forwardness.

The woman's lip quivered before speaking. "I sorry." She turned away and laid back on the bed without another word.

It was evident to Hailey that she shouldn't push. This may be the only friend she would have in this place, and she didn't want to overstep. So instead, Hailey rose up off the floor, grabbed a blanket from the third cot, went over to the woman sitting on the floor, and draped it over her shoulders. The woman again didn't move, and it seemed like she didn't even notice Hailey or any of her surroundings.

Hailey returned to her cot and tried with her own small, thin blanket to ward off the chill, which was quickly taking up residence in her bones.

I hate this place.

CHAPTER 15

Hailey awoke to screaming. She scanned the room, trying to regain her bearings. A little disoriented, Hailey shot out of bed and was hit with the reality of the situation. The woman who didn't speak English was still sitting in the same spot, seemingly unmoved. The other woman, who she talked to the day before, was huddled near the far end of her cot. Her knees were pulled up to her chest, and she was screaming.

Hailey followed her line of sight to the door. Three guards were standing there, one fiddling with keys. He unlocked the bars and swung them open. The other two guards entered, assault rifles slung over their shoulders. They approached the woman on her cot. Before they could get to her, she leaped off and ran to the back corner of the cell, opposite Hailey's cot.

The guards quickly closed the gap. The woman grabbed the small, protruding, metal pipe that was leading from the wall to the toilet. The guards each grabbed one arm and pulled, but the woman held on. They gave one swift yank and finally pried her off. They dragged her towards the door, her heels grating the concrete floor. She started kicking and twisting, desperate to break free. It was then that she caught a glimpse of Hailey. It seemed to act like a pause button as they exchanged glances.

Hailey's face held a look of dread and confusion. The woman, who a moment ago held terror in her whole being, went limp and stopped fighting. She continued to hold Hailey's gaze as tears started silently sliding down her cheeks. The sight caused Hailey's own eyes to tear. Just before the woman was hauled out of the cell, she closed her eyes and hung her head, fully relinquishing the fight.

The first guard returned his keys to the lock after swinging the bars closed behind them. Once the bars were secured, he turned and started walking away. Hailey rose off her cot and went to the bars. She pushed her cheek against them and strained to see down the row of cells. She was only able to catch one small glimpse of the woman's feet and the back of one guard before they disappeared around a corner.

Hailey never saw her again.

- - - - - - -

A whole day passed with no sign of her friend. Hailey knew it was silly to hold out hope, but with every sound that came from down the hall, she lifted her head in anticipation it would be her. They had only spoken once and hadn't shared much at all really, yet Hailey felt a dreadful ache in her stomach for her. It was interesting to Hailey how intensely bonding these terrifying experiences had been.

After a quick trip to the toilet that morning, Hailey had stepped on a small pebble as she was making her way back to her cot. She was now sitting on her cot with it in her hands.

As Hailey scratched three little lines into the wall, she smirked to herself. Something about people in prison movies had always bugged her. When she saw the prisoners making a notch in the wall for each day they were in their cell, she couldn't understand why they would want to keep track of such a thing. She always thought that it would only serve to point out how dire their situation was. But now, as the pebble cut its way into the wall, she felt a bit of sanity return and now understood that there was comfort in this small action.

She dropped her hands to her lap and looked at the small three lines that were etched into the wall. Oddly, the task evoked the exact opposite feeling she had previously thought it would. While residing in a place where she had no control, keeping track of her time somehow helped her regain just a small portion of the freedom she had taken for granted just days before.

Hailey saw movement in her peripheral vision. She turned to see the silent woman rise off the floor and make her way over to her cot. The woman moved timidly and slowly but with grace. She sat on the cot and placed her hands on her knees, resting her feet flat on the floor. The woman took a deep breath, and as she was releasing it, she turned and smiled at Hailey.

"Hello."

Hailey was shocked. "Um... hi. How are you feeling? I wasn't sure you were OK."

"I was praying. I'm sorry if I worried you and for my rudeness."

"No, not at all. Your English is excellent. Are you from Saudi?"

"Yes, I'm from a small town not far from here. My father actually had me tutored in English, you are kind to notice. My name is Sarna."

"I'm Hailey. It's nice to meet you. Ah, do you know what happened to the other woman?" Hailey longingly looked towards the bars. "They took her, but it's been a long time. I don't know what happened." Hailey paused to regain control over her shaky voice. "They just came and took her... she... seemed so scared."

"I'm not sure what she did, but I do know that she will not be back. You should put her out of your mind. May I ask why you're here?"

Hailey told Sarna about the past week. It felt good to finally share it with someone who wasn't holding her fate in their hands.

"I just don't understand your country. I don't mean to be rude, but I don't even understand why I'm here. I'm not from here and I kind of thought that they would be a little lenient with me. I wouldn't know your customs or rules, so... why am I expected to abide by them without a warning?"

"I'm sure many foreigners feel the same in your country. I am sorry for what you've had to endure. Some of the men you've encountered are a disgrace to our country, as I'm sure you feel about the same kind of men in America. Saudi is a very complex country. A lot of conflicts are created when trying to retain thousands of years of tradition and yet simultaneously needing to adapt to the world we are now surrounded by."

Hailey's heart softened a bit, Sarna's explanation had never occurred to her before.

"Do you have any idea if or how I can get out of here?"

"I'm sorry there is nothing you can do. Your life now lies in the hands of others. Women in our country don't have the same liberties as you have in America. Some of these I'm thankful for and some I struggle against. So all we can do is trust Allah and wait."

Hailey grunted sarcastically, "Right."

"You don't believe in God?"

"Not anymore. I used to believe in the Christian God when I was a kid, but... let's just say life hit me over the head and I woke up from that daydream."

"I'm sorry to hear that you've been through such times that changed your heart so drastically. You could use faith and hope when in a place like this." Sarna looked around the cell and shuddered.

They spent the rest of the day chatting about their different childhoods, their families and their life back home. Hailey found Sarna quite funny and liked her very much. Hailey guessed she was in her mid to late thirties. Sarna had simple features and long, dark hair. Her smile parted to show two rows of slightly crooked teeth, but her smile made her eyes squint a bit and twinkle. As the time passed, Hailey's heart lightened, and for a moment the fear of her predicament was replaced by giggles.

The difference between their cultures was vast, but they found some common ground as they talked. They enjoyed the lightheartedness of the distraction from everything around them, and Hailey was amazed at how Sarna carried herself. Her outlook on her life in Saudi was so different from what Hailey would have assumed. It seemed free of burden, and this unexpectedly caused Hailey to have a slightly more positive outlook.

A sound entered their ears.

Simultaneously, like deer in a meadow sensing danger, the two jerked their faces towards the bars. Heavy footsteps echoed down the hall, drawing closer. Three guards approached, one fiddled with keys, the others stood at attention. The first officer unlocked the door to their cell and slid it open. The other two guards entered.

The blood drained from both girls' faces.

- - - - - - -

She had been gone for over an hour, but to Hailey, it seemed a lot longer. The fear she felt for her new friend seemed to make time stand still. Since the guards escorted Sarna out of the cell, Hailey had virtually started to wear a track in the floor where she had been pacing back and forth.

Please come back, please come back. I can't handle being here alone.

Then she saw them.

Sarna was not walking on her own, as she had when she had left the cell. Sarna's legs were trying their best to walk, but they were moving at a slow-motion speed compared to the gait of the guards. The two guards were essentially dragging her. Something was obviously wrong.

They entered the cell, walked over to Sarna's cot and flung her down. Sarna let out a little cry of pain. The guards left.

As soon as they were gone Hailey ran over to Sarna's side.

"Are you OK? What did they do to you?"

"Yes, yes I'm OK."

From her slow, strained words, Hailey could tell she was in a lot of pain. Sarna rose off the mattress slightly and onto her elbow, she winced. Hailey's eyes immediately dropped to the cot. Spots of blood dotted the mattress.

"You're bleeding!" Hailey said alarmed.

"Can you help me undress?"

She helped Sarna rise slowly off the cot. Hailey, as gently as she could, helped Sarna remove the abaya. As it fell to the floor, Hailey gasped. What her eyes beheld didn't resemble a back. The smooth, dark skin on Sarna's shoulders fell away to a grotesque chaos of flesh and blood. The tracks, which were left by a whip, crisscrossed in all direction over Sarna's back and it was hard to tell just how many times she had been struck.

"Sarna, I'm so sorry."

"Could you please," she paused to take a slow breath, "help me clean up a bit?"

"Of course."

Hailey went over to the vacant cot and removed the blanket from off the mattress. After wetting it in the sink, she returned to Sarna.

"Now this is going to hurt, but let me know if it's too much or when you've had enough. We can take a break anytime."

Hailey spent the next twenty minutes cautiously dabbing Sarna's back, then rinsing the blanket intermittently as it filled with the sopped up blood. Once she was clean, Hailey helped her lay on her cot face down so her back could be exposed to the air.

Hailey bent down and retrieved Sarna's abaya from the floor and returned to the sink. The blood swirled around the basin as the water rinsed the cloth. Once the water ran clear, Hailey rung out the garment and draped it over the empty cot to dry.

Sarna slept on and off for the rest of the day, but Hailey stayed close to her just in case she woke and needed something. As she watched the rise and fall of her back as she breathed, Hailey wondered what Sarna could have done to deserve such a punishment. She also hoped that this would be the extent of her reprimand.

- - - - - - -

A couple of days passed, thankfully without any more visits by the guards. In the meantime, Hailey had learned a lot about her cellmate. Sarna had been arrested after being caught in public talking to a man without a male relative present. Sarna was speaking with some old friends outside of a shop and was spotted by the Mutawa. She tried to explain to them that her brother was just down the street and would return for her shortly, but the Mutawa would hear nothing of it, and she was hauled to the prison. When Hailey was accused of the same crime at the holding office, she had been confused, but Sarna explained to her that this type of behavior has been severely condemned in Saudi.

Hailey was completely shocked, but apparently, it was quite common to receive lashings while in prison, sometimes even before sentencing. Sarna also explained that as her in case, a formal sentence may never be given. She would most likely remain in prison for a few days, maybe a week or two and then be released. Both she and Sarna were thankful but shocked that no one had come for Hailey yet.

"The number of lashings are not a set thing. I hope and pray that mine are over."

"How can you live in such a place?" Hailey questioned.

"Remember, you are coming from a very different world. Saudi is soaked with tradition, and while there are many problems in our country, there are also some benefits. I know it is easy to look at someone who is different from you and be confused. It confuses me at times as well, but don't forget, there are problems in your own country that we often don't have to deal with here. You may see our rules as a lack of freedom for woman... and yes that is true in a lot of regards," Sarna admitted with a sad smirk, "but not entirely. For example, take the fact that women aren't allowed to go anywhere without a male relative. Usually, that rule... well... apart from the time that led me here," Sarna chuckled at the irony, "is a great comfort to me. In your country, your women are often left alone. The world is full of monsters, regardless of geography, and this has led to many problems for women everywhere. But here, I don't have to worry about who is around me. I can relax wherever I am for I'm protected by being with my family. I don't have to look behind me as I walk down the street or keep my eye out for questionable characters." Sarna smiled and shrugged. "I know the world sees our abayas as a prison, as do many of my friends. However, I see them as a shelter I can take with me wherever I go. Men are very visual creatures, and they allow themselves to be... led too much by this. Nevertheless, Allah loves his daughters and doesn't wish for them to be gawked at. I see my abaya as a provision from God."

"Huh, I never thought of it like that. So you are happy here in Saudi?"

"This is the only place I've ever known, so it is hard for me to judge that accurately. I will be honest though, there are many traditions our country holds onto which I don't agree with and I hope we learn to let them go before they destroy us. There are also some traditions which have been taken and distorted by evil men, and I hope the world will learn to see that for what it is and not condemn us all."

Hailey nodded, she knew what Sarna was referring to and they both exchanged a knowing look and nothing more needed to be said about it.

Sarna continued. "Some of the world would assume we would have a very low crime rate because of our very strict laws and punishments. However, we have our fair share of evil lurking in our midst, just as all cultures do, regardless of traditions. Which I know I don't have to tell you."

She leaned forward and gave Hailey's shoulder an

understanding squeeze.

"Some also think that Saudi has no regard for women. This is a very tricky issue. There are a large number of men who gladly add to the ill view from female rights activists. However, there are also many men in our country, like my father, who respect women as treasures. I'm certain the same dichotomy is true in all countries, and I hope the world would understand our struggles are the same. The good and the bad have a constant battle. In the hands of good men, our laws and traditions can protect us. In the hands of evil men, we are doomed. Wouldn't you say that it is the same in America?"

"Yeah, I guess it is. I understand what you're saying, but I have to say I don't know how I would give up the freedoms I enjoy every day. Ones that you and other Saudi women will never know."

"Well, I hope it comes to be that we all learn to treat others, regardless of tradition or sex, as Allah would desire."

"Yes... um... well... hey, would you like some water?" Hailey diverted the conversation.

"Yes, please."

Hailey could see where this conversation was heading and she had no desire to allow it to go there. God wasn't going to be the subject of their conversations now or later. Hailey knew that if they kept talking about the differences between their countries, it was easy to see that they would inevitably end up discussing the differences between Allah and God. Hailey didn't believe in or trust God anymore, and she didn't want to discuss it.

Hailey rose off of Sarna's cot and walked over to the sink. She took down two of the three tin cups off the back of the sink, filled each with water, and returned to Sarna.

"Can I ask you something?" Hailey said without looking up.

"Hailey, of course. You can ask me anything you wish."

Hailey slowly glanced up. "What do you think happened to the other woman?"

Sarna hung her head and looked at the small cup between her hands.

"I heard some of the guards discussing it when they took me." She set her cup on the floor. "It turns out she was arrested for adultery and was beheaded shortly after they took her from our cell."

"What? You guys still behead each other?" Hailey's voice showed her full shock at the news.

"For one, I didn't behead anyone." Sarna's voice was almost screaming. "My father, brothers, and mother didn't behead anyone. Do not label us for the actions of others. I fully disagree with how the punishment was carried out but not with punishing those who choose to do wrong. I don't believe in killing, but I do view marriage as sacred."

Sarna's chest was heaving with livid frustration.

"Sarna, Sarna, I'm sorry." Hailey held up her hands to signal her regret. "I actually believe the same thing. People shouldn't get away with things. But... beheading? It caught me off guard. I'm so sorry. I know I've only been in your country for little more than a week and my judgments are naïve." Hailey burst into tears. "But I'm so scared... I don't know where... my friends are or even if they know... I'm in trouble." Hailey paused to catch her breath so she could speak clearer. "I know I shouldn't be so inclusive with my judgments, but I don't understand. But now I'm forced into needing to understand everything, instantaneously, and my body and mind are revolting. I don't know why they punished you and not me or if it means that I'm stuck here forever or if there is an even worse punishment waiting for me."

Sarna's eyes filled with tears.

Hailey continued. "I don't mean to take out my fear on you or your family, and it was stupid for me to talk like that. I'm just so scared."

Hailey's shoulders shuddered.

"Hailey, come here." Sarna opened her arms.

Hailey went to Sarna. Being careful not to touch Sarna's back, she hugged her around her neck. Both women held onto each other and cried until their tears dried, and their bodies relaxed. They found understanding in their shared situation and choose to let the differences melt away.

The women gathered up their blankets and curled up together on Sarna's cot. Hailey's mind filled with images of her mother and her heart ached. Nevertheless, she was thankful to have Sarna close. Sarna started to sing. It was low and beautiful. Hailey didn't understand the words, but she could feel that the song was mournful yet lined with hope. It soothed her soul, and she soon drifted off to sleep.

CHAPTER 16

The last three days haunted Hailey. She wasn't in her cell anymore. She now sat quietly on a lone metal chair in the middle of a concrete room. There was no window in the door, no squat toilet, nothing but her and the chair. Every time she didn't actively keep her mind on something else, it would drift to the events of the previous few days. She tried to keep her mind on thoughts from back home, but her mind once again betrayed her.

The memories flashed in front of her eyes again. Her stomach lurched, and she had to lean forward and put her head between her knees to keep from vomiting. Once her nausea had passed a little, she closed her eyes. This was a mistake. The images flooded her mind again.

- - - - - - -

The previous days had gone the same way as the day when Sarna received her first lashing. Men came, took Sarna, beat her and then Hailey would help clean her up. Then they would sit, talk, sing and sleep. Hailey dreaded how long her friend might have to endure this. But after yesterday, they both wished Sarna could just go back to the lashings.

The women had woke up about an hour before the lights had come on. They remained in their cots and talked about the first meal they would have once they were released. This was one of their favorite topics of discussion. Sarna described again each of her favorite dishes causing Hailey's mouth to water. While Hailey was describing cheesecake, the lights flicked and came on.

Footsteps.

Alarmed, both girls sat up and looked towards the hallway. It seemed much too early for a beating. A lone guard appeared and slowed his pace as he walked by their cell. He looked right at Sarna and smiled. Sarna immediately dropped her gaze and stared at the floor, but Hailey's eyes remained on him. He was smiling in a way that made Hailey shiver, and she wished she could move and hide her friend from his gaze. After a few more seconds, he continued down the hall and was gone. The girls exhaled with relief.

However, an hour later the same guard made another pass and then another. Then shortly after their lunch had been delivered, if you could even call it that, the same guard walked by again. This time he stopped and faced them. He yelled something down the hall, reached into his pocket and withdrew a set of keys. Moments passed, and he just stood there staring, jingling his keys through his fingers. He was soon joined by another guard. The first guard unlocked the door, and the other swung it open. Both men quickly entered the room and came straight toward Sarna.

"No!" Hailey yelled.

These were not the men who dished out Sarna's daily lashings and Hailey's protective instincts were in overdrive. As soon as Hailey saw the guard the first time that morning, she knew she didn't want him anywhere near her friend.

Hailey yelled at them a second time, while simultaneously moving to insert herself between the men and her friend. It was foolish really, what did she expect to happen with two strong guards? The back of his hand connected with Hailey's right cheek and spun her around so quickly, she lost her footing and collapsed to the floor.

Sarna reached towards her and grabbed her hand to help her up. The guards snatched both of Sarna's arms. Hailey tried to hold on to Sarna's hand, but the second guard gave Hailey a swift kick to her ribs. She let go, recoiling in pain.

"Hailey!" Sarna screamed and tried to reach for her, but she could barely move under the guard's power.

Hailey, ignoring the pain, leaped up again, but the second guard came at her. He grabbed her and pushed her back to the ground. His left hand was tightly gripped around her throat while he sat on her thighs. Her body burned under his weight. The more she struggled, the tighter he squeezed. Hailey forced herself to not fight, and he eased up on his grip just enough so she could breathe. She turned her eyes back towards Sarna.

The guard from this morning had her pushed up against the wall by her wrists and was kissing her neck. The fear in her eyes was overwhelming to see, but Hailey kept looking at her, willing for Sarna to look at her. Sarna met her gaze, and they silently offered each other a moment of strength. The moment didn't last long.

The guard sitting on Hailey watched as his comrade removed Sarna's clothes, his face amused. Hailey couldn't watch. She squeezed her eyes shut when he dragged Sarna over to the cot. Screams filled Hailey's ears, but she was unable to speak or open her eyes. She demanded her body to cooperate so she could give

Sarna some words of courage or strength, but her body betrayed her, and she lay there silent.

When the other guard had finished with Sarna, the guard sitting on her released her throat, stood and followed the other guard out the door. Apart from the injuries inflicted to keep her away from Sarna, both guards had left Hailey untouched.

Once the guards were out of sight, Hailey ran over to Sarna's cot. Sarna was weeping and huddled into a little, protective ball, shaking like a leaf. Hailey grabbed a blanket and covered her nakedness and lay down beside her. Without a word spoken, Hailey sang and held her friend as Sarna soaked the mattress with her tears.

- - - - - - -

Hailey sat back up and slowly stood. The memories faded and the room came back into view. Movement, maybe if she kept moving she could clear her head. She made a few laps of the room and started humming 'Henry the Eighth I Am.'

The realization about how much darker her circumstances had become since she sang that song the last time, came and hit her hard. When she had been in the holding room at the airport, her situation seemed so much simpler. It was still just a small misunderstanding. But now, now it seemed utterly hopeless. She fell back against the wall farthest from the door and pulled her knees to her chest. A few silent tears fell from her eyes and wet the sleeve of her abaya.

She wished she was back in her cell with Sarna, but she had no choice when the guards came for her that morning. Sarna still had not uttered a word since the attack and her eyes were so vacant. The light that had previously been there was now gone.

Hailey hated being away from her. She had no idea why they had moved her to this new room, and she feared she was about to find out what her sentence was.

Maybe, because I'm a foreigner, they weren't allowed to punish me until the sentence came in. Can a sentence be given without a trial? Would I even get a trial? If Saudi guards dealt with their own people in such a horrible way, what might they do to me?

The different scenarios started to flood her mind.

A knock.

Hailey didn't bother to look up, she stayed huddled where she was. She had no strength to fuel her resolve, and as a result, she wasn't up to meeting her fate head on. She stayed still and kept crying softly. The door opened, and footsteps entered. Two men were talking, and one of them sounded upset. The door closed, but Hailey didn't move. Footsteps drew near, and Hailey squeezed herself into a tighter ball. She wished she could press hard enough to implode and disappear forever.

A hand stroked her hair and Hailey jumped, causing her to come face to face with a man. He was smiling at her. She pushed herself harder against the wall to gain another half an inch of distance from the stranger.

"Are you hurt?" The man asked in a soft tone, and if Hailey wasn't mistaken, he seemed almost concerned.

Hailey remained silent and just stared at him. He was a lot older than most of the guards and actually not in a uniform at all. He was dressed similarly to the other men she'd seen around the airport. He had on a brown robe and had a red and white checkered head covering with one of those black, braided cords holding it in place. His salt and pepper hair peeked out around his ears, which matched his full beard and small mustache. His nose was slightly large and sat between big apple cheeks and his eyes squinted when he smiled.

He reached out and touched her cheek, causing her to flinch; it was still sore.

"I'm sorry for that awful bruise, you were not to be harmed. I guess some things are unavoidable."

He briefly moved his attention towards the other man still standing at the door and pursed his lips.

Turning back to Hailey he spoke softly. "Are you well enough to stand?"

Hailey allowed him to help her to her feet and usher her to the chair. She sat willingly: no strength and no hope, meant no protesting.

"Once we are out of here I will get you some clean clothes and allow you to get cleaned up and get some rest."

Hailey's head snapped up and realized that this man might have come to rescue her. "Are you my lawyer?"

The man paused a moment then smiled. "Why yes. Didn't anyone inform you that I was coming?" Again he glared at the man at the door. "Well, no matter. I'm here now, and I'm going to get you out of here."

"I mean no disrespect if this is overstepping, but I was wondering if I could quickly stop at my cell before we go." Hailey couldn't bear to leave without saying goodbye to Sarna.

The man looked again at the man at the door, who nodded in return.

"Certainly we can arrange that."

Her lawyer's words were soothing, and her body relaxed a bit back into the chair.

- - - - - - -

The prison got smaller and smaller as they drove down the road and a few tears fell onto her cheeks. Her goodbye with Sarna wasn't what she had hoped.

After Hailey had explained that she was leaving, she bent down and gave Sarna a kiss on her cheek and hugged her. She then had no choice but to turn and leave when she hadn't gotten a response from Sarna. Hailey didn't blame her.

Once the door to the cell was closed, and Hailey had heard the clang, she stopped to turn back. She opened her mouth to speak, but before she had a chance to say a word, her lawyer came up to her side, gently held her arm and whispered in her ear.

"She is getting out tomorrow morning. Better not stir any emotions up. She will be all right."

Hailey nodded and kept walking.

Although now seeing the prison disappearing behind a hill, her heart ached with regret. Sarna had been a source of strength and a break from the loneliness she had felt ever since she was arrested.

I should have said something else, anything… there is just so much to say. Why did I leave things like that? Remorse raged through each part of her. When it started to reach its peak, Hailey forced herself to turn away from the car window.

"I just realized that I don't even know your name," Hailey said as she turned and looked at her lawyer.

"My name is Ehsan Al-Ma'mar, but you can call me Ehsan."

"Hailey. It's nice to meet you." She paused for a moment. "Ah… where are we going?"

"We are heading to my house. I thought you could clean up there and rest. Then in the morning, we can talk about how things are going to proceed. I have a large house, and my wives have already prepared for your arrival."

Wives? The fact that he had more than one made her feel a bit uncomfortable, but she shook it off and thanked him for his generosity.

As the car continued, Hailey stared straight ahead. When her mind started to drift again, Hailey tried with all her might to solely focus on the fact that she was going home. She knew that if she allowed herself to think of anything else, even for a moment, she would vomit from the realization that she just abandoned Sarna.

- - - - - - -

Driving up to Ehsan's house was shocking. Hailey wouldn't even call it a house due to the size of it. To her, it looked more like a small country club. The entrance to the property was protected by a large black iron gate with a small light colored, stone guard station to the left. The entire property was surrounded by a ten-foot, cream stone wall which extended from either side of the gate and around the back of the house.

The three-story house rested at the end of a long driveway, with two large, well-kept gardens on either side. The outside of the building was made of a similar stone material as the wall surrounding it. However, there was a bit more yellow added to give it contrast. White columns and arches accented parts of the front façade. In keeping with the architectural style of Saudi, the windows were all square at the bottom and arched at the top.

Hailey's eyes diverted from the house to a small Filipino man standing at the bottom of the front steps. He greeted the car as they pulled up and once the car had come to a full stop, he opened Ehsan's door. Ehsan got out, straightened his robe, and then turned to help her out of the vehicle.

As soon as Hailey was out of the vehicle, she noticed a second car had pulled up behind theirs.

"Who's that?" she questioned.

"Oh, nothing to worry about. These men are my security detail. You will be completely safe here Hailey."

Ehsan spoke to them for a few moments, and then they dispersed. Ehsan turned his attention back to her.

"Hailey, I want to welcome you to my home. This is Daib," Ehsan said as he introduced the man who had opened the car door when they pulled up. "I guess you would call him an... in-house mechanic."

Hailey nodded her hello.

Ehsan guided Hailey up the four steps to a massive, engraved, wooden door. As they approached, it opened before them, and they entered. Along each side of the entryway stood groups of people - the house staff.

"These are our other drivers" Ehsan introduced her to the three men.

He moved on to introduce each group: housekeepers, cooks, groundskeepers, and serving staff. After all the introductions had been made, Ehsan spent the next hour giving Hailey a small tour.

The entry way was spectacular. There were two grand, marble staircases curving around either side of the foyer and set in the back wall. In between the two, was a glass elevator. Ehsan didn't show her every room, much to the disappointment of Hailey's curiosity. She had never been in a place even close to something this grand and she wished she could explore every inch.

They did, however, visit the kitchen, the music room, the

dining hall, the two sitting rooms and three of the eight public bathrooms. Apparently, there were also private bathrooms in each of the bedrooms. Hailey found it fascinating that the sitting room on the ground level was only used by the men in the house and the one on the second floor was only used by the women.

I don't think I will ever get used to how different this country is.

After the tour, Ehsan steered her towards a small sunroom on the second floor. It was completely walled on two sides by glass windows. There on the floor, resting on satin pillows, sat two women in colorful wraps. There was a very short table, just a foot or so off the floor, set between them. Each was lounging gracefully and drinking tea. As Hailey and Ehsan approached, each woman rose and bowed their heads, keeping their eyes to the floor. Ehsan spoke for a moment to them in Arabic, and then he turned towards her.

"These are my wives, Maya and Ghada." He gestured towards each as he introduced them.

Hailey exchanged quick nods with each of the women as they made quick eye contact with her before returning their eyes to the floor. Ehsan turned and continued down the hall to a second staircase. Hailey followed.

"These stairs lead to the guest rooms on the third floor. This is where you will be staying. They are just down the hall from Maya and Ghada's rooms. You have your own facilities in the room so you should be quite comfortable there."

"Oh, I'm sure I will be. A cardboard box sitting at the roadside would have been an upgrade compared to that cell. I'm so grateful to you for inviting me to your beautiful home. Thank you."

As they reached the top of the stairs, Ehsan's phone rang. He answered it and talked for a few minutes. He was obviously not pleased with the conversation. He returned the phone to his pocket and carried on down the hallway. Hailey could see he was a bit rattled, but she followed without question.

He led her to her room.

"One of the servers will bring you your dinner. I'm sure you would prefer to get some rest rather than be bombarded with all the questions my family will undoubtedly throw at you."

"Yes… thank you, that would be great. I'm really exhausted."

"That is understandable. Good night."

Hailey watched as he bowed his head and backed out of the room. The door slowly closed and she turned toward the bathroom. Before she had taken one step, a blood-chilling sound pricked her ears… the click of a deadbolt sliding in place.

CHAPTER 17

She frantically tried the door a couple of times, called for him, but no answer came. Hailey, realizing she was trapped, desperately looked around the room for a tool or anything she might use to try and open the door. She only found a pair of large tweezers, but they wouldn't even fit into the lock.

Hailey decided that if she had any chance to get out of the room, it would have to be by brute force. She sat on the floor, rested her hands behind her as a brace and kicked the door with both feet. Each kick shook the door and the walls around it, and although she kicked as hard as she could, it wasn't showing signs of breaking. Frustrated, Hailey kept at it.

A small knock interrupted her next kick. She stopped and listened. Another knock came.

"Yes?" She said hesitantly.

"Stop, please. I in?" the voice was male and had a very strong accent but was kind.

"Yes come in," Hailey replied tentatively as she backed away.

Keys unlocked the door, and it slowly opened. In came a thin, African man carrying a glass of water and a plate of food on a silver tray. He wouldn't look at her but handed her the tray. Hailey noted that he made sure to keep himself between her and the door.

"See paper please."

Hailey could barely understand him, but he motioned to the tray as he spoke, so she looked down at it. There was a small folded red piece of paper with her name on it, sitting beside the glass of water.

Hailey looked up, the man was already making his way through the door. He closed it behind him and locked it. Hailey stood there for a moment and hesitated as she heard the sound of the man's footsteps diminish down the hallway.

She took the tray over to the bed, set it down and picked up the note.

> *Hailey,*
>
> *Please forgive me. There was an urgent matter I needed to attend to right away. I know it must seem so strange, but I had to lock you in your room for your safety. Please don't be frightened, you will be safe here. I will return soon to explain everything.*
>
> *Ehsan*

Hailey relaxed. The whole situation seemed so odd, but she trusted Ehsan. He had gotten her out of that awful prison and to be honest she was just too tired to think through any more possible scenarios.

She took a long hot shower, ate her dinner and crawled right into bed.

She snuggled warmly under a large blanket to ward off the chill of the air conditioning and, despite the concern that tried to flood her body, she was utterly exhausted. She forced herself to be consoled by the fact that Ehsan had things under control and would clarify everything in the morning. With that thought, she allowed sleep to take her.

Her dreams were mixed, some were of being back home and some about the prison, neither remained long or disrupted her sleep.

- - - - - - -

The sun rose and poured into the room. As it touched Hailey's face, she opened her eyes. The clock resting on the side table said it was 5:30 a.m. Her lip and her cheek still hurt slightly when touched, but she was surprisingly refreshed. She rose up onto her elbows and looked around the room. As her eye scanned the room, her ears searched for any sound.

Silence.

Hailey lay back down and pulled the covers up to her neck. Maybe she could grab a few more hours. Who knows what this day might hold, so she might as well be rested.

She didn't get to rest long.

After an hour of tossing and turning there was a noise at the door. Hailey quickly got off the bed. She ran over to the armchair in the corner, grabbed the silk robe she had left there last night, all the while being careful not to trip on the pile of pillows sitting under the window. Draping it around herself, she sat on the edge of the armchair and waited.

Ehsan entered, smiling. In his hands were five books.

"Good morning. Did you sleep well?"

"Yes, thank you. Ehsan…," she said cautiously, "what's going on here?" Concern was etched all over her face.

He strode over and took a seat on an identical armchair,

sitting opposite to her. A small round table sat between them. He set the books on the table and leaned back into the chair.

"I'm sorry for all the security. You see my family doesn't understand me 'taking my work home with me' as you would say. Some of them aren't exactly happy with this arrangement, but others, if they found out, would not stand for it. I couldn't risk them harassing you as you have already been through so much. There is only one key to this room, so you will be safe.

"Bringing you here to my home was truly the only way I could arrange for you not to stay in prison longer. You have been placed in my custody, and you are my responsibility until your court date. It is less than a week away and, I'm sad to say, you will need to remain in this room until then."

"For a whole week?" Hailey didn't really like the idea of that.

"It's only five days. I know it might seem like you've just exchanged one prison for another, but I assure you this is not the case. You were not locked in here as a punishment, only as a means for your protection. My brother would be the main objector to you being here. He returned home last night unexpectedly, and I just think it would be best if you remain in here. Would you be alright with that?"

Hailey thought for a moment. "Why didn't you just go over this with me last night?"

"I wish I had the time. Do you remember the call I took just as I was bringing you to your room?"

Hailey nodded.

"It was from my office. My brother works with me, and he was supposed to be out of town. However, they called to tell me that he was on his way home at that very moment. He wasn't due for another two weeks, which would have been well after you were safely back home. With the news of his arrival, I had to leave you and ensure the rest of the house didn't mention you. I came to check on you, but as you were already asleep, I thought it best to wait until morning. Do you understand?"

"I guess so." Hailey wasn't entirely comfortable with this arrangement, but she didn't want to ever go back to that prison, so she didn't protest.

"I've brought you some books, and if you need anything else to pass the time, please let me know. All your meals will be delivered to you. If they aren't to your taste, please let me know, and I will have the cooks prepare something else. I promise you can come out once my brother leaves or for your court date, whichever comes first."

They spoke pleasantries for the next few minutes. After which, Ehsan left the room with a promise to return later that afternoon.

- - - - - - -

The five days in her room passed by quicker than she was expecting. The joy of having fantastic food, a comfortable bed, hot showers, a familiar style of toilet, and the lack of unwanted visitors was extremely welcomed. Hailey was relishing the time so much that she wasn't bothered by the fact that she was locked in the room.

Hailey awoke with excitement, today was the court appearance. Yesterday, Ehsan had graciously spent time translating a document for her. It was a statement agreeing that she had offended the king and his people and that she was innocent of prostitution. It also stated that, by already serving time for the other charges, she was requesting to be released. Ehsan said that it would aid in a quick dismissal. Hailey thought it sounded quite reasonable, so she signed it.

Hailey had taken her breakfast back into bed with her and was sitting there when she heard someone in the hallway. She put down the piece of bread she was eating and strained to hear.

Yup, there are the keys and… the lock.

The door slowly opened, and a small, old woman peeked around the corner. Her face burst into smiles. She entered the room and made her way over to the end of the bed. She was in a black abaya which covered her feet, so it seemed more like she floated into the room. Hailey couldn't help to smile back. She looked like a wrinkled, Arab version of the pudgy fairy godmother in Cinderella. The woman was carrying a small covered basket. She laid the basket on the table between the two armchairs.

The woman turned back to face Hailey and started speaking a mile a minute in Arabic. Hailey, of course, had no clue what the woman was saying, but she was certainly excited about something. She came over to Hailey, removed the tray from her lap, grabbed her by both arms and forced her to stand. The woman only came up to her shoulder and had to be the cutest, most wrinkled thing Hailey had ever seen.

Rounding Hailey, she put both hands on Hailey's back and pushed her towards the bathroom. Once they were both standing on the cold tile. The woman reached around her and snatched both ends of the tie holding her robe closed and untied it. The woman worked quickly and started to undress her. Hailey tried to keep herself covered, but the woman would have none of it. She looked directly into Hailey's eyes and cupped her face in her hands. She said something in Arabic and then with two fingers she wiggled Hailey's nose and patted her cheek. Hailey smiled back, and as her shock vanished, she tentatively let the woman continue her work.

Now standing naked in the middle of the bathroom, Hailey, a bit embarrassed, tried to use her arms to cover herself. This for some reason delighted the woman, who, after shaking her head, broke into rolls of laughter. Hailey even chuckled herself. The woman turned away from her and glided to the bathtub. She bent down, closed the stopper in the bottom of the bathtub and turned on the tap. Steam filled the room.

The woman then left the room but returned shortly with a small bottle of purple colored liquid. Returning to the bathtub, she carefully lifted out the glass cork and poured some of the liquid into the running water. A sweet lavender and spice scent filled the room.

The woman turned towards Hailey and guided her with one hand towards to the bath and motioned her to get in. Hailey lifted one foot and slowly dipped a toe into the water. It was so hot that Hailey quickly withdrew it. Again this also delighted the woman. Laughing again, she adamantly nudged Hailey to get into the bathtub.

Ever so slowly Hailey complied and put both feet in the water, paused and waited till they adjusted to the heat. The woman grasped the tiny bottle with both hands in front of her bosom, hugged it and beamed at Hailey. Hailey smiled back. After a few moments, she turned off the water, shrugged her shoulders, sighed, and quickly left the room.

Hailey leisurely lowered herself into the steaming water until her toes touched the far side of the large, porcelain bathtub. When she was fully submerged, the water rested just under her chin. She let out a contented sigh and looked around the room. Hailey thought to herself that if she were able to build her own house with unlimited funds, this would be the kind of bathroom she would want.

The bathtub was a huge oval and fit her perfectly. There was nothing worse than a really short bathtub that kept your knees slightly above the water level when you tried to submerge your shoulders. The tapware of the bath and the sink were a shiny, yellow gold. Hailey wondered if they were made of real gold. It wouldn't have surprised her. All of the elements of the bathroom were exquisite: a marble benchtop, porcelain sinks, slate tiles, and ebony cabinets.

Resting her head on the slow-rising curve of the back of the bathtub, she closed her eyes and relaxed.

Hailey was almost drifting off when she heard the door to the bedroom open again. There were multiple voices, all talking rapidly, and all female. Moments later five women entered the bathroom. The old woman was amongst the group, as well as Ghada. Hailey didn't recognize the other three.

Hailey now wished the purple liquid the woman had poured into the bathtub had been a bubble bath mixture. She was totally exposed and felt very awkward with so many in the room. Thankfully, none of them gawked at her. They just kept talking and pointing to each other, hardly acknowledging her at all. Ghada came over and delicately sat on the edge of the bathtub.

"This is Haffafa, Ehsan's mother," Ghada whispered, introducing the older woman who had made her bath. "And this is Sabira, Trana & Pari. They are Ehsan's aunts."

Pushing past the aunts, Haffafa came towards her and motioned her to stand.

A sixth woman entered the room. It was Maya, Ehsan's other wife, and she had Hailey's robe clutched in her hands. Hailey stood and stepped out of the bathtub. Dripping wet, she made a tiny puddle on the floor around her feet but couldn't see a towel close by. The aunts, after giving her a quick smile turned and went to the wardrobe beside the sink and removed three dark red towels.

They were chatting excitedly and teasingly pushed each other as they dried off Hailey's body. If Hafaffa was the fairy godmother in Cinderella, these three were like the three fairies in Sleeping Beauty. It was like the scene when they were arguing over what color Sleeping Beauty's wedding dress should be. Hailey chuckled as they finished drying her off. Once she was dry, they left the room.

Ghada then helped Maya dress Hailey in the silk robe. The three of them, with Hafaffa trailing them, followed the others and left the bathroom.

When Hailey entered the bedroom, she noticed that the three aunts had stripped the comforter off the bed. A black, silk sheet now lay over the mattress, and the aunts were now standing in a row to the left of the bed.

As Hailey's eyes admired how the black of the sheet brought out the intricate carvings on the headboard and the four posts, Maya moved to the right side of the bed, and Ghada left the room. Haffafa came up behind Hailey and guided her gently to the bed. She motioned for her to sit on the edge. The silk was cool on the backs of Hailey's legs as she sat down.

Hailey watched curiously as Haffafa moved to the table. A white bath towel sat with a large, glass jar resting on top of it, along with some white gloves. Haffafa's basket now rested empty on one of the armchairs.

Assisted by one of the aunts, Haffafa picked up the table and brought it to the left side of the bed, in front of the other two aunts. She removed the lid to the jar and brought out a small almost translucent ball, comparable to the size of a baseball. She set it on the table.

As Haffafa was putting on the gloves, Ghada returned. She was pushing a small cart with a huge pot filled with steaming water resting on top. She entered the room slowly as to not slosh the water and joined Haffafa next to the bed.

"Please take off your robe and lay back on the bed," Ghada spoke softly and slowly to ensure her pronunciation was perfect.

"Why?"

"Please do as I ask," Ghada said with pleading eyes and gave Hailey a weak smile. "It's akin to… a… spa treatment in your country. Please lay back."

Hailey was unsure but hesitantly complied. Swinging her legs up on the bed she scooted up, removed her robe and lay on the bed. She again felt awkward being naked under so many pairs of eyes but didn't want to offend her hosts, so she only crossed her arms in front of her chest.

Haffafa turned back to the table and picked up a ladle which was resting next to the pot. She placed the small ball on the ladle then lowered it into the steaming water.

The next few movements escaped Hailey's notice. She was so focused on what Haffafa was doing. The three aunts and Maya had moved to space out around the sides of the bed. With a shared glance, they lunged at her. One aunt took hold of her right hand, the second took her right leg, and the third grasped her left leg. Maya seized her left arm. Hailey was pinned down. She struggled to break free, but they were surprisingly strong, and her fighting didn't amount to anything. After a few moments of struggling she stopped to look at Haffafa, eyes pleading for an explanation.

Haffafa bent down to her, patted her cheek and gave her an empathetic smile.

"Shhh." Haffafa cooed to her.

Haffafa returned her attention to the pot and removed the ladle. With one gloved finger she poked the ball. When she saw that the spot she poked gave way a bit and had left her fingerprint, she glanced to each of the other women and nodded. Then Haffafa rolled the ball out of the ladle and into her hand.

The women's hands gripped tighter. After setting down the ladle, Haffafa turned back to the bed and took one side step, so she was level with Hailey's feet. Slowly Haffafa lowered her hands and placed the steaming ball on Hailey's right leg, just above her foot. Haffafa rolled it one full turn of the ball towards her knee.

Searing hot pain flashed up her leg. It caused her to jump, but the aunt who held the limb had braced for it, so Hailey's recoil merely looked like a small flinch. Her scream was not contained, however. It shot from her lungs like a freight train.

Haffafa removed the ball and brought it up to Hailey's face so she could see it closely. It was covered in leg hair.

"No! No! You can't be serious. What is this?" Hailey looked back at Ghada, who had remained next to the cart. "What is this?" Hailey repeated pleadingly.

"It's for..." Ghada started to respond.

Maya yelled at her, so Ghada stopped talking and looked at the floor.

Haffafa turned back to the cart. She picked up the towel, wiped off the hair, repeated the heating process, and then she returned back to Hailey's leg.

"Please," Hailey whimpered, "why are you doing this? It really hurts. Please, stop."

None of the women answered or moved from their task.

Again and again, Haffafa ripped strips of hair off of Hailey, and after one leg was done, she did the other. Then Haffafa moved onto her arms.

Except for a small break to retrieve another ball when its predecessor got too small, or for Ghada to return with more hot water, Haffafa didn't rest until the only hair left on Hailey, were her eyebrows, her eyelashes, and the hair on her head.

Hailey's yelps and whimpers punctuated the whole treatment, which took two hours to complete. After the final pass over her top lip and cheeks, the women released her. Hailey tried to coil into a protective ball, but her skin hurt too much, so she returned to lying flat and still.

She listened as the women cleaned up and, once Hailey had heard the door open and close, she opened her eyes. Maya was still in the room, standing by the door. Hailey turned her head away from her.

"I left you some new clothes on the table. The wrap is called a khimar, and you can drape it around yourself, as well as use it to cover your face when a male is present. Please dress as soon as you are able." She paused. "I'm sorry that that was painful. I still remember my sugaring. It isn't the most enjoyable process but needed nonetheless."

Hailey didn't look at her or respond, so Maya continued.

"The balls Haffafa was using are mostly made of sugar. The hot water slightly melts the top layer and allows it to grip the hair as the ball is rolled over it." Maya spoke with a directness that was void of any apologetic tone or real empathy.

"Swell, and you were doing that to me because...?" Hailey made no attempt to hide her anger.

"Look here child," Maya snapped back. "You might want to change your tone with me. Ghada and I will most likely be the closest things you will have to a friend from now on and..."

Maya's frustrating uproar stopped short. "I shouldn't have said that. Ehsan gave us all strict orders not to talk to you about this, but I do want you to know that I'm not happy with the situation."

Hailey felt Maya take a seat on the bed. Hailey spun her head around.

"What are you talking about?" She tried to keep the fear out of her voice, but it snuck through.

Maya sighed. "Do you really have no idea what is going on here? What did Ehsan tell you?" Maya said, her voice softening a bit.

"Since I met him or just about what's happening today?"

"Why don't you tell me everything?"

For the next hour, Hailey told Maya the full story.

"… and when I woke up this morning and Haffafa came in I thought she was here to help get me ready for court. And unless I'm required to be naked in court, then I completely don't understand why you all had to rip off all my body hair. Wait!" Hailey's blood drained from her face. "I'm not going to be naked am I?"

Maya's shock appeared all over her face. "What? No, of course not. That's preposterous!" Maya paused and hesitated before continuing. "Child, today isn't your court date." She shook her head in disbelief. "It's… your wedding day?"

CHAPTER 18

The call, of course, hadn't been from Ehsan's office. Ehsan didn't even have a brother. It was the court official's office calling to say the schedule had unexpectedly changed and that the official wouldn't be available until Thursday. Ehsan had desperately needed to see him right away, and so he had panicked when he realized it would still be five days away.

Locking the girl in her room seemed like the only option. He had initially regretted that action, but he didn't want to tell her of his plan just yet. He wanted to avoid having a screaming girl in his house for five days. But after he came up with the ruse of his 'brother,' it had all worked out. She would remain safely locked in her room, and there would be peace and quiet in the house.

- - - - - - -

He visited her every day, and they talked for hours about imaginary court rulings, imaginary procedures, and her imaginary case. Ehsan enjoyed himself immensely and, as the five days were almost up, he was coming to see why the West liked dating. He had never been permitted to even have a conversation with his wives without their parents present, directing the whole exchange.

The time alone with Hailey actually heightened the anticipation. She was his, but he still couldn't have her. It was exhilarating.

- - - - - - -

Ehsan chuckled to himself as he locked the door after spending Wednesday afternoon talking with her. It was captivating and refreshing how forward and open she was. Sadly, his other wives had lost that sparkle. Hailey would be a welcomed addition to their house, and the other two would accept her soon enough.

Maya and Ghada were furious and confused when he had come home with the news. After a stern reminder that he was not asking their opinion but merely telling them of the change that would soon occur, they quieted their protests at once. Now finally, that change would be tomorrow.

He chuckled to himself again. His plans had come together quicker than he expected and he was pleasantly surprised. He honestly was expecting it to take a full two weeks, maybe more. Yet here he was, back at home only a week and a half after that first day at the prison. He replayed the events again in his mind with pleasure as he made his way back downstairs to his office.

- - - - - - -

Originally the request the king had made for him to go to the prison had annoyed him. Thankfully the day had not dragged on much longer, and it looked like he would be at the palace very shortly. Ehsan signed the last page of the report, waited for a copy to be made, thanked his host and rose to leave. His muscles ached from sitting so long. He knew his age was catching up with him, but it was during these long days that it seemed undeniable. He was no longer a young buck.

They exited the prison and made their way over to the side gate where their vehicles sat. Ehsan was always surrounded by his security team. Some of the other council members disputed their need for such protection, but Ehsan enjoyed having them around. They gave him a constant sense of importance and, with the increased threats and security issues regarding the royal family, having them with him gave him a welcomed sense of safety and pride.

Ehsan's attention was on the sky when he heard the shriek from his left. Turning, he saw a line of women being ushered towards the building. They were crossing a small field, a few yards away.

"They are new prisoners, council member. Nothing to worry about."

Irfaan seemed to always know what he was thinking and saved him from needing to even ask questions most of the time. Ehsan appreciated Irfaan, he was by far the best driver he had ever had, and Ehsan trusted him implicitly.

Ehsan returned his gaze to the line of women. One woman was limping, one was holding her side, and the next... Ehsan stopped walking. Her eyes weren't looking directly at him, but their brilliance instantly caught his attention. As the green caught the light, they sparkled. Her skin was fair but not a pasty white, it was creamy like the marble he had picked out for his foyer. The girl leaned forward and said something to the woman in front of her but then leaned back and turned her eyes to the ground. Ehsan futilely moved his head to try to acquire another glance of those green eyes. Soon the line of women disappeared into the building.

"I have forgotten something. We must return and speak with the warden at once," Ehsan said to his men.

His entourage turned with him and followed him back inside.

It had been two years since his third wife, Fareefta, had died. Even though he was pleased with his decision, he missed her and with now only having two wives, it seemed like his house was empty. He had wanted another wife to share his bed for some time now, but the king had been keeping him so busy that he hadn't had a chance to look.

He picked up his pace as they walked down the hall. Seeing the girl in the field was the first time in a long time that his heart jumped and caused his body to tingle like that. His anticipation of having her for his own was invigorating.

Of course, the arrangements would take some finesse to work out. Ehsan was sure he'd have to collect on many debts and favors, but it would be well worth it. Even in light of all the work he possibly had ahead of him, he looked at it, not as work per se, but something similar to the satisfaction one feels after returning from a grueling hunting expedition with your trophies. This would be by far his greatest conquest. With all the passion that was surging through him, he had to purposely force himself not to run down the hallway towards the warden's office.

The warden was still sitting at his desk. He looked up, surprised to see him return.

"I'm sorry to disturb you again my friend, but there is an urgent matter that I must discuss with you." Ehsan had to pause and steady himself as he was a bit out of breath.

"Is there something wrong with the paperwork?" The warden questioned.

"Oh no, everything regarding that is fine, and the king will be most pleased. However, there is another arrangement of sorts that I need to discuss. Would you have a moment now? This is very time sensitive I assure you and I would not ask lightly."

"Of course, my friend. Please, sit."

The warden's office was richly decorated and sat in stark contrast to the rest of the prison. The warden gestured towards a large brown armchair opposite him and the massive, dark oak desk where he was seated. After excusing his entourage to wait for him in the hallway, Ehsan accepted the offer and slid into the chair.

Ehsan leaned forward and rested his elbows on his knees. Spreading his fingers and pressing the tips of each to the matching finger on the other hand, he took a deep breath.

"We've known each other for some time now, haven't we?"

The warden nodded in reply.

"And you know I would never ask to collect on the favor you owe me unless it was an absolute necessity?" Ehsan paused. "Well, that time is now, and it is why I've returned to your office."

"Yes, yes my friend. Please, ask anything, and it will be yours. Your graciousness with that previous matter will never be forgotten," the warden said.

Ehsan smiled. "I was hoping that is how you'd see it. What I have to ask is a lofty request and will require your utmost discretion. Do you understand?"

"What you discuss with me now will never leave my lips into the ears of another soul, as Allah is my witness."

Ehsan leaned back into the chair. "When I was leaving, I

noticed you were receiving more prisoners. I wanted to ask you how often do you receive white foreigners?"

"It is quite sporadic. I think we've only had three in the last six months. Usually, the Americans and Europeans stick relatively close to the compounds. Those that don't, usually are so wary of alerting the police or Mutawa, they stay out of trouble, and I rarely see them here. Why do you enquire about such things?"

"Well, you see my friend, I have spotted one of your transfers just moments ago. She looks to be an American, and she has to be one of the most beautiful creatures I've ever seen. Now my request is this: you must hold her. It will be, at the most, a week… maybe two. I'm not sure what her crimes are or what the judge will rule, but whatever the case you can't allow her to leave or be transferred. Do you understand?"

"Ehsan, may I ask why you are making such a request and why the need to keep her here for so long?"

Ehsan hesitated then said, "I wish to make her my wife, and I need to discuss the matter with a few individuals to make that transpire. Now, will you do me this favor, my friend?"

"Yes, of course, but please don't delay. With the sensitivity of this situation, we need to handle this as quickly as possible."

"I strongly agree. There is one more thing, which I'm sure you can understand. Please see to it that she doesn't receive any beatings or special visits from the guards. I already see her as my wife, and I would appreciate that you handle her as such. Do we have an agreement?"

"Yes, indeed, Ehsan. I will see to it. She will not be harmed, and she will be here waiting for you, untouched."

Ehsan thanked the warden and left the prison. The drive to the palace passed without him even realizing it. His mind was consumed with thoughts of the girl, and anything else would have had to fight hard to get hold of his attention. He was transfixed.

- - - - - - -

Upon exiting the vehicle, Ehsan realized the full extent of his excitement. Leaving the prison last week without that beautiful creature had made him very uneasy, so he was thrilled to finally be back at the prison.

If he were an ordinary citizen some of the obstacles which stood in his way would not have existed and as such would have sped up the process even more. However, seeing how he was a council member and she a foreigner, he required a special dispensation from the royal family before he could make any further plans.

Such obstacles took most of the week. Although seeing how it was the first downside that Ehsan had come across to being in his profession, he didn't let it bother him. Thankfully, the other preparations for the wedding ceremony didn't pose any further time delays.

Unlike his other weddings, this one would, naturally, prove to be a bit more difficult, but the anticipation of it intrigued him. The other women had been easy to procure as wives. With Ehsan being such a powerful and wealthy man, the women's fathers had agreed quickly to the terms and, as each of the women was a good Muslim girl, they showed no objections. This girl would be a whole other story.

On top of the other arrangements he had to put into place, he had spent a considerable amount of time working through the events of today: the day he would collect his soon to be bride and return home with her. She wouldn't come easily, and he wasn't expecting anything less than a full out battle. She would obviously need to be broken... like to a wild horse.

Ehsan smiled as he thought of the metaphor again while he headed away from the vehicle. He was confident that the fight in her wouldn't remain for long and she would soon accept her fate and comply.

Ehsan wasn't worried about the actual ceremony. He had a plan that would ensure she would not make a scene. The ceremony would be small and tweaked due to the circumstances. It would not involve the pre-parties like his other weddings, much to the disappointment of his mother and aunts. It would be a simple gathering of his family, where the court official would witness the signing of their contract. Getting her from the prison to his house would prove to be the most difficult obstacle.

His confidence soared as he mounted the steps of the prison. It was nice to have the hardest part of this whole thing behind him, and he was grateful that only the enjoyable parts were left. He was even excited to see how much fight this girl actually had in her. He needed to watch her closely to see how he might use her fear and weakness to his advantage and get her to understand her role.

Ehsan had no doubt in his mind that seeing her that day last week was a blessing and he was not about to back down from such a gift. Even if she caused a scene as he escorted her out of the prison and all the way to his house, he was not giving her up.

As his eyes adjusted to the dim light of the prison entryway, he looked beyond to see the warden quickly approaching.

"My friend your timing is impeccable. I have had to work to

keep her here, but I was successful. I 'lost her paperwork' and reported her 'misbehavior.' The courts were patient with my excuses, but if you had waited any longer, I would have had no choice but to meet the next court date, which is only two days away." He paused, looked at his feet, and cleared his throat before continuing. "I assure you Ehsan she was not harmed intentionally."

"What? Do you mean to say that she was harmed unintentionally?"

"There was a small incident yesterday morning when she attacked one of the guards. The guard had to defend himself, but I assure you, apart from a few bruises, she is exactly the way you left her."

Ehsan was not pleased, but his friend had put his career and freedom in jeopardy to do him this favor, so he let it pass.

"Thank you, my friend. Where is she now?"

"We have moved her to a small secluded room in the east wing."

"Can you…" Ehsan paused and mustered all of his self-control, so he didn't appear like a hormone crazy youth, "take me to her?"

Once he was back in the vehicle with her, Ehsan sporadically glanced over at the girl. Not as much as he'd like to do but just shy of what might alarm her. She was so beautiful. Her creamy skin was so pure, so vulnerable.

He couldn't believe his good fortune. This girl's assumption that he was her lawyer had erased so much of the difficulty this trip could have posed. He eagerly took the gift she presented, and he was surprised the option hadn't occurred to him before.

The trip to the house would be almost too easy now. However, knowing he would still get to enjoy her fight later did take away any potential disappointment. This was, by far, the better way for it to play out. Now they would get to enjoy a quiet drive back to the house without the eyes of others gawking at the scene she might have made.

After he had introduced himself, he could see that the word 'wives,' plural, caused a bit of discomfort even though she tried covered it up. Ehsan shook her hand gently and had to force himself to release it.

Yes, this would do just fine. Eshan would let Hailey rest, and then tomorrow he would inform her of the truth... all the glorious details of her new life with him.

- - - - - - -

Ehsan's memories dissipated as his hand grasped the knob of his office door. He had to focus on going over the final details of this arrangement before the morning, and he couldn't keep his thoughts in the past any longer. There was much work to be done.

CHAPTER 19

Maya's demeanor changed after the talk she and Hailey had following the sugaring. Not that they were best friends now, but she did seem to have softened towards her. Maya's angry stare was gone. Now only a kind of leeriness remained. She now appeared to just view Hailey with an understandable apprehension. Maya justly wasn't thrilled to share her husband with yet another woman, but her anger looked as if it had melted after learning that Hailey wasn't choosing to be there.

Maya spent all morning in Hailey's room talking. First, it was more of a screaming match. Back and forth they went. Even after all of Hailey's efforts, she couldn't seem to get Maya to understand how ludicrous this all was and that Maya needed to help her escape.

"You should be honored that a man like Ehsan would choose you to be his wife."

It was the only major point Maya kept making as if Maya truly believed Ehsan's wishes really were the only thing that mattered. Hailey tried again and again to get her point across.

"But I don't want to be here. It's kidnapping, and I would never in a million years marry a man like him."

That comment outraged and appeared to greatly offend

Maya. It sent her into a rant of listing off all of Ehsan's accomplishments.

After about an hour of arguing, both ceased. They made their way over to the two armchairs and flopped into them. Hailey looked at Maya.

Maya was a strong and proud woman. She was beautiful. Her eyes had a serenity and wisdom to them and sat under thin dark eyebrows. Her smile was broad and revealed two rows of perfectly, straight white teeth that shone against the backdrop of her caramel skin. Her smile also amplified her small round cheeks and a few of the wrinkles on her face. The wrinkles didn't detract from her beauty, they added to it. Hailey could see why Ehsan had chosen her for his first wife.

Maya was one of those women who knew how to run a household but wouldn't try to rule it. It was evident she genuinely believed in and seemed not to be bothered by, the role women had in Saudi. She was actually honored by it. Hailey couldn't understand her point of view. Nevertheless, despite Hailey's confusion, she found herself respecting Maya.

"Are you a... Christian?"

Maya's question threw Hailey, and she wasn't sure what to say or where Maya was going with it.

"Why... do you want to know?" Hailey stalled to hopefully give her a bit more time to search for an answer.

"You seemed so opposed to our ways and, although I don't know much about Christians, don't they have a similar view? Women are to submit to men. It is the way it is in a lot of cultures, so why throw so many judgmental, poisonous arrows at Saudis?"

"Well... I used to be a Christian. But I wouldn't call myself one today. It's a long story and one..."

"Were you… I don't know the English word. Thrown out?"

"Excommunicated?" Hailey chuckled. "No, nothing like that. It was a personal choice one that I made long ago. But to answer your question, yes, Christianity does have submission. But it's not the kind you experience. You see biblical submission, or as I've had it explained to me, is a choice and just as much a sign of strength as a man shows in leading. I would assume you don't have dancing between the sexes here, but have you ever seen ballroom dancing?"

"Yes, when we were in London last spring we walked by a dance studio, and I saw a class through the window. Honestly, it was shocking to see."

Hailey returned her smile. "Well, in dance, it only works if one leads and one follows. The man proposes a step, but it's the choice of the woman to accept. It takes a lot of strength to choose to accept the step the man offers. The dance is only possible if a) the man makes the step and b) the woman accepts. Submission in Christianity is never about fear or domination. It's about a mutual respect to work toward a common goal, just like dancers moving across a dance floor and creating something beautiful. A woman dancer never looks at her role as demeaning or somehow less. It's just a different role. One is not more important than the other. I know using a metaphor you're unfamiliar with maybe isn't the best, but do you understand what I mean?"

"Ah… I think so. I have to look past the strangeness of the public contact of a man and a woman, but I can see the idea of it and, in a small way, you are right: it does sound beautiful. However, you see in my house the same is true, except if we do not submit and accept where my husband leads, he ensures we still proceed towards his goal. His means of doing this is different depending on the situation, but…" Maya briefly looked at the floor but soon regained her composure, "… he does get what he wants and what is right."

"Well, it seems to me that the two versions of submission are very different. You don't get to choose to submit because you don't have a choice to do anything else but submit."

"I know you think this is foolish of our culture, but I can honestly tell you that I'm glad to know I will always be cared for. As much as I know my place, Ehsan also knows his responsibilities and will never rescind or fail to uphold them."

"Do you love him?"

"Oh child, our definitions of love are probably just as different as our definitions of submission. The love which you have in the West, what is played in your movies, is not real. Love isn't an emotion, it's a fact. I'm a wife, so I love my husband."

"Well, I don't think it is a fact. I believe that it's both an emotion and a choice. There is no way I will ever love Ehsan. Do you really not see how wrong all of this is?"

"You sound like Ghada." Maya chuckled. "Now, I don't agree how Ehsan has gone about this, but you don't seem to understand that it doesn't matter. Ehsan looks to Allah for wisdom, and we look to Ehsan. That is the chain of how things work. Allah has put Ehsan in charge, and Allah put us on earth for our husbands. It's an honor. You'll see. After a few months in this house, you will come to understand… just as Ghada has. Trust me, Hailey, your life here will be more fulfilling than anywhere you would have ended up in North America."

Hailey could see that Maya fully believed in what she was saying, so she wasn't going to push the topic further; there seemed to be little point. Saudi was literally worlds away from home and trying to understand everything at this moment would only prove to distance Maya from her. Hailey remained silent and just shrugged.

"Don't fret so! You will soon see that your life here will be better than you think. You will not want for anything. Ehsan loves to spoil us."

"Maybe you're right," Hailey lied. If she were to get out of this house, Maya was obviously not the person to help her.

"I don't mean to pry, but can you tell me," Maya readjusted in her chair, "what choice led you to leave your faith? You seem to know a lot about Christianity and when you talk about it doesn't appear to be coated with disdain."

Hailey's heart sank, and her nose started to tingle with the threat of tears. The resolve she had built around those memories was crumbling. If Hailey was back home and safe, she could easily use distractions to fortify those walls. However, at that moment, she felt completely defenseless.

"I'm sorry. But no, I... can't talk about it." Hailey quickly turned her head and discretely wiped the tear that had escaped from her eye before Maya could see it.

CHAPTER 20

– London –

Eight years earlier

Hailey burst through the door and headed straight for the kitchen. It was the 30th of March, Hailey's day to finally turn seventeen. This was a day she had agonized over with much anticipation for years now. Entering the kitchen, she caught sight of her mother standing by the sink rinsing off a dishcloth. Hailey stopped in her tracks and smiled. Bethany, her mother, was singing one of her favorite hymns 'Be Thou My Vision.' It was a favorite of Hailey's as well.

Hailey and her mother were close, and Hailey appreciated her mother's candid, open outlook on parenting. Bethany seemed to have figured out the balance between being a friend to her children without forsaking the respect a parent needs to maintain for discipline to be effective. She accepted her humanity and didn't place herself above her children so as to portray she was infallible. She asked for forgiveness and gave it freely. Hailey admired her and prayed that God would teach her how to be a parent just like her mother.

"Oh, hello sweetheart." Her mother turned to face her. "How was school?"

Watching her mother dry her hands so nonchalantly on a towel and cross the room towards the table, Hailey's excitement rose to an uncontainable level.

"How can you be so calm, Mom? I'm seventeen, do you know what this means? The freedom! I mean I'm practically an adult." Hailey bounded after her mother.

"Whoa, slow down there grandma. Don't be in such a rush," her mom teased.

"Oh haha, Mom." Hailey paused looking around the room. "Hey, where are Claire and Ben?" Hailey had a volleyball practice that morning and had left the house before they woke, and she hadn't seen them since last night.

"They are next door playing, but they should be home soon. I told them they had to be back in time for supper."

Claire, who was fourteen and Ben, who was ten, were great younger siblings. Usually, in a family of three children, there were arguments by the hour. Shockingly, though, the decibel level remained relatively low most of the time in the Pearson house. This is something which Hailey attributed to her parents rather than to their good behavior.

"Hi, we're back," voices called out in unison from the front door as if in response to Hailey's question.

"Is Hailey home yet?" Claire shouted throughout the house as they came noisily jogging down the hallway.

"We're in here!"

The evening was filled with Hailey's birthday celebration. After the candles had been blown out and the cake passed around, Hailey's dad, Oliver, finally broached the plans for the evening, much to Hailey's delight.

"So monkey, you ready for tonight?"

Hailey loved that her dad still used the nickname from when

she was little. "You bet, what time do we go?"

"I want to come too!" Ben interjected.

"Hey, if Ben gets to go there is no way I'm staying home," Claire whined.

Hailey didn't mind, she would love to have them all there. Being able to drive for the first time was a big deal.

"Well, as soon as the dishes are done and the kitchen's cleaned up, we can all head out. If that works for your mother," Oliver said as he lovingly looked at her mom.

All three children's heads snapped around to look at their mother on the opposite end of the table.

"Of course, but you're not all leaving me behind. This is a big event," she smiled at Hailey, "and I'm not going to be stuck at home alone."

Hailey's heart soared. She looked around the table at each member of her family. "Thanks guys for being so excited about this; it means a lot to me."

Oliver had picked Hailey up that day during her lunch break and took her to her driving exam. Hailey knew that spending a few months studying was a little overkill, but she just couldn't take the chance and fail it. She desperately wanted to drive and couldn't waste any time with retaking tests. Her hard work had paid off. She aced it, and now she couldn't wait to get back behind the wheel.

Hailey typically hated doing dishes but worked at full speed to help, and she pushed her siblings to do the same. In no time the kitchen was spotless, they had their coats and shoes on, and were all piled into the car.

It was a quiet evening, and the air was cool and crisp. After Hailey snapped her seatbelt on and adjusted all her mirrors, she put the key in the ignition and turned to look at her father.

"OK kiddo, this is it. You ready?"

"Yup."

Hailey worried she wouldn't be able to drive in a straight line. There was so much adrenalin in her that her hands were shaking from all the excitement.

"OK now, shift the car into neutral and turn the car on while keeping the brake and clutch pushed in all the way and then put the gear shift into reverse." Her dad kept his voice calm and patient as she followed each step. "Great, now slowly back out of the driveway and make sure to check behind you and down either side of the street for other cars. That's it, slowly does it. Now shift into first and slowly add some gas while releasing the clutch."

The car started out smoothly, but as Hailey got excited her foot came off the gas a bit and the car lurched back and forth and then finally stalled. Laughter filled the car.

"I guess that wasn't the best start in the world huh?" Hailey groaned.

"Don't worry about it, just try again and this time, give it a little more gas."

For the next twenty minutes, Hailey practiced stopping, starting and shifting right up to third gear. She caught on quite quickly with only a minor stall here and there. Soon her father said it was time to leave their neighborhood.

The feeling was strange, but Hailey loved being in control of the car. They drove around town for another twenty minutes when Ben offered a wonderful suggestion.

"Ice cream! We didn't have any with the cake, and it's only right. I mean it is almost wrong not to have them together. Please, can we go get some?" Ben pleaded.

They always went to the same place. It was run by an elderly couple who made all their ice cream from scratch.

Outside the store, there were a few park benches to sit on so customers could enjoy the fresh air. The front of the store had the name "Grandma's Ice Cream" lit up in red, neon lights. There was a red and white striped awning which covered the length of the store and gold bells that hung over the door to announce the coming and going of the customers.

The inside was decorated like an old-fashioned ice cream parlor. The employees even wore those little tiny white caps and red and white striped aprons. There was an old wooden piano set up in the middle of the store where kids could come and play three songs to get a free ice cream. High backed benches lined the walls for ample seating. During the summer, the lineup went through the store, out the door, and around the corner. Fortunately for the Pearsons, the store was open year-round and was quieter this time of year.

Everyone agreed, and Hailey started to make her way over to the shopping center a few blocks away.

"Oh no Dad," Hailey said as she began to approach an intersection at the top of a hill and saw the light turn yellow.

"It's OK honey," he said trying to calm her. "Just come to a stop, and when you see the light turn green, you will let off the brake and step on the gas, while slightly easing off the clutch. You will roll back a bit, but there is no one behind you, so it's OK. As you add more gas, you will start to pull forward, and you can fully ease off the clutch."

Hailey's eyes remained glued to the lights with an occasional glance in the rearview mirror.

Oh God please don't let anyone come up behind me, please, please.

But just as the words were going through her mind a small

compact car pulled up right behind her.

"Ah, Dad, he's too close." Hailey's voice clearly conveyed her trepidation.

"Monkey, it's OK. Just ignore them and do what I said. Just step on the gas as soon as you take your foot off the brake and you won't roll. Trust me we've all been here, and the driver will understand, so don't even think about him or worry if you stall it, you can always try again, and you will get it."

"OK," Hailey whimpered and looked at the opposite light and saw it turn yellow.

OK, here we go, don't stall Hailey, don't stall.

As their light turned green, Hailey eased her foot off the brake just as her dad told her to. As she started to move her foot to the gas, the car began to roll backward, and she panicked.

"AHH."

Worried she would slam into the other car Hailey let her foot off the clutch before she had a chance to add some gas and the car stalled.

A small snicker escaped Ben's lips.

"Ben!" Her mom shot a look at her brother to silence any further teasing.

"Sorry.," Ben apologized, then remained quiet.

"Try again, it's alright."

Hailey heard the positive tone of her dad's voice, and it eased her a bit. She took a deep breath and tried again. This time went much better, and she was able to make it farther up the hill and into the crosswalk. However, as Hailey was still only going a few miles per hour, the driver behind her lost patience and leaned on his horn. Alarmed, Hailey lost her concentration and slammed on the gas, and rather than gearing into second she went into fourth. The jerk of the car startled her, and she hit the brake without putting in the clutch, stalling again. The whole family was now wide-eyed and sitting in the middle of the intersection. The driver honked again and blew passed them, barely missing their van.

"Yikes, that was close," she said through quick breaths. "Sorry guys. Dad, can you take over?" Hailey begged.

"Nope, this is the hardest part about driving a stick. Once you get this, and you will, you will be flying. Now put the car back into neutral and start it up."

A few more drivers passed them with curious looks and a few honks, but Hailey decided to ignore them. Her father just smiled and gestured forward for her to try again. She shifted into neutral and started the car.

But then it happened

"HAILEY.........!" Her mother's scream filled her ears.

As Hailey started to turn towards her mother, she was blinded by the headlights that were encircling her father's head. Then there was blackness filled with horrible sounds of tearing metal, squealing brakes, and screaming. Then came a dead, silent nothingness.

The next thing Hailey experienced was pain, a deafening, white-hot, searing pain that seemed to engulf her whole body. Someone was moaning, and there were strong smells of disinfectant. She soon realized that the moan she was hearing was trickling off her own lips. It filled her ears, but it was also accompanied by a quiet ringing. Hailey tried to open her eyes, but even that seemed to take energy she didn't appear to have.

What's going on? Ah, I'm so tired and why am I hurting so much.

She was exhausted and drifted back to sleep before she thought of how to answer herself or how to call out for someone.

Then there was that pain again. It gripped her body as she

tried again to roll awake. Little by little sunlight started to creep in under her eyelids as she forced them to open. The instant the light hit her eyes, terror grabbed her.

"No! Dad, watch out!" The response surprised her as it emerged from her with such volume and power. Nevertheless, realization met her full force.

We were in an accident, weren't we? The tears came then, along with a wounded whimpering cry. *Where is everyone? Are they OK? Do they know I'm OK?*

"Hailey?"

Hailey fully opened her eyes to see she was, in fact, lying in a hospital bed as she suspected. A woman was peeking around the door, concern etched on her face.

"Are you alright sweetheart?" The woman's voice was gentle and sweet.

"Where am I?" Hailey's voice was hoarse, and speaking made her throat lurch, and she started coughing.

Pain seared through her whole body as it was racked with coughs. The nurse ran over to her side and helped steady her until she stopped and was able to relax back against the bed.

"Honey, you are in St. Mary's Hospital. You were in a car accident, but you're going to be OK. The doctor knows you're awake and he should be here soon to answer all your questions. Is there anything I can get for you?"

"Water?" Hailey made sure to whisper this time as she didn't want to aggravate her throat again.

"Sure thing love, I will be right back."

The nurse left the room, and Hailey watched her go. She was young, less than ten years older than Hailey, maybe mid-twenties. She had blonde hair with a few dark roots starting to show. She was tall and slender, and she seemed sweet.

"Hello?"

A man's voice came from just outside her door. As he entered the room, Hailey assumed this was her doctor based on his appearance. The man had a gleaming white coat that hung open. Underneath the coat was a light blue dress shirt, adorned with a dark blue striped tie which matched his dark slacks. He looked to be in his late forties. His hair was a sandy blonde and was cut short. He had crystal blue eyes and a kind face that helped put Hailey at ease.

"My name is Doctor Stewart. I'm here to answer the millions of questions that you've probably been asking yourself. But first, I'd like to talk to you about how you are doing. Then I will let you ask as many questions as you would like. Is that's OK with you?"

"Sure," Hailey whispered.

"You were in a a very serious car accident, Hailey. You sustained some very severe injuries, but we were able to stabilize you, and after some intensive physiotherapy, we expect you to make a full recovery." He spoke while maintaining an encouraging smile.

So what? I don't care, where's my family? Hailey was dying to interject, but she refrained and allowed the doctor to finish.

"Now I am going to be straight with you, it will be a lot of hard work, but we should have you out of here in a couple of months. We contacted your aunt, and she arrived a few days ago, she will be back in..."

"Wait! How long have we been here?" Hailey interrupted.

"It's been five days. You were in a coma, but you started to make an amazing turnaround yesterday. You have a badly bruised liver, a torn spleen, and a few other internal injuries which we don't need to go into right now. You also have quite a few fractures."

Hailey could feel her left leg and right arm in casts, and she assumed a few ribs were broken as it hurt to breathe.

"But like I said, with work we expect you to make a full..."

It was then that Hailey's head started spinning. Spots seemed to take over the room, and Dr. Stewart's face went blurry, and his voice grew faint. The sensation was like falling into a hole filled with black cotton. Before exhaustion overtook her completely, Hailey heard the nurse return.

"Does she know?"

Even with her best effort, Hailey found it impossible to remain present to ask what they meant; sleep came and took her.

When Hailey awoke, she didn't know how long she had been asleep, but there was now no light coming through the window. Everything was quiet apart from the sounds coming from the machines circling her bed. A faint shuffle of feet and whispers filtering in from the hall beyond her door.

She tried to grab as deep of breath as her ribs would allow and slowly shifted onto her elbow. Pain seared through her other arm and in her abdomen, so she had to freeze until it passed. When it let up, she was able to shuffle around enough, and with the assistance of the adjustable bed, Hailey sat up a bit.

Even with such a usually mundane task, Hailey felt completely worn out. Her stomach lurched from a bit of nausea due to the lightheadedness swarming her head. She assumed this was fairly typical for someone who had been lying down for almost a week. She hoped it wouldn't last long and that she would be able to regain her strength quickly. Once her nausea passed, she realized how hungry she was, and she started searching for the call button.

Within minutes there was a knock on the door, and the same

nurse appeared.

"Hi, love, is there something you need?" The woman said softly.

Remembering to whisper, Hailey responded, "Yes please, I was wondering if I could get something to eat? Oh, and could you send my mom in if she is well enough, or tell me what room she's in?"

Immediately, Hailey saw the color drain a bit from the nurse's face. Even though she tried to hide it, Hailey saw concern flash in front of the nurse's eyes.

"Of course I can get you some food. You must be starving. Oh, I'm so rude I haven't even introduced myself. My name is Hope. I will be back in a few minutes, OK?"

Hailey watched her exit the room and was a bit confused as to why Hope seemed unsettled. Her mom was OK, wasn't she? Isn't that what the doctor had said? That with some work they would make a full recovery? Her mind seemed so fuzzy still, probably due to the pain killers. As she tried to sort through the fog to remember her conversation with Dr. Stewart, her head started to spin again. She didn't want to pass out again, so she closed her eyes and tried to clear her mind.

Stay calm stupid!! Hope probably is just exhausted from a long shift. You need to stay lucid, don't be paranoid!!

After hearing a few whispers outside her door, Hailey saw Hope enter the room. There was another woman in tow, but she hung back and remained in the doorway. The woman was dressed professionally in light gray slacks and a black turtleneck. Her hair was pulled back with a large black metal clip which left a few tendrils of her red hair fall to frame her face. She wore small dark rimmed glasses, and her face bore a small smile. Hailey smiled back and then turned her attention to Hope, who was approaching her bed.

Gently touching Hailey's shoulder, Hope spoke softly. "Hailey, this is Dr. Gloria Strodder, she's the resident Psychologist at St. Mary's Hospital, and if it would be alright with you, she'd like to talk to you for a bit. Would that be OK?"

"Sure."

Hailey tried retaining her smile, but with the concern starting to course through her, she found it difficult. Hope excused herself with the promise to return with food. Dr. Strodder approached and took a seat in the chair beside Hailey's bed.

"Feel free to call me Gloria, Hailey. Thank you for agreeing to talk with me a bit." Her voice was sweet and calm.

Hailey nodded.

"Now I want you to take a deep breath and understand that I am here to talk to you about something very serious. It won't seem real at first, but I also want you to know that as it sinks in you are not alone. Do you think that is something you can do?"

"Yeah… I think so," Hailey replied hesitantly. She closed her eyes and took a deep breath.

It was a surreal moment, and Hailey felt exactly as she did when she was about to jump off the platform when she went bungee jumping with her youth group. Their youth leader had used it as a lesson in faith. His words flooded her mind.

- - - - - - -

"Now we all technically know the rope attached to our feet will hold us. However, only in us jumping does our faith mean anything. We can say we know the rope is strong, but if we are unwilling to trust that strength, then our faith is meaningless. Just like the book of James says 'Faith without deeds is dead.' So as you jump, feel the outworking of your faith and think how it's like a symbol of your faith in Christ. Think about all the other applications this practical and exhilarating event has for your walk with God."

- - - - - - -

The memory faded and Hailey opened her eyes.

"I have been told that your doctor has explained to you that you were in a car accident and that he has gone over most of your injuries with you. What I would like to do now is tell you what happened and then answer any questions you have." Gloria leaned forward and rested her hand on the edge of Hailey's bed.

Hailey felt fear and urgency rush over her as the woman continued.

"This information has come through your aunt, the witnesses, and from the police investigators. You were driving and were having some trouble getting going after stopping at a light, which is a situation we all have been in." Dr. Strodder smiled slightly to convey her understanding. "Upon entering the intersection, through no fault of yours, there was another vehicle approaching the intersection from your left. The driver of that vehicle, a lorry, had been driving since the night before and had no right to be on the road. He had momentarily nodded off and didn't see the red light or your vehicle. He hit you at full speed. It is an absolute miracle you survived, sweetheart. It took the rescue workers a very long time to even get you out of the car, and after the assessment of your injuries, they were almost certain you wouldn't pull through. Hailey, look at me, honey."

Hailey had glanced down to her cast leg, wondering if she

would ever run again, but she returned her eyes to the doctor as asked.

"Hailey, your family did not make it."

CHAPTER 21

The doctor's words hit her in the chest like a sledgehammer hitting a glass vase. It threw her body into uncertainty and denial. Hailey lost control as one side tried to panic and flee while the other side remained in disbelief and doubt. All Hailey could do was sit by and watch to see which side won. It was like moving through molasses, but finally, she spoke. "Wait you must be mistaken. Dr. Stewart told me that after some rehabilitation we'd be OK."

"Hailey, he didn't say 'we' he said 'you,'" Dr. Strodder replied, keeping her voice calm, even and compassionate.

"No... no, he said 'we.' You're wrong! They are at home or in a different room. Go ask Hope, she'll tell you." Hailey screamed her conviction. "No, they are all OK, you'll see. No, no you're wrong, you're wrong!"

Hailey then realized her body was shaking and as she looked up and saw that Dr. Strodder had tears in her eyes, Hailey panicked, and it was becoming obvious which part of her was starting to win.

Hailey sat straight up, ignoring the pain that stabbed through multiple parts of her body, she grabbed at the I.V. lines with her good arm and ripped them off of her.

"I will find them, you'll see. This isn't happening… it can't be, it just can't." Hailey's words poured out of her, mixing with the sobs battering her soul.

"Hailey, stop!" Dr. Strodder leaped off the chair grabbing onto both of her shoulders.

The feeling the coldness of the doctor's hand through her hospital gown was enough of a shock to jolt Hailey fully into the moment. But it was a moment Hailey's mind and body were not willing to be in, and they revolted.

With eyes darting about the room like a cornered animal looking for freedom, Hailey's breathing launched into an irregular rhythm. She couldn't get a full breath in and the more she tried, the more her lungs protested and burned. Her rib cage was heaving against her bandages, and the pain that seared from them was blinding. Hailey's vision was filling with flashes of blackness as her fear started to strangle her.

"Hope, Hope!! Get in here we're losing her," Gloria screamed towards the door.

Hope must have been waiting in the hall as she appeared instantly with an orderly in tow. Together Dr. Strodder and Hope worked fast to get the oxygen mask over Hailey's mouth, while the orderly tried to keep her still.

"Breathe all the way out and then take fresh air in, Hailey," Hope coaxed her.

She tried to follow her direction, but her body wasn't cooperating. Her limbs were still fighting to get off the bed.

The orderly had been instructed to be gentle due to her injuries, but it was proving difficult for him to restrain her. The pain from her fighting body proved to be too much, it engulfed her, and she collapsed. Multiple alarms from the machines around her rang in her ears.

=======

"What happened? I thought you said she was out of the woods." Norah didn't even try to control her frustration as she ran into the hospital and approached Dr. Stewart and Gloria, who were waiting for her.

Norah had spent hours talking with both of them in the past few days, going over Hailey's diagnosis and recovery schedule. She had been so thankful to them for spending so much time with her and taking such amazing care of Hailey. However, all that now faded into the background after she received the message to come to the hospital immediately.

"Norah, calm down."

Gloria's reassuring tone usually had the most calming effect, but now it only aggravated her.

"Don't tell me to calm down. Tell me what happened." Tears welled up in her eyes.

Dr. Stewart explained. "She had a severe panic attack. Normally, this wouldn't be serious, but with Hailey's injuries and state of mind, it was just too much for her body and she..."

"Oh God!" Norah slumped down into the closest chair.

"No, she's alright now. She coded, but we were easily able to bring her back. We gave her a sedative to calm her down so she could get some much-needed rest."

"Why in the world did she have a panic attack?"

Gloria bent down to eye level. "I told her about her family, and as expected she took it hard, very hard. Her body wasn't in a state to handle that, but she's OK now."

"What? You told her without me here? What were you thinking?" Norah looked back and forth between the two looking for an explanation.

Beep Beep.

Dr. Stewart's pager interrupted them. "I'm sorry I have to go. I will be back as soon as I can."

Gloria took a seat beside her. "I know we discussed that, but the doctors thought she would sleep till morning. When she woke up and started asking questions I thought it best to tell her. In my opinion, it would have done more harm to wait."

Norah rolled her eyes.

"I know it may not make sense to you, but this was the best course. I didn't think Hailey would respond quite so powerfully, but now that everything is back under control, she can start processing it. She will need your help for that, and you still need some coaching on how to help her through this. I know you're upset with me, but can you put that aside and move forward so we can help Hailey recover?"

Norah knew she was right, but the anger still ran through her. She rose from her seat and walked a couple steps. Turning back towards Gloria, she agreed. "Of course."

=======

She awoke to find her aunt sitting next to her and Dr. Strodder knocking at the door. Hailey closed her eyes. She never wanted to open them again. How could she face a world that didn't contain her family?

"Is she awake?"

"Yes, she just stirred, but I don't think she's ready to talk to anyone."

"I'll come back later."

Over the next few weeks, Hailey's aunt stayed glued to her

side. She helped her through the beginning of her recovery and tried to aid her in understanding how to survive the realizations which assaulted her each day. After a couple months Hailey's aunt had to return to the States. So as soon as Dr. Stewart signed off on her transfer, the arrangements were made, and they moved her to New York. Under any other circumstances, Hailey would have protested profusely. She didn't want to leave her friends or her home; they were the only thing left in her life. However, she had no emotion, will or energy to fuel the protest, she was a hollow tube, and so no objections were spoken out loud.

As per Dr. Stewart's assessment, she did make a full recovery. It was a painful and long process, but Hailey survived, though only physically. Hailey lost herself that day, and she blamed three people for taking away her family: the driver of the truck, herself, and God, whom she had not spoken to since.

CHAPTER 22

Maya had left her room during lunch, and Hailey was thankful for the rest. Time was passing quickly, and she needed to think of some way to change the circumstances she was being pushed towards.

Rising from the chair after pushing around the remaining food on her plate due to her low appetite, Hailey made her way to the bathroom. She washed her hands and dried them on the towel hanging near the door. Turning back to the mirror she gripped the porcelain sink and leaned forward so she could closely look into her own eyes.

Hailey, you can do this. You have to buck up. This is your life at stake, and you are not going to spend it here imprisoned in this psychotic household. Now, what are your options? Think!

From their conversation that morning she knew Maya would be impossible to collaborate with. Ghada might be a different story. From what she could gather from Maya, Ghada was less than impressed when she became Ehsan's wife. Maybe that was something Hailey could use to befriend her, and they could find some common ground. Ghada always looked so defeated whenever Hailey saw her and maybe she was also looking for a way out.

Do I have enough time for that? There must not be that much time left until this so called wedding. What if I can't even see her at all before then? What if I do see her but couldn't get her alone?

Hailey's heart rate started racing, her knuckles were turning white from the grip she had on the sink.

Relax Hailey. Don't lose it. There has to be a way to talk to Ghada. Hailey took a deep breath and lowered her head, so her chin rested on her chest, a few tears traced down her cheek.

Come to me all who are weary.

Hailey's head shot up.

"*No!*" Hailey whispered as she glared into the mirror.

It had been so long since she stopped listening to that voice and she hadn't heard it in years. Hailey pushed back from the mirror and angrily stomped back into the bedroom.

She threw herself onto the bed and buried her face in the pillow. The memories of her family crawled up onto the bed with her and pressed her so hard into the bedspread that she could hardly breathe. Hailey didn't know how long she laid there, but as the time ticked by the memories lifted. Little by little she felt lighter and lighter.

A knock came at the door, startling Hailey.

She jumped off the bed and looked frantically around the room until she regained her bearings. She must have drifted off to sleep, and it took her a moment to realize where she was. Hailey looked down and saw her disheveled appearance.

It took Hailey a bit of finesse to get the hang of looping the khimar around her head. Hailey much preferred it to the thick, dark fabric of the abaya. She was able to wear somewhat familiar type clothes underneath and then just have this colorful, four-foot fabric draped around her. The khimars Hailey was given were relatively plain, yet the khimars she'd seen the other woman wearing were beautiful. Some were patterned, and some were just solid, but all of them were brightly colored and embroidered with intricate designs.

Adjusting her khimar, she cleared her throat. "Uh, come in."

Each of the women who were present during the sugaring returned and drifted into the room. Hailey craned her head to try and look around them hoping Ghada would turn the corner. She didn't. Instead, a woman, who Hailey hadn't met before, entered the room last. She was carrying a small, oddly shaped, wooden table.

The three aunts, Sabira, Trana, and Pari each brought an item: a jug of water, a drum, and what looked like a bag of flour.

Haffafa was holding a small wooden stool in one hand, which matched the table the stranger carried. She was no longer in an abaya but also wore a khimar. It was bright blue and made Haffafa's appearance seem even more joyful than before. In Haffafa's other hand she carried a green khimar, embroidered with gold thread. When she unfolded it, Hailey could see it was slightly sheer.

Maya came near her and explained. "This is called Lailet Al-Hinna, a Night of Henna. Normally this would be an all-night party, but seeing how these circumstances differ from normal tradition, we've altered them a bit." Maya pointed to the stranger. "That woman is a henaya. She is very skilled at applying henna. You will be impressed."

Maya guided Hailey over to the wall by the bedroom window and coaxed her to sit on a large blue pillow which was sitting on the floor. The other woman gathered around. Haffafa came over, set the stool down and removed the plain khimar Hailey was wearing. She then draped the green khimar over Hailey's head and face and let it float down over her shoulders.

The Henaya, a woman even older than Haffafa, came over to Hailey's right and set the little table down. It looked like a small wooden chest with legs, and it had a split down the middle. The small woman reached in with one hand on each side and pulled the flaps apart. Inside was a bowl, a wooden spoon, a small plastic mat that looked like a flexible cutting board, and five brown tubes. The woman then folded down the other two sides of the table. The part that was previously a cube-like chest was now a flat work surface.

The two aunts, who held the bag and water jug, came over, chatting excitedly. Hailey would be surprised if the three of them spent even a full hour throughout the day not talking. They placed the items near the feet of the Henaya and moved back.

Hailey's suspicion that the bag held flour was confirmed. The Henaya took the bag and water, poured them into the bowl and stirred it with the spoon until it formed a dough. She finished off the mixing with her hands. After she had seemed satisfied with its consistency, she replaced the dough back to the bowl, covered it with a small black cloth and nodded to Haffafa. Who then shrugged her shoulders up in excitement, turned and left the room.

Pari, the aunt who had been holding the drum, had settled herself on a pillow to Hailey's left, a few feet away. She rested the drum between her knees and smiled at Hailey.

Maya remained beside Hailey, on her left, and had lowered herself onto a large red pillow. She cupped her chin with one hand and rested on her elbow. She was smiling and talking with the other two aunts while they pushed the furniture in the seating area, the two chairs, and the table, off to the side.

The Henaya remained quiet and continued to keep her eyes

on the floor. Hailey was about to interrupt Maya and ask what was next when the door to the room flew open.

In came Haffafa carrying a blue, pottery bowl and two hand towels draped over her arm. She had ten or so women trailing behind her. They all poured into the room. All of them seemed to be very excited, and they were all talking at once. Each of them was carrying a pillow and found a space around the room on which to perch themselves. Once everyone was seated, stillness blanketed the room. Those who continued to talk only did so in a soft voice. However, most sat silent and watched Hailey.

Maya leaned over and whispered, "Keep your eyes on the floor, it's a sign of respect."

Hailey lowered her head and, for the most part, did as Maya asked. She only sporadically stole a glance here and there. Her curiosity was just too overwhelming not to.

Haffafa bent down in front of Hailey, removed one towel from her arm and placed it on the floor. She uncrossed Hailey's feet and rested them on the towel. Then she took the other towel and put it on Hailey's knees. She took each of Hailey's hands and rested them on top of the towel. Haffafa placed her hand on Hailey's head, said something then returned her attention back to Hailey's hands. She picked up one of Hailey's hands and put it into the bowl of warm water and washed it, then did likewise with the other. Afterward, she dried each of them with the towel. Haffafa took the same care to wash and dry her feet. Next, Haffafa took the bowl and towels to the bathroom and then returned to sit with the other women.

The Henaya then moved her hands to the bowl with the dough and pulled off a small piece of the dough. She placed it between her hands and rapidly moved her hands back and forth to roll the dough into a long strip. Her speed was impressive, and her skill was immediately evident. After the dough had been rolled, she moved it over to Hailey's hands that were now resting on her thighs. The Henaya worked with precision and arranged the pieces of dough into shapes and patterns, covering Hailey from her fingers and up past her wrists. After each piece had been placed, it was pressed lightly against her skin so it wouldn't roll off. The process was continued on Hailey's feet until all four sections were beautifully decorated.

The Henaya placed the small amount of remaining dough back into the bowl and then grabbed a small canister from a small drawer in the front of the table. It had a tiny aerosol tip. She uncapped it and moved back toward Hailey but paused. She looked at Maya, spoke a few words, and waited.

Maya leaned forward. "Hailey, usually henna takes a while to stain the skin. However, this spray will open up your pores to allow the henna to set more quickly. She would like me to warn you so that you won't be alarmed. It does sting a bit."

Hailey nodded her head, and the Henaya continued. The spray did sting, it felt like rubbing alcohol being applied to a small cut. Once the spray was applied the Henaya then moved back to her table and removed one of the tubes. She unscrewed the lid, carefully placed it back on the table and turned back to Hailey. Pressing the end of the tube with her right hand, while using her left to guide the tip, she expelled a dark paste from the tube. Hailey assumed this was the actual henna. The Henaya filled in the spaces between the dough until everything was either black from the paste or white from the dough.

The Henaya rose, replaced everything back to its place, and closed up her table. As she did so, one of the women seated on the other side of the room began to sing. The others joined her.

Pari started to hit the drum. They all clapped and broke out into very high-pitched vibrating yelps.

Hailey jumped, startled.

"It's called ululations. It's how Arab women express joy. They are praising Allah for your beauty and your upcoming marriage. You should be very honored," Maya said, trying to comfort her.

Hailey knew she'd never go through with the wedding, and yet she found she was in total awe of what she was seeing and hearing. Surprisingly, in a weird way, she did feel honored.

Hailey knew no one from home would understand her compliance. Yet, in light of all she had experienced in Saudi so far, she now realized that waiting quietly for the right moment proved a better option than expressing her feelings and opinions as they occurred. She willed herself to remain seated on the floor, careful not to disturb the dough, and continued to listen to the women around her.

The celebration continued, and after the women had finished singing, some of the older women sitting around Haffafa got up and went over to the other side of the room. There were two young girls, maybe in their late teens, sitting there. The older woman bent down and pulled them up into the center of the room and then took their seat again. The young girls looked around a bit embarrassed at first, but they soon got on board and started belly dancing. All the women clapped and cheered. There was laughing, singing and the rhythmic sound of the drum filling the air. Hailey was actually exhilarated by the scene and found herself smiling at the sight.

As the girls continued to dance, the door to the room opened. Hailey reluctantly pulled her eyes away and glanced towards the door. Her smile slowly fell away. Ghada entered the room, and Hailey instantly noticed the cut above her eye and the bruise on her cheek. She was carrying a large silver tray which she brought over to the bed.

The young girls stopped dancing and came over to the tray, they picked it up and passed it around to the older woman. It was filled with a variety of different fruits and nuts. There were a few other items on the tray. Hailey couldn't distinguish what they were, except that they were sweet and among the first choice of what was taken from the tray. The women soon emptied the tray and continued to chatter while they ate.

No one seemed to even pause at the sight of Ghada's face. Hailey moved to take off the green khimar, but Maya stopped her hand and shook her head. Hailey complied and returned her eyes back to the door, but Ghada was already gone.

The sight of the women before her no longer intrigued her, no longer exhilarated her; it scared her.

What was I thinking… that I would just go through the motions and wait until later to try and escape? Or wait until the ceremony? But why would anyone listen then? How could I possibly think that having an audience would make any difference? Neither the number of people there nor the officiant would be guaranteed to listen or to care. These women didn't seem to.

The smells and sights and the kindness she had been shown, apart from the sugaring, had been almost hypnotic. Maybe that was why she had been so calm before. Yet there was no calmness now. Hailey's flight instinct had kicked in again when she had seen Ghada's face and Hailey knew she had to get out of here immediately.

But how when I'm in a room with many eyes smothering me?

After another hour of talking and eating, the younger women started another round of songs and dancing. They were soon joined by everyone in the room, leaving Hailey sitting alone on her pillow. Everyone was enjoying themselves and paying no attention to her. Hailey looked at the door.

CHAPTER 23

The taxi weaved its way through the compound's streets and made its way to the main road. A right turn, then two lefts and another right. The heat mixed with the rhythmic rocking of the cab made Ryan sleepy. He dragged his hands over his face and rubbed his eyes. The drive wouldn't be long, and he didn't want to doze off.

The cab reached the gate, and the driver waited for the cast iron fence to roll slowly out of the way. Ryan's patience was already failing him. He nearly had to stop himself from getting out and pushing the gate so it would open faster.

After it fully opened, the cab then attempted to turn left. It was almost finished the turn when a white truck screeched around the corner, barely missing the cab. Ryan's fingers dug into the seat to keep his balance. His heart raced.

Woah, that was close!

The cab driver yelled something at the truck and shook his hand out the window. Before their vehicle had a chance to advance any further, another white truck sped around the corner and raced after the first. Then two more, identical to the first two, followed suit.

"You...?"

The driver stopped his attempt to find the word and just gave Ryan a thumbs-up sign. His accent was thick, and it was obvious he didn't speak much English.

"Yes. You?"

The cab driver nodded. He waited a couple seconds before pulling out, undoubtedly waiting to see if there were going to be any further maniacs racing around the corner. It was clear, so they continued on their way.

As the cab sped towards the airport, Ryan leaned his head against the headrest. His heart was still pounding a bit. The blistering air merged with the smells of the market they were passing. As the smell wafted through the open window, Ryan's head started to spin. He closed his eyes and tried to go through the things he wanted to discuss with George. He hoped it would distract him so his body would settle down.

He couldn't wait to finally get some answers. The drive should only take another twenty-five minutes, so Ryan had plenty of time to run through everything. He leaned forward to grab a pen and paper from his bag to make some notes.

Ten minutes passed, and he was surprised at how many questions he actually had.

The cab driver said something in Arabic and Ryan looked up. The man reached for the radio and turned up the volume quite loud. It wasn't music but a man talking, Ryan guessed it was the news. Whatever the report was about the cab driver was not happy. After every statement, he yelled and shook his hand at the radio. When the talking had stopped, and music filled the car again, the cab driver looked at Ryan through the rear view mirror. His eyes were sad.

"What's wrong?"

"I no English."

But it was clear he wanted to tell Ryan something. The cab driver used his knees to help steer the car. He placed both hands together then swiftly moved them outwards.

Ryan had no idea what the man was doing. The man kept making the same motion again and again. The car crossed the centerline, causing the driver to quit his effort as he swerved the car back into their lane. The man huffed, checked his mirrors and slowed the car. He pulled a tight U-turn after just enough speed had been taken off as to not flip it, and headed back the way they had come. After Ryan had recovered from being slammed into his door, he looked back to see if there had been a cause on the road to explain the change in course. Ryan saw nothing.

"See? See?" The cab driver said as he motioned towards the roof of his car.

Ryan looked up and to see a picture of three children clipped to the visor and then looked back at the man. The driver's expression was pained, and he had tears in his eyes. Ryan finally understood. Something must have happened to his family, and the man wanted to race back to them. Ryan undid his seat belt, leaned between the two front seats and pointed to the picture.

"They... no OK?" he asked as he showed the man a thumbs-up sign.

The man looked at him confused. Realization soon graced the man's face, and he shook his head 'no.' He pointed to the picture again, looked at Ryan and shook his head "no" again.

No, nothing with his family...

The driver then placed a few fingers on Ryan's chin and guided his face to look forwards. The man pointed past the picture and through the front windshield, towards the sky. Ryan followed the angle of the man's finger.

Smoke.

Tons of billowing black smoke filled the sky a few miles away. Ryan could also see flames, just visible over the tops of the closer buildings, licking at the smoke.

"What happened?" Ryan looked pleadingly at the man.

Again the man made the same motion with his hands. Ryan's face paled… bomb. The man was trying to signal the motion of a bomb exploding.

"I sorry."

The man took one hand off the wheel and gripped Ryan's shoulder. Ryan dropped his gaze to the man's large hand as the man gave his shoulder a squeeze.

"Sorry?" Ryan questioned and returned his eyes slowly to the man's eyes. "Why are you stop…"

Ryan stopped and jolted his attention back to the sky. He traced the space between the car and the smoke and calculated the distance they had traveled. The realization physically pushed him back into his seat, wrapped its hands around his throat and started to choke him. He couldn't breathe. He started to panic.

The cab driver pulled over, but Ryan grabbed his shoulder over the seat before the man could exit the car.

"No, please keep going. Go!" Ryan gestured with his hand towards the smoke.

They sped through the streets back to the compound. They couldn't get very close. Police and emergency vehicles were blocking most of the street. The cab driver pulled up a few yards away and stopped the car. Ryan threw the door open and raced towards the gate.

Minus the gate and four feet of the high stone fence, three feet on the left and one foot on the right, everything else was enveloped by smoke. Only for a brief moment, here and there, could Ryan catch a glimpse of a burning building through the billowing inferno.

Ryan was running at top speed and was able to maneuver around three police cars and around a handful of officers without being impeded. Ryan turned to see them making chase. Unfortunately, it was at this moment a man stuck out his foot and tripped him. Ryan crashed to the ground.

The rocks on the pavement scraped his hands and tore a hole in the knee of his right pant leg. He had been running so fast that he wasn't able to adequately brace his fall and his left cheek slightly skidded along the dirt. He winced in pain.

Ryan was only able to rise a few inches before they were on top of him. One officer slammed his knee into the middle of Ryan's back and took hold of both his arms, pinning them behind his back. A second officer lightly pressed the sole of his shoe onto the side of his face, and a third had a hold of his feet.

Ryan's tears cut their way through the dust on his face.

"Get off of me! I have to see if they're all right," he sobbed as he strained against the officers.

Once the man had his hands cuffed behind his back, the other two backed off. They dragged him to his feet and slammed him, back first, into the door of a police car.

"Who are you?" an officer shouted at him.

"What are you doing?" screamed another.

Ryan answered their questions but never made eye contact. He couldn't take his eyes off the gate. It was ludicrous, but he was waiting for the Haringtons to run out.

Any moment now. Come on, guys. Any moment... Any moment now.

But no one came, everyone inside the compound was dead.

- - - - - - -

Everything had been destroyed: the trees, streets, stores, homes. It was all gone. The explosions had obliterated everything. Except for ash and rubble, there was nothing left.

Ryan sat stone still on the curb across the street, a cold, untouched coffee in his hands. The police had un-cuffed him and placed him there an hour ago, and he hadn't moved since. His body, numb to the chaos raging around him, just sat there in shock, eyes transfixed on the gate.

An officer approached him a while ago and explained what had happened. Ryan heard everything the man said, but he offered no nod, not even a change in expression. Shock imprisoned him. The man gave his condolences then moved onto another group to deliver the same message.

There had been four bombs, each encased in a white truck driven by a suicide bomber. They had been perfectly placed around the compound to ensure complete ruin. No one had stepped forward, as of yet, to claim responsibility and the list was long of those who disagreed with such compounds being in Saudi.

White trucks! White trucks!

Ryan kept repeating that fact again and again in his mind, each repetition cut deeply through him.

Most of the large fires had now been put out, but the compound still crackled with smoldering embers. Ryan's lungs burned from the smoke he had already inhaled, and that continued to swirl in the air. His face was still covered in dirt, and a bit of mud from where it had mixed with his tears. The scrape from his cheek had been bandaged, but it had stopped bleeding. If he had been able to register any feeling in his own body, the gash on his knee would have still stung considerably. Although with the gaping hole in his heart and his shock, he could have been missing a limb and he still wouldn't have noticed.

Ryan blinked and then blinked again. He heard someone crying, then sounds of footsteps running, people screaming, sirens. His surroundings were finally coming alive to him. He glanced around, truly seeing them for the first time.

Soldiers and police were running every which way, emergency workers were yelling back and forth as they worked, and blood... lots of blood. Even though the compound had been completely destroyed, the nearby buildings were only partly affected, and this had caused a lot of non-fatal injuries. Ryan realized he was sitting on the edge of the triage area. Women were sobbing. Men screamed as they held hurting, dying, or dead loved ones. Children wailed or remained still, as if comatose.

The wounded sat in groups awaiting treatment. The injuries varied, but it seemed to Ryan that most of them consisted of shrapnel gashes, burns or injuries from falling debris.

Two small eyes were looking at Ryan. Ryan looked back. She must have been only around four years old. Her head was laid softly in her mother's lap, and a slender hand stroked her dark curly hair. Ryan nodded a hello. She blinked slowly, and a slight smile pricked at the corner of her mouth. The child's eyes slowly closed and she drifted off to sleep. Ryan started to turn away but stopped. He noticed her legs, one was missing. Turning away quickly, Ryan vomited violently.

How could men do such terrible things to one another?

Ryan sat up and looked around once more at the horror that surrounded them all. He wiped his mouth with the back of his hand and took a deep breath to steady his nausea. He tried to keep his eyes away from the girl, but they returned.

The girl's mother sat, staring expressionlessly and continued to gently caress her daughter's hair. The girl was so small.

She shouldn't be here.

Ryan looked at her wound again. The leg didn't continue down past her knee. There was a crude tourniquet tied tightly around her thigh, but the gauze which covered the stump was already getting spotted with blood. Concerned, Ryan wondered if the medical team needed to be alerted. He urgently looked around. No one seemed available. Everyone was helping someone in worse shape than the little girl. Ryan didn't bother to flag them down, there would be no point. There were just too many wounded. His eyes slowly filled with tears as his mind and heart filled with despair and hopelessness.

Oh God, help us… help us all.

CHAPTER 24

Hailey rose silently off the floor then stopped. She surveyed the room to see if any eyes were made curious by her movements. Not one eye was on her. The women continued to dance and laugh. Everyone was immersed in their fun. Hailey's eyes looked at the door again.

It is less than twenty feet away. Could I make it? And if I do, what's on the other side? Is there a guard?

When Ehsan showed her around the house, she hadn't paid very close attention and quickly got turned around. The house was a mansion. She wondered if she'd be able to find her way out.

And even if I did get out the door and out of the house, where in the world would I go? Easy, Hailey, one step at a time.

She closed her eyes and bit her bottom lip to steady her nerves and muster up some courage. All she knew at this point was that she had to get out of there. She would just have to take it as it came.

She took one small step, then another. Keeping her back to the wall, she slowly made her way around the room, then around the bed. And yet still no one noticed her. As she passed the last corner of the bed, she carefully bent down to pick up her abaya and tucked it inside the bottom of her top at the back. A few more steps and she had the door handle in her hand behind her back. She went to turn it, holding her breath.

It turned! She continued twisting just enough, so the door released, fortunately without a sound. Hailey quickly opened the door and slipped, noiselessly out of the room and into the hall. She clenched the handle to keep it turned and braced the door with the other as she swung it closed behind her. As soon as the door touched the door-jamb, she eased her grip to allow the handle to turn back.

She glanced down the hallway, first to the right... empty. Then she looked to the left... empty. She finally released the breath she had been holding and tentatively jogged towards the staircase. She tiptoed down each step and hugged the wall as she went. All the while, she constantly scanned all directions to keep a lookout for anyone who might appear. She made it all the way down the stairs without a soul in sight.

Hailey slid along the carved, oak wall at the bottom of the stairs. Without slowing, she looked behind her before she reached the corner. Hailey wanted to give herself as much time as possible to run if she were spotted. Her head was still turned when she reached the corner.

The two women ran full into each other, sending a tray of teapots and cups crashing to the floor. They stood, unmoving and stunned for a moment.

"Ghada!"

Ghada didn't respond but grabbed Hailey's arm, opened the door of the nearby room and shoved her in. Hailey was about to protest when Ghada raised her finger to silence her.

"I will be right back." Ghada smiled a quick grin and left the room.

Hailey paced in front of the door like a large jungle cat at a zoo.

Shoot.

Hailey had just gotten out of one room only to be trapped in another, but she made no attempt to leave. She realized she, almost definitely, would need some help to get away. Yet being put in another room was disheartening nonetheless.

Hailey pressed her ear to the door and heard Ghada picking up the tray and tea items. A moment later the door opened, and Ghada slipped in and hurriedly closed the door behind her.

"I was hoping you would think to leave when you did. I've been trying to find ways to separate you from the others, but now you've done it yourself," Ghada whispered excitedly. "And I'm so glad because I wasn't able to think of anything."

"You... can help me then?"

"Of course. What Ehsan is doing is irrational and wrong. You are not meant to be his wife no matter what he says. But you must leave immediately. I heard some of the drivers talking and, the court official, the one who is to marry you, will be here soon. If you have any chance to get away, it would be now." She turned to go, but Hailey grabbed her arm.

Hailey looked deep into her eyes with as much gratitude as she could. "Thank you."

"You're welcome." She flashed Hailey a smile. "Come, we must go now."

Ghada took her hand and didn't let it go.

The women made their way, hand-in-hand, out the door and down the hall. They snaked their way around corners, through hallways and into rooms that connected to other rooms. It seemed like Ghada was a pro at getting around the house undetected. Hailey had no idea where they were in correlation to the front door, but she assumed Ghada wasn't headed there anyway. She kept silent and followed.

Finally, they went through a small, frosted glass door which led into a large pantry. Hailey heard voices and dishes clanging about as they scurried along the tile. They must be right next to the kitchen. At the end of the wall to the left was an open archway, through which the kitchen sounds emitted. A few feet past the archway was a thin wooden door, which was set into the wall at the end of the room. Next to the door was a tiny, four-pane window and Hailey could see trees through it.

Trees!

Hailey's heart soared. They were so close.

Ghada stopped. "Stay here a moment."

Ghada dropped Hailey's hand and peeked around the wall of the archway. Hailey heard a male voice address Ghada. As a precaution, Hailey hid behind a few large bags of onions and potatoes in case the man made his way into the pantry. Her heart raced. Ghada didn't glance back at her but kept walking casually around the wall, into the kitchen, and out of sight.

The man and Ghada talked for a moment, Ghada raised her voice slightly and then there was silence. Hailey stared at the section of the wall where she'd seen Ghada disappear.

Footsteps.

Hailey's eyes started to water as they remained unblinking, willing the spot to reveal Ghada and no one else. She held her breath, knowing she couldn't make a sound or move from that spot not matter what.

More footsteps.

Her thighs burned and protested under her weight, but she remained where she was. Hailey wished she could become smaller and crouch lower.

Ghada!

She came back around the corner, her voice showed her confusion. "Hailey?"

Hailey came out from her hiding place.

"We're safe to go. Come."

Ghada reached out her hand again, and Hailey took it. Ghada guided her past the archway. Hailey gave the kitchen a quick glance. It was empty. Relief flooded Hailey as they made their way to the wooden door.

The sun was incredibly warm on Hailey's face compared to the coolness of the house. She breathed in deeply, and although the hot air burned her lungs a bit, she welcomed it. There were two sets of large windows in her room, which she opened regularly. But it was nothing compared to having the outside surround her and feeling the earth under her feet.

Ghada guided her along the house and over to a small shed next to a large garage. They went in, and each took a seat: Hailey on two tires stacked on each other and Ghada on a large red paint can.

"The drivers are still in the garage washing off the cars. But they should be finished soon, and when they are, you can take one of the cars. Here are the keys." Ghada threw a set to Hailey.

"What? You aren't coming with me?" Hailey said after catching the keys.

Ghada looked stunned. "Come with you? Are you crazy? I…" Her words trailed off, and she paused. It was obvious the thought had never occurred to her. "How?"

"What do you mean how? You get in the car and come with me. We will work out the rest later. You don't want to stay here do you?"

"No… but I couldn't possibly. Could I?" Ghada's face was

painted with hope as she considered the possibility. Then she shook her head. "OK, yes! I will come with you."

Hailey watched as Ghada rose and went over to a small work bench. She bent down and grabbed a bag that was hidden behind jars of nails, bolts, and screws.

"I hid this bag here the other day," she said as she pulled some clothing from the bag. "I thought that if I ever managed to get you out of the house, then you could use these. I brought you an abaya for later, but I also took some clothing and a hat from Ehsan's closet for you to wear over it. We will draw less attention if it appears that a man is driving the car." Ghada glanced down at her clothes. "Oh, I will need to run back into the house and get my abaya. I will draw less attention if I am fully clothed. I assume you can drive?"

"Yeah, I can drive. But I can do more than that." Hailey smiled and withdrew her own abaya from behind her back.

Ghada beamed.

The women changed and waited. The sun started to set, but there was still plenty of light. The voices eventually grew fainter and then disappeared altogether.

"It sounds like they are finished. We can go now."

Ghada went first to make sure the coast was clear, and then Hailey joined her. Hailey pressed the unlock button on the key fob. The light on a tan Mercedes near the far wall flashed. They made their way over to it, passing a handful of other luxury cars that Hailey couldn't name. She imagined that their combined price tags were more than she would spend in her whole lifetime.

She hopped in the front, and Ghada took a seat in the back on the passenger side. Hailey started the car, and both held their breath as the engine jumped to life.

Hailey didn't hesitate, she couldn't risk someone having enough time to return to the garage to investigate. She threw the car into drive, pushed the garage button clipped to the leather sun visor and sped out as soon as the door was high enough to clear. She made a hard left but needed to compensate quickly to the right to avoid hitting a large copper fountain sitting in the middle of the driveway. After correcting her course, Hailey tried to take a few deep breaths to slow her racing heart but was interrupted by an awful sound.

When the car made the abrupt turn, the tires spun on the gravel causing hundreds of the small stones to be thrown into the air. Each piece of gravel ricocheted off of the side of the fountain with a loud ping. It sounded like someone was using soda cans for target practice. She looked in the mirror to check to see if Ghada was OK. Ghada's face held the same expression as Hailey's, shock and fear.

"Quick, take the driveway to the right."

Hailey obeyed and turned the car right as she came to the fork in the road.

"The left goes to the main gate. It is a quicker route out of the grounds, but I'm sure everyone is alerted now, and we can't chance it. We'll have to keep right now. We can follow it to the West gate. Daib was working on it today, so I think it will still be open."

It only took them a few minutes to loop around the garden to the side of the house. They soon saw that Ghada had been right. The gate was open. There was only one man in sight. He was sitting under a tree drinking some water. Hearing the car approach, the man lowered the bottle and looked towards them.

"But how are we going to make it past him?" Hailey agonized.

"Don't worry, Hailey. That's Daib. He is a very kind man, and he won't stop us."

Hailey thought she noticed a slight smile as Ghada spoke, but before she could ask more questions, Hailey had to return her attention back to the road.

The sight of the two of them reflected in Daib's stunned face would have made Hailey chuckle, were it not for the fear and adrenalin shooting through her. They drove past Daib, who merely raised his hand slightly to say goodbye. His eyes were sad, and he made no move to alert anyone or to intercept them. Again, thankfully, Ghada had been right.

Freedom was now just a mere fifty-or-so feet away. The gate was so close, and the main road lay just beyond that.

"Ghada we're almost there."

Hailey looked in the mirror once more to check on her new friend. Hailey could tell she was upset. Ghada's eyes were damp and pained.

Alarmed, Hailey questioned, "Ghada what's wrong?"

"No, everything is fine. I'm happy to be leaving this place. But…. there are some… some… things I will miss. Please don't slow down, I will be o…. HAILEY LOOK OUT!"

Hailey's eyes bolted forwards again to see a dark vehicle turning into the driveway. She turned the wheel sharply to avoid a collision. The tires screamed in protest. Hailey panicked and mistakenly slammed her foot on the gas instead of the brake. The car lurched forward in a burst of speed. The shock of the momentum slowed Hailey's reflexes, and she was unable to compensate quickly enough.

The car slammed into a large tree. Hailey was thrown forwards, and although she had her seatbelt on, her head made a hard impact with the steering wheel. Pain exploded all over her forehead, throughout her head, into her eyes, down her face, and into her neck. Her vision went dark, and she slumped back against the headrest with a hard thud.

CHAPTER 25

The wreckage of human lives that surrounded him added to his own sadness, and it was almost now entirely consuming him. Ryan had to do something, or he wouldn't be able to hold it together for much longer.

He did whatever he could to help those around him. He ran to find bandages and water and passed them out, assisted medical personnel in holding pressure on wounds, and consoled those who would let him. Ryan wasn't sure how many hours had passed.

After dusting off the dirt from his pants, Ryan stretched his hands over his head, made one more sweeping look around him, and took as deep of breath as the lingering smoke allowed. Lowering his hands, he moved to leave the area to find more to do. But soon stopped, as an officer approached.

"The area has been cleared. If you'd like to go inside, you're welcome to have a look around. But please walk carefully as the debris is very unstable. You must not, under any circumstance, remove anything from the scene. Once our investigation is complete, we will instruct you when you can return to your home and start sifting through your property. Do you understand?"

"Are there..." Ryan choked back tears which were threatening to break through again, "any survivors?"

"No, I'm sorry, it doesn't appear so. The explosions destroyed everything, and you shouldn't even hold out any hope of salvaging any personal belongings."

Ryan cleared his throat. "OK, thank you."

The man moved onto the next group of people standing a few feet away. Ryan didn't know if he should take the man up on his offer or continue to the airport. He made no attempt to move towards either option. He felt stuck.

On the one hand, his plane had long ago taken off. He would have to reschedule because once George had realized that Ryan hadn't made his flight, he most likely would have gone back to his office. There would probably be another flight later that day, but it was extremely unlikely George would still be there. So there was now no rush to get to the airport. Ryan looked towards the gate again.

On the other hand, heading into the rubble seemed so overwhelming that it terrified Ryan to take even one step forward. The ruins before him were all that was left of his second family, and he questioned if he'd even be able to face that truth right now.

Somewhere in the midst of his indecision, his foot made the choice for him, and it stepped off the curb. One step after another and soon he was gripping a piece of the twisted gate to steady himself. He was surprised when he got there. He hadn't consciously made the decision to go into the compound, but here he was.

Looking past the gate and down, what used to be, the road which led into the compound, brought new waves of shock. Everywhere Ryan looked there was nothing but debris. Ash, twisted metal, crumbling bricks, burnt wood, and broken glass were strewn everywhere and dripped with water.

He passed a family sitting on what had once been their front lawn. They were all huddled together holding each other and crying. He wondered if there had been someone left inside or had they all been fortunate to be out when the bombs went off.

There were numerous houses Ryan passed that had no sign of anyone mourning their loss. Ryan shuddered as he wondered how many bodies might lie underneath.

It took Ryan quite a while to wind his way through and make it over to where the Harington's house sat. He knew he was just a few yards away, but his vision was blocked. Some large chunks of a building that had once been the gas station across the street from their house were blocking his line of sight. As he scaled the debris and looked over towards their lot, he literally saw nothing. It seemed like an enormous dark hole in the earth had swallowed up the house.

Ryan stumbled backward from the devastation, and it caused him to lose his footing. His heel caught the edge of the rock, and he landed hard on his elbow. Blood trickled out and mixed with the dust covering his arm. Ryan made no attempt to cover the wound or stop the bleeding. He just sat there, leaning back on his hands, refusing to take his eyes off the sight that lay before him. Everything was gone.

The full reality of what he saw, stripped away the last bit of hope he had that they might still be alive. His body threw him forward as it was ravaged by heaves. There was nothing in his stomach to empty, but his body didn't seem to care. It was trying to rid itself of the pain and misery that was suffocating him. After his stomach had settled, Ryan sat and sobbed.

He knew there was no point in going any closer. The officer

couldn't have been more right in his case, there was absolutely nothing left, nothing to salvage. With understanding starting to sink in that his friends were gone and seeing that there would be nothing left to retrieve, he knew he wouldn't need to return later. There was also no point in staying here sitting on this mound of debris. His friends were dead, but Hailey still needed him.

He picked himself up and looked once more at the sight.

"Goodbye, my friends... I will miss you. Father, not that they are... worrying about such things, but let them know I'm... not... giving up. I will find her." His whisper through the tears was barely audible.

With that, he ripped off the sleeve of his t-shirt, tied it to the wound on his elbow and cautiously made his way back to the gate. He needed to get to the airport and track down George. He was his only lead and connection to Hailey.

=======

At the last minute, he had been summoned to the office. Generally, Ehsan wouldn't have been bothered by such a request, but today was different. He was looking forward to tonight, and it greatly upset Ehsan to have to go to work just hours before the court official was to arrive. Fortunately, he was able to sort out the dispute quickly and had only been gone an hour.

Ehsan was happy to be on his way home, and soon the frustration was gone. Tonight was what now consumed his thoughts. He was thrilled. In only a few hours he'd have a new wife.

The ceremony was just a small road bump, one he hardly

considered necessary as he already deemed her to be his. But he would patiently endure it.

His driver, Irfaan, slowly completed the last turn towards the house. They were almost at the gate.

"Ah... Councilman?" Irfaan interrupted his thoughts and pointed to the main entrance.

A dark town car had just pulled up to the house.

"Slow down!" Ehsan commanded.

Irfaan obeyed. Ehsan watched as the driver of the car jumped out and opened the back door, closest to the house. From inside the car, the court official emerged. Ehsan swore and shook his head.

"He's early."

Ehsan had already used all of his pull to find an official who'd perform such a ceremony, and he couldn't chance to let the official think he was coming home late. He couldn't afford to offend this man. The whole situation already rested on egg shells as it was, and so Ehsan would have to sneak into the house and be there to greet him. The end was so close, and he refused to let it slip through his fingers now.

"Quick! Go to the west gate."

Most of those involved were terrified of Ehsan, and so his word was truth. On the other hand, to those in his family that were still so traditional, he would have to put on a show. He'd have to be sure to demonstrate that this was a godly marriage and to do that, he would need a happy official.

Eshan turned around to see how close the official was to the house. Thankfully, it seemed he was still instructing his driver on what to do with his bags. The staff was all lined up on the steps ready to greet him, and the official would have to take the time to greet each one before entering the house.

Thank Allah for such pompous traditions.

Upon realizing that he'd still had time to get inside to make his greetings, Ehsan relaxed back into the seat. Yet, almost immediately, the sound of squealing tires filled the car. Ehsan was shocked when one of his Mercedes sped down the driveway and had to swerve to miss them. He had fired drivers for much less, and this driver would be no different. Ehsan was about to jump out of the car to flag the driver down and give him an earful when the car accelerated and smashed into a tree. His raged boiled.

Imbecile! That car was a gift from the king.

Ehsan bolted from the vehicle and stormed over to the driver's side door of the crashed car. He threw open the door. The man laid still, his head turned away from him. Ehsan bent down and ripped his hat off. Confusion gripped his face as locks of flowing hair were released from under the hat and drifted down over the driver's face and shoulders.

Ehsan was only frozen for a moment. He grabbed the driver and turned him over. The driver's head flopped over, and her face came into view. It was Hailey. Ehsan's attention was soon averted to the back seat as he heard the door open. A woman in an abaya was exiting the car on the opposite side from where he stood. She scrambled out and started to limp away from the car. Ehsan yelled at Irfaan to pursue her and then turned his attention back to Hailey.

Blood was seeping from a gash on her forehead and streaming down her face. Eshan removed his guthra from his head and pressed it against the wound. The blood immediately saturated the red and white cloth. As he waited to see if the pressure would stop the bleeding, he looked down at her. Compassion only graced his face for a moment until he took in the whole scene.

She was trying to get away?

He looked through the passenger window to see his driver dragging the woman back towards them. Fury replaced the last ounce of his compassion. Not only did his new bride try to escape, but there was also a member of his household who had helped her.

Ehsan removed the cloth and the blood, once again, flowed out. He gave Hailey a little push back into the car before turning away, her head flopped back away from him. He removed his cell phone and called up to the house. After a few rings, one of the staff answered. Ehsan sighed with thankfulness: it was Labeed. He was very compliant and followed orders impeccably.

"Get Maya to meet me immediately at the staff entrance. The others are not to be alerted, only directed to keep celebrating. Secondly, Instruct the kitchen staff to make sure that no one runs out of food or drink.

"As soon as the court official has finished his greetings, I want you to bring him into the sunroom in the east wing. He is to be offered everything that might potentially make him comfortable and happy. And I mean everything. He is only to be told that I am dealing with a crisis in the kitchen and that I will be along shortly. You must convey my deepest apologies. Lastly, get... oh... what is the name of that annoying kitchen girl? The one with the medical training?"

"Nia?"

"Yes, get Nia to get the medical kit and go to the guest room next to my office."

"As you wish."

Ehsan clicked off the phone. He turned back towards the woman struggling with Irfaan. She was kicking and yelling at him to let her go, and Irfaan was having difficulties to keep ahold of her. He went over to them and immediately the woman stopped fighting. She dropped her eyes to the ground, and Irfaan let go of her. She instantly fell to her knees and started kissing Ehsan's feet. Ehsan bent and raised her chin with one hand and used the other to rip off her veil.

"Ghada!" Ehsan made no attempt to hide his shock.

A fresh wave of anger shot through his chest, down his arm and out through his hand. He hit Ghada with such force that she went sprawling backward. Ghada coiled into a ball to protect herself, but Ehsan made no further advances towards her. Instead, with a haunting calm, he told Irfaan to take her into the house and lock her in her room.

"Of course," Irfann replied.

"Then return and put the car away. And get someone to help you clean... this up," Ehsan said as he gestured towards the wreckage.

It was then that Ehsan saw Daib standing by the gate, mouth agape. As Irfaan pulled Ghada to her feet, Ehsan motioned for Daib to come to him. Daib jogged over.

"Take Hailey into the house and lay her in the guest room next to my office. Be gentle and be sure not to speak to anyone. Nia will meet you there."

Daib nodded and bent to remove Hailey from the vehicle. She was still unconscious, and her head fell awkwardly back over his arm, but Daib readjusted, so her head rested on his chest.

Ehsan followed them to the house with clenched fists.

CHAPTER 26

He was now pacing back and forth in his office. Hailey was still unconscious in the guest room, and Ghada was sitting quietly in her room.

You fool!

Ehsan chided himself for thinking this day would continue down the path he'd initially thought it was headed. His original plan had been to show Hailey his firm hand and teach her to sit silently through the ceremony. But then when Maya had disobeyed him and revealed the truth to Hailey, she had seemed so compliant. It shocked him that there was no cries or protest of any kind from Hailey and so he, against his better judgment, took the easy path.

How could I be so foolish? I should have taken the precaution of being firm with her from the start, regardless of her response. Fear would have ensured something like this would never happen. How could I even think for a moment that this girl was anything like Saudi women?

Ehsan's rage built with each thought.

A wild horse, although appearing tame, will always run the first chance it has. Ehsan you know this. She doesn't know her place yet. She's a Westerner.

Ehsan then knew he needed to correct this mistake immediately. He checked his watch. Maya and Nia should be finished cleaning and bandaging Hailey up by now. He moved towards the door. As his hand clasped the gold handle, he hesitated. The anger that surged through him was threatening to overtake him.

Things felt as though they were crumbling around him and he wasn't a man that was used to being surrounded by things which were out of his control. Both of these women had to be taught a lesson. Each needed to be shown force to put them in their place, and it needed to happen before the ceremony.

He let go of the door handle as he realized he would need to get control of his emotions before proceeding. Ehsan went to the window and looked out. Seeing his land stretching out before him had in the past, helped to remind him that he was the master of this house. And thankfully, now was no different, he felt calm and strength return.

I can still set things right.

With that thought wrapped around him, he left the room.

Nia was leaning against the wall outside his door. She stiffened and stepped away from the wall as he closed the door behind him.

"Yes?"

Nia shakily delivered her report. "The girl is regaining consciousness, and her wounds seem relatively superficial. There is no need to bring her to the hospital. I stitched and bandaged the wound on her forehead. I gave her something for the pain, so she is a bit groggy. Someone will need to keep an eye on her, due to a possible concussion. Maya has returned to the guests. Is there anything else you need?"

"No no, that should be just fine. Go retrieve Ghada from her room and bring her into the guest room Hailey's in. Ghada can watch over her until the ceremony. But make sure she brings Hailey some new... appropriate clothes."

Ehsan shuddered again as he thought of Hailey in his clothes. He dismissed Nia without a glance, just a wave of his hand. Ehsan then made his way to the guest room.

After unlocking the door, he quietly slipped into the room. The lights were off, and there was minimal daylight slipping through the curtains. Hailey was lying on the bed, moaning and moving slightly.

Ehsan made his way around the bed and took a seat on a chair set in the far corner. He braced his head on his right hand. His thumb supported his chin and his finger frame the side of his face. His eyes narrowed, not to avoid bright light, but in anger. He sat there motionless.

After a few minutes, Ghada entered the room carrying a small bag. She gently closed the door and then rushed over to the bed.

"Oh Hailey, I'm so sorry. I'm so, so sorry. Does it hurt? Can you open your eyes?"

Ghada never even looked towards Ehsan, so he remained silent. She was completely unaware of his presence.

Slowly Hailey raised her eyelids. "What...," she coughed, "happened?"

"We crashed, and we're back at the house. Ehsan is furious. I should have never assisted you, let alone gone with you. Compared to how we've now affected things, your life would have been much easier if we just obeyed. I'm so sorry."

Hailey cleared her throat. "No, it's not your fault. I would have just gone on alone. What do you think he will do to us?"

Ehsan smiled to himself. It was quite enjoyable watching this exchange without their knowledge of his presence. His hand was starting to cramp a bit, but he didn't dare readjust in case they noticed the small movement. He persisted with keeping still and continued to listen as he remained hidden in the shadows.

"He should be coming any time now, but… please do whatever he says. Keep your eyes to the ground and be as submissive as you possibly can. Ehsan has a great temper, and the last time he was disobeyed like this…" Ghada sniffled. "Well…" she struggled to continue.

"Ghada, what? Tell me!"

"All I will say is that it is why he now only has two wives and now wants to marry you."

"Ehsan had three wives? Ghada you need to tell me. Where is she?" The fear in Hailey's voice seemed to add more darkness to the room.

"Ehsan killed her," Ghada blurted out in a sob.

"What?"

Ghada regained her composure and explained. "Her name was Fareefta. She was only sixteen when Ehsan married her. She was a sweet girl, but her beauty betrayed her. Ehsan had a business partner that took notice of her. And as a favor to him, Ehsan allowed Fareefta to share her bed one night with the man. He was passing through on a business trip. Afterward, Fareefta's spark was gone. She was an empty shell of a once wonderful, full of life, young girl. After a few months, Fareefta's withdrawal changed, and anger replaced every empty corner of her soul. She was patient and dedicated to getting her revenge. She worked hard and finally found five men who would testify with her."

"Wait, what? Why?"

"You see, in Saudi if a woman is going to accuse a man of rape, she needs four or five men to testify with her. The courts do not take a woman at her word. But when the men were summoned to give their accounts, they changed their minds. Fareefta was then charged with prostitution, and it was left to Ehsan to choose the punishment."

"He's a monster." Hailey's disgust coated each word.

Ehsan's body tightened, but he remained in control and stayed silent.

Hailey continued. "But why didn't anyone stop him? That has to be illegal, even here."

"Not at all. Fareefta belonged to Ehsan. The punishment wasn't done in secret and even had an audience of several Mutawa, our religious police."

"Yes... I'm... familiar with them."

"Ehsan made an example of her and forced many of us to stand and watch. He made it clear that if anyone looked away, there would be a punishment waiting for us as well. Hailey, it was the most terrifying day of my whole life. Fareefta was dressed in a white gown, her head uncovered. They no longer looked at her as something to protect or value, just an item that needed to be disposed of. Ehsan slowly walked her over to the large tree in the center of the west garden, and we all followed. Fareefta didn't even fight or protest, but then neither did any of us.

"Everything seemed to go in slow motion. Ehsan pulled out a small handgun from this black case one of the Mutawa were carrying, and simultaneously Fareefta kneeled. The crack of the gun jolted my soul. It haunts my dreams and some nights I still feel it shake my insides. It seemed like it took an eternity until she stopped twitching. They all stood quietly. I whimpered until Ehsan turned and led the way back to the house."

"So... are you saying that he's going to kill us?" Hailey's

voice was trembling with fear, and it saddened Ehsan to hear his young bride be so afraid.

"Oh my dear, how wrong you are," Ehsan said as he rose and came out of the shadows.

This caused both women to shriek from shock.

"Ehsan, I'm sorry. Forgive me, forgive me." Ghada backpedaled off the bed. She came around to him and sank to his feet. She started kissing his feet and asking him for mercy.

"Child," he bent towards Ghada, "your actions today are inexcusable. I've given you a good life. You have never gone without anything and to pay me back with such disobedience and disrespect will have consequences. But I will address that in a moment. For now, go sit in the chair."

Ghada complied.

He returned his attention back to Hailey who had sat up and was now cowering in the farthest corner of the bed from where he stood. He slowly rounded the bed and sat next to her. She recoiled but remained where she was.

Ehsan leaned over to turn on the bedside lamp. It filled the room with a soft glow. He reached his hand towards her and stroked her cheek. There was a large bruise forming, and she winced slightly at his touch.

"I'm sorry you were hurt. How are you feeling?" He said compassionately.

"Fine!" Her curt reply stung and Ehsan wished she would look at him.

"The ways of my country must confuse you greatly. I want you to know that I'm a respected, God-fearing man. I won't deny that I have a strong hand, but I wish for you to also know my compassion. I am willing to overlook these events on one condition."

Hailey slowly turned her eyes to him.

"You must sit through the rest of the evening completely silent. If one word escapes your lips, then your punishment will be reinstated and carried out swiftly. Do you understand?"

"What is it?" Her voice quivered in fear.

"What is what? Your punishment?" Ehsan chuckled to himself.

Even now she shows her boldness. She really is my wild horse.

"I've just come to learn that a woman's empathy is much greater than her fear for herself. This is a tool, which I now see, is a better teacher. With the situation with Fareefta, I used fear to be a lesson to my house and, thanks to Ghada, I see that it did have the desired result I had hoped for."

He turned and smiled at Ghada who was sitting still, her eyes to the floor. Ehsan looked back at Hailey, she had lowered her head and was looking at her hands. He raised his hand to elevate Hailey's chin and forced her to look at Ghada as well. She tried to fight his grip but soon gave up.

"For example, take Ghada. I could again solely punish her for her transgression. She would be corrected, and the house would once again be reminded that I'm the head of this house. However, if I punish someone she cares for…"

Ghada's head shot up, dread and tears filled her eyes. As soon as Ghada made eye contact with him, she dropped her gaze again to the floor.

Ehsan continued. "…not only will those things never happen again, but another reminder will not be needed later on. Unlike a lesson in fear from the punishment of self that wears off, fear of the punishment of another… will never fade."

Ehsan dropped his hand from Hailey's chin and turned back to face her.

"One might choose to rebel if it is only their self they have to worry about. They... weigh the risk. However, if it is someone else who will be on the receiving end of that punishment... well, now what woman could ever choose that? So, my dear, you were wondering what your punishment would be? The better question is who will be receiving that punishment? And the answer to that... is Ghada."

Ehsan let his words sink in for a few moments before he spoke again.

"Now then, the ceremony is only an hour away, and I must go meet the official. Ghada, I assume that bag contains Hailey's clothes?"

"Yes, Ehsan."

"After she's changed, take Hailey back to her room. Both of you are to celebrate with the guests. Hailey, you are to keep a khimar on for the rest of the night. I'm in no mood to explain your cuts and bruises. Do you both understand?"

He looked between the two until they both nodded.

"Good. Ghada we will discuss your insolence later."

Ehsan rose off the bed and moved towards the door, but he paused and turned back to them.

"You both should feel honored. Many women would do anything to be a part of my house. I've chosen you, and nothing will ever change that."

CHAPTER 27

The Riyadh airport was insanely crowded. It seemed like there were thousands of people moving about. Ryan had a difficult time picking his way through the crowd after exiting his gate, but after ten frustrating minutes, he finally found his way to a wall of pay phones.

Diving into his bag, he retrieved George's number. Ryan deposited the correct coins into the slot, punched in the numbers, and waited for the phone to connect. Two foreign ring tones sounded in his ear. The phone clicked, and an Arab voice came on the line, said a short sentence, and then the phone clicked off. Ryan couldn't make out any of the words in the short sentence, but it was evident that it was a recorded message. Ryan tried again and had the same outcome.

Frustrated, Ryan motioned the phone towards a man standing off to his right.

"Help?" Ryan pleaded.

The man nodded and took the receiver. Ryan deposited more coins and dialed the number. He held his breath as the man listened.

"Uh, sorry, bad... number." The man said as he handed the phone back to Ryan.

"OK, thank you." Ryan tried to steady his voice, but he felt deflated.

He replaced the receiver and slumped away.

This can't be happening. If I don't have George's number, where in the world do I go from here?

Ryan slowly moved back through the crowd. He felt so crushed and lost. Hailey was still out there somewhere. Looking around him at all the people moving past, his chest started to constrict. A slight sweat broke out on his forehead, and he began to feel dizzy. Ryan walked over to the far wall.

Ryan realized he should call Norah and give her an update, but he couldn't bring himself to walk back over to the pay phones. He knew his resolve would betray him and he just couldn't handle talking about Anna. Not yet. Scenes from the compound bombarded him, and panic was threatening to take over. He leaned his forehead against the wall and closed his eyes.

Do not fear, I'm with you, even until the end of the age.

The reassurance calmed him. After a few more deep breaths, the fear cleared, and Ryan raised his head.

If God is still guiding me, then there must be a way to keep going.

Ryan pushed off the wall and, after getting some directions from one of the airport staff, he made his way to the security office.

It was a lot farther than the one at the Dammam airport. He had to go outside and around a large part of the airport, but he soon found it. It was a huge office attached to the airport, not just a desk like at the Dammam airport.

Ryan entered through the front doors. Inside, on his right, were a set of glass doors and a set of metal ones to his left. He took a spot in the line which was in front of a long counter straight ahead of him. The line moved painstakingly slow, but Ryan tried to keep his mind engaged with people watching.

There was a lot of foot traffic in the office. Officers, Mutawa, detainees, and civilians, all bustled about. The busiest part of the room was the glass doors. It was here that Ryan's attention was most directed. Not more than five minutes passed between the doors opening and closing. At the moment a man was being led through by two officers. He was in handcuffs and was being forcefully escorted through the middle of the office, between the line and the front doors. The man looked scared and pulled against the officers' grip.

Ryan was so engaged he didn't notice that someone was speaking to him. There was so much Arabic in the room, and it all seemed to blend together in his ears.

"Excuse me, sir? Can I help you?"

The English words broke through the din in the room and pulled Ryan's attention away from the detained man. Ryan turned to look. It had been more than an hour of waiting but noticed he finally was at the front of the line.

"Oh, sorry. Yes." Ryan approached the counter. "I'm looking for a friend of mine, and I'm hoping to find someone here to help me track her down. She flew into this airport but never made it onto her connecting flight to Dammam."

The officer was nodding along while making a few notes on the notepad sitting on the desk in front of him.

Ryan continued. "Her name is Hailey Pearson, and she flew in from Germany just over two weeks ago. Is there someone I can talk to?"

The officer stiffened, stopped writing, and looked at him.

"I sorry, no English. Come back tomorrow." The officer looked over Ryan's shoulder and motioned for the next in line.

"Wait, please anything you can tell me now would be a big help. Is there anyone else I can talk to?" Ryan pleaded.

"No, no one here speak English." The officer raised his voice. "Now go, come back tomorrow."

Everyone in the office was now looking at him. Ryan glanced around quickly and saw a tall guard standing by the glass doors taking a few steps forward, his hand moving to rest on his gun.

Not wanting to cause more of a scene, Ryan nodded his apology to the man at the desk and removed himself from the line. Frustrated, he walked back towards the door. Ryan peered over his shoulder towards the guard and saw that he was no longer near the doors but was now making his way after Ryan.

Ryan, not wanting to instigate a chase, slowed his pace and allowed the guard to reach him.

"I'm sorry, do we have a problem here?" The officer's voice thundered loudly.

"No sir, I'm leaving."

The man's English was clear, but Ryan didn't want to make matters worse and press him for answers about Hailey. He would just have to come back tomorrow if he couldn't reach George. He gave the same nod of apology to the guard and moved to leave. The guard grabbed his arm.

"I think I should escort you out to make sure there isn't a problem."

Ryan complied and didn't object or pull away. With his heart racing, he fell in step with the guard.

As they reached the exit doors, the tall guard leaned down and whispered in his ear, "Go to the Mutawa holding office, northeast of here."

Before Ryan could question his directions, the guard pushed him through the doors and moved back inside. Out in the hot afternoon sun, Ryan stood there stunned. He doubted if he had heard the guard correctly.

If I did, then Hailey must have run into trouble with the Mutawa. Maybe she was still at their holding office? Could they have kept her there so long?

Hope filled his heart and Ryan jogged back around to the front of the airport to the line of waiting taxis.

CHAPTER 28

Hailey understood little of what was happening. After Ghada had escorted her back to her room, she sat silently on the same pillow, while the others continued to celebrate. No one offered any explanation or even talked with her, so she just sat and watched with little interest.

After a while, all the women quieted down. They rose off the floor, and Haffafa came over and pulled Hailey to her feet. All the women ushered her out of the room, down the stairs and into the sunroom.

Ehsan was standing in the middle of the room in front of an old man in flowing robes. Ehsan was dressed in what Hailey guessed was traditional groom's attire. Hailey numbly allowed Haffafa to guide her to her spot. All the women left the room, leaving the three of them there. Soon four other men entered and, once they had made a small circle around them, the old man started talking.

The next hour was full of tradition and different ceremonies. Hailey never spoke and only nodded when someone looked at her. She never knew if they were just looking or if they were actually waiting for a response from her, so she nodded every time just to be sure. Hailey wanted to cry out or run, anything to get away from what was being forced upon her. But Ehsan's threat to punish Ghada was like duct tape over her mouth and a lead weight to her feet. And so she stayed silent, sat when Ehsan sat, and stood when he stood.

After the old man had stopped talking, Ehsan led her to the sitting room on the main floor. The other men followed. There was another handful of men already sitting around the room when they got there. Hailey recognized a few from the day she arrived, but the rest were strangers. They started celebrating with Ehsan.

Hailey thought the whole thing was similar to a bachelor party back home. She felt so awkward being there, as she was the only woman in the room. But again, fear kept her sitting on the small chair that Ehsan had led her to.

Hailey had no idea how much time had passed, but eventually, the men finished singing and eating. Ehsan came back over to collect her and then led her to the sitting room on the second floor. There all the women were gathered. A similar celebration took place to what had occurred in Hailey's room before she was led down to the sunroom. Hailey paid little attention to any of it and mostly just stared at the henna designs on her hands.

After the party had died down, Ehsan led Hailey out of the room. As soon as the sounds of the voices from the guests trailed off as they made their way down the hall, Hailey burst into tears. Her body started shaking. She tried to stop it, but the more she fought for control, the more she lost it. Ehsan used both his arms to support her as he guided her down the hall.

"Shhh, my young, wild mare. Once you are tame, you will come to see that things aren't as bad as you think. I bet you will even start to enjoy all the comforts and luxuries that I bestow on my wives. Some, I would imagine, are beyond anything you could have even dreamt."

Ehsan led her to the end of the hall to a staircase. When they reached the top floor, they continued down another hallway until they came to a large, wooden double door. He opened them and showed her in.

It was a large bedroom, twice, maybe three times the size of the one Hailey had been staying in. There was a kingsize bed in the middle of the far wall. The wall was completely comprised of windows. Heavy, black velvet drapes with gold embroidered, paisley designs hung down each side. A large, double-sided, electric fireplace crackled on the left wall: one side faced the bed and the other side faced into the bathroom. Apart from the fire, the only light in the room was coming from a thin floor lamp beside the bed. Large paintings and wall sconces adorned the walls. The floor was thickly carpeted and had smaller rugs placed around the room: under the bed, under the large sitting area and in front of the fireplace.

Ehsan rounded Hailey and went over to the fire. The flames lowered as he turned a small dial on the wall. He turned back. His face was slightly in shadow, but she could see a small smile on his face. He started at her, unmoving.

Hailey wished she could melt into a puddle and be soaked up by the fibers in the carpet. Anything to escape his gaze, anything to avoid what might take place in the next few moments. Hailey lowered her eyes to the floor. She couldn't bear to look at him. Hailey's mind was reeling with how she could possible escape, but each plan was met with thoughts of Ghada. There was no doubt that Hailey's safety was at stake here, but with the threat of Ghada's punishment looming over her, she continued to remain frozen where she was.

Ehsan moved towards her, and her heart raced faster and faster with each step he made. Hailey closed her eyes. She couldn't watch him. She tried to retreat into her mind, but the crackling of the fire filled her ears and kept her present. It sounded like a wild clock ticking off beat.

Once he reached her, each of his movements removed a piece of clothing and yet she didn't feel completely naked. As each piece hit the floor, it was replaced with layer upon layer of fear. After she was completely covered with fear, she was led to the bed.

The black sheets were cool against her bare skin. She cringed and willed her body to comply, yet she questioned if it would it be even possible for her not to fight back.

How is this happening? Ghada I'm so sorry. How am I supposed to do this?

After Ehsan had laid her on the bed, he left her side and walked slowly over to the lamp, clicked it off, and then moved to a chair beside the fireplace. In the flickering light from the fire, she could see he was relishing every movement.

Resting over the back of the chair was a large red blanket and, after Ehsan had retrieved it, he leaned forward towards the fireplace. Hailey hadn't focused on it before, but on the wall was a small handle next to the fireplace. Ehsan pulled it towards himself. The black top of the fireplace, which led up to the ceiling, pulled back to uncover a high, glass enclosure. Instantly, a warm, soft light emulated from it. The light seemed to be coming from the glass itself and faintly illuminated the room. The light had the opposite effect on Ehsan's face. In contrast to the room, now that the light was coming from behind him, it encased him in darkness.

Hailey could no longer see his features and, as he advanced

towards her, she felt her mind scream out for someone to help her. Surprisingly no sound exited her lips. Her mind and her body, her very being, was screaming at her to protest, but she remained still, lying exactly where Ehsan had placed her.

When Ehsan knees touched the footboard, he swept the blanket above the bed. It floated towards her as if in slow motion. As it covered her face, she tried to remain still, but it only increased the feeling of being trapped. When the feeling grew beyond what she could handle, she slowly raised her arms and slid the blanket down past her chin. Ehsan by then had moved to her right and was slowly undressing. Hailey turned her face away, towards the wall and squeezed her eyes shut.

The pain and loneliness she felt were threatening her resolve to not bolt for the door. As Ehsan raised one side of the red blanket, she felt his weight lower the far side of the bed as he climbed in beside her. Her mind screamed again.

Help me, someone, please. I can't do this.

Ehsan's hand pressed softly onto her bare, right shoulder and slid down her arm, pricking her skin with revulsion and disgust. Hailey squeezed her eyes tighter and kept her head turned away. She could smell his cologne mixing with his sweat and a slight aroma that lingered from the cigar he'd smoked early. The smell made her stomach sway.

His hand moved back up her arm and then moved to grip her left shoulder and slowly pressed down. He gradually pulled to turn her towards himself. As his face was just coming into view, he stopped.

CHAPTER 29

Ryan reached the Mutawa holding office and, after paying the cab driver, he entered the brick building and went over to a long oval desk.

"Excuse me, do you speak English?" Ryan spoke slowly to the man who sat behind the desk.

"Yes, how may I help you?" His English was clear.

"I am looking for a friend of mine. I think she may have been arrested at the airport and brought here. Is there anyone I can ask about her?"

"Please go through those glass doors," he gestured to a set of frosted doors beyond his desk. "There are chairs just beyond those doors where you can wait. I will let someone know you are here."

"Thank you."

If Ryan was honest, he was quite shocked. He was actually getting somewhere. He followed the directions and sat on one of the five small wooden chairs.

There was activity everywhere he looked, not unlike the inside of a bee hive. He sat there watching, elbows on his knees, hands clasped. He glanced at his watch again, ten minutes had passed. He leaned back. Maybe this wouldn't be as easy as he had hoped.

After another half hour, he stretched and looked back towards the frosted doors. He was going batty sitting there.

Maybe they forgot about me.

Ryan rose, made his way through the frosted doors and returned to the guy at the front desk to question why there was such a delay.

"My apologies sir, insha'Allah Bakora." The man returned to some papers on his desk.

"Wait, I'm sorry I don't know what that means."

"Oh pardon me. It means 'tomorrow, God willing.'" Again the man returned to the papers.

Ryan made sure to choose his tone and words carefully. "I don't mean to be a bother. But please... she's been missing for over two weeks. Is there any way someone could see me now?"

"No, I'm sorry, insha'Allah Bakora." The man gave him a quick smile and went back to his work.

Ryan didn't want to make any enemies here until he got some answers, so he thanked the man and turned to leave. He would have to find a hotel for the night and return in the morning. Irritated, Ryan exiting the building.

The bright desert sun hit his eyes, and he immediately squeezed them shut. He didn't see the small woman about to enter the building.

She practically bounced off him and fell backward. Luckily she wasn't alone, and the man at her side reached out and caught her arm, keeping her upright. Ryan blinked a few times to adjust his eyes and finally focused on the couple.

"I'm so sorry. I'm so sorry."

The small woman's eyes were the size of saucers, but a huge smile soon ran across her face from ear-to-ear.

"No bad done. You OK?"

"Yes, of course, I'm fine. The sun hit my eyes, and I didn't see you. I'm so sorry."

"Don't worry my friend. My wife... tough girl." The man said as he flashed a smile to his wife.

"You American?" The woman's voice was sweet and her accent thick, as was her husband's, but Ryan could still understand them both.

"Yes, I'm from New York."

"Why you here? You in trouble?" concern was in the man's eyes as he pointed to the building behind him.

"No, I'm... here for a friend."

"We here for our son. Sweet boy but in trouble because of our choices." A tinge of regret held onto the woman's words.

The man raised his hand to Ryan's shoulder. "You eat yet?"

Ryan realized he hadn't eaten much that day.

Only breakfast actually... breakfast with the Haringtons.

"Um... no." Ryan cleared his throat and continued before his mind had the chance to go any further down that path. "I actually haven't eaten since breakfast."

"You too skinny. Come, we eat."

The little man had him by the hand and was towing Ryan across the street before he could protest.

They spent the next two hours at a small café across the street, telling each other their stories, and eating. The thought of sitting in his hotel room until the next day did not excite Ryan, so he was thankful for the short distraction.

Their names were Zaara & Zayan, and they had two children: a son and a daughter. They seemed to be a very happy family. However, the story that brought them to the office that day was tragic. The husband had lost his job a few years ago, and so they had gone to work for a wealthy family in the heart of the city. Unfortunately, the master of the house had taken a liking to their daughter when she turned fifteen and asked for her to be given to him in marriage as his fourth wife. When Zayan politely refused, the man punished them all by kicking them out. And if that wasn't enough, he accused their son of stealing some jewelry when they left.

Zayan explained that an accusation like that was trouble enough for anyone, but that it was even more so in their son's case. When their boy was little, he had been caught stealing an apple from a market vendor. They were thankful the court had just given them a warning at the time, but this would now be his second offense. It would not be overlooked.

The Mutawa were now holding him for a few days until the court sent over the paperwork to process a ruling. Zaara & Zayan were at the holding office to visit him. As the couple talked, he saw they were trying to remain positive, but Ryan could see they were scared about what their son's ruling would be.

"I'm so sorry about your son." Ryan's voice dripped with sympathy.

"Thank you!" Zaara bowed her head as she replied. "Now, now... tell us about your friend."

After Ryan had told his story, it was indecipherable which of them was more shocked.

"That so sad. When you go back tomorrow, ask for Ahmed. He big man of the office. He know everything that happen at office."

Zaara nodded emphatically as she listened to her husband speak.

"If your friend there, he know. If not, he know where she

might be."

Ryan thanked them for everything, and after they had finished their meal, they parted ways. The couple headed back across the street to see their son, while Ryan asked the server to call him a cab.

Ryan's heart ached as he walked over to the waiting cab. He had left out the part about what happened to Anna and her family from his story. He wasn't ready to talk about it with anyone. But now the pushed aside facts raged back into his mind. He clenched his jaw during the entire ride to the hotel to keep his composure.

- - - - - - -

When Ryan woke the next day, he was stiff from sleeping on the unfamiliar mattress. He gingerly got up. As he stood, he hoped he would get something more than just a brush off when he went back to the Mutawa office. He showered, dressed and headed out the door. Hopefully, this Ahmed would be there and would agree to see him.

The same man from yesterday sat behind the desk. He looked up as Ryan approached, but his smile fell a bit when he recognized him.

"Can I please speak to Ahmed please?"

The man was taken back and wrinkled his brow in confusion. "Let me… check if he's available. What is your name?"

"Ryan Foster."

"And who is it that you are missing?"

"Hailey Pearson."

The man picked up the phone, pushed a button, and spoke for a couple minutes. Ryan stood still and held his breath. The man hung up the phone, nodded to him, picked up the phone again, pushed another button, and spoke for another few moments. Upon replacing the receiver on the base, the man shot him a forced smile.

"Yes, he will be out in a moment. You can go have a seat," the man dismissively waved him towards the glass doors, "in the same place."

"Thank you."

Ryan took a seat on the same wooden chair and again watched the busyness of the office. A few glass-encased offices lined the two far walls, with a few cubicle type desks in the middle of the room. Ryan was scanning the glass offices when he noticed a set of eyes watching him from the far corner office.

He was a tall man with a goatee and was dressed as a military officer. His arms were folded across his chest, and his eyes were squinted. The man was obviously assessing Ryan and made no attempt to try and hide it. Ryan felt uncomfortable under the weight of his stare, so he averted his eyes and continued scanning the rest of the offices. It was clear that the man had seen Ryan looking at him, but Ryan tried to casually look around as though he didn't.

"Excuse me, Mr. Foster?" The deep voice came from right next to Ryan, and it startled him.

"Yes, are you Ahmed?"

"Yes, please come with me."

Ryan followed the man to the largest office, which was on the opposite wall from where he had sat. Ahmed then proceeded to explain to him that Hailey had in fact been there two weeks ago, but that he couldn't release any information as Ryan was not an immediate relative.

"So by immediate, you mean that only a father, mother or

sibling can ask about her? Ryan was trying to keep the panic from his voice, but it peeked through.

"Yes, exactly. I'm sorry Mr. Foster, but we can't help you."

"But her family is dead, and the only family she has left is an aunt." Ryan was scrambling. "Couldn't she request the information?"

"Unfortunately that won't suffice. Would you by any chance have any of her documentation with you?"

"Like what?"

"Her visa, her passport, or anything to substantiate why she is in my country?"

It was evident by the man's tone that he was getting impatient, but Ryan didn't care.

"No, she should've had all that with her. The friends she was going to stay with while she was here had her sponsor papers all arranged for her before she came. And I know she would never have traveled without them... or her passport."

"Do you have their contact information? Someone I can call to confirm her purpose for being in Saudi?" Ahmed readjusted himself in his seat. "I would like to help, but we have a protocol I must follow. I'm sure you can understand that."

Ryan put his head in his hands.

"They're all dead." Ryan's whisper was faint.

The response must not have reached the man's ears, that or he didn't care. But either way, it seemed Ahmed had had enough.

"I'm sorry, but I can't help you. As I told your friend when she was here, my hands are tied. I would suggest talking with security at the airport, maybe they can help you. Or maybe the American Embassy. However, the Embassy might be a bit overrun at the moment. We have had some... security issues arise yesterday."

Yeah, no kidding. Ryan thought to himself.

Ryan was furious. Here was a man sitting just a few feet from him that knew where Hailey was and had even talked to her. Ryan wanted to go over to him and beat it out of him. As his anger level rose so did he, and quickly. He knocked his chair to the floor. With clenched fists, he started to move toward the man.

Be still and know that I am God

Ryan knew better than to fight against the reminder. He stopped advancing, just as the man was about to call out for assistance.

"I'm sorry to have bothered you," Ryan hissed between clenched teeth.

Ryan couldn't believe it, but his feet started to leave the room. It made no sense to move, but with each step he took, he began to understand and calm down. God had a different plan and using force against one of the officers was obviously not it.

Once outside Ahmed's office, Ryan once again looked around. He squinted to his right, towards the corner office. The goateed man was no longer in the doorway but seated at his desk. He was immersed in his work and was no longer paying any attention to the rest of the room.

Seek Me first, and all these things will be added unto you

Feeling compelled to question the man who had been staring at him, Ryan moved towards the man's office. He had no idea what he would say once he reached the door, but he kept walking.

Just breathe.

Ryan couldn't begin to fathom where this could possibly lead, but he wasn't going to pause and question it. All that lay on the other side of this act of obedience belonged to God. The past had taught him that. He had experienced many times how one simple act of obedience could open up the door to God doing incredible things. And so, again… now… in this instance, he would choose to obey. He took another deep breath to steady himself as he got closer.

As Ryan came into the doorway, the man raised his eye to meet him.

"Mr. Foster, I assume?"

Ryan was a little thrown. "Um, yes."

"Please sit." The man gestured to the padded wooden chair opposite him. "I know why you're here and I may be able to help you. My name is Faisal."

CHAPTER 30

Hailey was surprised to wake up to the sun pouring in through the open curtains. With the unbelievable fear and confusion that gripped her last night, she hadn't expected herself to fall asleep. Yet here she was rubbing her eyes and rising off the bed. To Hailey's relief, Ehsan hadn't returned to the room that night.

Even before her feet hit the floor, her body was chiding her for the decision to get up. Running the car into that tree had obviously done a number on her, and her muscles were screaming at her to keep still. She chose not to heed to them and continued making her way gradually to the bathroom.

She flicked the light on and looked at the ghastly reflection staring back at her. There was a long cut on her right cheek, bruising from a black eye forming around her left eye and her hair was extremely matted. The paleness of her skin was haunting.

Yikes, I look awful!

She lightly touched the bandage the woman had put on her forehead, but the pain from it caused her to wince. She dropped her hand and let it be. She splashed some water on her face and brushed her hair. After replacing the brush back on the side of the sink, she stared at herself again.

There was barely any emotion in her eyes, apart from confusion. She wasn't shocked at seeing that particular expression staring back at her. Last night played out completely differently than what she had been dreading. None of it made any sense.

Her mind naturally went into replay mode.

- - - - - - -

As he was turning her over to face him, she saw Ehsan's smile, and it chilled her to her bones. She started shaking. He began to shift his weight towards her, but in an instant, he stopped. His smile fell, and his face scrunched into an angry glare.

Ehsan dropped hold of her shoulder, rolled away from her, swung his legs over the side of the bed and sat up. He paused only for a moment before he stood, grabbed his clothes, got dressed and walked over to her side of the bed.

Hailey was so confused about what was happening, she didn't divert her eyes or try to move. Ehsan just stood there looking at her. Then in one swift swoop, his hand flew from his side and connected with the side of her face. Ehsan always wore a big ring, and it united painfully with her cheekbone. With her head still resting on the bed it had no place to recoil, and so she felt the full force of the impact. She yelped and withdrew away from him to the far, top corner of the bed.

Ehsan made no further advances towards her. With the same speed as he had approached her, he left the room.

- - - - - - -

The present came back into view.

So now here she was, alone in his room, standing in complete silence in his bathroom. She had no idea what to do, so she remained at the sink staring at her gloomy image.

A small tear fell from her left eye, rolled itself down her cheek, curved down her mouth and paused on her chin before releasing and falling. As it hit her hand, which was gripping the sink, it took her attention away from her reflection. She looked down at her hand and watched the little tear roll down towards the far side of her hand and onto the edge of the porcelain sink, where it rested, unmoving.

The sight of the tear, for some reason, caused the confusion to be pushed back. It allowed a feeling of utter defeat to engross her. Hailey breathed out a shaky sigh. She felt so lost and, apart from the fear of Ehsan's return looming over her, she felt completely numb and cold.

Hailey!

"What?" Hailey whispered slowly.

It had been a long time since she had even allowed herself to listen to that quiet voice. Usually, her anger would push it away, but she was exhausted and terrified, and so surprisingly, she didn't resist.

Where do you have left to run?

More tears gathered in her eyes.

"Nowhere."

I have never left you, nor forsaken you.

"Yes, you have. What about my family? You left me all alone." Her defeated, pained voice echoed slightly off the cold tiled walls.

Did I?

"Yeah, you did. My life was perfect, and you took it all away.

You destroyed it. And now you've allowed all these things to happen to me. Where's your so called love, your protection?"

It's been here all along. It's been the driving force for all that I've allowed you to choose and endure. Open your eyes, Hailey.

Hailey hadn't realized she had closed them and so she slowly opened them. Her reflection was gone. Steam now covered the massive mirror. She raised her hand to wipe it off but hesitated. There was movement in the mirror.

Beyond the steaminess on the mirror there was something moving, shimmering. Hailey strained her eyes to see past the steam to try and make out what she was seeing. She questioned if her eyes were playing tricks on her or it was actually happening. She then saw something move in the top left corner of the mirror.

The steam was being wiped away, and a word formed: *HOSEA*. There was a slight pause, and then a number *two* took shape.

Hailey's mind flooded with memories of learning about this part of the bible in high school. She remembered thinking how stupid it sounded for God to command Hosea to marry a prostitute: *Sure God was trying to show Israel that they had gone away from Him and were now running after false gods, but couldn't God have just left poor Hosea alone and got their attention a different way? Even if it was destroying them, He could have used something else.*

There was more movement on the mirror and Hailey continued to watch as word after word was written into the steam. She pulled away for a moment to rub her eyes. When she looked back, the image before her remained. The whole second chapter of Hosea actually was being written into the steam on the mirror.

As her eyes passed over each section, individual scenes from her own life started to unfold in her mind. He was calling her attention to specific verses and then to specific parts of her life.

She recognized each event, each moment, as it was shown to her. However, there was a profound difference from that of a typical memory. The perspective wasn't through her own eyes or through her emotions: it was through God's. It was hard to explain, yet undeniable.

> Verse 5: "For she said, 'I will go after my lovers, who give me my food and my water, my wool and my linen, my olive oil and my drink.'"

She saw a mosaic of flashing images: In the first image her mother was standing at the sink singing, and she saw her younger self run into the room to tell her mom about something. In the second image, she was in the center of a group of teens from school talking about how to be a "good Christian." They were all looking at her with envy, and she savored it.

> Verse 8: "She has not acknowledged that I was the one who gave her the grain, the new wine and oil, who lavished on her the silver and gold,"

Then a third scene came. It was more complex, and it confused her. She was standing by three girls. But she was purple - from head to toe - purple. Likewise, the other three were the exact same shade. She soon turned and walked away from them.

A few feet from the purple girls were three other girls. They were orange. As Hailey approached them a trail of blue fell from her and left her a soft red color. As she got closer, some yellow seeped off the others, enveloped her, and turned her orange. She now matched their particular shade. It was like reverse color blending done by children in elementary school.

Before Hailey could question it, all three scenes started merging together, like photograph negatives being placed one on top of the other.

Her eyes continued reading.

> Verse 13: "... but me she forgot, says the Lord."

Hailey then saw the pride she was feeling in each scene personify, increase, detach from her, grow wings, and soar above the three images. It was then Hailey noticed Jesus standing next to her in each of the scenes. Witnessing the pain on His face almost destroyed her right at that moment.

Her mind was then flooded with other scenes: scenes of herself ignoring the hurts of people around her in exchange for social status, or for comfort and scenes of her chasing after crushes and popularity.

The scene when she got news of her family as she was lying in the hospital came into view. She saw Him holding out His arms to her, but she spit in His face and turned away. Then scenes from a trip she took to Europe after high school grabbed her attention. These filled her with shame and made her blush with regret. She dropped her head as a sickening feeling filled her middle.

After a few moments, the feeling passed, and she returned her eyes to the mirror.

> Verse 6 & 7: "Therefore I will block her path with thornbushes; I will wall her in so that she cannot find her way. She will chase after her lovers but not catch them; she will

280

look for them but not find them."

Hailey then saw Jeremy standing there in a suit, looking handsome. His eyes pierced her soul.

Verse 10: "... no one will take her from out of my hands."

She saw herself start running after Jeremy, but without making any movement of his own, he moved farther and farther from her, like he was being pulled away.

Again and again, her eyes were led from one passage to another and then her mind was directed, correspondingly, to a moment in her life. The anguish she experienced compounded with each realization. It soon became too much, and she diverted her eyes from the mirror.

Her heart whispered softly, "So it was you who caused all these terrible things? You were punishing me?"

Hailey, it's your choice to turn away in anger at this moment and go back to the path that you've been on all these years. But first, I request that you honestly ask yourself – how has your life gone so far?

"If the accident never happened, everything would have turned out fine." She didn't attempt to hide her anger.

You may think your life was perfect before your family died, but you've actually just been hiding behind that. Then when things ended with Jeremy, you used that as something else to hide behind. If you look at your life from start to finish, you'll see.

His words escorted her mind to the time before the accident. The realization of who she was before the accident floored her. Her pride had been running rampant since she was little and her need for acceptance had grown insatiable. In truth, she had always been frightened, terrified of rejection.

It was so clear to her now what the scene of her changing color was about. She had become a chameleon to such a degree, she barely knew who she was anymore. She, herself remained "red" which signified that she still kept a few parts of herself intact. But she adapted and added everyone else's "color." Each one of her choices was delicately calculated to ensure acceptance and to manipulate everything, so she remained in control.

Slowly, Hailey allowed the Lord to turn her mind from the memory and her eyes back to the words He was writing on the mirror.

> **Verse 14:** "Therefore I am now going to allure her; I will lead her into the wilderness and speak tenderly to her. There I will give her back her vineyards, and will make the Valley of Trouble a door of hope."
>
> **Verse 18-21:** "Bow and sword I will abolish from the land, so that all may lie down in safety. I will betroth you to me forever; I will betroth you in righteousness and justice in love and compassion. I will betroth you in faithfulness, and you will acknowledge the Lord. In that day I will respond,"
>
> **Verse 23:** "I will plant her for myself in the land; I will show my love to the one I called 'Not my loved one. I will say to those called 'Not my people, 'You are my People'; and they will say, 'You are my God,'"

As soon as Hailey's eyes read that last word, the mirror cleared and now she only saw her reflection. For a moment she just stood there blinking with shock. She was taken aback with disbelief by what she had just witnessed. After a moment, she took in all that had just happened, and further understanding seeped in. From the very start, she had been so similar to Hosea's wife, Gomer.

With her pale face staring back at her, she shook her head at herself. She now saw her life as a whole. Her faith had not been a way to communicate with, learn about, honor and love her creator. It was a free pass into a club where she found acceptance. It became a way to relate to others, to keep control of her life, and to manipulate circumstances, so criticism and rejection never came to her. She was just like Gomer.

Gomer had had a husband at home who would give her the love she desperately longed for. But instead, she had run after love in the embrace of many arms. Likewise, Hailey had run after acceptance and self-preservation, instead of finding rest in the arms of the One who had created her, the One who had sacrificed everything to rescue her and to draw her to Himself. She had stolen control from the only rightful owner of it.

Hailey?

"Yes?" She answered hesitantly.

She felt unsure of how He felt about her. With the blinders of self-pity and pride now stripped away, the weight of the truth about her past weighed heavily on her.

You have always been incredibly petrified that someone might reject or judge you. To keep that from happening, you do one of two things. You either push them away and run or you strive to attain perfection. The first, leaves you feeling isolated and unacceptable. The latter is an impossible task. This type of perfection is elusive because it's undefinable. You will never reach it, and when you fail to do so, you are only left with fear and shame. You feel like you're not enough and are unlovable.

Hailey felt exposed and scared. She dropped her chin to her chest, it was too much to keep looking at herself.

Hailey, you have never truly believed this, but when I look at you, I see you as pure. Right from the moment you returned to Me and gave Me your life on that rainy day while sitting on your bed when you were ten, and up to this moment. I washed all the sins away: past, present, and future sins. My son meant it when He said 'it is finished.'

Hailey raised her head and looked in the mirror again. "Really?"

Before the foundations of the world, I knew you. I rescued you back and now... now I see what I first created.

The idea of what He was saying sounded so fantastic. As a teenager, there were many times she heard people reading things like this from the Bible, but she had never allowed herself to get too close to it. Her doubt and her lack of measuring up to others had kept her back.

"So... what do I do now?"

My definition of perfection, for My children, is to stop striving, to know Me, and be truly known. You have been living so long believing lies, lies about who you are and about who I am. I want to teach you how to renew your mind so that you can see truth. This is a process, and it is done on a journey that is only possible when it's walked with Me. The journey I call each of My children to walk is as unique as each person who chooses to walk with Me, yet the requirement is the same for all My children.

"What is that?"

Faith!

"But... but my faith is so weak."

Many think fear is the opposite of faith, but it's not.

Mistrust is the opposite of faith. I can do unimaginable things with even a small amount of trust. So I want to ask you, Hailey will you trust me with that room?

The strange question startled Hailey. "What room?"

In your life, you have built up this beautiful house. This house is who you portray yourself to be to the world. You allow others in and give them tours and even used to invite Me in sporadically. However, there is one room you keep hidden. You don't show that part of yourself to anyone. It is locked up tight and taped off. What lies behind that door... terrifies you to such an extent that not even you enter it.

The blood drained from Hailey's face. The panic rising in her chest was causing the room to tilt. She grabbed the sides of the sink again to steady herself.

"But I can't let you in there. What if, when the door opens, everything in there comes out and destroys everything? What if I can't get it to go back in?"

Even so, will you trust me with it?

"How can I decide that when I'm trapped in a place like this?"

I have allowed you to come to Saudi... to enter this 'Valley of Trouble' because it is your 'door of hope.' I have bigger plans for it. You need to choose this day whom you will follow.

Hailey turned away from the mirror, slowly walked back to the bed, and perched on its edge. Everything He had said to her rolled around in her mind. A quote from Einstein she heard in one of her English classes came to her mind: "The definition of insanity is doing the same thing again and again and expecting different results."

Hasn't that been what I've been doing this whole time, the same actions again and again, the same thoughts again and again?

Hailey felt so exhausted. Not just the exhaustion she felt building from all that had happened to her since she left home but from years of regret.

If there is even a small possibility that He could be trusted, is it worth letting go of everything?

Hailey scanned the whole room, panning each wall, each piece of furniture. Then slowly she lowered herself to the floor. The carpet was soft on her knees as she sat on her calves. She leaned forward and rested her forehead on the carpet. Tucking her hands around her middle, she grabbed her elbows with each opposite hand and hugged them close to her herself.

All the walls of her self-preservation crumbled at that moment, tears of pain gushed violently through each crack. The façade was gone. Every wound and hurt she'd experienced or caused, every regret, each feeling of guilt, all her fear-ridden choices, and every moment of shame she had clung to... they all broke through the control that had held her together for so long. She acknowledged and repented for each one.

Hailey paused. She realized she was in very unfamiliar territory. Without her façade, she felt dangerously unprotected. That small, locked room was the only thing that remained. She sat there unmoving, dreading to move any further.

Will you trust Me?

Hailey's hesitation only lasted a moment more when she realized all her resolve was gone.

"Yes. I will trust You. You can go in."

There was another pause.

Fear started to crawl back across the floor towards her. Hailey held her breath. Just before it had its hands around her again, in poured His power. His forgiveness and grace met her, it flooded in and engulfed her. He hemmed her in and protected her.

And after a lifetime of sorrows and fear, Hailey felt peace and hope. She had no idea what was down the road. Usually, this would terrify her, but at this moment her soul relaxed as she rested entirely in His hands.

Hailey rolled over onto her side and rested her cheek on the floor. She sighed, closed her eyes and slept.

CHAPTER 31

A smile crept across Faisal's face as he scanned the man in front of him. Ryan was tall, well built, and if Faisal was honest, a bit intimidating. Faisal didn't let that derail him. He knew he was the one coming from the place of power and that was all that mattered.

During the couple days when Hailey was here, Faisal had tried to make it back to her, but he was averted every time. Then when the choice was made to transfer the girl without his authorization, Faisal had been furious.

He knew she couldn't remain in his office forever, but the realization that he wouldn't get another moment with her frustrated him to no end. It had been two weeks since she had left and still, he lay awake at night thinking about her.

Faisal gestured again for the man to take a seat across from him.

"But even though I know why you're here, why don't you tell me the whole story." Faisal leaned back into his chair and folded his hands in his lap to listen.

"Well… on April 29th, about two and a half weeks ago, a friend of mine…"

"Hailey Pearson, correct?"

"Yes, yes that's right. She left the States and came to Saudi. She was supposed to transfer in Riyadh and catch a connecting flight to Dammam. We have..." Ryan paused, a brief sadness flashed in his eyes, "... had friends who lived in a compound there."

He paused again and cleared his throat.

"You see she wasn't supposed to leave so early, but she decided it would be fun to surprise them. That's why I only found out she was missing after a full two weeks had gone by. I've talked to everyone I can think of, but no one will help me. This is as far as I've gotten. I know she was here in this very building, but I'm at a dead end if I can't find someone to help."

Ryan looked at him with pleading eyes. As soon as Faisal saw the hopeful, yet desperate look in the man's eyes, he knew he had him. Ryan would be an easy target.

"Oh, no! Were your friends in the compound bombing yesterday?"

He didn't need to wait for a response, the look in Ryan's eyes confirmed it.

"I'm so sorry. I want to assure you, everything is being done to find those responsible. The Palace is furious, and everyone that is available has been tasked with finding and punishing those who are to blame."

"Thank you for the reassurance. But honestly... I have to keep all of that in the back of my mind right now. If Hailey's in trouble, I need to keep my focus on finding her. You..."

Faisal could hear the frustration in Ryan's voice rise.

"... you said you could help with Hailey?"

"Yes, well... this is a very, how would you say... temperamental situation." Faisal chose his words carefully.

Just as Faisal was about to continue with his plan, someone

walked past his office. Faisal glanced from the door to Ryan and back again. He realized that this was not the place to discuss this. To avoid raising suspicion, he continued talking, making a point to raise his voice just a bit to keep it natural.

"You see, we have a lot of protocol in our country and even though we want to assist you…" Faisal pulled a sheet of paper from his drawer and a pen from the holder on his desk, "…I'm sad to say it, but our hands are tied."

Faisal saw Ryan's eyes narrow with confusion and anger. Faisal made no attempt to explain. He kept talking about procedures and red tape as he continued writing. After he had raised the pen from the page, he folded the paper and looked at Ryan.

"I'm sorry, but I can't help you."

Faisal handed the paper to Ryan. Faisal looked down at the paper Ryan was holding and smiled at Ryan when he looked back up with raised eyebrows. Ryan looked a little stunned, but it was obvious he got the message – don't talk, leave and read it later.

Faisal rounded the desk as he gestured for Ryan to get up.

"I hope you find what you're looking for," he said while shaking Ryan's hand.

After Ryan had disappeared through the frosted doors, Faisal returned to his desk. Turning around he opened the filing cabinet and reached in and took out Hailey's passport. Resting his elbows on his knees, Ryan leaned forward, being careful to keep his back to the door. He gazed at her face.

"Well my beauty, it was a pity we never got to continue from where we left off, but… I will cut my losses for now. At least I'll benefit a little from our meeting." His whisper was barely audible.

Faisal leaned back into his chair, keeping Hailey's passport in his hands. He needed to get rid of all her papers and soon. It would be much too incriminating if he were caught with them. Yet, thankfully, it was Saturday so he would still have a bit more time. He would have to try and make a copy of her picture to keep as a memento before then.

Replacing the passport back in the drawer, he smiled. He was happiest when there was a plan or a plot in the works. And as things came back under his control, it felt like silk running over his soul. He relished the feeling.

=======

Things were different; Hailey was different. Her heart still feared what might be in store for her, but at the same time, she felt safe. It was quite a contradictory sensation.

The whole morning passed with no sign of Ehsan. The door was locked. She had already tried it twice. As she sat on the bed, she looked around. She soon realized that she couldn't just sit and wait. She would lose her mind wondering when he would return.

Hailey stood up and tightened the knot on her robe. She then made the bed. She wasn't sure why, it wasn't like it mattered, but at least it was something to do, and it helped to keep her hands busy. She looked around again. There were no books, no paper to possibly use for doodling, nothing.

Well, now what? Ooooh, a shower!

Hailey headed to the bathroom. She held her breath as she looked on the back of the handle for a lock.

Yes!

She locked the door before dropping her robe.

The hot shower stung her cuts, but it soothed her aching muscles. With nothing else to do, she stayed under the water until her body was too tired to keep standing. She needed to rest so, reluctantly, she turned the taps off.

As she was drying herself while coming back into the bedroom, she noticed a folded piece of paper sitting under the door. She walked across the room to retrieve it.

Hailey,

Make no mistake, the fault of my quick departure last night lies with you. You displeased me, and I had to remove myself. I was planning on returning to you this morning, but sadly, I have been summoned to go to Dammam, a city to the East. It was an urgent matter and one I, regrettably, could not put off.

I instructed Nia to give you this letter, and she is now waiting outside the door. Once you are ready, knock on the door. She will check your injuries and bring you back to your own room. Breakfast will be there waiting for you.

Now that you are my wife, you are free to roam throughout the house. You are not, however, permitted to leave the house alone. I have assigned Daib to be your driver for now. I will hire you a permanent one when I return.

In Saudi, women aren't permitted to travel far without papers signed by their husbands, giving them permission to do so.

So, seeing how you have no papers of your own, I know you will be smart and stay close to home.

Make no mistake, upon my return, you will be corrected for my departure last night. In the meantime, I want you to plan out how you are to alter yourself and your behavior, so you don't displease me again.

I know you won't make any trouble for anyone in my house when I'm away... Ghada thanks you for that.

I hope to be back by the end of next week.

Proud you are mine,

Ehsan

Hailey let the letter tumble from her fingers and drift to the floor. She raised her eyes to the door.

At that moment she knew this would be her window to escape, maybe her only one. She couldn't stay and wait to find out what Ehsan's punishment involved or what her life here might consist of. Hailey shuddered as a few ideas crept to the edge of her mind.

Wait! What about Ghada? I can't leave without her. But what if she's too scared to try again?

Have faith!

Hailey blew out a long breath to steady herself.

Right! Stop and let go. I can do this. He'll take care of that.

She took a few more deep breaths. It would take everything in her not to bolt for the stairs as soon as Nia opened the door. She knew this escape would need to be planned out, not spontaneously like her previous attempt.

293

Hailey got dressed and knocked on the door.

"I'm ready."

She heard the keys in the lock.

You have no idea just how ready I am.

=======

Ryan shook his head as he slammed the door open and stepped outside. The conversation he had with that man, Faisal, was so infuriating. Faisal was all over the place. First, he surprised Ryan by knowing his name, and he made it seem like he could help. Then, Faisal asked him to tell the whole story, only to say then that he couldn't help.

He clutched the note in his hand as he jogged across the street to the café.

This note better be worth it.

Ryan sat down at one of the outdoor tables and carefully unfolded the note. His eyes made quick work of the words.

Yup, it was worth it.

The man was obviously not a good man, his extortion was evidence of that. However, at this point, Ryan didn't care what kind of character or integrity the man had. If Faisal could help him find Hailey, he didn't care how much money it took.

The weekend would be painful to endure, but by mid next week, he should have enough information to help track her down.

CHAPTER 32

The weekend was filled with plans. Hailey had already familiarized herself with the layout of the whole house, the names, and schedules of all the staff, as well as taken quite a few trips out of the house with Daib. The plan of escape was coming together nicely.

Hailey was thankful Ehsan had assigned Daib to be her driver. The other men in the house frightened her, and she never would have had the guts to do half of what she needed to with them near.

The only negative was that Daib had been instructed by Ehsan to only drive her to markets, clothing and food stores. He was also told to keep her from speaking too long to any one person. Be that as it may, Hailey had made the most of the length of leash she was given.

She took drives around the property and ventured into the city to explore. All the while asking question after question to Daib.

"Where does this road lead?"

"How much money am I allowed for purchases when we go shopping?"

"Do you have family out of town? How long does it take to

get to the airport to pick them up?"

"Do you feel safe in the markets? If you had someone harass you there, would it take long for help to come... like... how far are we from the nearest police station?"

Hailey, of course, didn't make these questions too obvious. She was careful to casually slip them in amongst normal conversation. Daib was sweet and answered them all. And if he was at all suspicious, he didn't show it. Hailey soon saw why Ghada liked him.

Hailey knew Ghada trusted Daib, but she couldn't be certain about his feelings about her being in the house. And she couldn't be confident about his loyalty to Ehsan over a foreigner. It was for this reason Hailey was very careful not to push the boundaries too far with him. She couldn't risk Daib revoking her privileges, or locking her in her room, or worse, calling Ehsan to alert him.

Hailey had hoped she would be able to plot with Ghada, but she hadn't seen her all weekend.

She questioned Daib about it when they went to the market Monday morning.

"She's in England visiting her daughter. All of Ehsan's children go to a private boarding school in England. Ghada goes up once a month to visit her."

Hailey was shocked, and worry started to burn the edges of her plan.

"Do you... know when she'll be back?" Hailey said, trying to sound casual.

"She should be back late this afternoon."

Hailey breathed a sigh of relief and leaned her head on the seat's headrest. She couldn't possibly leave without Ghada.

- - - - - - -

While walking around the market, she had overheard one of the street vendors talking to a group of tourists. Hailey moved in closer so she could listen. The man was telling them about a small tour company that chartered adventure excursions to Westerners.

Hailey couldn't believe it. She had worked out most of her plan already, but crossing the border had still been a bit of question mark.

After the tourists had moved on, Hailey scanned for Daib. He was at the next stall looking at some gold watches. She hurriedly seized her chance. She grabbed a small rug from among the many items the vendor was selling and approached him.

"Oh, I give you a good price for that," the man said has he gestured to the rug in her arms.

"I'm not interested in the rug, but please listen."

The man's confusion showed all over his face. Hailey quickly continued in the hope of changing his expression so Daib wouldn't notice and come over to assist her.

"I'm in trouble, but please keep motioning to the rug as though we are bartering. I will pay you for your time."

"Yes, yes of course."

Thankfully the man picked up her cues and mimicked her motions towards the rug. They silently acted out a common market interaction, giving Hailey the opportunity to talk to the man.

"A friend and I need to get out of Saudi quietly without alerting the authorities or my driver. I heard you talking about that travel company. Do you think they could help me?"

"Yes, yes. The owner is my brother. What kind of trouble are you in?" The man looked over her shoulder towards Daib.

Hailey dropped the rug she was holding and picked up another to get his attention back to her.

"Please, you can't keep looking at him." Hailey's heart raced. "I can't get into explaining, I don't have time. But is it possible to see if there are any openings on one of those trips? I can pay your brother whatever he wants.

"Yes, yes. I call him right away. I know he find something."

"That would be amazing. Thank you."

Hailey looked over, Daib had left the watch stall and was heading their way.

"I need to go now, but in about an hour I will return to your stall."

The man raised his hand just as she was about to turn away. Hailey paused.

"You OK?" There was genuine empathy pouring off of the man, but he soon remembered to cover it with more gestures to keep up their little charade.

"I will be."

- - - - - - -

Upon returning to the man's stall in the market, Hailey learned that his brother had come through in surprising ways.

Within that hour they had found a spot on one of their tours. The bus would pass through that area on Thursday as it continued its circuit around Saudi to Jordan, then onto Egypt. The whole trip sounded a bit wild to Hailey, but she didn't care. It didn't matter what she would be doing or where it was going, as long as it helped get her closer to home and away from Ehsan.

Hailey wasn't given the details, but the man's brother had

even arranged a way to avoid the passport check at the border. She was given directions to the tour company and was told to go there tomorrow where a package would be waiting for her. It would contain everything she would need.

It seemed like God really was going before her, and with no way of contacting Anna, this would most likely be her only chance to get out of Saudi.

- - - - - - -

Hailey collapsed on her bed after removing her abaya. She was hot and sweaty and should have jumped right into the shower, but she was exhausted. Even with the reprieve of the air conditioning in the car, the heat had drained most of her energy while she walked around the market. She had time before Ghada got home, so she curled up on the bed to wait.

Unintentionally, she soon drifted off.

> ...He was after her. She tried to run, but it seemed like her feet were treading through invisible wet concrete. She tried to scream. No sound came out; her voice was gone...

Hailey shot awake. Her body was shaking. Relief finally broke through her panic when she realized it was just a dream. She laid back down until her breathing slowed and her heart relaxed back into a normal rhythm.

I can't wait to get out of here.

She took a quick shower, then headed down to the kitchen to find a bit of rice. Her stomach couldn't handle anything heavier.

It was late in the afternoon by the time she returned to her room. There was still no sign of Ghada. Upon closing and locking the door behind her, Hailey bent down at the edge of her bed. She retrieved the papers she had safely tucked under the mattress and spread them out on the bed. Seeing the whole plan laid before her was a bit overwhelming.

How am I supposed to make this all work?

I know the plans I have for you. As you walk, you will hear my voice. I will tell you which way you should go.

The words were like balm to her troubled spirit.

A knock. Then another.

Both caused Hailey to jump. She froze and listened.

"Hailey?"

"Ghada?"

A thrill surged through Hailey.

"Are you alone?" Hailey questioned.

"Yes, can I come in?"

"Yeah, just a sec."

Hailey threw a thin blanket over the bed and ran to the door, cracked it a bit, then opened it just enough for Ghada to slip through. Hailey closed the door and threw her arms around her friend.

"I'm so glad you're back."

Ghada returned the hug and then pulled back and scanned Hailey head to toe.

"I'm so sorry I wasn't here. Are you alright? Did he hurt you? Oh, that's a foolish thing to ask, of course, he did. Are you OK?"

Hailey chuckled. "Actually… I'm alright. I'm… actually more than alright. Nothing happened. It was the strangest thing. God… saved me. Oh and I'm getting out of here. Actually… we are getting out of here and soon."

"Wait, wait. God? Maya said you didn't believe in God. And

what are you talking about... getting out of here? Are you mad?"

"No." Hailey chuckled again. "You won't believe what happened to me." Hailey continued and told her friend about what had happened.

"You say you have spoken to God? How is that possible? Allah does not speak directly to creation. You... actually heard him?" Ghada's disbelief was evident.

"No, Ghada I was not speaking with Allah. I was talking to God. I don't say that disrespectfully. I was talking with the God of the Bible, the God of my mother, God the Father, Son and Spirit. And... well not exactly in the way you're thinking. It wasn't audible or anything like that. I know people who have, but it wasn't like that."

Hailey paused to slow her voice, which was gushing with excitement.

"I guess the only way I could describe it is to compare it to how a blind person "sees." A blind person can't see with their eyes. But if they use their hands and trace a person's face then they can "see" what the person looks like. That is what it's like when I talk with God. I don't hear His voice with my ears, my soul and heart feel His words. And He also spoke to me through the scripture He showed me. It was incredible."

"If what you say is true... what do you think God wants you to do now?"

"Leave this place. And you have to come with me. I have it all here, the whole plan."

Hailey led Ghada over to the bed and removed the blanket.

"See?"

Ghada spent a few minutes scanning all the pages and asking a few questions.

"Hailey, this is incredible... but I'm sorry. Since our last attempt, I realized how foolish I was to think I could go with you. My daughter is coming home after her studies in a few years. I can't leave. My place is here with her, and there is no way to arrange for her to be safe if I leave."

Both women stood there silent for a moment. Hailey felt sick to think of Ghada not coming with her. She grabbed her friend and pulled her into a tight hug. They both clung onto each other tightly and wept as the full awareness of the situation hit them.

"I get that you... can't leave... your daughter." Hailey sniffed. "But how am I supposed to... to leave without you? Or do this without you? What if... Ehsan's hurts you?"

"Hailey, this isn't my path." Ghada pulled back and held both of Hailey's shoulders. She gave them a little shake. "Don't worry about me. Sure he will be upset, but I know he won't do anything drastic. Especially if you leave. It would mean that he would only have Maya left. It's a source of pride for Ehsan to have more than one wife. There is no way he would... I mean... I know you're scared because of what he did to Fareefta, but he did that because she shamed him publicly."

"How can you be sure?" Hailey interjected.

"I know it sounds distorted, but he does love me. I will be all right."

Ghada pulled Hailey towards her. They hugged and continued to cry together.

- - - - - - -

After their tears had dried up, they remained in Hailey's room, talking. Ghada was fascinated with all Hailey was saying about her God and Hailey was happy to share everything she knew about Him.

The whole evening was bittersweet. There was an indescribable joy as Ghada's curiosity bubbled over, but there was also a looming sadness as their impending goodbye drew closer.

"I'm so glad to have met you," Ghada said. "With you leaving... yes it does take a dear friend away from me. But please know, you are not leaving me the same. I am very interested in learning more about your God, and I will seek for Him... as you have been saying. If I do find Him and He has the power you speak of, then I no longer need to fear Ehsan.

"This idea that life is more than the physical is fascinating. If Ehsan only has control over my physical world, then my daughter and I will be able to survive. You have left me with a curious and intriguing gift." Ghada paused for a moment, kissed Hailey on the cheek, and rose off the floor from where they had been sitting. "For the first time, I look at my path with something other than fear and sadness. It isn't your path to remain here. So you go when it's time, and I know you will find your freedom."

Hailey allowed Ghada to help her to her feet and walked with her over to the door.

"I will miss you Ghada."

The two friends hugged each other once more and, as more tears fell down each of their cheeks, a small bit of peace fell over them.

CHAPTER 33

When the Monday sun poured through the open window of Ryan's hotel room, his eyes shot open, and his feet were on the floor a split second later. He was hoping the banks would be open early. He desperately wanted to get the money as soon as possible so he could meet Faisal that afternoon.

The meeting was set for three o'clock, but Ryan assumed the transfer would take a while to go through and he didn't want to be late. Faisal had written down the name of a large bank in the center of town, and as soon as Ryan was ready, he headed downstairs to find a cab.

After he was tucked into the back seat and had instructed the driver, Ryan sat and nervously played with the small piece of paper in his hand as the car snaked through town.

The bank wasn't much different from other big banks Ryan had been to around the world. Aside from the differently dressed men and woman coming in and out, it looked familiar. He swiftly mounted the five steps that led up to the large gold metal doors, pulled them open and went inside.

Commonly, a guard was posted in such a large bank back home. However here, an armed officer was standing slightly to the side. He was in the same fatigues as the men at the airport and the holding office and was also holding an assault rifle. He eyed everyone who entered.

All these little differences were constant reminders to Ryan of how far he actually was from home. He nodded to the officer as he passed.

Ryan approached the counter, and he hoped this exchange with Faisal would finally be the road that led to the end of his search. Once Ryan had the information Faisal was holding hostage, so hopefully, he wouldn't run into any more roadblocks or detours.

Three hours later, Ryan unhurriedly came back down the five steps outside the bank. Tears threatening to break through. The transfer would take at least a day or two.

Reaching the sidewalk, he paused and raked his fingers through his hair.

What if Faisal wouldn't wait? What if he asked for more money and then Ryan would have to wait another few days for the difference to come through? What if....

Remain in Me. I will draw near to you.

The soft words reminded him just how little control he had. He allowed peace to take hold and he ignored all the other 'what ifs' that were vying for his attention.

Shaking off the worry, Ryan stepped to the edge of the street to catch a cab. He decided to go back to his room and wait until it was time to leave for the park where the meeting was being held.

I hope he's OK rescheduling.

- - - - - - -

The meeting with Faisal was less than pleasant. Faisal had

been irritated that Ryan didn't have the money. However, after a long sigh through pursed lips, Faisal agreed to hold onto her papers until the following day.

As Ryan watched Faisal leave the park, he prayed the bank wouldn't delay the transfer any longer. The only thing he could do now was trust, wait and return to the bank tomorrow to see how this played out.

Ryan remained in the park for a few hours. Mostly he just strolled along the paths which wound past rock gardens and patches of trees, sand, and bushes. Momentarily, he would pause to watch families playing, businessmen on their phones or groups of veiled women huddled together chatting.

He felt so small. Even though Ryan understood that none of this was in his control, it was during these times of waiting in which that truth seemed to smother him. The heat wasn't helping.

He crossed the street and approached a small vendor selling delicious, spiced-smelling food. He bought a bottle of water and returned to the park. He found a small bench in the shade of a large tree, where he sat and slowly drank the water. As he felt the cold liquid falling down his throat and through the center of the chest, he relaxed.

It will be three weeks tomorrow since Hailey left.

He started to chuckle with disbelief at how ridiculous all this was as he replayed the last few weeks in his mind.

He still didn't have any confirmation that she was OK or even alive for that matter, but regardless, he felt this crazy, barely containable drive to continue to look for her. It wasn't a desperate, frantic urging to track her down but a calm compulsion that seemed to flow through his veins.

He knew for a fact God was leading him. So as long as he

continued to obey and follow Him one step at a time, then he knew he would find her.

Ryan just prayed he would find her as he wanted to: whole and not harmed in any way.

=======

Hailey spent most of the night tossing and turning. Sleep was hard to find in amongst her bouts of tears. She understood why Ghada couldn't come with her. But the thoughts of what Ghada might have to endure when Hailey was found missing were hard to ignore.

Hailey finally drifted off to a deep sleep in the early morning hours. She awoke a few hours later as the sun crept over the bed and touched her cheek.

I can't believe it's already Tuesday.

If it weren't for her travel plans delaying things until Thursday, Hailey would have already left. She shook her head. Thankfully it helped dislodge the fear that was trying to get her to focus on how fast time was ticking by. Hailey had to fight to keep her thoughts from wondering when Ehsan would come back. Today was the...

One thing at a time.

Today she needed to go to the tour company. She made herself focus on that. Then the rest of today and Wednesday would be spent on getting things she had put off doing yesterday. Hailey rolled over and caught sight of the clock.

Yikes!

Within the hour, Daib would be ready and waiting to drive her as she had requested. She didn't want to cause him to have to wait for her. She got up, dressed quickly and went downstairs to grab a simple breakfast.

As she sat on a small stool in the kitchen, finishing off the last few bites in her bowl, she huffed to herself. She had tried to be completely covert this whole time and to be so careful, especially around Daib. But her cloak-and-dagger act had turned out to be ultimately futile after last night.

They had just finished dinner when Ghada pulled Hailey aside. Ghada told her about Daib's view of Ehsan and, with a little more reassuring and prompting, Ghada then convinced her to tell him everything.

Hailey set down her bowl. Thinking about her conversation with Daib, filled Hailey with immense solace again. She was still shocked that Daib was fully willing to help her with anything she needed. Understandably, he had made it very clear that he would only help her to a point. He had to protect his place in the house, and he wouldn't risk threatening that, regardless of how much he agreed with her choice to leave.

As Hailey thought about his choice of words and his tone, she wondered about the reason for his loyalty.

I bet it has more to do with Ghada than with Ehsan.

Hailey smiled.

It's tragic they didn't meet under different circumstances. They sure would have been cute together.

As Hailey finished off her tea, she went over the shopping list in her head.

Her first stop would be to the tour company to pick up the package, then to a mall on the other side of town to buy a set of clothes. There was no way this would work if she showed up wearing a full black abaya. She needed to make sure she blended into the tour group as much as possible.

Afterward, she'd ask Daib to drive her to her favorite market so she could pick up some color contacts, hiking boots, sunscreen, scissors, an electric razor, and a backpack. The pack had to be large enough to show she was not just on a day hike, yet small enough to pass as a seasoned traveler. The contacts, scissors, and razor might be pushing it a bit, but Hailey didn't know what snags she might run into. So just in case, she thought the more she could change her appearance, the better.

Hailey also needed to reserve a hotel room close by to the house, which they could do on the way home. She had already purchased a camera, a journal, hair dye, a few nonperishable food items, and a baseball cap on the weekend. So those were already scratched off her mental list. These, she assumed, now made perfect sense to Daib.

As she thought about how strange her purchases must have looked to him, the scene from the market yesterday morning came into her mind. She had been so scared that the man at the stall would alert Daib. The humor of it now drew the corners of her mouth into a small smile.

You're a real '007 Hailey.

"What are you finding so amusing?"

Startled from her thoughts, Hailey turned to see Maya coming into the kitchen. Hailey watched as she went over and poured herself some tea. Maya smiled over her shoulder at Hailey, still waiting for a response.

"Oh nothing," Hailey lied. "How was your sleep?"

"Fine, thank you. Are you going out again today? I saw Daib cleaning your car this morning."

"Um yeah, I thought I would be finished yesterday, but the heat got to me, so I came home early. Actually, it's been kind of hard finding some of the ingredients. I sure hope you all like it."

Hailey was glad she had thought of the idea of throwing a

dinner party for everyone. It was the perfect explanation for why she needed to be out so much: searching for American ingredients. Everyone was excited about coming, and they seemed to be leaving her alone so she could prepare. This was another upside to the plan. The ruse would also ensure she could go out Thursday morning. With the supper scheduled for Thursday night, she could say she was going to the bakery to pick up some fresh bread.

Maya smiled. "I'm looking forward to it. But please be back for lunch today. I have some women from our family coming over who you need to meet."

Hailey was frustrated but made sure not to convey it in her tone or expression. "Sure, I shouldn't be too long."

After Maya had left the kitchen, Hailey rolled her plan out in her mind again while she waited for Daib.

After Wednesday I will have everything I need. Then the only thing left to do is try and get some sleep and wait for Thursday morning to come. Hmm... that's going to be tough.

I will have to take extra care that morning to be as laid back as possible. It's going to be hard, but vital... I can't raise anyone's suspicion. I will eat my breakfast, casually check with Maya and Ghada to see if they need anything and then go meet Daib.

Daib will then drive me to the hotel... I hope they still have room. I will change into my regular clothes as we drive and I'll use the headscarf to cover my head, neck and most of my face.

Hailey snickered as the potential irony hit her. Usually, she found irony amusing but only to a point. Getting arrested again for not covering her head was going far, far beyond that point.

There is no way I'm going to forget to pack one this time.

OK, what's next? Right, I'll check into the hotel. That will give me the privacy and time I need to dye and cut my hair. Oh... my hair.

Hopefully, a small cut job will do, and I won't have to use the razor. Ah, who cares, I'll shave it if I need to… just as long as I don't look too much like me when I'm done.

Then once I'm all cleaned up, I'll head back out to the car and Daib will drive me to the pickup spot for the tour. After I board the bus, I'll try my best to blend in as much as I can until we reached the Jordan border.

But then… the next steps… how am I…?

Hailey shuddered.

What if…?

Seek after Me earnestly. My right hand will uphold you.

The events after approaching the Jordan border were completely out of her control, she couldn't even contemplate the possibilities. They were unimaginable.

He will deal with those and so there is no sense in me trying to deal with them now.

Hailey moved to place her dishes into the sink. Her stomach fluttered with excitement as she thought again about the beginning of her plan.

Could that part really go that smoothly?

Sure it was easy to play through each step in her head, but with so much out of her control, her fear began to lick at her faith again.

She gripped either side of the kitchen sink and hung her head. It was now only two days away and, with each day that it grew closer, she felt it was getting harder and harder to keep from panicking.

God, I'm finding it hard to be calm in all of this… to even think straight. I know whatever happens on Thursday is going to be better than anything that might happen if I stay. But then I guess fear is never rational. I'm scared.

I have already gone before you.

Show me how to trust you so that I can make it home. I know I need to leave this in your hands, but I'm weak. Thank you for being patient with me each time I take it back. I need your strength and look to you to give me wisdom and courage – to give me everything I need. In Your name, Amen.

After the last word had rolled off the lips of her mind, she felt refreshed. Redirecting her focus on Him allowed her to see again how big He was and, in turn, it made everything else seem smaller. He was big enough for any circumstance that she might find herself in. Her fear died down again.

Two quick honks sounded from outside. Daib was signaling for her. She jogged to the front entry way to grab her bag. Once it was over her shoulder, her hand clasped the door handle. She glanced over her shoulder and caught sight of someone standing at the top of the staircase.

Her heart jumped.

Ghada's silhouette came into full focus, and Hailey relaxed. Her smile conveyed both of their hearts and Hailey returned the sentiment – two more days and Hailey would be free. They held each other's gaze for a moment longer, silently savoring it for as long as possible. But when Daib beeped the horn again, Hailey nodded a goodbye and left the house.

=======

Ryan's return to the bank was depressing, and as he came back down the stairs of the bank for the second time empty handed, he couldn't help but feel utterly defeated. The man at the bank apologetically informed him that the transfer could take another day or two and Ryan dreaded bringing that news to

Faisal.

Faisal's words slithered back into his mind from their meeting yesterday.

"I am a patient man, Mr. Foster. However, if you can't get the money, I can't see how dedicated you are to find your friend. If you are wasting my time... it will cost you much more. I will wait another day. But if you postpone again, and I'm sure you can understand, I will have to be compensated for my time."

If Faisal was true to his word, and Ryan assumed he was, then this delay in the transfer could result in setting him back a lot further. Reaching the last step, Ryan sat down and rested his elbows on his knees, clasping his hands in front of him. As he watched all the people scurry from place to place he thought about all the ramifications.

If he came back to Faisal with no money and the price went up enough, then Ryan would have to ask for another transfer, which would take even more time.

How is this going to stop?

Faisal was not the kind of man Ryan would ever choose to deal with, but circumstances made it impossible for Ryan to walk away. He was Ryan's only link to Hailey, and without that information, Ryan was at a complete dead end.

When his eyes pricked with the threat of tears, Ryan refused to give in to the black hole that this situation had turned into.

Father, you have led me to this point, but it seems to be leading nowhere. I'm scared, and I need to find her. What if it is already too late? Where is she? I have to be honest, I'm starting to get angry, but I don't want that to turn me away from Your guidance. Help me. I know that You've already gone before me. You knew I would run into these delays even before I left home. Show me your provision in the midst of them.

=======

The drive was short and passed without Hailey even realizing it. Her mind was so immersed in the final details that needed to be completed.

They came to their first stop, and Daib turned off the car.

The bells on the front glass door sounded as she entered. A man was talking with two Aussies from behind a desk at the back of the store. He signaled to her with his hand that he would be just a moment and returned his attention back to the couple.

The other two workers were busy organizing brochures on the shelf to her left and didn't even look up. Hailey moved further inside of the shop to where two tan wicker arms chairs sat and took a seat in the one closest to the door. Daib had stayed in the car, so she sat silently and waited.

Hailey looked around the shop. The walls were filled with advertisements for different travel and adventure packages: sand surfing, temple tours, rafting trips, camel races, desert cave explorations.

Hailey was shocked to see all that Saudi offered to tourists. She always thought Saudi was a very closed off and private country and as such, they wouldn't want to entertain visitors. She started to realize that all of her assumptions had been way off. Hailey took a deep breath as she looked at the posters. These activities would be among the things she'd be doing on her trip.

She looked down at the small table between the two chairs, picked up a brochure and skimmed the pages. This was more to keep busy than out of interest.

Ten minutes later the couple left the store, and the man behind the counter signaled to her.

When she reached the counter the man started speaking in Arabic. He apparently thought she was a Saudi from her clothing. In keeping with custom, he hadn't made eye contact with her, so he didn't notice her piercing green eyes and the pale skin surrounding them.

She waited till he paused. "Are you the owner?"

"Oh, an American, my apologies."

"You are... Latif?"

"Yes...," he replied tentatively. "Do I know you?"

"No, but I met your brother at the market. He said you would have something for me today," She said as her breath caught in her throat.

The man lowered his voice and leaned towards her slightly. "Hailey?"

"Yes!" She smiled and nodded as relief poured over her.

"I don't know what you've gotten yourself into Miss, but I hope this helps." He reached under the counter and removed a large envelope. "Take this, but don't open it here. I left you instructions and included everything you need."

"I can't tell you how thankful I am to you both."

Hailey set a large number of bills on the counter, but Latif put his hand on the bills and started to slide them back towards Hailey.

"This is far too much."

"No... it isn't."

Latif looked at the other two workers, then continued in a natural tone. "Thank you for your business, and please come again."

Hailey nodded and tried to convey her deepest gratitude with her eyes, then left the store. Daib jumped out of the car as she approached.

"Did you get it?"

"I'm all set. Let's get to the mall as quickly as you can. I can't be late getting back."

Hailey shoved the envelope into her bag and jumped in the car as Daib held the door open for her. They pulled away from the travel shop.

"Daib," Hailey paused, "you will take care of Ghada when I'm gone won't you? You will protect her once he knows I'm gone… right?"

Daib looked at her in the rear-view mirror and nodded. "With my life."

CHAPTER 34

"The market is very busy today. Would you like to try to start closer to the north end?"

Hailey hadn't made it up that far during the previous visits so the north end might be more productive.

"Yeah, that might be a good idea. Thanks, Daib."

The crowds thinned a bit as they slowly made their way through the narrow streets next to the market. Daib finally found a spot and stopped. He got out and rounded the car to let her out.

After grabbing her bag, Hailey proceeded through the crowd. Daib trailed slightly behind. She walked for about ten minutes, then stopped.

Through all the usual sounds of the market, there were others that seemed a bit out of place. Hailey strained to separate them from the vendors calling out their deals and the chatter of the customers. She walked a bit further, and it became increasingly clearer.

Screams mixed with cheering.

Hailey walked on her tippy toes to try and get a glimpse of what was going on. The small market streets seemed to open up to a large square a few yards ahead of them.

Hailey stopped and glanced back at Daib to ask him what was going on. He was quite far behind her. He had slowed his pace and was talking on his cell phone. Hailey's curiosity turned her attention back to the commotion, and she continued to walk towards the open square.

The screams and cheering became louder and louder as she approached. There must have been a hundred people gathered around, which made it near impossible to see anything. Hailey weaved her way through the crowd to get closer.

As she passed the last line of onlookers and reached the front, the crowd fell silent, apart from one woman. She was much older and was about twenty feet to Hailey's left. She was sitting on her knees, rocking back and forth, and wailing. Hailey pulled her eyes from the woman and looked around to the rest of the crowd surrounding the square, before looking to the center.

Ten men were standing out in the open, hands clasped behind their back, unmoving and staring straight ahead. They weren't looking at anything in particular, just standing and looking very official.

A pile of small, jagged rocks sat slightly beyond the men's feet. Fifteen feet beyond that, lay a young woman. Her face was turned towards Hailey, and her eyes stared blankly in her direction. As the full sight reached Hailey's eyes, her stomach lurched, forcing Hailey to wince and look away.

The girl's body lay in a twisted heap, and her hands were tied behind her back. She would have been naked apart from being dressed in her own blood and some shredded material. Blood pooled around her, it seeped into the dust covering the square and coated the strewn rocks around where she lay.

She had been stoned.

After a few moments, Hailey was able to compose herself.

She slowly turned her attention back to the body. Hailey had never seen anything so gruesome. The stones had cut their way through the girl's skin and left deep gashes and welts all over the girl's body.

The older woman's cries echoed in the square and shook Hailey's core. Hailey's own tears were now pouring from her eyes. She didn't move to wipe them away; they were soaked up by her veil.

The men started walking towards the girl. Hailey watched as two of them loomed over her, bent down, and each grasped one of her arms. The girl's head flopped forward, breaking the dead gaze she had towards Hailey. The men dragged her from the square, leaving two trails of blood as her legs were scraped over the ground. The crowd parted to let them through.

Apart from one man, the rest followed in two lines on either side of the blood trail. The last man remained and paced back and forth along the edge of the watching crowd. As soon as the other men were out of the circle, he started speaking.

Interspersing his comments, the crowd broke their silence and cheered. They made short comments and gestures with their fists. A few seemed to be out of objection or contempt, but mostly they were of ones of support.

The man continued talking for a few minutes, then he motioned towards a section of the crowd. Those standing in that direction moved aside and allowed two officers to enter; they were not alone. In their grasp was a young boy. Hailey would have guessed he wasn't more than fourteen. He was not struggling, but tears were rolling down his dirt-smeared face.

The man spoke again, and as he did so, he moved over to a cart Hailey had not initially noticed. From the cart, the man pulled out a four-legged, brown stool, a hatchet, and something else that Hailey couldn't quite see from the angle of where she stood.

The boy was brought to the center of the square by the officers and was made to kneel. The crowd cheered and shouted. The boy raised his eyes and started intently in a direction towards Hailey's left. Hailey pulled her eyes away from him and saw what the boy was looking at.

There were three people on their hands and knees: an older man, an older woman, and a beautiful young girl. All of them were intently staring back at the boy. They were all in unison whispering to him. Hailey looked back at the boy who was now nodding and smiling back.

The man stopped speaking and walked over to the boy. One of the officers, knelt beside the boy, slightly behind him on his left. With one hand, the officer reached under the boy's right arm and clasped his other hand, which reached over the boy's left shoulder. It looked kind of like a backward hug. The officer braced himself. The other officer took the boy's right arm and stretched it straight out to the side.

The man spoke again and leaned down. The third item was now visible to Hailey. It was a rope. The man placed the stool beside the boy and tied the rope around the boy's wrist. Then the officer pushed the arm down to rest on the stool.

It was then that Hailey noticed the stool wasn't actually painted brown, it was covered with dried blood. Hailey's stomach pitched: she finally realized what was actually happening. These men, these horrible men, were about to cut this boy's hand off.

Hailey's eyes darted around the crowd, looking and expecting someone to stand up and put a stop to this. But those that weren't cheering and clapping were just looking on with curiosity.

Does anyone realize this is just a boy, a child? Why isn't anyone doing anything?

The man turned back to the crowd and spoke as he raised the hatchet high over his head. After walking in a full circle, he moved back to face the boy. As the hatchet started to swing downwards, Hailey had to turn her face. She just couldn't bear to see this.

As the view of the boy moved out of her sight, it just as quickly came back into view. A large hand had come around her face, painfully gripped her chin and turned her head back towards the boy. Another hand gripped around her back and held her arm. She tried to struggle against whoever was behind her, but she couldn't move. She was forced to watch.

The crowd fell silent, the hatchet came down, but it stopped an inch above his wrist. The man again lifted his hand high above him. Hailey tried to turn away again, but the hand squeezed harder, keeping her face forward. The hatchet came down again, but this time it didn't stop.

In one quick motion, the hand was severed from the boy. As the boy's scream forcefully broke out of his chest, it also broke Hailey's silence. She cried out. No one looked over at her, no one even noticed – the crowd had started cheering again and the sound was deafening.

Hailey struggled again to turn her face away, but the hand squeezed even tighter, causing her to yelp. Laughter filled her ears as a mouth came up the side of her face and close to her ear. Her blood chilled as a voice spoke.

"I'm glad you got to witness this, my dear. This is Chop Chop Square, a place that will await you if you ever disobey me again."

The hand around her face released as the other hand spun her around. Ehsan's horrible face filled her view.

Hailey tried to back away, but his hand held her tightly.

"No... no. No!" Her defeat poured out through each no.

"Isn't it to all our good fortune that I returned when I did? You and Ghada would have come to greatly regret it if you had tried to leave. It saddens me to think that you don't yet understand what a privilege it is to be in my house, to be part of my family."

The boy had stopped screaming. Hailey looked over and saw he was now being led through the crowd and out of the square. Ehsan jolted her arm to get her attention back, but he made no attempt to leave.

"You see that is what I have done, Hailey. I have welcomed you into my house. Given you everything you could have ever needed and this is how you repay me?"

"I... I... I..." Hailey had no response. She could only look with terror into Ehsan's cold and angry eyes.

The crowd again grew silent, and Ehsan's eyes looked away towards what was happening. His hand remained on her arm with a tight grip. Hailey took the chance to look for Daib. He was standing on a small step near the back of the crowd. His eyes held hers in deep sadness. Then as his eyes started to water, he hung his head and looked away.

It must have been Ehsan on the cell, and Daib had to tell him where we were.

She kept her eyes on Daib.

But why did you have to tell Ehsan about my plan? Couldn't you just have said that we were coming back soon? The plan wasn't ruined just because he got back? Why did you tell him?

Hailey wished he could hear and answer the questions that

were pouring into her head. She didn't understand it. This must be the line that Daib meant after Ghada had convinced her to bring him into their confidence.

Ehsan jerked her arm to move her attention back towards the square. A woman was being dragged into the center. Her demeanor was exactly the opposite of the boy's. She screamed, kicked, and thrashed to try and get away, but the officers that were escorting her were strong and held their grip.

A few more officers had entered the square as well. Hailey assumed it was for crowd control as everyone was getting rather worked up. They spaced themselves around the square and faced the crowd.

Again family members revealed themselves as they reacted to the scene. In this case, it was an elderly woman, probably the woman's mother. There were three younger men with her straining to hold her back. They tried their best to silence her, but she was not having any of it.

When Hailey's attention had been on Daib, the stool and hatchet had been removed, and now there were other items in the square. A wooden apparatus had been placed in the center. It had a crescent cut out of the base, and a large blade hung from the top, between large upright lengths of wood. Upon realizing what it was, Hailey tried to pull back and run, but Ehsan held her in place.

The same man who had announced the last punishment was speaking again.

"You see," Ehsan leaned towards her again, "this woman was caught in the act of adultery."

The smell of his hot breath made her nauseous.

"She will now be punished for her crime by beheading. I am glad this case came before us today. For if you ever try to leave me again… this will be your fate. So watch closely."

Ehsan gripped her face again so she'd be forced to watch. Hailey started to weep. It was a horrible nightmare, and she had no way of waking up or getting away.

Help me. Oh God, please help me. Help her.

The woman was led towards the crude guillotine. She now fought with everything she had. The officers were now having a hard time even holding onto her, let alone getting her to kneel. The man stopped speaking and quickly closed the distance between himself and the woman. His fist came up so fast, Hailey didn't even have time to close her eyes.

The man punched her so hard, her head snapped backward. Blood poured from her nose. The hit had dazed the woman so considerably that her fighting stopped immediately and her screams ceased.

Apart from the elderly woman who cried out in horror, the crowd also now stood silent. The awful crack his fist made with the woman's face seemed to have shocked everyone. But a moment later, they snapped out of it and returned to their cheering.

After the officers finally secured the woman to the apparatus, they released her and gripped either side of the wood that ran up to the blade.

The announcer spoke again as he walked around the edge. He raised his hand, and the crowd grew silent.

"Here we go," Ehsan whispered into her ear. He sounded practically giddy.

Once the crowd had quieted down, the man lowered his hand and walked slowly over to the woman. Hailey was actually shocked that the woman hadn't been knocked out completely from such a hit. She remained awake, and her head rested in the crescent shaped cut out. She didn't strain against the restraints, and so no one needed to hold her down. She was slowly blinking, and any movements she was trying to make were nothing short of pathetic.

When the man reached the woman's side, a deep scream came from the woman's mother. Hailey strained against Ehsan's hand to see her. She was struggling against the men who were trying to hold her.

As the man grasped the long rope that ran down the length of the guillotine, the elderly woman managed to break one of her hands free and reached under her abaya. Everyone barely had time to react as the woman pulled out a gun. She raised it into the air and pulled the trigger. The shot rang out, and everyone either hit the ground or started running. Chaos ensued.

From the perspective of others in the crowd, everything moved quickly. But for Hailey, it almost seemed to be in slow motion. As soon as Ehsan released her to cover his head, she turned and ran. Ehsan yelled at her and then yelled for someone to stop her.

Hailey didn't turn back or slow her pace. She ran as fast as she could.

Hailey easily found a fast path through the crowd, and before she knew it, she was through. She paused and glanced back. Hailey momentarily caught Ehsan's eye. It was gutsy, but she couldn't help flashing him a quick glaring smile of defiance. As it hit its mark, she saw his anger burn towards her.

Another shot rang out, then another and another. Each one caused more screams and greater panic. Hailey turned and ran again. She was far from getting away, and she didn't want to push her luck by keeping still too long. Ehsan would not have come alone, and she needed to keep moving if she were to have any chance of evading them.

She exited the square quite quickly and started to run in and out of the market stalls. She didn't want to run in a straight line and stay in Ehsan's line of sight, so she made sure to weave a crazy route throughout the market.

Her lungs burned, and her body raged at her to stop. She wasn't used to running in such intense heat, especially under so much fabric. It was stifling, but she forced herself to keep going. The screams from the square diminished as she went on and now she was the only one running. Hailey had managed to get ahead of everyone.

At last, she reached the top end of the market and ran around the corner of a large building. She was about to adjust her speed so she wouldn't draw any attention to herself, but it was a moment too late.

CHAPTER 35

The pain of running into someone at a full run isn't unlike running into a brick wall. Hailey sat on the sidewalk completely stunned, but the shock was increased tenfold as she heard his voice.

"Oh my goodness, I'm so sorry. Here let me help you."

He bent down and grasped her elbow to raise her off the ground.

Hailey was utterly speechless. The wind had been entirely knocked out of her, and she couldn't breathe sufficiently, let alone form words. Her head was spinning, and things looked a bit fuzzy. At first, she wasn't sure if she saw things correctly.

As he started to pull her to her feet, her foot caught on the edge of her abaya. She tripped and fell into him.

"Uh, are you OK?"

By his tone, it was evident that he was feeling incredibly awkward with having this strange woman hang onto him. It was clear he didn't know who she was.

Hailey giggled but refused to let him pull back. She just leaned into him and breathed in his smell. He smelled of home and of safety, and she refused to let go.

=======

Ryan stayed on the steps of the bank as he thought things over. As he watched people pass by and go about their day, he wondered if there was a way around the hurdle that sat unmoving in front of him. After an hour, his stomach started to do flips. He didn't have to meet Faisal until much later, so he reluctantly raised himself off of the steps and set out to find an early lunch.

He crossed the street, jogged down the sidewalk and along a beautiful, gray brick building. But just as he got to the corner, a woman dressed in a full black abaya rounded the corner at a full run and smashed right into him. He stumbled backward, and the woman ricocheted right off of him and crumpled to the ground.

Ryan was thoroughly embarrassed. Apologies stumbled out of his mouth as he tried to help the woman to her feet. Tripping, the woman fell into his arms and held on tight. Ryan tried to back away and help her to stand up straight, but she wouldn't budge. She clung to him. Awkwardly, he held her, unsure of what to do. He clumsily looked around to see if there was someone who could assist him. But as there was no one with the woman, there was no one to help him.

Yet someone was watching him. Ryan didn't notice at first, but a man across the street from where they stood was staring at them with great interest. As Ryan looked around, he finally saw him. They locked eyes.

When it became apparent that the man wasn't going to look away, it made Ryan feel even more embarrassed. He tried again to pull the woman off but with no effect.

The man yelled something at him in Arabic and started to cross the street.

He was momentarily delayed as he was forced to wait for some traffic. When the man returned his eyes to Ryan, he touched something hanging from around his neck, bringing attention to the badge he wore.

Ryan's heart sank as he realized that this man was a member of the religious police.

Oh no... Mutawa.

Ryan looked down at the woman in his arms and then back at the Mutawa, then back once more to the woman. Ryan then realized what this all must look like to the man who was now impatiently waiting for the last car to pass so he could proceed towards them.

Ryan instinctively let go of the woman and raised his hands above his head to show his innocence. Releasing the woman still had no effect, she continued to cling to him. This seemed to anger the man even more as he now was glaring and yelling at Ryan.

"I think we need to leave." He whispered quietly.

The woman raised her head slightly off his chest and looked towards the street. She stiffened instantly as she saw the Mutawa. She then pushed herself upright, grabbed his hand, and moved past him.

"Run!" she yelled.

Ryan didn't protest. He couldn't chance getting detained by the Saudi religious police and miss the meeting with Faisal.

The woman pulled him behind her. She was fast, and he had trouble keeping up with her.

They made their way past a few buildings and across another street, easily leaving the slightly large Mutawa behind them. As they increased their distance, the man called out after them. The man's voice was loud as it boomed against the buildings. This alerted some of the guards outside the bank. They started to pursue them.

The woman veered to the left, away from the bank, almost jerking Ryan's shoulder out of the socket as she changed direction. They ran down the street as fast as they could, but the guards were gaining on them. They released each other's hand to help aid in their speed, but it wasn't enough. Ryan saw they were getting closer and closer.

"Cross!" Ryan yelled to her.

She immediately changed course and started to cross. Ryan had not seen the car.

The sound of screeching tires echoed through the streets.

The woman screamed.

The guards kept running.

The woman's hands slammed on the hood of the car, but it managed to stop just inches from her legs. Ryan couldn't believe that she was still standing. For a moment neither of them moved.

Ryan glanced towards the driver and was about to return his attention to the woman to make sure she was alright, but he stopped. With eyes full of shock, the old man from the holding office sat behind the wheel of the car.

"Zayan?" Ryan said in disbelief. He looked at the passenger side. "Zaara!"

They smiled at each other briefly before their reunion was cut short. One of the guards yelled at them again to stop. They were only seconds away, so Ryan grabbed the woman's arm and shoved her into the car.

"Drive!"

Zayan needed no more persuading. He hit the gas, and they sped away.

Ryan leaned forward between the two seats and relayed what

had just happened to Zayan and Zaara as they made their way out of downtown. "I can't believe we ran into you. You have no idea how glad I am to see you," Ryan said beaming.

Zayan looked at him. "Where we go?"

"Actually I have to go back to the park by the holding office."

"Ryan no. I think you not go back there. Those guards that chase you... will be there right now. They make report."

"But I have no choice. It's my last lead to finding Hailey."

As he finished saying her name, the woman's hand slowly rested on his back. Ryan leaned back to explain and apologize, but he stopped. It was the first time he looked directly at her. Those eyes! His heart raced, and without speaking, he raised his hands and frantically removed her veil.

"Hailey! Oh God, how? What are you...? You're here?"

The questions poured out of him, some not even coherent. He couldn't believe that Hailey was actually sitting here before him.

Tears were spilling down her cheeks. She didn't hesitate to answer him. She leaned forward into his arms. They embraced each other tightly.

As he held her, he glanced towards the front seat looking for some explanation. Both Zayan and Zaara were smiling at him. Zaara nodded to him in confirmation.

This is actually happening. God, thank you... thank you that she's safe.

He held her tighter as she sobbed quietly into his shoulder.

"Ryan, don't let go... OK?"

He held her tighter. "OK."

After her shoulders had stopped shuddering from crying, he pulled back, but his hands still held her shoulders. He looked into her eyes, those beautiful green eyes.

"You're actually here? I mean right here?"

She chuckled and shrugged her shoulders. "Yup."

They embraced again.

=======

The four fugitives weaved their way through more city streets. Zayan suggested it might be best to return to his house before making any decisions and Ryan and Hailey agreed.

Zaara retired to the kitchen to make some tea as soon as they all entered the house. Their house was small and cozy. It was the exact opposite to Ehsan's house, and Hailey instantly felt at ease within its walls. It was made out of that tan, clay stone which Hailey had expected to see in Saudi.

Zayan led them into a small living room near the front of the house.

"Please, sit," Zayan said as he gestured to the small couch at the edge of the room. Then he sat on a large chair in the corner.

Ryan hadn't taken his eyes off Hailey since he had removed her veil and it was now making her blush.

"Ryan, I'm not going anywhere." She smiled a teasing smile.

"I know, but I just can't believe you're here. I mean you're right here. Hailey where have you been?"

Hailey glanced down at her folded hands, and a tear escaped from the corner of one eye.

"Well…" Hailey paused, unsure of how to start.

"I go help Zaara. I return soon." Zayan smiled at them both, nodded and left the room.

With a deep breath, Hailey started from the beginning. She told him about how she had been feeling, why she had decided to go early, and admitted her foolishness. She told him about the plane ride and her getting lost at the airport. She told him about the nice businessman and about getting arrested. She told him about the holding cell and about Faisal.

Hailey couldn't help but notice Ryan tense up, but she didn't stop.

She told him about the transfer to the prison. She told him about the murder of the woman in the shower room and about her friend Sarna. She told him about the hope she felt when she first met Ehsan.

Hailey noticed the same hope she had felt fill Ryan's eyes as she spoke. She had to look away as that hope evaporated when she told him who Ehsan really was.

She told him about Fareefta and about Maya. She told him about her escape attempt with Ghada. She explained all the details about her plans to get away a second time and what had brought her to the market that day. Then she finished off with the events that had made her run: about Chop Chop Square.

"But then I ran into you and just like that we were back together. God is good."

Ryan had been looking at the floor during the last part of her story but raised his eyes.

"God?" Ryan questioned.

"Yeah, I found him again." Hailey looked away and shook her head then returned her eyes to his. "Or I should say… He came for me." She chuckled.

Ryan leaned forward and hugged her again tightly. "I'm so glad you're OK."

"You have no idea how happy I am that I don't have to try and make it out of Saudi alone. Hey, we should call Anna and let her know I'm OK. Her number was taken from me at the airport, and I haven't been able to call her yet. But you've talked to her right? She must be totally freaking out."

Ryan's eyes darkened, and his chin quivered. He dropped his eyes to the floor and started to cry. It was obvious he was trying to stop, but his shoulders heaved, and the sobs poured out of him. Hailey moved closer to him. She pulled him to her and rested his head on her shoulder.

Even hearing herself tell the whole story was upsetting. Hailey realized that for Ryan, hearing it all for the first time, all in one shot, must be completely overwhelming. It was clear he needed to let it out. She held him and stroked his hair but said nothing.

After a few minutes had passed the sobs slowed, his breathing returned to normal, and he sat up. Ryan moved to wipe his tears with his shirt, but Hailey stopped him. She took the edge of her abaya and wiped the tears from his eyes and off his cheeks. As his eyes held hers again a few more tears pooled in his eyes. He forced himself to look away.

"Ryan, what's wrong? I'm here for good. I'm OK... I'm not going anywhere." She tried to reassure him.

He sighed and looked at her again. He raised his hands and cupped her face. The empathy that moved across his face scared her.

"Ryan..." She couldn't finish, a large lump had formed in her throat.

"Anna is..." He paused.

Fear seared through her. "Ryan what? What's going on?" She didn't like the anger that came out through her tone, but she needed to push him.

"She's dead, Hailey."

"What? Who?" Hailey tried to piece together what he had said, but her mind was racing all over the place.

"Anna!"

Hearing her friend's name drained all rational thought and control from her body.

Ryan tried to hold onto her, but she pushed him away and stood up. She walked to the other side of the room. It seemed as though every one of her emotions was trying to get out all at once and it was suffocating her. She paced back and forth along the far wall. She felt dizzy and trapped.

Suddenly she couldn't breathe, and the abaya seemed to tighten around her like a snake. It was squeezing the life out of her, and she had to get it off. It was a flurry of fabric and the harder she fought to get it off, the more tangled she got. She screamed.

"Hailey, stop fighting. I can get it... let me help." Ryan was at her side.

She didn't listen. She kept thrashing at the blackness that was now surrounding her face. But somehow through all her panic, the abaya fell away. Ryan now held it in his hands. He let it drop to the floor as he backed away to give her some space.

"Hailey, that urgent matter that pulled Ehsan to Dammam that day was a bombing. Someone drove trucks into Anna's compound, and it was completely destroyed." Tears again dripped from his eyes and off his chin.

Hailey stopped moving and just stood there, staring at him as he finished the description of what had happened. Then, her own floodgates failed. Ryan was instantly at her side. He caught her as she crumpled to the floor. They held each other tightly as they grieved together for their friend. The only sounds in the house were their sobs echoing off the walls.

CHAPTER 36

After a simple yet delicious meal of chicken and rice, Ryan and Hailey helped Zayan and Zaara clean up the kitchen. Then they all sat around the table to make a plan.

"Hailey, things are going to be just too difficult to leave the country together. You don't have your passport, and I can't come on that bus tour. I think you may have to keep to your original plan. We can meet in Jordan." As Ryan spoke, he could see her deflate.

"Ryan, I don't want to be alone again. Try and understand, I'm not trying to be difficult. I'm terrified to try to make it to Jordan alone. The chances that I won't run into a major problem for not having any papers are slim at best. I really don't think I can do it alone."

Ryan felt at a loss.

What are we supposed to do?

He had now missed his meeting with Faisal. Even if the money came in tomorrow, who knows how Faisal would react or what he might demand now. Hailey needed to get out of Saudi as soon as possible, and he couldn't handle keeping her fate in that man's hands.

"I actually almost had my hands on your passport." Ryan

tried to chuckle, but it fell flat.

"What do you mean? How?"

"Yeah, that was actually why I needed to go to the park today. I actually had met Faisal, and he was going to sell it to me. I was going to meet him at the park."

"You're joking, you actually met him?" Hailey was openly shocked.

"Seriously, I did. I was just leaving the bank when I bumped into you. But now that I missed that meeting there is no way he will accept the original amount. He was already pretty upset that I was taking so long to get the money. The money will come in tomorrow, but with his increase, it could take another few days."

Zayan voiced what they all felt in their hearts, "Ah... no good to stay in Saudi. Hailey, you need leave now."

They all worried that the longer Hailey stayed in Saudi, the easier it would be for Ehsan to close all their exits. Without knowing how much pull he had in the city, they just couldn't chance it.

"Zayan, I know we can't wait, but what choice do we have?" Ryan looked back at Hailey. "If you don't want to go alone then you need your papers so we can fly out of Saudi. But to get your papers, we need to wait for more money. But if we wait it could put you in more danger. I don't know what to do."

Zaara started to sniffle and wipe her eyes. "I so sorry. We too poor. You so sweet, but we no help."

"Are you kidding? You two have helped us so much." Hailey patted her hand. "You saved us. Thank you for letting us in your home. We will be forever grateful. You may have put your lives in danger, and we don't expect anything more from you. Please don't feel bad."

Hailey handed her a tissue from the small box sitting on the counter. As Ryan smiled at her for her compassion, she unexpectedly rose and left the room, leaving them all a little confused. After a few moments, Hailey returned with her bag.

"I'm sure glad I didn't drop this. I don't know if it will be enough or what Faisal was asking for, but would this work?"

Hailey turned the bag upside down and dumped its contents on the table. Out came stacks of cash and a large envelope.

Ryan was visibly shocked. He counted it.

"Hailey, this is actually almost triple what he was asking for. Where did you get it all?"

"Hailey, that a lot of money," Zayan said with huge, wide eyes.

"Yeah, I was given an enormous expense account and, for almost a week now, I've been slowly taking out a bunch of it."

"Nice job," said Zaara.

"On second thought, I think it's stupid to even try and fly out of the Riyadh airport. It will probably be too dangerous. But maybe we can make our way to another city close by. Well, that is if we can still get your papers." He looked towards Zayan for ideas.

"Sorry my friend, don't know. I only know Riyadh airport. We always stay close to home."

Ryan leaned back and raked his hands through his hair. He was out of answers.

=======

Hailey saw how tired he was. She wanted to say that he could leave on the next flight out of there and that she'd be OK to go on the tour, but she just couldn't get past the fear of going without him.

Father there just has to be another way. I don't want to leave him. Please have mercy, show us another way.

They all sat there in silence, each racking their brain for a solution. Unfortunately, no one was offering any. Ten more minutes passed, and the silence was wearing on Hailey.

"Hey, what's this?" Ryan leaned forward and picked up the envelope.

"Oh, the owner of the tour company gave it to me. It's my bus ticket and details about the trip."

Not that they're much use now.

She watched as Ryan opened the flap and dumped out the contents. The paper with the directions floated to the table, followed by her ticket. They landed silently, but it sounded like a thud to Hailey. It was like they were mocking her.

She sighed.

Ryan took the paper and read it. "Woah, are they really going to hide you in a secret compartment when going through the border checkpoints?"

"Really? Actually, I had never gotten around to reading that yet. They did tell me they had a way around passport check. So... I guess that's it." Hailey shuddered. She didn't like small spaces.

Ryan picked up the envelope again and looked inside. Hailey watched as he reached his hand in and withdrew another ticket.

God, could it really be that simple?

"What's this?" Ryan questioned again.

Tears pooled in her eyes, and she had to blink a few times to see Ryan.

"It's Ghada's ticket. I totally forgot about it. Originally when I was talking to the man at the market, I told him I would need two tickets. I totally forgot about it when Ghada said she couldn't leave."

"We now no need another airport or see that bad man." Zaara laughed.

"Actually, I'm still going." Ryan's confession stunned them all.

"Why?" Zayan questioned.

"I don't want anyone at that office to have your information, Hailey. Who knows, it could make its way into Ehsan's hands and I don't want him knowing where you live or anything else about you."

"I never thought of that." Hailey's heart sunk and cringed at the thought.

"Nope," Zayan said. "Too dangerous for you go. So... I go instead." Zayan held up his hand to cease any protest, so Ryan didn't offer any. "I need go to town to pick up my son, Aahil. He finish at hospital tomorrow, and I stop at office on way home. OK? OK."

Zayan didn't bother waiting for an answer but rose and waved for Zaaya to follow. After a quick explanation of the sleeping arrangements, she left the room with him.

Ryan and Hailey stayed up most of the night talking, mostly planning out the next two days. While Zayan was out getting the papers, Ryan would run out and get some things to disguise them. He would also try and find some provisions they'd need on the trip.

After the plans had been laid out, they moved into the living room and took a seat on the couch. Ryan told her how he had met Zayan and Zaara and then they talked, like old times.

"Talk about home," Hailey pleaded.

"Well... OK then. Let's see. The first thing you're going to do is have a hot shower and get into some of your own clothes. And while you're doing that, I'm going to run out to Papa's and get you the biggest 'Gobs of Greek' you've ever seen."

Hailey smiled, leaned back against the couch, and allowed her head to fall back. She closed her eyes as she pictured taking a bite of her favorite pizza.

"Mmm... that sounds so good." She kept her eyes closed. "You sure know how to treat a girl right Ryan Foster."

Hailey felt Ryan shift, and she slowly opened her eyes. The room was dim, but his face filled her view. He had moved closer and was now inches away from her. He raised his hand and slowly moved a strand of hair off her forehead, then stroked the backs of his fingers down her cheek and along her jaw.

"I missed you so much, and I was so scared I wouldn't find you."

Hailey was speechless. The air between them was intense, and her heart was beating fast. He looked into her eyes and slightly raised his eyebrows. Even though no words were spoken it was obvious he was asking if he could kiss her.

She nodded slightly.

Ever so slowly, as if giving her time to change her mind, he leaned towards her. She didn't want to change her mind. She didn't want to pull back. As he came closer, neither of them closed their eyes. As his lips pressed tenderly against hers, they continued to hold each other's gaze.

Hailey had never experienced such an intimate kiss. It wasn't passion that made it intimate but honesty. They remained totally open and aware of each other. It was as though they were silently agreeing to be completely vulnerable with each other, knowing it was completely safe to do so.

At that moment Hailey realized how completely in love with him she was. The emotion in his kiss told her he felt the exact same way.

After the sweet, soft kiss had ended, Ryan pulled back but continued to look into her eyes.

"I love you," he said.

Hailey didn't even need to hesitate. "I love you too," she echoed.

Hailey realized she had felt that way for a long, long time and, if it weren't for her stubbornness, she would have realized it a lot sooner.

They embraced each other. Ryan held her quietly for another hour until she fell asleep. The day had been filled with such a kaleidoscope of emotions, and she was exhausted.

=======

Ryan looked down at her small form curled up against him. Her hand grasped a bit of the bottom hem of his shirt. It was if, even in her sleep, she didn't want to let him go. His heart was so full to have her in his arms again. She had been through so much, and he was so thankful that God had brought her back to him.

He would have stayed there until the sun came up, but he knew she would sleep better in a bed. He lifted her slowly off the couch, trying hard not to wake her and carried her to the back of the house.

After he had laid her down, he noticed some of her hair had fallen over her face. As he bent down to move it and cover her up, he knew for certain that very soon he would ask Hailey to be his wife. He just couldn't possibly last another day without her.

CHAPTER 37

The next day started fairly late. Hailey and Ryan were both still asleep when Zayan left. He didn't mind, though; they must be exhausted. These next few days were going to be very intense for the both of them, and they needed as much sleep as possible.

After kissing Zaara goodbye, he left the house, started the car and drove into town. The money had been left for him on the table with a note to try and stick as close to the original price as possible, but they gave him permission to pay whatever it took to get Hailey's things.

The drive into town was surprisingly slow. The traffic was worse than normal, and it irritated Zayan. He continued his way through the streets until he made it to the hospital. He found a parking spot and jogged up to the front doors. His son was already sitting in the waiting room waiting for him. As soon as their eyes met, they teared up, and they ran to hug each other.

Pulling back, Zayan looked down at his son's injury.

"I'm so sorry my son."

"It's OK papa. I wouldn't change a thing. And hey… it's a good thing I'm left-handed."

They both chuckled bitter-sweetly.

Zayan loved his son's humor, and it never ceased, even in

situations that seemed so bleak and depressing. Zayan was still ashamed because he couldn't protect his son from such a punishment, yet he was happy his son appeared to be OK in light of it all.

His heart started to ache as thoughts of his daughter entered his mind. It had only been a day, but he was already missing her. Zayan knew it was the right choice to send her to his brother's until everything died down. He needed to ensure that his old boss would not come after her. Zayan would have sent her away sooner, but his daughter had insisted she be at the square to support her brother. He would send for her in a few weeks, and then they could move on and put this all behind them.

"I can't wait to get home to see Mama. Is she doing OK?"

"Well, Aahil, you won't believe what happened. After dropping your sister off, we ran into two Americans. It's a long story, I'll tell you on the way. We do have to make one stop. I have to go the Mutawa holding office before heading home."

Zayan leaned over and tousled his son's hair.

"It will also be nice for you to be home so you can translate for us. They don't speak any Arabic and your mother, and I are having a tough time with our English."

"I'm sure you've done fine."

Aahil smiled at him and off they went.

=======

When Hailey woke up, she tidied the little room and went to see if Ryan was awake yet. Sadly, he had already left the house.

The afternoon passed by painfully slow and there was no word from Zayan yet. Hailey was sitting in the kitchen alone while she waited for Ryan to get back with the supplies.

The house was quiet. Zaara was out back in the small garden collecting some things for supper. Hailey was a bit shocked that anything could grow in this heat. However, the couple had set up a little garden and received a nice return for their efforts. Hailey had already explored the extent of the small house. It was a tiny two-story. Downstairs contained the living room, bathroom, kitchen and the kids' bedrooms. Both rooms were tiny and could pretty much just fit a bed, a little table and a small dresser for clothes. There was no sitting room and very little walking room. Upstairs was only half the size of the downstairs. Zayan and Zaara had made it into a bedroom for themselves and put a small desk by the one window.

So there she sat, tapping her fingers impatiently on the kitchen table.

A few hours later, after something to eat and a lot more painful waiting, Ryan came through the door. He had half a dozen or so bags grasped in his hands and two large hiking backpacks, one slung over each shoulder. Sweat was pouring down his face.

"Yikes, it's hot out there today," he panted.

Hailey brought him a glass of water, and they went into the living room to go through the purchases. Hair dye for them both, scissors, a set of colored contact lenses, clothes and hats. Pretty much everything Hailey had spent the last few days collecting.

"Oh, I got a cell phone too," Ryan said.

"Really?"

"Yeah, I think we've got to call home. Everyone must be going crazy with worry. I haven't talked to anyone in like... a week."

Hailey watched and listened as Ryan called Thomas and gave

him their number, along with instructions to call Norah.

"Ryan, what about calling the American Embassy? They should be able to help, regardless of how powerful Eshan is."

"That's a good idea."

Ryan's eyes darkened, and his expression fell a few seconds after dialing the number. He hung up.

"Well?"

"It was just a recorded message saying that due to the bombing, no one was available at the moment to take calls. It said that we could leave a message and that they'd try to call us back soon."

=======

Zayan and his son returned early that evening. Hailey's heart sank when she saw the boy. He was the same boy who was in the square yesterday. She hadn't realized that Zayan and Zaara were the people she'd seen.

"Does it hurt?" Hailey's eyes gestured to his stump.

"No, not much anymore," Aahil said.

"I guess the doctors gave you some pretty powerful pain medication huh?" Hailey smiled.

The boy dropped his gaze momentarily.

"No, that type of thing is really expensive, but I can handle it." The boy said as he glanced towards his father.

Zayan dropped his eyes to the floor.

Seeing his father, the boy added, "Yes, my father taught me what it means to be strong."

Zayan raised his head and beamed with pride, then nodded to the boy.

Hailey again saw the same love she had seen in the square

pass between the two of them as they looked at each other and silently reassured each other that everything was going to be okay.

"Where is the girl?" Hailey questioned.

"What girl?" asked Aahil.

"There was a girl with your parents at the square."

"Oh, my sister. She's with my uncle for a few weeks."

"How was the meeting?" Ryan said as he entered the room. He had been in the kitchen helping Zaara.

Zayan nodded towards the boy, signaling him to fill Ryan in.

"Honestly, better than my father expected. The man did hold out for more money, but after my father had pushed to expose his extortion, he backed down quite quickly and agreed to the original price. My father wanted to make sure you had lots of cash in case you run into any trouble. Money is a great tool in turning away heads and opening doors. There is one thing, though..."

Hailey's breath caught in her throat.

"There are actually warrants posted for both of you." He looked at Hailey. "It seems that man, Ehsan, isn't going to let you go easily. He is saying that you are traveling with a man who stole you from him. He must have seen the report from the Mutawa about Ryan, and you escaping and put it together. They are charging Ryan with kidnapping another man's wife and you with adultery. These are no small accusations. Does Ehsan have a picture of you?"

"I don't think so."

"Well, that is at least something. But all the police around the city will have your descriptions by now." The boy let that sink in a bit while he went to the front door. He retrieved a large envelope from his bag, which was sitting up against the door frame. "I'm sure you will be glad to see these again."

Hailey took it and peeked inside. "Thank you so much, all of you."

Smiles went around the room.

"Supper ready," Zaara called out from the kitchen.

Hailey noticed the amazing smells emanating from the kitchen. She, Ryan and the boy all followed Zayan into the kitchen.

The food was delicious. It was a lamb, rice, tomato, green pea dish with a ton of spices. Hailey devoured two servings, and Ryan had three. Everyone talked and laughed throughout dinner; momentarily forgetting each of their worries. Hailey was thankful that she and Ryan were there. It seemed to bring some joy to the family amid their own personal devastation.

"I'm sorry to cut this short, but we really have to start getting ready." Ryan apologized again and helped Hailey to her feet.

During the last few hours before heading to bed, they worked to help each other change their appearance. If the police were on alert for them, then they had to make sure they made as many changes as possible. Ryan reached into one of the bags and grabbed the scissors.

"Do you want to do it or should I?"

Hailey winced. "No, I'll do it," she said.

Even though she was sad to see it go, seeing her hair fall to the floor piece by piece did relieve a bit of the stress she was feeling from traveling tomorrow. After a quick hack job, she tidied it up.

"Wow, you actually did a really good job." Ryan smiled.

It was obvious he liked it; a huge smile was spanning from ear-to-ear. Hailey looked at her reflection again, and after a few more snips, she was reasonably satisfied with it herself. It was a messy, pixie cut that surprisingly complimented her face very well.

Ryan again dug into one of the bags and this time took out the three boxes of hair dye.

"So do you want to be a blonde bombshell, the racy redhead, or black and mysterious?"

She smiled, it was nice that he was attempting to make this as fun as possible.

"Um, I think I will go for red. Might as well go extreme."

He must have seen regret flicker in her eyes again. "Hey, you look beautiful, and this will work." Ryan smiled as he spoke.

He bent down, tilted her chin upwards and kissed her again. This kiss wasn't as gentle as the first. Both of them released some of the stress they were carrying. When they came up for air, both gasped for a quick breath. The simultaneous sound caused them both to burst into laughter. It helped lighten the mood incredibly, and they returned to the task with a more playful air.

They dyed Hailey's hair first, and it turned out great. She even considered keeping it that way for a while once they were home.

Ryan decided to go blonde. After Hailey had rinsed the dye out of his hair, she did a quick trim. Hailey didn't allow him to check the mirror until she was all finished. She was actually having a hard time not showing any emotion so she wouldn't give away anything while she worked.

"OK all done."

Ryan turned around and looked in the cloudy, cracked mirror over the sink. For a moment neither of them said a thing. But as soon as they caught each other's eye in the mirror, both broke into rolls of laughter. While Hailey looked like a hip rock chick, Ryan looked like a member of a corny boy band from the 90's.

"Well… it's different," Ryan said after catching his breath. "But… I'm sad to say, I just might have to change it back once we get back to the states."

Hailey giggled again.

"Hey now, no complaining. I know you love it but… you're just going to have to get used to the fact that this… this hotness… just has to go."

"Aww. It's going to be so tough to let it go." Hailey leaned towards him and gave him a quick kiss. "Come on stud, let's finish up and call it a night."

There was no one in sight when they returned to the kitchen, but there was a note on the table:

> *Ryan and Hailey,*
>
> *My father will be ready early to drive you to the meeting point. Ryan, please use my room again as I will go stay with a friend tonight. Oh, and my parents wanted me to tell you that they are happy to hear you both laugh, as am I. I wish you all the best.*
>
> *Aahil*

"So I guess this is it. Are you scared?" Ryan held her and smiled.

"Actually, if I'm honest… I'm terrified." Hailey's voice quivered.

"Head to bed. I have something for you, and I will be right there."

"OK…" Hailey left him in the kitchen and headed back to the girl's room. She got ready and climbed into the bed to wait.

A few moments after she was tucked in, a soft knock sounded on the door.

"Come in."

Ryan slowly opened the door and came over to the bed. Hailey moved her legs over so he could sit on the edge.

"Hey, when was the night Ehsan left you in his room?"

"Ah... last Thursday. Why?"

"You won't believe this, but I had a dream that night that you were in trouble. I think God wanted me to pray for you."

"Now... that all makes sense."

"Wow," Ryan huffed.

They sat there in silence for a moment as the facts settled in.

"It's getting late, and I should let you get some sleep. But read this first OK? I will see you in the morning."

Ryan bent over and kissed her forehead and each of her cheeks. He pulled back just a bit to catch a quick look at her eyes, then leaned in and kissed her lips. It was sweet and caused her to melt. She was already tired from the day, and his kiss stole the last bit of energy she had.

He said goodnight and left. Once the door clicked, Hailey opened the tiny, folded piece of paper.

ISAIAH 58:11

"The Lord will guide you always; he will satisfy your needs in a sun-scorched land and will strengthen your frame. You will be like a well-watered garden, Like a spring whose waters never fail."

Sleep well Hailey, my love. He is with us and goes before us.

CHAPTER 38

Hailey took one more look around the small house. Everyone was already outside, so it was quiet, peaceful and, for the moment, she felt so safe. Ryan was saying goodbye to Zaara, and Zayan was getting the car loaded with the backpacks, so she took a few minutes to relish the calm.

"Hailey? We need to get going," Ryan called for her from the front door.

"Just a sec. I will be right there."

Hailey moved around the kitchen and found a small piece of paper and a pen. She scratched a short thank you note and left it on the counter with a fair size stack of bills. Hailey wished she could leave it all, but they needed some for food and possibly bribes. She consoled herself knowing they would be shocked and blessed by what sat there.

Bless and protect them.

And with that, she joined Ryan outside.

After saying her goodbyes to Zaara, they all piled in the car and headed to the pickup spot. As soon as Hailey was in the car, she covered her head, popped in her contact lenses, and put on her sunglasses. She was dressed like a Westerner but covered her clothes to avoid drawing attention to herself. It was similar to what she wore when she first came into the country. Although in contrast, she would make sure to have that scarf glued to her head until they were out of Saudi.

The drive was uneventful, but with each horn honk or siren, Hailey jumped. Ryan grabbed her hand and squeezed it after she jumped the third time.

"Remember that verse. We will be OK," Ryan whispered to her and squeezed her hand again.

Hailey relaxed. Her head knew that he was right, yet her heart was a little slower. Although now having Ryan's reassurance, her heart was starting to catch up.

They reached their stop, and Hailey was surprised at how many people were already waiting. She did a quick head count... twelve men and seven women. They should blend in easily.

Ryan got out and held the door for Hailey, then closed it behind her. He then went to the back, removed their bags from the trunk, and joined her again beside the car. She moved to take hers, but he insisted he take them. They said their goodbyes to Zayan.

"You be careful," Zayan said as he patted each of their cheeks.

The old man hurriedly got back into the car and drove off but not before they saw a few tears in his eyes. Ryan and Hailey watched him go and then turned to take their place in line.

They tried to match the excitement of those around them, but with the amount of adrenalin pumping through their bodies, it was hard to relax. Fortunately, they were able to stand in the sea of all the others and were barely noticed.

There were Aussies, and Americans, and a few Asians. Hailey even heard a British accent at one point. They had waited for about fifteen minutes before a large bus pulled up. Hailey saw the number on the side: seventy-two. She looked at the page of directions.

"This is our bus," she said with a sigh.

Ryan loaded the bags in the storage compartment under the bus and joined Hailey as she was passing the tickets to the driver.

"Oh, star passes... fantastic," the driver said lowering his voice a tad as he pointed to a small star on each of their tickets.

Hailey hadn't even focused on them before.

"We are glad to have you." He winked, confirming he understood who they were.

Hailey took a deep breath and returned the smile. "Thank you."

"But I was informed there were to be two women." The man tried to keep an upbeat but quiet voice.

"Yeah... there was a slight change in plans. Is... that OK?"

Hailey briefly glanced around to the other waiting passengers and saw that no one was even paying attention to their conversation.

"Yes or course. Welcome aboard."

The man's face still showed his hesitation, but he smiled a tight-lipped smile at her. He nodded for them to get on as he handed their tickets back to her. Before boarding, Hailey passed them to Ryan, who returned them to the small pack he was keeping with him on the bus.

The bus was similar to one of those big Greyhound buses back home. It wasn't in the best condition and smelled like fish. Hailey didn't care, she would have boarded it even if it had no wheels and they had to carry it out of Saudi.

Hailey followed Ryan to a seat near the back of the bus and

settled in. After putting her bag in the overhead compartment, they sat silently and watched the others pile in and find their seats. A few glanced their way and smiled.

After the last person had boarded the bus, the bus driver came back on, stood near the front of the bus, and faced them. He was a very tall, thin man. It was evident he hadn't shaved in a couple days, and the stubble gave him a disheveled look. He had small round eyes, set closely together, but they were kind. His crooked little smile showed off a few missing teeth, they kind of added to his endearing, scruffy appearance.

He waited till everyone noticed him and became silent.

"My name's hard to say in English, so you all can call me Joe. The first part of our trip will be very long so hunker down and relax. As we pass through the next couple towns, we can all get out and stretch our legs a bit. But please don't wander off because we will only be stopping for about ten minutes in each place. Does anyone have any questions?"

A small Australian man sitting right in front of them raised his hand. Joe nodded towards him.

"When does the in-flight movie start?" He chuckled to himself.

"When you go ten minutes without talking or... when pigs fly... whatever comes first." Another man sitting at the very back heckled him.

The whole group started laughing. Joe flashed them both a smile, took his seat and started the bus. It roared to life and sputtered a bit. Joe worked the gears, and it lurched forward. It reminded Hailey of an old school bus she rode as a child when it tried to make it up the hill to her house. Within a few minutes, they were on their way.

Ryan looked at her and grabbed her hand. He squeezed it

and grinned at her.

"This is it... you ready?" He whispered.

"You bet. If it were possible, I would sprout wings right now and fly out of here, but I guess this bus will have to do." She replied with a nervous smile.

They both grinned at each other and held one another's gaze. Ryan leaned over and kissed her lightly on the forehead.

"Ahem," the Aussie in front of them cleared his throat.

Ryan and Hailey turned their attention forwards. He was leaning over the seat with the hugest grin on his face.

"Sorry to interrupt, but you guys are new to our group. So... what's your story?" He looked from Ryan to Hailey and back again.

"Um, we were just traveling around and found out about the tour. It sounded fun so we thought we'd join you," Ryan explained.

"Ace! I'm Jack, and this is my girlfriend, Holly." He gestured to the girl sitting beside him.

She was small, like Hailey, and had long brown hair. Hailey unconsciously reached up and touched her own hair. Even though she liked her new look, seeing Holly's hair made her miss her long hair. Holly was reading something and didn't turn around. She just raised her hand and waved. Jack shot out his hand over the seat.

"Uh...I'm Ryan."

"Hailey." As soon as Hailey said her name she wondered if it was a mistake that she hadn't used a fake name. *Shoot!*

They both shook his hand.

"Hey, everybody this is Hailey and Ryan. Hailey, Ryan... this is everybody. We're from all over. I won't overload you with everyone's names right now." Jack glanced down at Hailey.

"You know you can take all that off if you want," he said as he gestured to her clothes.

"Really?"

"Yeah, as long as we're on the bus, you don't need to bother. Even when we stop, you just need to put on your head scarf. The Saudis don't mind as long as we all stay together."

"Oh... OK..." Hailey was a bit hesitant but excited to get out of it. She made quick work of it and then settled back in her seat.

"Better?" Jack said.

"Much better. Thanks."

"Have you guys ever been on a Patetagi Tour before?" Holly said from her seat, again not looking back.

"No, this is our first time," Ryan replied.

"Ah... I hear you guys get up to some pretty wild stuff," Hailey added as she squeezed Ryan's hand. She realized she had forgotten to tell Ryan about what they were in for.

"Oh yeah! Life is too short to be boring. Am I right man?" Jack leaned down and punched Ryan playfully in the shoulder.

"Yeah, sure... sure thing." Ryan awkwardly shifted in his seat.

"Last year we went to Thailand and did sport climbing and diving. It was epic. The year before that we went to South America for white water rafting, and that's where we almost lost James." Jack pointed to a big, black man sitting two rows up.

The man turned around and shrugged towards them.

"Hey, now... how was I supposed to know that a guy my size could still bounce out of a boat?" His voice was deep and boomed in Hailey's ears.

Jack answered him, "Gravity doesn't care how big you are James. You shouldn't have tried to lean out and catch that fish." Jack laughed as he turned back to them. "And now onto this adventure. We're glad to have you both along." With that, Jack shot them a smile and turned back in his seat.

"Dang it, Ryan, I'm so sorry." She leaned closer to whisper in his ear. "He caught me off guard. I shouldn't have used my real name."

"Hey, it's OK. I really don't think it will be a big deal." Ryan leaned towards her. "So when Jack said 'now onto this new adventure'... what exactly does that mean?"

Hailey looked at him with a guilty frown. "Ah... yeah, this isn't exactly a senior's tour group. They kind of are extreme-sporty types. Patetagi Tours cater to thrill seekers."

Ryan pulled back and looked at her with raised eyebrows.

Hailey pulled him back towards her and continued to whisper. "It's not like I was choosing a vacation for us. I couldn't have very well been picky when trying to run from my crazy "husband."" Hailey did air quotes with her hands, but she dropped them slowly to her lap as the realization hit her. "Oh no. Am I really married? I mean was all of that legal?" It sounded so much worse when she said out loud. Her heart sank further.

"What? No!" Ryan said.

"Are you sure. I mean we had a ceremony and everything. I signed papers."

"Yeah... I'm pretty sure none of it would hold up. But if you're worried, I'll look into it once we're home. Don't worry... it will be alright." Ryan's assurances lifted her heart back out of her stomach.

"OK... but yeah I think we should check."

"So... what exactly are we going to be doing on this trip?" Ryan said.

Hailey was thankful for the change of subject. "Well... a

couple of things," Hailey said hesitantly. "But don't worry most of the really crazy stuff is going to happen in Egypt and we will be long gone before that. But in Saudi, well... we're going sand surfing, camel racing, riding these dune buggy things and scuba diving." She paused. "It actually could be kind of fun."

"You've got to be joking... that's the calm stuff?" Ryan looked at her with this stunned, bewildered look. He poked her side and said, "Hmm, I had no idea I was in love with such an adventurous woman.

It finally hit Hailey of how stupid it sounded. Here they were running for their lives, or at least for their freedom, and here she was thinking about doing fun, crazy activities.

She put her head in her hands and moaned. "Oh my word, you're right! This is so ridiculous."

"No, it's OK, you're right. It doesn't sound that bad. Whatever will get us out of here, I'm game." Ryan leaned down to kiss her, but just before he was able to connect, the bus lurched, and they bashed heads.

"Ouch," Hailey yelped.

They both burst out laughing, while they rubbed their heads.

"Sorry, can I try that again?"

Hailey nodded, and he leaned back into her. The kiss was filled with hope and excitement. They would soon be out of Riyadh and the further and further they got away from the city, the better off they would be.

=======

The bus was hot and sticky. Hailey had fallen asleep on his chest not long after Joe had pulled away from the meeting spot. They were quite a way across town.

The majority of the other passengers were now huddled around James. He was showing them pictures of his trip to Africa, something about climbing Kilimanjaro. Jack had offered for Ryan to join them, but Ryan declined. He was glad Hailey was leaning on him as she slept because he liked having her near him. It was also a good excuse to stay in his seat and rest.

The traffic was surprisingly quite clear, as was the sky. Ryan peered up out the window. The sky was a brilliant blue, and the yellow sun hung in the center of a sundog. Ryan always thought it was a stupid name for the colorless rings that sometimes circled the sun, yet he loved seeing it.

The bus bumped along. The potholes seemed twice as big as they knocked the bus around. Ryan rested his head on the back of the seat and continued to look outside. After a few moments, the bus pitched again and caused Hailey to stir. He leaned his mouth close to the top of her head and shushed her until she settled again. He moved his arm around her to help keep her steady. Ryan was glad she was relaxed enough to sleep, and he hoped she would sleep until they left the city.

They weren't so lucky.

The bus stopped, then went a few feet more, then stopped again. Ryan returned his attention back outside. They were still on one of the major roads and close to the outskirts of the city.

"Sorry folks," Joe called from the front of the bus, "but it seems like we've run into a checkpoint. We might be here awhile."

A groan sounded from everyone else, and alarm blasted through Ryan.

"Hailey, wake up."

"What is it?" She said groggily.

She had only been sleeping for twenty minutes and was

having trouble waking up.

"Get up, we may have a problem. There's a checkpoint ahead."

Ryan didn't even try to keep the fear from his voice because he knew his concern was etched all over his face.

"What!?" Hailey jolted upright and looked at him in fear.

"Shhh," Ryan reminded her.

The others glanced at her but then returned their attention to James. Ryan broke his gaze with Hailey and looked towards the front of the bus. There was a huge line of cars in front of them. He rose from their seat.

"I'll be right back."

Ryan made his way to the front of the bus. As he walked up the aisle, he looked out the side of the bus. There were already officers positioned sporadically along the road. There would be no way they could sneak off the bus without getting noticed. He returned his eyes forward once he reached Joe's seat. He did a quick count of the cars. There were twelve cars between the bus and the checkpoint.

"Sorry, I have no idea why they're here. In my five years doing this route, I have never seen them set up a checkpoint like this."

Joe's tone matched Ryan's concern.

"Hey," Joe's whisper was quiet, so Ryan had to lean down to hear him, "I'm not sure what you two are into. I was only told that you ran into some trouble and you needed safe passage out of Saudi. But... I need to make sure that there isn't anything... ah... illegal that they might find on you or in your packs."

"No no... nothing like that. We didn't do anything wrong. My friend just got into trouble, and we need to get out of here."

"If they decide to search the bus... I'm sorry, but I don't think there is anything I can do to protect you."

"Wait, the man at the market told Hailey that you had a way to avoid the passport check in Jordan, why can't you do that now?" Ryan questioned.

"That's a very different situation." Joe nodded to an officer as he walked by the bus, then continued. "There is a small town just on the border that we were going to stop at and you were going to go underneath the bus. I have a hidden compartment behind the luggage storage. And if you haven't noticed, there are a lot of officers lining the street, so that's not really possible right now."

"So what are we supposed to do?"

"I have no idea," Joe said as he shook his head.

CHAPTER 39

If Ryan's face was any indication of how his discussion had gone with Joe, Hailey was not optimistic.

"What happened?"

"Joe has no idea what to do. He has this great little hiding place for us under the bus, but that isn't exactly an option now." He gestured outside to the officers.

Hailey had already noticed them. They had passed three officers already, and there were more posted every couple of meters between the bus and the checkpoint.

"Ryan what if they are looking for us?"

They had both been thinking it was a very possible explanation for the checkpoint, but when Hailey said it out loud, their anxiety increased. Getting into Jordan was now not their biggest concern.

What are we going to do if we can't even get out of Riyadh?

The bus moved forward painfully slow as the number of cars ahead of them lessened. It was an excruciating countdown and as they got closer Hailey's fear grew. Tick, Tick, Tick. Ten cars, nine, eight.

"Ryan, I can't take this. We have to get out of here."

She stood up. Hailey had no idea what she was going to do,

yet she knew she couldn't just sit there.

Ryan grabbed her wrist. "Sit down," he said.

His whisper was quiet but stern, so she listened and sat down with a hopeless thump. She understood Ryan's desire not to bring attention to her fear, but she was frustrated with him.

"We can't! You know that. We just have to wait."

Hailey looked at him with disbelief. Was he actually suggesting they just willingly go to their capture? They at least had to go down fighting.

"What's truth?" His eyes drilled into her.

"What?"

"What's truth?" He said with even more determination.

"I have no idea what you're talking about?" She turned her head to look outside.

Ryan touched her chin to turn her back to face him.

"I'm asking you to focus, not on your fear but on what's true." Ryan paused to see if she understood.

She didn't.

"I... I don't know." Her frustration rose.

Here we are in the worst situation possible, and he wants to play twenty questions?

"Truth... is that God is here." He paused. "Right?"

"Yeah..." she said hesitantly.

Where is he going with this?

"And He has led us this whole time." He paused again. "Right?'

"Yeah..."

"So... what else is true?"

Hailey's eyes darted to the front of the bus again, but Ryan's hand came to the side of her face and turned it, forcing her to look at him.

He repeated his question, "What is truth?"

"Um..." She tried to clear her head to think, "... God is good."

"Right! What else?"

"God loves us and will watch over us no matter what happens."

Hailey looked at Ryan with pleading eyes. She started to understand what he was doing, but she was still having trouble verbalizing it over her fear.

Another officer passed by their window, and she squeezed her eyes shut. Again his hand touched her face. She opened her eyes. His compassion filled her view.

"Hailey, the truth is that nothing happens outside of His control, good and bad. His will is what remains."

Hailey looked around the bus again and allowed Ryan's words to sink in. Everyone was still huddled around James. She closed her eyes and took a deep breath, and at that moment, peace draped around her. It covered her and drove out the debilitating fear that had taken hold. She took another deep breath and opened her eyes. She turned back towards Ryan.

"OK," she said as she nodded her agreement with him.

He took her hands in his and held them for a moment before bringing them up to his lips. He kissed both of the backs of her hands and took a deep breath himself.

"I have no idea what will happen or what we are going to do about it. But I do know that we don't need to be afraid. Are you with me?"

Hailey took another deep breath and allowed the last bit of fear to pass through her. As it dripped off of her, she looked deep into Ryan's eyes.

"Yes... I'm with you" Hailey glanced towards the group

again. "What are they all doing?"

"James is just showing them some pictures. Are you OK?"

"Yeah. Thanks for helping me see through this. But I have to say this really sucks. My body won't stop shaking."

Ryan chuckled. "I know. I'm not all peaches and ice cream over here you know."

Hailey grinned at his bizarre choice of words.

Ryan winked at her. "I know we can make it through this," he said.

=======

The group around James parted, and everyone took their seats. They were laughing and talking. Jack and Holly, inspired by James's photos, were animatedly starting to plan their own trip to Africa.

Jack looked at Ryan. "Hey, you guys alright?"

"Perfect," Ryan lied. There was no reason to alarm him or get him involved.

"OK... then," he said as he turned towards Hailey. "Hey, you sleep well?"

"Yes, just not long enough." Hailey smiled back.

Jack nodded, sat back in his seat and picked up his conversation with Holly. Ryan was glad he didn't initiate more conversation.

The bus pulled forward again, and Ryan looked up towards the front. The small tents set up on either side of the checkpoint were surprisingly close now. He squinted his eyes and peered through the windshield. One, two, three, four... four cars to go and then it would be their turn.

Neither of them said another word to each other as he leaned back against the seat. Ryan prayed and just stared straight ahead. He prayed they weren't even looking for them but, that if they were, then Hailey would stay safe no matter how it all played out.

Hailey leaned her head on his shoulder and closed her eyes. He kissed the top of her head and took her hand.

"We'll be alright," he whispered to her through her hair.

One, two... there were just two cars to go now. The bus pulled forward and stopped. A moment later it pulled forward again and stopped. Then another moment after that, it pulled forward again. Ryan closed his eyes.

Here we go.

Joe opened the door. A large officer with a long beard came up the steps and stood beside Joe. He looked down the aisle of the bus, and he momentarily glanced at each of them as his eyes scanned the length of the bus. No one spoke.

Ryan couldn't see his eyes but just knew they were surveying and assessing each of them from behind the large sunglasses that sat on the man's face.

The officer turned to Joe. They talked back and forth in Arabic for a few minutes. Joe's voice started to rise, but the officer's remained steady. Again Joe raised his voice slightly, and the officer responded, then he pointed to the door. Joe dropped his head, sighed and left the bus.

Ryan peered outside to see where Joe was going. He didn't go far. Joe remained beside the bus. He was upset and was kicking the dirt with his foot. Ryan returned his attention to the officer still standing at the front of the bus.

"We are looking for someone," his voice was deep and serious, "and if you are not that person you have nothing to fear and you will be on your way shortly."

Ryan shot Hailey a "stay calm" look. Her eyes were two large saucers filled with panic. He squeezed her hand to remind her to relax.

"Now, I'm sorry for my rudeness," the officer continued, "but I must request that the women not put on their head coverings. We need to ensure that you match your passport picture. If everyone stays seated and silent as we do our search, this won't take long. Please have your passports and tour passes ready, and we will be along shortly to check each of you." The officer then turned and left the bus after thanking them for their cooperation.

The other passengers started to rummage around to get their stuff out. Ryan leaned against the window and looked outside again. The officer motioned towards another to join him. They talked for a moment, and then they both came on the bus. Both officers stood at the front and waited till everyone took their seats. With their backs to each other, they started to move down the aisle. It created another painful countdown.

"Quick switch places with me, I need to get our passes out." He pushed past Hailey and went to open the overhead bin.

"Sit down now!" the older officer yelled at him.

"Sorry, I'm just getting my pass."

The officer frowned and glared at him. "Hurry up and then take your seat."

Ryan quickly found the passes, closed the bin and sat down.

"Yikes," he whispered to Hailey.

They sat there silently and waited for their turn.

Beep… beep.

The older officer's walkie-talkie went off. He returned James's passport back to him and walked to the front of the bus to answer the page. The younger officer continued checking papers. Soon he reached Jack and Holly.

The young officer tried to hide it, but Ryan caught the slight pause as he saw Holly. He took her passport and tour pass and looked at them. Ryan's heart sank when he realized that Holly's hair was really similar to Hailey's before she had changed it. They were even the same size. It was obvious now that they were looking for Hailey. The officer looked from the passport to Holly and back again. He handed it back to Holly.

Ryan took a deep breath.

OK, here we go, our turn.

The younger officer rested his hand on the back of their seat. He didn't acknowledge them. Instead, he looked to the front of the bus towards the older officer, who was still talking on the walkie-talkie.

Catching the younger officer's eye, the older officer nodded. He spoke a moment more, turned one of the little black knobs and returned the walkie-talkie to his belt. The older officer looked back up and started down the aisle towards them.

The two officers spoke for a few moments.

"Can I see your passport and tour pass again please?" The older officer said to Holly.

Holly held them out to him.

"Is there a problem?" Jack's concern was obvious and understandable.

Ryan looked at Hailey. He shook his head slightly.

Don't say anything, just wait. Ryan pleaded with his eyes.

"Have you been near the downtown bank or Deera Square in the last few days?"

Jack glanced at Holly. "No, at the rest stop we stayed with the bus. You can ask anyone."

"No... that won't be necessary. We don't have a problem." The officer said as he reviewed her papers again. "You're from

Australia?"

"Yes sir," Holly said shakily.

"Look at me, please. I need to see the color of your eyes."

Holly slowly looked at him. The officer leaned towards her.

I'm so glad I didn't forget those colored lenses.

The older officer then looked at the younger one, who shrugged his shoulders in response. The older officer frowned at him and shook his head. He shoved the passport at him. The older officer was openly frustrated, said something to the younger one, and then returned to the opposite side of the aisle. He continued to check the few remaining passengers on the far side.

The younger one paused for a few moments to regain his composure, before handing Holly's papers back to her. Then he turned towards Hailey and Ryan.

Ryan held out their tour passes, and he took them. Hailey was the last girl on the bus left to be checked, the other passengers were all men. The older officer barely looked at their passports before continuing on and had already reached the last seat.

"Where passport?" The younger one asked.

The other officer looked up for a moment but quickly returned his attention back to the man who had teased Jack just before they left.

"Well... they actually are... ah... under the bus in our packs," Ryan said, shrugging his shoulders.

The older officer finished off with the last passenger and joined them. He took the passes from the younger officer and dismissed him. Hailey watched as the younger officer walked back up the aisle."

"Your passports are under the bus?" The officer said,

annoyed.

"Ah... yes, sir."

"How long have you been in Saudi?"

The officer looked back and forth between Ryan and Hailey.

"Ah, not long." Ryan tried to steady his voice, but it was a bit shaky.

Keep it together man.

He knew he couldn't allow his voice to betray them.

The officer glanced down at the passes again and then looked around the bus. He was obviously thinking things through. Ryan's heart almost stopped.

What if this officer had incredible instincts? What if he already could tell something was up with them. Father, help us.

"You two," the officer called towards Jack and Holly, "turn around!"

Jack and Holly turned and looked at him, eyes wide.

"How long have these two been traveling with you?"

CHAPTER 40

Hailey's mouth was dry. Her heart was beating so fast that her ribs were almost hurting. Here they sat, Ryan and her in a hot bus in Saudi Arabia and their fate was about to be sealed by two strangers. Everything about their situation seemed so absurd, and it appeared to move in slow motion.

Jack looked at Ryan, Hailey squeezed Ryan's hand, and for a moment no one moved or said a word. To Hailey, it seemed endless, but then finally Jack smiled at Ryan and nodded.

"Oh... Sam and Ava? Lovely people. They've been with us since the start of the tour." Jack looked at Holly. "What has it been now, love... one week? Two?" Jack didn't wait for her answer but continued chatting away.

The officer never took his eyes off of Ryan and Hailey while Jack spoke. Hailey found it too intimidating to look at him, so she kept her eyes glued to Jack while he re-lived a few of their adventures.

Hailey soon realized that being too still didn't seem natural. This needed to be convincing, and she didn't want to throw Jack's cover story out the window by avoiding eye contact with the officer. She smiled and nodded along with Jack and, intermittently, did a quick glance at the officer.

"It was ace! We started in Dubai. Have you ever been there? The sand-boarding on Big Red is amazing." Jack, a man they had barely met, was actually covering for them. Hailey couldn't believe it.

"No... I've never been," the officer answered slowly and finally stopped staring at them and looked at Jack.

"You know, if you need our passports, we can run out and get them. It will just take a bit. We were the first ones here, so our packs are at the back." Ryan's tone was light-hearted and convincing.

Hailey looked at the officer to see if it resonated.

"No, that is fine. But when you stop next, get it out and keep it with you at all times. It's not safe to travel in Saudi without it." The officer handed the passes back to Ryan, then turned and started making his way to the front of the bus.

"Yeah, no kidding," Hailey responded. Her voice came out louder than expected.

The officer turned around. Hailey's heart sank. He looked at her and sneered.

"Sorry." Hailey tried to put on her sweetest apologetic smile.

The officer shook his head but said nothing. He just turned and left the bus. Hailey kept her eyes on the door, dreading he might come back.

Dang it, why did I say that? Don't come back, don't come back.

When Joe's head bobbed into view as he climbed the few steps back onto the bus, Hailey signed with relief. Joe looked back at them. Hailey and Ryan shook their heads, showing him their mutual disbelief. Joe shrugged his shoulders, took his seat and started the bus.

The actual meaning of Hailey's comment was totally lost on the Aussies and the officer. As the bus pulled through the checkpoint, Hailey leaned back against the seat with Ryan. When she glanced at him, their eyes met, and they both burst out laughing.

"I can't believe that you said, 'Yeah, no kidding.' You're gutsy, I'll give you that."

Hailey moaned. "I know. I can't believe I said that."

Ryan pushed off the seat and cupped her face. "I love you, Hailey." He continued to hold her face and leaned in to kiss her.

Hailey couldn't believe it. She was finally safe, and at last, she was heading home. With no fear of any more "what ifs" looming over them, she sunk into his kiss and enjoyed it.

"Ahem," Jack cleared his throat.

Hailey and Ryan broke off their kiss and looked at him.

"Ok, you two love birds... what's your story?" Jack asked as he leaned on the back of his seat.

Holly popped up right next to him. "Are you two the reason for that stop?" she questioned.

Ryan looked at Hailey. "Ah... yeah, we are."

"Actually... I am," Hailey corrected. "It's a really long story."

"I bet it's a ripper." Holly's curiosity was almost tangible. She looked like an antsy kid.

Hailey reached out her hands and placed one on each of their arms. "Thank you so much for covering for us. You have no idea what that meant to us." Her eyes started to water.

"Ah, no worries mate," Jack said.

Holly put her hand over Hailey's and squeezed it. "But hey, it's obvious you guys have had a tough go, why don't you get some rest. You can tell us all about it later. How does that sound?"

Hailey was thankful for her suggestion. "That would be great. Thank you."

With one more huge grin from them both, Jack and Holly disappeared behind their seats.

CHAPTER 41

The landscape was uniquely beautiful and unlike anything she had ever seen. The bright Saudi sun was just starting to set. It highlighted the sand and caused it to look as if it were on fire: a blaze of red rippling from dune to dune. The small ripples in the sand left by the wind reminded Hailey of the effect water had on the ocean shore back home.

Hailey instinctively looked over at Ryan to share the sight with him. When she saw that he was still sleeping, she remembered that he had fallen asleep soon after they had left the city. She didn't want to wake him, so she slowly turned her attention back to the window.

I can't believe I'm free, Hailey thought to herself.

You are free indeed.

God's reassurance brought warmth to her whole body and radiated throughout her soul. Hailey leaned her head on the back of the seat as she continued to look out at the view.

I am so amazed… and humbled… that You came for me.

I will always come for you, for I am your refuge and your strength.

God… all of this was so scary. I would have never imagined that going through something like this would lead me back to You or back to feeling hopeful about life again. I definitely wouldn't have chosen this or anything like it for myself, but I see how necessary it was.

Thank You for leading me here. I wasn't living... just running... from everything. If You would have left me to continue in my own choices... I would have gone my whole life not having a genuine connection with anyone. My fear of loss and my fear of rejection would have consumed and ruined me. I would have kept everyone just slightly out of reach.

Hailey took a quick glance at Ryan. She smiled, then turned back to look outside.

Oh and thank You for protecting me through it all. So many of those situations could have been so much worse... but I'm alive.

Hailey's heart lurched as her mind remembered that the same wasn't true for Anna. This had been the first quiet, peaceful moment that Hailey had had alone since Ryan had told her about the bombing. The deep sadness she had felt as Ryan held her after telling her started to force its way in. Hailey looked around. She didn't want to lose her composure and mourn here. This wasn't the place. Hailey bit her lip and shook the thoughts free. She pushed herself to think of something else. Ghada and Sarna!

God, what's going to happen to them? Please watch over them and call them to Yourself. Keep them safe.

I did not come into the world to condemn it, I came to save it. I will continue to call to them just as I have always done.

Hailey felt comforted. There was a small pause.

Hailey?

Yes?

We aren't finished yet.

Hailey's heart sank. *What... what do You mean?*

I have even greater plans for you.

Hailey looked at Ryan, around the bus and then returned her attention back beyond the window. As she watched the sand dunes stream past, she realized she had two options at that moment. Retreat and lean back or trust and lean in.

Her mind and emotions desperately wanted to draw near to the one of familiarity – the one that seemed safe. Although deep down, she knew that the shelter it offered was an illusion.

But it's what I've always known, Hailey tried to rationalize with herself.

The other choice was completely foreign to her and Hailey feared what might lie there. She felt panic start to rise in her chest and up into her throat. It began to tighten its grasp. Hailey's eyes darted about, and her breathing quickened.

Then something happened. Deep in Hailey's core, something changed. Staring straight ahead into the back of Holly's seat, Hailey sat up straight and slightly forward, off the back of her seat. With both hands resting on her thighs, she took a deep, slow breath.

"I trust You," she whispered.

Faithful am I who calls you, and I also will bring it to pass.

Before Hailey could ask any more questions, she was interrupted by a sound above her...

BRRINNG... BRRINNG... BRRINNG!

=======

Ryan jumped awake from the sound of a phone ringing. A little disoriented he looked around alarmed.

"That's... our phone." Hailey's words helped him get his bearings.

"Oh, right," Ryan said as he rose from his seat.

The bags in the bin had shifted, and it took him a bit to readjust things so he could reach the front pocket of his pack. He made quick work of the zipper and retrieved the phone.

Plopping back in his seat, he hit the answer button. "Hello?" There was no voice on the other end, just a series of crackles.

"Hello?" Ryan tried again.

"Ry... can... me... it..."

Hailey looked at him with questioning eyes. Ryan mouthed 'I don't know' in response. He couldn't make out a full sentence. Then the call was dropped. Ryan put the phone down in his lap but kept holding it.

"I don't know who it was. The connection was awful."

"Hopefully they'll call back."

No sooner had Hailey said the words then the phone started ringing again.

Ryan quickly answered, "Hello?"

"Ryan?" a weak voice questioned.

"Yes?"

"It's... Anna."

DID YOU ENJOY

VEILED

LOOK FOR THE SEQUEL:

THE SAND BRIDE

www.cyanagaffney.com

While you're there... check out the contest page for details about how to

ENTER & WIN

Be sure to follow Cyana on social media!

ACKNOWLEDGEMENTS

Colin, thank you for being an amazing partner and my best friend. Your support through all my crazy ideas means the world to me. Thank you for the encouraging talks that helped push me through.

Olivia, you bring me so much joy. The light you bring into my life is inspiring. Thank you for your ideas about the launch party. Your offers to help and your Facebook posts were beautiful.

Dad, thank you for your critiques and ideas. Thank you for your excitement.

Mom, thank you for late night talks. Thank you for your love, enthusiasm, and support.

Sister, thank you for your insights for this project. Thank you for the many hours you spent reading and giving me your feedback. I hope you know how much your contributions have meant to me.

Melissa, thank you for your work on the cover – it's beautiful.

Carla, thank you for your friendship. Your excitement jumpstarted a huge aspect of this project - it was mightily used.

74265677R00232

Made in the USA
Columbia, SC
30 July 2017